I0701755

ALSO BY EVAN GRAVER

<u>Ryan Weller Thrillers</u>

Dark Water

Dark Ship

Dark Horse

Dark Shadows

Dark Paradise

Dark Fury

Dark Hunt

Dark Path

Dark Prey

Dark Fraud

Dark Drone

Dark Country

Dark Order

Dark Cover-up

Dark Angel

<u>Standalone</u>

Liberty Brigade

<u>John Phoenix Thrillers</u>

Rising Phoenix

Target Phoenix

Rising Phoenix

© 2024 Evan Graver

www.evangraver.com

All rights reserved. No part of this publication may be reproduced, distributed, or transmitted in any form or by any means, including photocopying, recording, or other electronic, or mechanical methods, without the prior written permission of the publisher, except in the case of brief quotations embodied in critical reviews and certain noncommercial uses permitted by the Copyright Act of 1976.

ISBN-13: 979-8-9876681-9-1

Cover: Cover2Book

This is a work of fiction. Any resemblance to any person, living or dead, businesses, companies, events, or locales is entirely coincidental.

Printed and bound in the United States of America.

First Printed January 2024

Published by Third Reef Publishing, LLC

Hollywood, Florida

www.thirdreefpublishing.com

RISING PHOENIX

EVAN GRAVER

CHAPTER 1

Caracas, Venezuela

Miguel Tapia pulled his 1985 Mercedes coupe into the central stall of his three-car garage. He switched off the engine of the aging vehicle and breathed a sigh of relief before pressing the remote to close the garage door, shutting out the world.

Like every other night, it was a struggle to make it home through the poverty-stricken sections of the city to his luxurious country home after a long day of working in the Federal Legislative Palace, known to the Venezuelans as the *Capitolio*.

The government official often felt strained to the bone as he labored under his boss, the Minister of Economy and Finance. Yet, he felt good things were coming and that the minister would soon appoint him to a higher position of authority.

Tapia pocketed his keys as he slipped out of the car, then retrieved his suit jacket from the back seat. He hoped his wife, Isabel, had fixed something delicious for dinner tonight.

Stepping into the house, Tapia glanced around. Usually, Isabel was laboring in the kitchen, happily humming a tune while the scents of cooking meat, boiling rice, and grilling vegetables wafted through the air.

Tossing his jacket over the back of the couch on his way through the house, he called out to his wife. "Isabel! Where are you?"

She didn't answer. Their modern kitchen, filled with granite countertops and stainless-steel appliances, felt like a tomb without her presence. Isabel had freshly scrubbed the counters as if she were preparing to cook, yet the stove burners were cold. It was unlike Isabel to abandon her duties. She had faithfully prepared the evening meal for over thirty years, serving their children and grandchildren at the big dining room table.

Tapia shivered. Something was terribly wrong. The knowledge that Isabel might be in trouble made his bones ache.

The house was what many Americans would call a McMansion, a word Tapia had picked up during his days at the University of Miami before Hugo Chávez had made going to college in the United States all but impossible. Only government officials could travel to the U.S. anymore, and only if the State Department invited them. Although the U.S. had imposed harsh sanctions in the past, the two countries were trying to mend their relations because Venezuela had what the U.S. craved—black gold.

"Iz!" Tapia shouted again. "Isabel!"

Still, there was no response. The air felt stifling, and the house was so quiet that he could hear the air conditioner kick on. Cool air blew from the vents, but it did nothing for the sweat beading on the brow of the frantic husband.

Tapia headed for the courtyard, intent on finding his wife. The house formed a square around the courtyard where a sparkling blue pool was the center of activity anytime his grandchildren would stop over. Tapia had always loved the outdoor feel of the courtyard with the many potted plants and hanging ferns Isabel tended to each day. The relaxing atmosphere made the courtyard an inviting place to sit and reflect, but right then, the environment did little to quell the panic rising in his chest. Tapia didn't know what he would do without his beautiful Isabel.

He poked his head into the various rooms off the courtyard until he came to the master bedroom. Placing his hand on the doorknob, the knot of dread tightened in Tapia's gut. He had wondered when this day would arrive. For years, he'd been passing information to CIA spies who had operated out of the U.S. embassy until former U.S. Secretary of State Mike Pompeo had ordered it closed in 2019, forcing Tapia to resort to old school dead drops to communicate with his handler.

While Tapia loved his country, he hated seeing what Chávez and his self-appointed successor, Michel Zarate, had done to it, turning the greatest economy in South America, maybe even the world, into one of abject poverty and deprivation. In the early years, when Venezuela had been prosperous, there had been little information to pass, mainly technical specs on oil well production or new military hardware purchases, but the last few years had been fruitful, a variable spigot of information about the inner workings of Zarate's brutal communist regime.

Twisting the doorknob, Tapia stepped into the darkened bedroom. Isabel sat on the bed, her hands and feet bound, a gag stuffed into her mouth. Even in the low light streaming over his shoulder through the open door, Tapia could see the tears coursing down his wife's cheeks.

Slowly, Tapia took in the three other people in the room.

A man was on his knees beside the bed, a black bag over his head and his hands bound behind his back. Behind him stood two men who wore black balaclavas and dark clothing.

One held a silenced pistol at his side while the other carried an Israeli-made Uzi submachine gun at port arms.

"Glad you could join us," the man with the pistol said to Tapia in Spanish, their native tongue. "Close the door."

Tapia followed the orders, hoping this was just a simple ransom situation and not retribution for his work with the Americans. The only hitch in that scenario was that he had no clue who the man on his knees was.

"I have money," Tapia said.

"Where?" the *pistolero* asked.

"In a safe in my office," Tapia replied.

"Show me," the gunman said.

Tapia led the masked man through the house to his office and opened the safe hidden behind a large, framed photo of Simón Bolívar: The Liberator of Latin America. The safe contained passports for him and Isabel, various government documents, the deed to the house, and fifty thousand dollars cash in cherished U.S. greenbacks.

The *pistolero* tossed the money into a bag and, twitching the muzzle of his pistol, told Tapia that he should head for the bedroom. Much relieved that the man had taken the money, Tapia hoped this hostage crisis would soon end.

Inside the bedroom, the *pistolero* waited for Tapia to face him, then, without warning, raised his pistol and shot the kneeling man in the forehead, toppling him over backward, the hood capturing the spray of blood and brain matter that would have otherwise ruined the rose-patterned wallpaper, handpicked by Isabel decades ago.

Without being ordered, the man with the Uzi bent down. He pulled the hood off the stranger, revealing the bruised and battered face of Luis Garcia, Tapia's friend and CIA handler.

Isabel tried to scream, but it came out as a muffled cry behind her gag. Garcia had been to their home many times. He'd broken bread with the Tapia family, and now he lay dead on their terracotta tile floor.

Panic clutched Tapia around the chest like a vise, squeezing him slowly, causing his breath to come in quick gasps. The scent of cordite and blood hung thick in the air.

Tears spilled down Tapia's cheeks, and his bowels threatened to flood his pants with fecal matter. The SEBIN had discovered his treason, and he knew that seeing Garcia shot dead was just the beginning of the torture that awaited him.

Uzi smacked Tapia across the face to bring him out of the shocked stupor he'd fallen into at seeing his handler so mercilessly murdered. He shoved Tapia toward the wooden chair he'd pulled from under Isabel's dressing table. Tapia sank into it without question, thankful to be off his feet, but no sooner had Tapia's butt touched the velvet softness of the mauve-colored cushion than Uzi produced zip ties and cinched Tapia's right wrist to the chair arm. The government official didn't bother to struggle. He just wanted his life to end, but he knew it wouldn't be that easy.

The masked man continued to use zip ties to bind both of Tapia's wrists to the chair arms and then wrapped rope around his upper body, pinning his elbows to his sides. Once Uzi had Tapia's torso and hands secure, he moved to Tapia's ankles, using more zip ties to fasten him completely to the chair.

"Do you know who your friend is?" *Pistolero* taunted. He gave Garcia's body a brutal kick to the ribs. The air filled with the foulness of Garcia's bowels letting go. Tapia could taste the coppery odor of blood in his mouth, both his own from being slapped and that of Garcia's head wound.

Tapia nodded. "Luis Garcia."

"He is a CIA pig!" *Pistolero* shouted. "And so are you, *pendejo!*"

Tapia now understood that these men were from the *Servicio Bolivariano de Inteligencia Nacional.* The SEBIN was the equivalent of the FBI, CIA, Secret Service, and U.S. Marshals Service rolled into one unit. They didn't work the streets like common law enforcement officers but conducted counterintelligence investigations or performed security for the government. Tapia had routinely seen the SEBIN troops around the *Capitolio*, wearing their full black uniforms and facial coverings so no one would recognize them.

The men who had come for Tapia wore civilian clothing, but they were most definitely SEBIN. No other law enforcement agency in Venezuela would dare interfere with their work, especially when there was a CIA spy available for ready torture, which made Tapia wonder why they had shot Garcia so quickly. But judging from the bloody pulp of his swollen face and the fact that the masked men had ripped out all of Garcia's fingernails, told Tapia that the SEBIN had already gotten what they wanted from the American. The CIA case officer had given up Tapia's name, and now the SEBIN had come to torture him.

Pistolero waved his hand in front of his masked face as if to dispel the stink of the dead body. He ordered his compadre to grab Garcia by the arms while he gripped the dead man's ankles. Together, they picked Garcia up and carried him from the room. Unfortunately, they left a trail of blood and excrement on the tile that still reeked even with the body outside of the room.

Tapia tried to breathe through his mouth, intentionally blocking the smells from entering his nostrils, but he kept having to spit out blood or lick his lips, so he'd inadvertently suck air in through his nose. His olfactory senses triggered a gag reflex. Tapia fought down the vomit, trying to force its way out of his body.

He and Isabel were going to die. There was no doubt about it.

"Forgive me, Isabel," Tapia muttered, but she didn't seem to hear him, or if she did, she didn't understand why he was apologizing.

After disposing of Garcia's body, the return of the two

men prevented Tapia from explaining his traitorous actions to his wife.

Pistolero sat on the edge of the bed and held Isabel's hand. "This is all a terrible thing," he said calmly to her. "I know you are afraid, but we are not here to hurt you. We are interested in the information your husband has passed to the CIA."

Isabel's eyes darted toward her husband as she continued to cry. *Pistolero* wrapped his arm around her shoulder and held her close.

There was a strange juxtaposition between *Pistolero*'s caring demeanor toward Isabel and his harsh killing of Garcia that made Tapia shiver.

After several minutes of comforting her, *Pistolero* kissed the older woman on the forehead. He stood and paced the room, holding the suppressed weapon loosely in his hand as Uzi stood by complacently.

"Garcia told us everything," *Pistolero* said to Tapia. "Now you will do the same. We will torture you, but first, you will witness the pain you have inflicted on your wife."

He pushed Isabel flat on the bed, flicking open a folding knife. The blade caught the light and glinted for a moment. Tapia feared the SEBIN agent would kill Isabel. Instead of slicing her bonds, the man slid the knife under her clothing and slowly started to cut away her shirt.

Isabel struggled to break free from the man's grasp, but her bindings made it impossible.

Bile rose in Tapia's throat again. What he feared they were about to do to Isabel was worse than death, and no matter how much he wanted to look away, he couldn't. He tried silently to catch Isabel's gaze, but she bucked and kicked too violently in her own life-and-death struggle to worry about her husband.

Pistolero put a finger to his lips. "Shhh, angel. Don't move. I don't want to cut you."

Isabel's body went rigid as she stared wide-eyed at their captors. Her husband cried at being unable to help her. He had inflicted this pain on his beloved wife.

Pistolero kept cutting away her clothing until Isabel was completely naked. He ran the back of the knife blade over her delicate brown body, raising goosebumps on her flesh and causing her to tremble even more.

Without looking at Tapia, *Pistolero* asked, "Would you like to see my friend take advantage of this fine lady, or will you tell me what I want to know?"

"I will tell you everything," Tapia pleaded. "Just, please, leave her alone. She has nothing to do with this."

"But she has everything to do with your traitorous actions, *señor* Tapia. You sold your soul for a big house with a swimming pool and cabinets full of food while our people suffer. I assume you did all that to protect your wife and your son and daughter. What about your grandchildren? Do they know you are a traitor?"

Tapia looked away, unable to meet the man's harsh gaze.

Pistolero snorted as he shook his head sadly. "They will learn soon enough."

With a quick twist of his wrist, *Pistolero* sliced the rope holding Isabel's legs together. Uzi took the action as his cue, and he was suddenly atop her. The bond holding Isabel's hands together fell away under the knife as Uzi pinned Isabel to the bed.

Standing behind Tapia, *Pistolero* twisted the traitor's head up, forcing Tapia to watch as Uzi violated his wife. Isabel did not fight but lay still on the bed, her brown eyes staring unblinkingly at the ceiling, almost as if she'd gone into a catatonic state. Tapia closed his eyes as Uzi grunted and strained over Isabel's naked body.

Tapia felt the pressure release from his head. When he opened his eyes, he saw *Pistolero* standing at the head of the bed, gun barrel pressed to the skin between Isabel's unseeing eyes.

"No, please!" Tapia screamed. "Please don't kill her."

"But she is in such great pain, *señor*. Do you not wish to spare your wife such indignity? Everyone will soon know the suffering you have caused her, and they will all blame you. Your children will never look you in the eye again, and your grandchildren will hate you for causing such distress to such a beautiful lady."

"I beg you. Don't do anything rash. I will tell you everything."

"You will tell us anyway," Uzi grunted from atop Isabel, hips still luridly grinding into her flesh. He grinned at Tapia. "First, I will finish my work."

Tapia closed his eyes and tried to push away the vision of the Uzi's naked buttocks thrusting against Isabel's inert body, but there was no way to unsee the image of the masked man violating his wife. The knowledge that he had caused such graphic pain settled heavily upon Tapia's shoulders, a burden he would forever bear.

The sound of a muted pop caused Tapia's eyes to snap open.

Isabel lay unmoving on the bed as Uzi continued to have his way with her. She stared impassively at her husband, a third eye opened in her forehead from the suppressed pistol shot, weeping blood to mix with her drying tears. Tapia's heart broke. He wanted very much to die.

Once Uzi had finished his necrophiliac act and he'd buckled his pants around his waist, he and his fellow SEBIN officer lifted Tapia, still fastened to the chair, and carried him through the house. Tapia knew he would never see his home again. He would never hold his wife and children again, and if he were to face a living Isabel, deep in his heart, Tapia suspected she would never forgive him for helping the Americans.

Tapia wanted to ask where they were taking him, but he knew all too well the horrors of their destination. While Tapia and *Pistolero* waited in the garage beside the silver Mercedes, Uzi disappeared out the side door.

The sound of a diesel engine heralded his return. *Pistolero* draped a black hood over Tapia's head. The interior stunk of blood and sweat and fear. There was a bullet hole in it, allowing Tapia to see a small tunnel of his world. He realized with startling clarity that the hood he now wore had been over Garcia's head. *Pistolero* dropped something into his lap, which Tapia guessed was the bag of money by the heft.

They slid Tapia into a van on his back, still bound to the chair.

Tapia knew the men would take him into the heart of Caracas to *El Helicoide*, the massive SEBIN prison. Initially constructed in the 1950s, then President Meina Angarita had envisioned the three-side pyramid as the world's first drive-through shopping plaza and a symbol of Venezuela's modernity. But the mall had not been completed once Angarita had been ousted by a coup, and after languishing for years as an empty shell, Zarate had ordered the SEBIN to take command of it. They had turned it into one of the world's most notorious prisons, renowned for its human rights abuses.

Over the years, Tapia had heard many horror stories from inside *El Helicoide*. There were nicknames for some of the overcrowded cells: The Fish Tank, Little Tiger, and Little Hell, but the one the prisoners feared the most was known as Guantanamo. Tapia had never heard of a reason for the name, suspecting they had copied it from the American prison on the island of Cuba. The Guantanamo cell had a reputation as a nightmare of hellish proportions. Blood and feces coated the walls of the twelve-by-twelve-meter room. Hot, cramped, and airless, the room had no lights, no toilets, and no running water. Inmates urinated into plastic bottles and defecated onto old newspapers or into plastic bags referred to as "little ships." When they had nothing else to use, they just shit in a corner.

Tapia closed his eyes and breathed in and out through his mouth, trying not to add his own brand of terror to the already sweat-soaked and bloody hood, but the torture that awaited him was all he could think about. Even the image of Isabel's catatonic body could not rouse him to anger.

This was all his fault. Tapia had known the consequences when the CIA had recruited him during college, and he had always suspected that, eventually, the SEBIN would catch him.

———

TAPIA FELT the van slow and come to a stop before the driver switched the engine off.

He didn't know how long he'd ridden in the vehicle through stop-and-go traffic and along winding bumpy roads. What he did know was that this was where the actual torture would begin. The purpose of being forced to watch the cold-blooded murder of Luis Garcia and then witnessing his wife being brutally raped and killed was just to soften him up. The SEBIN would pull out his teeth, his finger- and toenails, slowly peel his skin off his body, and shove random objects up his rectum. And that was just the beginning.

The two SEBIN officers dragged Tapia from the van and sat him upright in the chair. Blood rushed to the prisoner's hands and feet, causing them to tingle excruciatingly. He desperately wanted to be released from the chair and to take the hood off his head. To breathe deeply from the air inside his courtyard with the bougainvillea blossoms and the scent of Isabel's cooking would be heavenly, but he knew that was just a dream now.

There were two clicking sounds, metal striking metal—

knives snapping open—and then Tapia was being cut free of his bonds. The thought of one of those knives cutting off his wife's clothing sent a chill through Tapia's nearly immobile body. First, they freed his feet, then worked their way up to the rope binding his chest to the chair.

No sooner had the bonds fallen away than Tapia jumped up and tried to flee, but his feeble, blood-starved legs gave way just two steps into his flight, causing him to fall face-first into the dirt.

His two captors laughed at his crazy antics before hauling Tapia to his feet and marching him over rough ground. Tapia sensed they'd entered a building when his foot struck what he took to be a threshold.

Pistolero and Uzi thrust Tapia forward, and he tumbled onto hard-packed dirt. They pulled the hood from his head, and Tapia blinked rapidly against the light inside the cell. He had expected *El Helicoide* or even *La Tumba*, the prison of solitary confinement cells five stories below the new SEBIN headquarters on Plaza Venezuela, but this was neither of those places.

Miguel Tapia found himself in a makeshift prison cell. The bricks that formed the walls were old and flaky. Moisture glistened on them as water seeped through the pores in the mortar and the brick. A bucket to do his business sat in one corner, and an old wood and green canvas army cot gave him a place to sleep.

His two masked captors slammed shut a wooden door made of stout planks and held together by iron strapping that had rusted and corroded but was still stronger than Tapia's fingers as he clawed at it. He broke two fingernails and embedded a splinter deep under his skin before he gave up and sank to the cold dirt floor. He would never get the splinter out without tweezers or some other tool. The pain was an intense reminder of why Tapia was in the cell to begin with, and it served as penance for the suffering he had caused his wife.

Pounding on the door drew no one's attention. Tapia could feel the walls closing in around him. There was no way out.

Then, the single overhead lightbulb in a metal cage winked out, plunging him into utter darkness.

CHAPTER 2

Ankoko Island, Venezuela

A DARK GREEN MIL MI-17 HELICOPTER LUMBERED OVERHEAD, flying just above the treetops as it crisscrossed the length of the disputed island.

John Phoenix noted the time and date of the helicopter's movements in his waterproof notebook as he swatted a mosquito buzzing his ear. Despite the heavy application of insect repellent, it didn't seem to keep the flying pests away.

"Fuck me," Phoenix muttered as he lay in the jungle near the end of the airstrip that the Venezuelan military had cleared in 1966, right after Guyana had received independence from the United Kingdom. Despite the many protests of the Guyanese government, the Venezuelans hadn't relinquished their new outpost. In fact, Venezuela claimed that over half of Guyana belonged to them in a long-standing territorial dispute that harkened back to colonial days.

Over the years, Venezuela had done little but lodge protests in international courts. Once ExxonMobil discovered major oil deposits off the coast of Guyana in 2015, dictator Michel Zarate had upped his rhetoric against his neighbor.

First, there were detainments of Guyanese fishing vessels by Venezuelan navy ships in Guyana's Economic Exclusive Zone, and then Zarate had issued a decree creating a "Strategic Zone for the Development of the Atlantic Facade" in an area that Guyana claimed encompassed its territorial waters. The most recent aggression by Venezuela was the flight of Sukhoi Su-30 fighter jets over the village of Etering-bang on the Cuyuní River just downstream from Ankoko Island.

And hence the reason John Phoenix was lying in the dirt, sweating his ass off in the jungle. He'd been to worse places like Iraq and Afghanistan, where the sand got into every-thing, including the crack of one's ass. Phoenix didn't mind the jungle, maybe because his mother was Colombian, and even in the brutal heat of Texas summers, he'd never seen her break a sweat.

The Mi-17 made another pass over the airstrip and then came in for a landing, spreading dust and debris across the barren airstrip. Usually, when the military helicopters set down, soldiers burst forth, fleeing the eggbeater like their lives were in jeopardy, but no one exited this bird. Phoenix suspected the occupants were conducting an aerial survey of the airstrip.

Phoenix fitted a pair of binoculars to his eyes and gazed down the length of the runway at the helicopter. Through the helos's front windows, Phoenix could see the pilots wore military green flight suits and white helmets, their dark visors down. The binoculars also contained a laser rangefinder, displaying the distance to the bird in the right lens, while the left lens housed a digital camera. Resting his finger on the shutter button, Phoenix documented the visitors.

Once the rotors had stopped turning on the Russian-made helicopter and the pilots had shut the turbine engines down, the door to the rear compartment slid open. Four men stepped out wearing khaki cargo pants and matching bush shirts with rolled-down sleeves. Phoenix pegged them for Russians based on their fair skin, rounded noses, and dirty blond hair. They had the ramrod posture of men who'd served in the military, and if Phoenix had to guess, they were probably on Ankoko to act as military advisors to the Venezuelan Army.

Driving out of the trees, a Tiuna UR-53AR50, a Venezuelan-made light utility vehicle similar to an American Humvee, pulled to a stop by the knot of newcomers. A man wearing the uniform of a general stepped out. He shook hands with the civilians, who were already appraising the airstrip and the surrounding environs. Phoenix wished he had a parabolic mic to eavesdrop on their conversation.

Eventually, the men all got into the Tiuana and drove away, leaving the pilots to walk, helmets in hand, to the small cluster of buildings that comprised the outpost.

Phoenix would have dearly loved to learn exactly who the newcomers were and what they were doing at the base, but he couldn't stick around. At least he had pictures of the entire entourage to send back to Headquarters in Langley, Virginia. And he'd have to write a report. One thing he'd learned at The Farm while undertaking the Clandestine Service Training program to become a case officer was that he would spend more time drafting reports than actually conducting field exercises, which was another reason he enjoyed being in Guyana. There was little oversight of his activities, and he only wrote reports once a week. Most of the time, he was in his hide, watching, waiting, and gathering intelligence.

He had to leave tonight, though. His supplies were running low, and he had a scheduled rendezvous with a fishing boat that would take him downstream to the town of Eteringbang. While it was still light enough to see, Phoenix checked his hide to ensure he hadn't left any trash or other litter behind that would warn others that he'd been spying on the base.

As Phoenix backed out of his hide, the suspected Russians reappeared and began unloading equipment from the helicopter. Their big yellow cases contained survey equipment, which they quickly set up.

Phoenix speculated on the rumors he'd heard on his way to Eteringbang. After Guyana had dispatched advisors to investigate whether Venezuela was about to broaden and lengthen the Ankoko Island airstrip, they claimed the rumors weren't true, but the CIA had suspected otherwise, and now surveyors were actively working the area.

After snapping off more photos, Phoenix wiggled backward from his hide and brushed leaves over the spot where he'd lain. Then, he quietly made his way to the river.

Squatting by the bank, Phoenix gritted his teeth. His idea of a fun time wasn't swimming through caiman-infested waters to wait for the boat to reach his pickup point, but he didn't want to hang around the water's edge either. He checked his watch, then cinched his waterproof rucksack tighter on his shoulders. With the survey crew working the runway, he had little choice but to exit the area lest they beat through the bush and find him.

Slipping on a pair of diving fins designed to go over his combat boots, Phoenix waded into the water and began kicking toward a distant island in the center of the river. It was more like a sandbar that trees had sprouted on, but it was better than treading water. The Cuyuní River was plagued with things that could kill a man in a heartbeat—caimans, giant snakes, swarms of piranhas, the occasional bull shark that had snuck in from the ocean, and of course the deadliest of all predators: man, and the many diseases infesting the shits they frequently took in the river.

The sound of an outboard reached Phoenix's ears as he swam. Before long, a nineteen-foot wooden boat appeared, being pushed by a seventy-five-horsepower outboard. The boat's owner had festively painted it with hues of bright green, blue, and orange. A lone man sat at the tiller and angled the bow toward Phoenix's position in the water.

Seconds later, the boat coasted to a stop, and Axel, the owner, reached out a hand to the CIA case officer. Phoenix recognized his contact, Axel, and swam toward the boat. Axel helped Phoenix clamor aboard and then returned to the tiller, swinging the boat in a wide arc before heading back downstream.

"Slow down as we pass the ferry," Phoenix ordered.

Axel dropped their speed to a mere idle as they approached the town of Ancón on the northern bank of the Cuyuní. The town was just a collection of huts in a long row, but at the eastern end, there was a ferry to ship people and supplies across the river to the military base on Ankoko.

The Venezuelans had a major advantage over the Guyanese. They had cut a network of roads through the dense jungle to bring in gear and supplies. A single dirt track led from San Martin just downstream out to join Route 10, a major paved road that stretched from the Brazilian border in the south to the Caribbean Sea in the north.

As the boat drifted with the current, Phoenix swatted at another mosquito that buzzed his ear. Despite the arrival of the helicopter at the airstrip, there was no enhanced guard presence at the ferry terminal. Axel cast a line, pretending to be fishing as the Venezuelan troops would quickly run off anyone who stopped along the river near their crossing.

Phoenix motioned for Axel to head out before someone took notice of them. The Guyanese quickly reeled in his line and restarted the outboard. He increased their speed, cutting through the silt-stained water, leaving a wide, creamy wake behind them.

Three miles downstream, the Cuyuní joined the Wenamu River, and another couple of miles through the twisting confluence, they came to Eteringbang. The tiny village wasn't much more than a single street beside the river, lined with brothels, nightclubs, and restaurants, with several convenience stores and a hardware supply. Most of the buildings and homes sat on stilts, but in the not-too-distant past, a flood had ravaged the city and destroyed many of the properties. However, the hearty settlers and natives had rebuilt, using whatever scraps of wood and tin they could find.

Living in the tiny outpost in what the Guyanese government called the "Hinterland" wasn't easy. With Georgetown an hour's flight away and no roads through the Essequibo Region, supplies were limited to what the ferries brought upriver. The primary occupation of the outpost was illegal mining in the mineral-rich jungle, and with no bank in town, the currency of Eteringbang had shifted to gold.

Axel steered his boat up to the concrete quay beside a long row of other such boats that contained plastic oil barrels, improvising a fleet of floating oil trucks that served the miners and the surrounding community.

Phoenix shouldered his pack, having tucked everything neatly away, and bumped fists with his native friend who knew Phoenix was a CIA officer, as Axel had worked with the CIA to keep tabs on the Venezuelan base on Ankoko for years.

"Not a blade of grass," Axel said.

The Guyanese had taken the statement from the song of the same name written by Dave Martins, an iconic Guyanese composer and comedian. Martins maintained that the song was purely about the Guyanese people's deep affection for Guyana and everything Guyanese, but others argued he had written it with the border threat in mind. Despite the disagreements over the song's origins, the Guyanese people sang the song as passionately as they did their national anthem.

Axel's statement meant that Venezuela couldn't take any more of Guyana's land beyond what they already possessed, but Phoenix knew that if Michel Zarate desired to conquer his neighbor, the forty-six-hundred-member strong Guyana Defence Force would be powerless to stop him.

On his way to his hotel, Phoenix waved to one of the police officers who occasionally patrolled the town. The officer had dressed casually in flip-flops and shorts with a machine gun slung over his bare chest. A large gold chain glistened around his neck, and Phoenix thought it was probably the result of a bribe someone had paid the cop.

Phoenix's hotel, another ramshackle building along the river that had been divided into sleeping rooms, also operated as a brothel. Many of the young women were Venezuelans tricked into believing they were signing up for a better life, but in reality, they had what they called "survival sex," earning half a gram of gold for each male they serviced— barely enough for room and board for a single woman, yet most sex workers had at least one child to provide for. It sickened and saddened Phoenix to see the levels of depravity these women had to stoop to in order to provide for themselves.

As he climbed the stairs to the upper deck, he tried not to think about the impoverished people he met or the plight of those around him. He yawned, wondering if sleeping in the bush was more comfortable than sleeping on the thin mattress in his room. But it didn't matter. The Army had taught him how to sleep just about anywhere.

A hooker named Bambi called out to him, propositioning Phoenix just like she did every time she saw him.

Waving her off, Phoenix continued to his room. As a precaution for this mission, he'd brought only what he could fit into his rucksack to Eteringbang and had carried everything with him into the bush. He was thankful he'd left nothing behind as he saw the door to his room was standing wide open. Phoenix entered, half expecting a hooker and her

John to be doing it on his bed, but thankfully, he found no one inside.

Not me, Phoenix mused, *another John.*

Phoenix had learned early in his life that his first name often had negative connotations, and he'd usually dealt with those situations with flying fists. People often referred to a person who could be easily taken advantage of as a "John," but John Phoenix was no dummy, and he was not a man many could take advantage of unless he allowed it. And there were few people in the world he would allow to use him. His employer was usually the one who bent him over the table and made him their plaything. He was the CIA's "John."

After closing the door to his room, Phoenix tossed his pack onto the bed and pulled out his satellite phone. Having turned it off several days ago, Phoenix figured he'd better check if his handler, Leslie Connelly—assistant chief of the Latin American Division and the only person with the number to his phone—had left him any messages.

Moving back outside, Phoenix let the phone connect to the satellites orbiting high overhead. He walked along the street, checking the phone as he stepped up to a counter attached to the side of a house that acted as a tavern. Through the open window, he ordered a beer. By the time he had his cold Banks DIH Caribbean Lager in hand, the phone was pinging irritatingly with text and voicemail messages.

Phoenix sipped his beer and opened the messaging app. He wished he'd left the phone off. A crisis had developed in Caracas, and Connelly wanted him to get off his ass and get moving.

Walking down the street toward a quiet corner, Phoenix sipped his beer and listened to the escalating voicemails, starting from "Where are you, Bowie?" to "If you don't answer the fucking phone, *I'm* going to kill you."

Being from Texas, Phoenix had picked up the codename Bowie after the knife maker and frontiersman who had perished so infamously at the Alamo. When his old boss at Ground Branch, Chris Miller, had bestowed it on Phoenix, the operator hadn't liked it at first, but the name had stuck, and he even used the first name of Jim as a cover alias.

Phoenix dialed the number for Connelly, then lifted the phone to his ear. He took another swallow of beer as the phone rang on the other end.

Connelly answered with, "This is Nightingale. Say ident."

Phoenix gave his credentials to verify his identity to his handler and then asked. "What's so important that I'm not watching a team of Russians survey the Ankoko airport?"

Unfazed by his revelation, Connelly said, "Get to the Eteringbang airport. I have a plane waiting to fly you to George-town, and I have a team locked and loaded."

"A team of Ground Branch shooters?" he asked.

"No. They're contractors. I'll explain everything when you get here."

"What's the mission?" he asked, wanting to have at least some idea of what Connelly was throwing him into.

Without hesitation, his handler said, "Bowie, you're going into VZ to retrieve our asset."

CHAPTER 3

"The team needs to come to me," Phoenix said into the phone.

If Connelly had a team ready to fly, then they should have been waiting in Eteringbang for him to return from the field.

"I want to brief you in Georgetown," Leslie Connelly replied.

Phoenix let out a long sigh. He was used to high-pressure situations and dealing with the whims and demands of his chain of command, but sending him on a hasty mission into the heart of darkness was something he could do without. Then again, that's why they paid him a below-average salary —to save the world. After all, he *was* the CIA's "John."

"Where's the asset?" he asked.

"Outside Caracas," Connelly replied.

"Eteringbang to Georgetown, Georgetown to Caracas. That's a lot of travel time, Nightingale. We're putting the asset in jeopardy by not being on the move already."

"You were in the bush, Bowie. And honestly, that's where you belong."

Phoenix snorted, used to Connelly sniping at him. That's what he got for having a relationship with his fellow case officer. How she had ever become his handler, he didn't know or like. He preferred sleeping with her to taking orders from her.

"But I need you here, so stop drinking beer and get on the plane already," Connelly added.

The phone went dead in Phoenix's hand, and he headed for his room, wondering how she knew he'd been drinking a beer. She had always been excellent at reading him.

Fortunately, no one had tampered with the lock on his door, and his pack was still on the bed where he'd left it. Phoenix didn't bother to inventory it. If someone had stolen from him, he'd never retrieve his property. He just slung the pack over his shoulder and headed for the exit. As he passed Bambi, who wore a bright pink bikini top and cut-off jean shorts that she'd trimmed so high that her boney brown ass cheeks hung out, she propositioned him once again.

With a pocket full of gold dust in one-gram bags, Phoenix could probably buy every hooker in the hotel and have one helluva party, but he wasn't about to dip his wick into any of the ladies he'd met on this trip. Pulling a couple of bags of gold dust from his pocket, he handed them to the woman. "Take the day off, Bambi."

She stared at the bags as he turned to walk off, then she jumped up and threw her arms around him, planting a big, wet kiss on his scruffy cheek. "*Gracias, mi amor.*"

After untangling himself from Bambi's amorous clutches, Phoenix hurried down the street to where the boats sat along the concrete quay. It took a few minutes for him to find Axel, who was lounging in the shade of a bar, drinking a beer. Once they linked up, they were in the boat moments later, speeding upriver toward the airstrip.

The ride through the muddy water in the high-horsepower boat was heavenly compared to the oppressive heat and humidity of the Amazon basin, and the wind kept the mosquitoes away.

Phoenix muddied his boots as he stepped from the bow of

the boat onto land. He turned and pulled more gold packets from his pocket and dropped them into Axel's hand, saying, "Not a blade of grass, brother."

Axel grinned as he took the gold. He put the motor into reverse as Phoenix shoved the boat off the bank, and then the CIA case officer headed up the wide trail to the dirt landing strip, a gash of ochre scratched into the verdant jungle landscape.

A Cessna 208 Caravan sat at the end of the runway beside another Cessna with the markings of Fenix Aviation on its side. Phoenix smiled at the misspelling of his last name and opened the door to the tiny building that served as a terminal. He immediately spotted his pilot, a fellow American who still wore his aviator shades indoors. Phoenix figured he'd been a hotshot Air Force jet slinger that the CIA had lured into flying for one of their many contract carriers. The paychecks were bigger, but the planes were a lot slower.

Phoenix motioned with a nod of his head toward the plane without stepping all the way inside the terminal building. The pilot stood up and came toward him.

Outside, the man asked, "You Bowie?"

"Yeah," Phoenix replied. "Let's get going."

"Good," the pilot said. "I've already filed the flight plan."

The two men walked to the Cessna Caravan and climbed in. They donned headsets, and then the pilot, who introduced himself as Orville Wright, started the engine. After talking to airport control, the pilot taxied them onto the runway, and moments later, they were in the air, flying at 214 miles per hour over the lush green jungle. Guyana had little in the way of roads or infrastructure in the interior. For centuries, the impoverished country had sparse money to spend on large projects, and carving roads through the Amazon basin was tricky at best and an expensive nightmare at worst.

Phoenix took his gaze from the passing scenery, leaned back in the seat, crossed his arms, and closed his eyes. He had other problems to worry about than how Guyana chose to spend its newfound oil wealth.

A man's life was in jeopardy, and the CIA had called Phoenix to save it.

———

John Phoenix's eyes snapped open as the Cessna 208 Caravan's tires chirped on the asphalt runway.

Glancing around, he saw they had landed at Eugene F. Correia International Airport at the eastern edge of Georgetown. Orville Wright taxied them off the main runway toward a small hangar.

Phoenix saw his handler standing beside a Toyota Hilux. Leslie Connelly still looked as beautiful as ever to Phoenix despite all the heartache they'd put each other through.

Nightingale wore charcoal slacks with a matching jacket and a white blouse. The wind teased her loose black hair, and her lips had a hard set to them. Phoenix had fond memories of being her lover, lying in bed, holding hands, admiring the espresso color of her dark skin against his own light brown.

Despite being part Comanche, Phoenix's father was as white as he could get, while his mother was Colombian. Phoenix had inherited his mother's black hair, brown eyes, and olive complexion. In the right light, he could pass as a Latino, or as an Arab, or just an average white guy. Able to speak English and Spanish by the time he was walking, he'd picked up some French in high school and conversational Arabic in Iraq to enhance his utility as a case officer.

Growing up in Texas, along the banks of the South Concho River, Phoenix's father, Hank, had been a skilled tracker and outdoor guide, taking people on hunting and fishing trips. It was on one of those guide trips that Hank had found a woman in the desert, badly dehydrated and left for dead. He'd brought her into his home and had nursed the young woman back to health. Marisol, an undocumented immigrant, had stayed by Hank's side, becoming his wife and giving birth to John. Their home had been a happy one. As a young boy, Phoenix had learned his father's trade, becoming a renowned tracker in his own right, and helped supplement the table by catching fish and hunting for game.

But the happy family had been torn apart when Phoenix was fifteen. A drunk driver had struck and killed his parents as they returned from San Angelo. At the time, John had been on an extended hunting trip and had missed the sheriff's deputy, who had come to give him the devastating news and take him to Child Protective Services.

Phoenix had hidden in the bush for months to cope. He often saw the sheriff's patrol cars stopping by the house to check on him, and had studiously avoided any interactions with law enforcement.

Then, one day, he received a visit from Paul Shaffer, whom Phoenix knew from attending church with his parents. Shaffer claimed he'd spoken to CPS, and they would allow the Shaffers to foster young John. After moving to San Angelo, Phoenix returned to school, but without the ability to escape into the bush, he often felt lost. Adrift in a sea of pain and loneliness, he began a torrid affair with Angela, the Shaffers' youngest daughter. Angela, trying to cope with her own demons, joined some friends for a night of partying and underage drinking in Abilene to celebrate their high school graduation, but the night had taken a wrong turn, and she'd called Phoenix for help.

In the process of saving Angela from the frat house, where she had been drugged and raped, Phoenix had accidentally set fire to the building. It hadn't taken the police long to track down the culprit, and they quickly arrested Phoenix. A lenient judge had understood Phoenix's righteous anger, and he'd presented the eighteen-year-old arsonist with a choice— join the Army or go to jail. Phoenix had signed his indoctrination papers while still in handcuffs, and two days later, he was on a bus to basic training at Fort Leonard Wood, Missouri. From there, it was Airborne School, a stint in the 75th Ranger Battalion, and then on to Special Forces. He'd picked up a bachelor's degree in Homeland Security from Embry-Riddle Aeronautical University and then joined the CIA. He'd been recruited to the agency as a paramilitary case officer, spent a few years downrange with the Special Activities Center, and then transitioned to case officer, running his own assets in the field.

But all that was ancient history to the John Phoenix who stepped out of the Cessna. Phoenix tried not to show any emotion at the sight of Connelly. The situation must have been desperate for her to fly all the way to Guyana just to brief him. Carrying his pack, he walked toward the Toyota, but before he could greet the assistant chief, she turned and headed for the open hangar door.

Phoenix had to let his eyes adjust to the darker interior of the hangar as he followed Connelly inside. Two men and a woman stood beside a table, checking weapons and gear. There were H&K MP5s, Glock 19 pistols, and two Russian-made SVDM Dragunov sniper rifles. They had also laid out an assortment of other kits on the freshly swept concrete floor, each row corresponding to a backpack, which corresponded to each member of the four-person team.

Connelly paused at the table. "John, you know Kendra, Sam, and TJ, don't you?"

Phoenix shook each of their hands. In the CIA, regardless of rank, everyone went by their first names as a security precaution designed to protect their true identities.

"Good to see all of you again," Phoenix said.

Not long ago, members of this same team had helped Phoenix with an operation called Dark Angel. They had prevented an Iranian front company from stealing advanced submarine propulsion technology from MCG Marine

Defense, an American corporation with its testing and assembly plant in New Amsterdam, Guyana.

While Phoenix knew better than to ask where the other members were, he couldn't help himself. Turning to TJ, he asked, "Where's Ryan?"

"He's somewhere on his sailboat right now." TJ shrugged. "I stayed behind with Kendra."

Phoenix had liked Ryan Weller, a capable and skilled troubleshooter for hire. The two men had worked closely on the Dark Angel operation, and he would have liked to have Ryan along for this one, but the group in the hangar had also proved their mettle during that op, and Phoenix knew he could trust them when things went loud.

Kendra and Slater moved off to check other gear, and Phoenix asked TJ a follow-up question. "What did Ryan think about you and Kendra? I know they had a history together."

TJ shrugged. "What's he going to say? He's married to Emily." He turned his back on the case officer to pack his gear into one of the black backpacks.

Phoenix walked over to where Connelly was looking over the gear selection, thinking about his history with her. Instead of bringing up better times, he asked, "How are we getting to Caracas?"

Connelly spread a map on a nearby workbench and pointed to a little dot on it. "There's a dirt strip near La Quintería. Orville Wright will fly the team up, and you'll drive from there."

"How long is the drive?" Phoenix asked.

"Eight hours, give or take," Connelly replied.

Phoenix rubbed his chin as he looked at the map. "Where's this guy being held? *El Helicoide?*"

"Nothing so nefarious," Connelly said. "Our tracker says the SEBIN are holding him in a small compound outside Caracas."

"You have a tracker on this guy?" Phoenix asked. "How did the VZs not catch it?"

"It didn't activate until the asset was taken," Connelly replied.

"Gear's all set," Kendra said, walking over to the two CIA officers.

From their previous interaction, Phoenix knew Kendra Diaz had once been a sicario for the Aztlán Cartel. She was good with a gun and even deadlier with a knife. At just 167cm, or five-feet-six-inches tall, Kendra was a beautiful Mexican woman with silky black hair and soulful brown eyes.

TJ Cab had black hair spiked up with gel at the front and sunbaked skin from working as a fishing guide in the Florida Everglades between jobs with Ryan Weller and his merry band of misfits at Dark Water Research. TJ had been a US Navy boatswain's mate who'd served in the combat-heavy Coastal Riverine Squadrons. He was compact and muscular at five-eight, 173cm, and his blue eyes scanned the gear with an economy of motion that said he'd been doing this kind of thing for years.

Slater Harden had married Kendra's younger sister after their arrival in Guyana. He'd helped them build a security company catering to executive protection, security monitoring, and armed airport escort services. He was a lean, tall man with long blond hair tied up in a man bun, looking more like a surf bum than a former Air Force pararescue specialist.

"When do we get the full mission brief?" Phoenix asked his handler.

"Right now," Connelly said. "I have briefing packets for all of you to read on the plane. Once you land, burn them completely."

"Copy that," Phoenix replied, inspecting the prearranged gear package before he stowed it into the provided backpack.

The hangar was owned by a CIA shell corporation,

allowing for quick flight service. Also, it provided Phoenix with a place to leave his own backpack until he returned from Venezuela. Phoenix placed his kit from the previous mission into a locker, confident he would be returning to Ankoko Island based on the photographs he'd handed over to Connelly on an SD card. He thoroughly inspected his new weapons, and then the team boarded the plane for Venezuela.

Staring out the window as the Cessna took off, Phoenix couldn't help but wonder how truly fucked this mission was.

CHAPTER 4

Caracas, Venezuela

PHOENIX LISTENED TO HIS PEOPLE CHECK IN OVER THEIR TACTICAL radio net, telling him they were all in position above the isolated hacienda where the SEBIN had the CIA asset known as Cobalt Panther locked away. It was just past four in the morning, and the guards were lethargic about their rounds, not expecting anyone to attack them.

So far, things had gone well. The flight to La Quintería had been uneventful. Once on the ground there, Kendra had used her good looks and a screwdriver to commandeer a Mitsubishi Montero for the drive to Caracas. The SEBIN safe house had been easy to find even though it had been a hard drive up the dirt roads through the mountains north of the capital city.

Phoenix rolled his shoulders to ease the tension building between them. He often had a knot in his muscles just between his right shoulder blade and his spine, where he carried all his pent-up emotions. A good masseuse or an acupuncturist could relieve the tension for a while, and he wished he had someone to stick a needle in the knot right then. He shook out his right hand, getting the blood flowing again and trying to ease the pain radiating up his spine. *I should have gone back to being a hunting guide instead of joining the CI-fucking-A.*

"Are you okay?" TJ asked quietly.

"Fine," Phoenix replied tersely, not wanting to dig into his psych profile right then. *Why couldn't you have left me in the bush, Leslie?*

The answer Phoenix knew was that he was the closest case officer to their under-siege asset. After reading the briefing packet three times, Phoenix still had a lot of questions, but the one that no one seemed to have an answer for was where Anaconda—the CIA handler for Cobalt Panther—had disappeared, too. Since Cobalt Panther had activated his emergency signal, there had been no communication with Anaconda. Phoenix figured he was dead. His team would be, too, if the SEBIN caught them in the act of rescuing their prisoner.

"Still just two guards?" Phoenix asked quietly into his headset.

"One at the front," Kendra piped up, acting as overwatch with one of the SVDM sniper rifles.

"One at the rear," Slater added from his position on the mountain on the far side of the compound, carrying his own Dragunov.

"Shit," Phoenix muttered. "Something is definitely wrong with this picture."

"We need to go now," Slater urged. "Two guards will be a piece of cake."

"Two guards are a trap," Phoenix replied. "Stand down."

"Stand down?" TJ whispered.

"All of you shut the fuck up," Phoenix stated. "Quiet on the comms."

Thankfully, silence greeted his admonishment.

"Stay here," Phoenix instructed his partner. "I'm going to have a closer look."

The old farmhouse sat on the saddle of a ridge between two higher mountains. There was only one road in, which could account for the small number of guards, but if Phoenix was running the other end of this operation, he might let an opposing force think it would be an easy snatch and grab—lure the rescuers in and then massacre every last one of them.

But only two guards to stand watch over what Phoenix had counted as five outbuildings besides the main house was just not enough. From his study of the satellite photos provided in his briefing packet, Phoenix knew there were two more houses nearby—one farther down the track near the base of the next mountain and one off to the right, just down the spine. Either of those could be barracks for a larger force.

The other problem Phoenix saw was there were a lot of trees surrounding all the buildings, blocking his snipers' view and that of the orbiting satellites, which Connelly had told him would provide a constant real-time feed, but they seemed to have gone on the fritz about the time Phoenix and his team had gotten into position—another bad omen in Phoenix's mind.

Phoenix flipped down his NVGs and scanned the mountain slopes on both sides of the property before changing them over to thermal imaging. He could see three heat signatures—two guards and the prisoner. Or at least Phoenix hoped it was Cobalt Panther.

It was just too damned quiet for his liking.

Pressing a button on his comms unit, he heard it click and buzz, and then Nightingale came on the line. "What's the holdup?" she asked.

"You got eyes on this compound?" Phoenix asked Connelly.

"Our sat feed is still out, but Cobalt Panther's emergency

beacon is squawking from the small storage shed behind the house," Nightingale replied.

"How many people did you count on thermal before losing the feed?" Phoenix asked.

"Three, Bowie."

"I'm going in to take a look," Phoenix said. "There is something definitely wrong with this picture."

"Just get it done." Nightingale terminated the communication with a click.

"All right, TJ," Phoenix said softly to his companion. "Stay put, and I'll be back shortly. If the shit hits the fan, you guys know what to do."

"Roger that," TJ said.

Phoenix worked his way down the hill toward the single-lane dirt road that ran through the property. Taking the road was much easier than beating through the bush, where he might stumble into a cactus or trip over a poisonous snake. The snakes didn't bother him. He'd been on many rattlesnake roundups in Texas. It was the danger of accidentally being bitten by one of the reptiles that he wanted to avoid.

"I've got you," Slater said.

"Eyes on," Kendra chimed in.

Phoenix stayed in the shadows of the larger trees, moving cautiously forward, sweeping his gaze side to side to spot trip wires attached to explosives or laser beams that would sound an alarm when broken. It disturbed him that he saw no sign of a military-style operation, and he had to wonder if the SEBIN felt ultra-comfortable on their home turf.

Once Phoenix reached the concrete apron at the front of the garage, he knelt and drew his suppressed Glock. He wanted to just sneak and peek, but he was more than prepared if the need for gunplay arose. Holding his breath, Phoenix listened to the wind moan through the trees. He heard the creaking of branches and the occasional tap, tap, tap of a twig against a windowpane. Long ago, as a boy on the hunt, his father had taught him how to quiet his body and mind, to still those parts of him that otherwise might give away his position to the quarry.

He'd expected to smell cigarette smoke from the guards or even hear the rustle of their gear as they moved, but no matter how much he strained, he couldn't hear or smell them.

Standing, Phoenix edged forward along the front of the garage. He wondered if there was a four-by-four they could use as a getaway vehicle inside. During their surveillance over the last twenty-four hours, they'd only seen a single black SUV come or go from the hacienda.

Phoenix tightened the grip on his gun in his right hand, his trigger finger laying along the slide. The suppressor made the gun cumbersome, but his forearm muscles quickly accommodated the extra weight. However, the knot in his back was screaming at him.

"Movement to your front," Kendra said.

Connelly's warning to get this done quickly echoed in Phoenix's ears, reminding him that Cobalt Panther's life was in danger.

"Take them now," Phoenix commanded.

He didn't hear any gunshots, but Phoenix saw the head of the guard at the front of the house snap back sharply as Kendra's bullet entered it. The guard lost his footing, and he toppled to the ground.

"Moving," TJ said, rushing from his position to join Phoenix now that the shooting had started.

Phoenix ran past the dead guard, angling for the shed where the SEBIN supposedly held Cobalt Panther.

"What the hell did you do, Bowie?" Slater asked. "The entire place is swarming with guards. It looks like you kicked over a hornet's nest."

Phoenix swore under his breath. He knew it had been too good to be true. It was a trap. He picked up his pace, running for what looked to be an old cold storage shed. The original building had been dug into the hillside to keep the interior cool. A single strand of what appeared to be an extension cord ran from a junction box beside the heavy wooden door back toward the house on rough wooden poles.

He raised his Glock and shot the cell's padlock, but all the bullet did was damage the lock's exterior. Without thinking, Phoenix grabbed a small clump of C-4 plastic explosive and jammed it into the corner of the door and frame. Stabbing a detonator into the plastique, Phoenix stepped out of the way and hit the remote to blow the charge.

Behind him, the hacienda grounds swarmed with SEBIN troopers. They wore black uniforms, helmets with night vision monocles, balaclavas, and chest rigs. One man took a sniper round to the throat—ripped off his feet like a giant had punched him. A team of six or eight SEBIN stacked up to head for the prison cell. Phoenix palmed a fragmentation grenade and hurled it sidearm at the men, blasting most of them off their feet.

Phoenix turned and kicked open the shed door that he'd blown the lock off just seconds ago. He had to snap on a flashlight to see the prisoner hunkered under his canvas cot. *A fat lot of good that will do.*

"*Vamanos!*" Phoenix ordered. "I'm here to rescue you."

The man had trouble standing and seemed to Phoenix to be taking an irritatingly long time to drag himself out from under the cot. Phoenix turned in the doorway and raised his MP5. He shot two men rushing toward him. He really was Jim Fucking Bowie. This godforsaken shed was going to be his last stand.

"What's going on?" Nightingale demanded in his ear.

"I told you it was a trap!" Phoenix shouted. "Now, get off the fucking net and let me do my job. Where the hell are you, TJ?"

"I'm at the far end of the compound. I can't get to you. The troops are forming a defensive position around the shed.

"Figure something out, double quick!" Phoenix shouted above the roar of automatic gunfire.

Cobalt Panther had just gotten to his feet when Phoenix dove on top of him, body-slamming the weary prisoner to the ground and driving the air from the man's lungs in an audible grunt. Just as they smacked into the hard-packed dirt, a hail of bullets tore through the front wall of the shed.

A ricocheting round knocked over the tin pail the prisoner had used as a latrine. While the air in the ventless room had been heavy with the smell of sweat, fear, and bodily fluids before, it absolutely reeked now as a puddle of piss spread across the dirt.

Phoenix could see another line of troops advancing toward his position through the door. They had their AK-103s braced against their shoulders, sending waves of lead into the shed. Gaping holes appeared in the walls, and debris rained down on the two men huddled there.

Spinning, Phoenix tried to use his body as a shield and the heavy door as a barricade. Shouldering his submachine gun, Phoenix returned fire. He could see men falling, presumably from shots from his snipers, and he hoped his meager 9x19mm bullets were penetrating the oncoming enemy as well.

Phoenix crawled off Cobalt Panther and dragged him by the collar of what had once been a dress shirt toward a far corner of the cell where the shed had been dug into the side of the mountain. He hoped the extra dirt would help shield them from the incoming rounds, but the front of the shed was still susceptible to attack.

An explosive crack split the air from a grenade, striking the top of the shed, causing Phoenix's ears to ring and the front of the shed to blow apart in spectacular fashion. Shards of metal and wood cascaded down on the two men trapped inside. A support beam fell from the roof and drove itself straight into Cobalt Panther's stomach, sticking out like a massive, quivering arrow before toppling over and ripping out the CIA asset's guts.

"No!" Phoenix screamed in frustration and anger.

Cobalt Panther reached up, grabbed Phoenix by the chest plate, and pulled him close. The man whispered hoarsely, *"Caballito del diablo."*

"What?" Phoenix cried, not understanding the man's words.

With his dying breath, Cobalt Panther spoke just a little louder, *"Libélula."*

Phoenix saw the man's eyes flutter, and then his body went limp, releasing what was left of his bowels in a long exhalation of gas and putrid stink.

There was little Phoenix could do now as the SEBIN force advanced on his position. Obviously, they didn't care about taking prisoners. Just hoisting the dead bodies of foreign invaders would bring them worldwide attention, claiming another invasion by the Americans to dethrone Zarate.

Slapping a fresh magazine into his SMG, Phoenix prepared himself for his last stand. He sat with his back to the cool earth, inhaling deeply to re-oxygenate his body. He could distinguish individual SEBIN troopers now, backlit by a raging fire near the main house. Smoke hung in the air, thick and cloying. With each breath, he inhaled the rot of a dead man and the stench of the fire. He blinked his eyes, realizing he was sweating profusely.

He'd been in some rough patches before, but this was by far the worst. Phoenix didn't bother to shoulder his gun. He switched it to three-shot burst mode, rested the barrel on a piece of wood that had fallen across his lap, and fired indiscriminately at the nearest enemy.

John Phoenix finally knew how he was going to die.

CHAPTER 5

TJ Cab knelt beside the rear door to the hacienda's main house, readying to breach.

Moments earlier, he had rolled a grenade under the large propane tank just meters from the house. The resultant explosion had nearly blown him off his feet even though he was ten meters away. A rolling conflagration had ignited another nearby building, turning it into a blazing inferno. He hoped the distraction would help Phoenix escape with Cobalt Panther from the shed at the rear of the property.

But the SEBIN troops continued unabated toward his team leader's position. TJ knew it had been dangerous to let Phoenix go alone, but he'd had little say in the matter. He couldn't figure out where the hell all the troops were coming from and how everyone had missed such a large force amassed near the target.

He stood swiftly and booted in the French door, shattering the feeble lock and busting out several panes of glass. Moving into the house, TJ shouldered his MP5, using his night vision goggles to aid in his sweep of the empty rooms as he headed for the garage. Phoenix had instructed him to figure something out, so he was going to steal a ride.

Entering the garage, TJ glanced around at the vehicles parked inside. A Mercedes G550 caught his eye. He checked the ignition, then the sun visor for the keys before finding them on a hook by the door he'd come through just seconds earlier. He grabbed the keys and jumped into the vehicle. The 416-horsepower twin-turbo V8 roared to life with a twist of the key. He didn't bother to open the flimsy carriage doors, just powering through them with the steel bull bar on the front bumper of the SUV, shattering the wooden doors from their hinges.

TJ spun the wheel hard over to the right. The rear wheels churned wildly in the dirt as they tried to gain traction.

"I'm coming, Bowie," TJ called over the radio, then added for the benefit of the others, "I'm in the G-Wagon. Don't light me up."

He didn't have to worry about his teammates riddling the machine with bullets because the SEBIN did an excellent job of it once they realized TJ was barreling toward them. The former boatswain's mate never let off the gas as he crashed into the knot of soldiers approaching the shed.

A SEBIN trooper rolled up over the hood, crashed into the windshield, and went spinning away. TJ felt the vehicle shudder as bullets smacked into the thin, metal skin, boring holes through the interior and shattering windows. The windshield imploded on itself and showered crystals of safety glass all over TJ, the front seats, and the floorboards. He drew his pistol and aimed it out the front, shooting at the SEBIN as he drove with his left hand.

Approaching the shed, TJ spun the wheel again and turned the G-Wagon broadside to the opening.

"Let's go!" TJ shouted, firing his pistol through the vacant driver's window.

Phoenix jerked the rear passenger door open and dove inside. No sooner had he landed on his belly on the supple leather seat than TJ stomped on the gas, throwing power to the rear wheels. He turned the G-Wagon around and headed out of the compound.

"Where's Cobalt Panther?" TJ asked, realizing Phoenix was his lone passenger.

"He didn't make it," Phoenix replied, getting to his knees and firing his MP5 out the rear window at the receding enemy, then called over the radio, "Rally Point X-Ray. All team members report. Rally Point X-Ray."

TJ kept the power on as they headed up the spine of the mountain. There was one road in and out of the Culebrillas housing development, which meant they would have to ditch the G-Wagon and go on foot through the mountains at some point. The longer they were in Venezuela, the greater their chances of capture were, and now that the SEBIN knew the team was in the area, they would stop at nothing to detain the Americans.

Instead of turning and heading down the mountain toward Caracas, TJ headed higher into the hills. The road was steep and narrow, nothing more than a rutted two-track that jostled and bounced the two men as TJ navigated their way toward safety. Under the trees, they were in pitch-black darkness, but in the open, the brightness of the Milky Way spilled out before them. With no headlights, the going was tough, and Phoenix had to turn on his flashlight so that TJ had light to see what lay ahead.

At a bend in the road, Phoenix ordered TJ to stop so they could abandon their ride. As TJ climbed out, he took his foot off the brake. The battered G-Wagon idled forward, then picked up speed as it careened pell-mell down the side of the mountain, crashing through the brush like a raging bull elephant.

Phoenix led the way on foot up the mountain road, the red lens on his flashlight casting an eerie glow over the trees and bushes. From where they were, it was seven miles as the crow flew across the Venezuelan Coastal Range, the northeastern extension of the Andes Mountains, to the Caribbean Sea. Trudging up and down the mountains, however, would make the trip much longer.

"What happened to Cobalt Panther?" TJ asked.

"KIA," Phoenix said simply.

TJ wanted to ask more questions but knew Phoenix wouldn't provide any answers, so he remained quiet. Part of him was thankful they didn't have to lug an injured man through the rugged hills. As part of their briefing, the team had discussed the possibility that the SEBIN might have tortured Cobalt Panther, rendering him sick or injured, and they knew moving with him would be slow going. So, they had planned to evacuate using several vehicles, but like most good battle plans, it had gone to shit just as soon as the first gunshot had been fired.

The two men walked silently along, moving away from the deadly ambush site and hopefully farther from the clutches of the terrifying SEBIN. TJ had only agreed to this mission because Kendra had said she was going. She had plenty of combat experience but wasn't as well-trained as TJ or even Phoenix, who had probably forgotten more about fighting than either of them knew combined. Phoenix was stoic and uttered few words regarding the mission briefing or his life history. What little TJ knew about the man had come from Ryan Weller, and Ryan had just touched on the man's career highlights in the Army Special Forces and then the CIA.

TJ prayed the man's experience could lead them out of danger now.

CHAPTER 6

Kendra Diaz crouched in the darkness, waiting for her brother-in-law to arrive.

She had made her way off her mountain perch after tossing the big SVDM Dragunov sniper rifle off the side of a cliff. She could run faster without it, and it wasn't a close-quarters combat weapon by any means. The 1.2-meter-long gun was hard to bring to bear in such situations. Besides, Kendra had run out of her limited supply of ammunition mid-firefight, and she had begun her exfil through the mountains even before Phoenix had called for them to head for Rally Point X-Ray.

Once Slater made it to the rendezvous, they would head for the rally point together.

She heard a twig snap and spun, leveling her suppressed Glock in the general vicinity of the noise. The Trijicon night sights glowed intensely in the dark. For a moment, Kendra feared they would give away her position, but then Slater hissed, "Hey, Big Sis. I'm coming in."

He'd been calling her "Big Sis" since the day they'd first met when she'd found him chatting up Yasmine at a waterfront bar near where they'd docked their liveaboard trawler.

Yasmine had a way with men, while Kendra was more stand-offish. Slater had told her she radiated a "go fuck yourself" vibe, which she attributed to her training and the residual effects of being a killer for the former Aztlán Cartel.

Now, Kendra breathed a sigh of relief to hear her fellow sniper's gruff male voice. She lowered her weapon but kept it ready in case it was another trap by the SEBIN. From the onset of the action, Kendra had wondered whether Phoenix and TJ would make it out of the compound. It broke her heart to think that her lover might have perished in the fray when she was just getting to know him.

Even though she'd seen the G-Wagon hauling ass away from the hacienda, she didn't know if Phoenix or TJ had sustained any injuries. Rally Point X-Ray meant the asset was dead, and the team was on their own instead of meeting with a Blackhawk helicopter that would have whisked them out of Venezuela to a U.S. Navy warship.

"You ready to move?" Slater asked.

"Let's go," she said without hesitation.

The former PJ led the way, having more land navigation experience than Kendra. Since it was so dark in the mountains that she could barely see her hand in front of her face, Slater had used a short length of rope to tie them together. It was just long enough to keep their feet from tangling as they walked, but not so long they could accidentally wrap it around a tree and bring their progress to a jerking halt.

Kendra kept a hand on the rope, and despite their attempts to be stealthy, they made a lot of noise moving through the brush.

"Did you see them get out?" Kendra asked, her voice barely above a whisper as she spoke into their comms unit.

"I saw a vehicle leave the compound, but I don't know who was in it," Slater replied.

"By the way it was shot up; I think it was them," Kendra said hopefully. Doubt about what she'd witnessed crept into her mind. If she thought about it too hard, it might just cripple her. Kendra had always believed that attachments made her weak, so she had formed few other than with her sister, but Slater had grown on her, and then TJ had come into her life. Worrying about TJ meant her mind wasn't on the mission, so she forced herself to think of him as any other man she'd previously encountered—an expendable asset.

"Once the vehicle left, the shooting stopped," Slater replied, "so it was probably them."

They fell silent as they struggled up a steep slope, breathing heavily with exertion.

The false dawn brought just enough light to make out individual trees, which they grabbed to aid in their climb. They had mapped this route on the plane after looking at satellite photos. But sometimes, the eye in the sky couldn't accurately indicate the ruggedness of the terrain, and Slater and Kendra were finding out firsthand just how true that was.

Pausing just below the summit of the next ridge, Slater called a halt to their climb. They rested under a dwarf tree, sipping water and watching the sunrise, spreading light across Caracas far in the distance.

Turning their backs on the magnificent scenery, the two infiltrators crawled to the top of the ridge. From there, they peered down at their destination—Rally Point X-Ray.

Slater removed his binoculars from his pack and glassed the distant mountain rendezvous. It appeared to be a ramshackle collection of rusted tin, and corrugated metal cobbled together into a small hut.

"Do you see anything?" Kendra asked, keeping an eye on their six.

"Nothing moving, but they could be inside."

"Or up in the hills, waiting for us to make the first move," Kendra replied.

"There's only one way to find out," Slater said. He let his

binoculars dangle from the neck strap as he slung his pack over his shoulders.

The two snipers headed down the side of the mountain, carefully searching for the best route through the brush and weeds. Full daylight made the going easier, and they covered the ground quickly, moving to within one hundred meters of the rally point before they stopped a second time to reconnoiter the area. Slater glassed the buildings again and then tried to raise Phoenix or TJ on the comms.

Kendra felt her heart sink when no one answered. She still worried about TJ's safety despite her trying to put him in a box at the back of her mind.

Slater pulled his pistol from its holster. "We go slow and clear the hut. Stay with me and move as one."

Kendra tapped him on the shoulder to indicate that she understood as she unholstered her pistol. From X-Ray, they were to hike over the central spine of the Coastal Range, then follow an old creek bed down to civilization, steal a vehicle, and drive the coast road to Guiria on the Paria Peninsula, where they planned to either steal a boat or pay off some pirates to take them across the sixteen kilometers of open water to Trinidad. But first, the two groups had to link up.

Reasoning out the scenario, Kendra decided that if Phoenix and TJ didn't turn up, she would take Slater south by any means necessary. It meant traversing the entire length of the Venezuelan countryside, but she felt it was safer than Phoenix's desired scheme. The problem was that Slater just looked like a big, dumb American. While that worked to their advantage in Guyana while running their security company, it didn't work so well when trying to blend in with the local populace in a hostile country.

As they approached the hut, the big blond surfer walked forward, gun up, sweeping the area before him and to his left. Kendra kept one eye on their six and swept the right side of their path with her weapon. The jungle seemed oppressively quiet and hot. Not even a bird sang in the trees.

Slater and Kendra arrived at the hut but found no one inside, and despite repeated calls on the radio, they couldn't raise their teammates.

"They're all right," Slater reassured her, reading the anguish on Kendra's face.

"Zulu?" Kendra asked, wanting to get moving to their next rendezvous point. If their teammates weren't there, she would start on her own plan to the south.

"First, we rest a bit," Slater suggested. "Let's get something to eat and drink."

Kendra knew Slater was buying time, hoping Phoenix and TJ would turn up soon. She hoped so, too.

Instead of sacking out in the hut, they moved a couple hundred meters up the slope and set up a bivouac under a camouflage tarp. A light rain began to fall just as they crawled under their makeshift shelter and settled in to eat protein bars and sip water.

Kendra found herself checking her watch every couple of minutes while Slater used his binoculars to study the far mountainside and the approaches to the hut.

"I gotta pee," Kendra announced and then wiggled out from under the tarp. The rain continued to fall, but her bladder was the most pressing need.

Just as she was about to pull her pants up, TJ whispered, "That's a sight for sore eyes."

Kendra nearly jumped out of her skin, quickly hoisting up her pants and buckling her belt. When she had both hands free, she lunged at TJ, wrapping him in a bear hug. "You nearly scared the shit out of me."

"At least you had your pants down," he mused, letting her go.

"That's not funny," she said, then hugged him again. "Where have you been?"

"We took the scenic route. Bowie wanted to get to a mountain top to call home on his sat phone. His encrypted comms gear got smashed during the firefight."

"Do you know if we're still going out through Trinidad?" she asked.

TJ shrugged. "Bowie altered the plan following a conversation with Nightingale."

"I still can't believe she went back to Washington instead of staying close by."

TJ replied that he didn't think she wanted to dirty her hands.

"What's the new plan?" Kendra asked.

"Bowie wants to powwow. He's down at the shelter."

Kendra led TJ through the woods to where she and Slater had set up their temporary camp. She was eager to get moving, but as they made their way down the slope, Kendra and TJ froze in their tracks at the sound of an approaching truck engine.

CHAPTER 7

Phoenix unslung his H&K MP5 as he left the bivouac and made his way toward the hut designated as Rally Point X-Ray. He, too, could hear the engine laboring up the steep hill over a narrow, rutted road.

They weren't expecting company, so these were either tourists looking to picnic in the jungle or SEBIN troops searching for Cobalt Panther's rescue team.

Phoenix suspected the latter.

The vehicle turned out to be an older model Toyota Landcruiser with extra lights on the front bumper and a carburetor snorkel running up the left-side A-pillar. Inside, four men in black uniforms rode with the windows down and gun barrels poking out.

Phoenix activated his comms unit. "Let them dismount. If we can secure the vehicle, it will help with the exfil."

No one answered nor fired their weapons as the SEBIN troops stepped out and began a systematic sweep of the small valley. Time seemed to tick slowly past as the men beat the bush. They came within three meters of where Kendra and Slater had erected their tarp, but luckily, the troops didn't spot it.

Rain continued to splatter down, deadening the sounds of the jungle and making conditions miserable for everyone involved. Fortunately, the leader of the SEBIN force decided he'd had enough of getting wet and headed for the hut, his men grouping up to join him. They huddled in the shack, several of them lighting cigarettes.

"All right, boys and girls, TJ and I are going to take them," Phoenix said over the comms.

He and TJ had the hut in a crossfire, and since they were the only ones sporting submachine guns, it was like shooting fish in the barrel.

"On three," Phoenix said, then counted up from one.

At the designated number, he and TJ let loose several quick bursts of fire, riddling the tin and quickly executing everyone inside the building. Phoenix didn't feel bad about catching the Venezuelans unawares. They would have killed him and his team just as quickly if they'd found them.

Phoenix let off his trigger and shouted for TJ to ceasefire.

As the echoes of gunfire died away, Phoenix trotted up to the hut, pulling his pistol out. Once inside, he put a bullet in the forehead of each man to make sure they were all dead. It was an old habit, and no one involved was going to call the Hague and complain about human rights abuse.

Exiting the hut, Phoenix ordered his team to mount up in the Landcruiser.

He got behind the wheel and handed his sub gun to Kendra, who took the front passenger seat. After turning the Landcruiser around, he headed down the trail, now a muddy mess from the still-falling rain. The windshield wipers hadn't been changed in a long time, resulting in the half-rotten rubber leaving streaks across the window with only small patches of clear glass to see through. Phoenix muttered a curse at whoever was in charge of vehicle maintenance.

The road widened several miles later, but tree branches still scraped the sides of the vehicle. Several times, Phoenix had to back up and charge forward even harder to make it up a slippery slope or through a giant mud puddle. Rain continued to pound down, increasing to a torrential downpour.

Passing several small clusters of homes, Phoenix hoped the occupants weren't paying attention to the passing vehicle. At least the rain would obscure their view and, hopefully, with it, their recollection that anyone had passed that way.

Even in four-wheel drive, the Landcruiser had trouble staying on the narrow track, wanting to slide down the mountain as they traversed its long slope.

Finally, the road rose to the spine of the mountain ridge. There was nothing to see but trees on either side and if the Landcruiser slipped off the road, they were in for a wild ride downhill. Phoenix concentrated hard as he drove, the knot in his shoulder making his whole arm ache, but he didn't dare take his hands off the wheel to stretch his muscles. He gritted his teeth against the pain and kept driving.

Just after passing a small farm with cleared land on both sides of the road, their journey came to a halt in a clearing about the size of a suburban cul-de-sac, except instead of houses, it was lined with banana trees.

"I thought you knew where you were going," Kendra said.

"I did. The map shows this road goes all the way into town," Phoenix replied.

"I told you to stop and ask for directions," Kendra joked, "but no, you're a man. You don't *need* to ask for directions."

Even though Phoenix knew she was just trying to ease the tension of the situation, he still gave her the middle finger salute and said, "Fuck you."

"Hey, that's my job," TJ piped up from the back seat, letting everyone know that he was the one who had a special relationship with the former sicario.

"What now?" Slater asked.

"I guess we're getting wet," Phoenix replied. "And not just in your panties, Kendra."

She smiled as she flipped him the bird.

Phoenix grinned back at her as he got out of the Landcruiser. Reluctantly, the rest of the team followed him into the pouring rain. Phoenix pulled a thermite grenade from his kit and tossed it into the Landcruiser. It would burn the Toyota to the ground, even in the rain.

Wet, miserable, and tired, the four-person team formed a conga line with Phoenix at the point, and Slater walking drags, now carrying TJ's MP5.

A half mile later, they came to a stream overflowing with turbid water. They followed it downhill and discovered a suitable spot to cross, avoiding the need to wade through the knee-deep water, despite already being soaked to the bone.

Phoenix navigated by compass, humping them over the low foothills toward the outskirts of Caracas. They crossed several roads, huddling in the bush until no vehicles were coming, then darting across one by one.

Eventually, they broke out of the trees into an industrial area. All four team members shed their combat gear and changed into the civilian clothing they'd brought, which included dress slacks and guayaberas for the men and jeans and a T-shirt for Kendra, then stowed their wet gear in their backpacks.

"Kendra and I will be right back," Phoenix told the other two. "Stay loose and stay alert."

Phoenix led Kendra into a parking lot, where they discreetly checked the doors of various cars and trucks to see if their owners had left them unlocked. Crime was high in the country, and it surprised Phoenix to find a ride that was both unlocked and had the keys under the floor mat. He couldn't help but wonder what was wrong with the old Buick station wagon.

Years of hyperinflation and a ban on the importation of

new cars and trucks had led Venezuelan car owners to cling to their vehicles much longer than they normally would have. It wasn't uncommon for cars to catch fire along the side of the road due to delayed maintenance or to crash from the same lack of care for the engines and brakes.

Phoenix started the Buick's rattling motor, hoping it would at least get them out of town. He noticed a cloud of white smoke pouring out of the tailpipe. Slowly shaking his head in disbelief and disgust that he'd picked such a rotten vehicle, Phoenix put the car in gear and backed out of the parking space. He cruised through the lot to where he'd left TJ and Slater, with Kendra jogging over to join them.

The ride out of town was not smooth as the car's shocks had worn out long ago, and the brakes squealed each time Phoenix barely touched the pedal. Trailing after them, the tale-tell cloud of smoke foretold a coming breakdown.

"You couldn't find a better car?" Slater asked.

"Next time, I'll let you pick the ride," Phoenix replied.

"Where are we going, anyway?" TJ asked.

"There's a heliport between here and Mampote," Phoenix stated, not giving them the rest of the details but purposely keeping them in the dark to prevent them from squawking if the SEBIN picked them up.

They hadn't gone more than a handful of kilometers before the Buick's engine coughed and belched a gigantic cloud of smoke from the tailpipe. Steam poured out from under the hood as Phoenix negotiated the station wagon off to the side of the road.

"Everyone out," Phoenix said, then glanced over his shoulder at Slater. "You're up, stud."

With the team in civies, all of them except for Slater blended in with the local population. The big American stood out like a sore thumb, towering a good head above the average Venezuelan male.

Not wanting to let the man get into trouble, Phoenix

ordered TJ and Kendra to stay with the broken-down Buick and keep their weapons out of sight while he accompanied Slater to search for a new car. The last thing they needed was for some good Samaritan to call the police to report strangers with firearms in their neighborhood.

In 2012, under the oppressive regime of Hugo Chávez, the Venezuelan government had banned all sales of firearms and ammunition to private citizens, mandating that only military, police, and security forces could legally own and buy guns. Once the new law was in place, Chávez had run a months-long amnesty program, urging his citizens to swap their arms for electrical goods. When that failed, forced gun confiscation and destruction began with the police and military going house to house, conducting invasive search and seizure raids.

Chávez, like other dictators before him, knew that to control the populace completely, he had to disarm them. The Venezuelan people were now suffering from the simple mistake of giving up their ability to protect themselves.

The destruction and collapse of one of the greatest economies in the world was not from a sudden armed over-taking of the government, but from the lies that Chávez had spread, and the Venezuelans had regretted their decision to give up their guns ever since. With no way to fight back against tyranny, a succession of demented and vindictive regimes had held the Venezuelan people hostage.

Still, Phoenix knew there were plenty of illegal guns on the streets, many the result of Venezuelan government officials confiscating them in raids and then reselling them on the black market. The weapons Phoenix's team carried would fetch a high price, but Phoenix wasn't interested in selling them. He wanted to use them to help his team escape before the SEBIN swept them up and killed them.

Following Slater through the narrow alleyways between rundown apartment buildings, Phoenix watched as the taller American searched for another mode of transportation to get the team to the heliport. Nightingale had told Phoenix to contact a man named Javier, who would fly them out of Venezuela, but first, they needed to get to Mampote.

Slater slowed and studied the cars parked along the curb. They were two blocks from where they'd left Kendra and TJ, and Phoenix felt totally exposed. Several people had taken an interest in the blond surfer. They leaned out open windows or catcalled from the streets. Women propositioned him, several fourteen years old or younger, and when Slater rebuffed them, an old woman, missing several of her front teeth, offered to service him.

Again, Slater turned the woman away.

Phoenix continued to hang back. He knew Slater could handle himself. He'd seen that firsthand on the two operations they'd worked together. However, an urban environment differed from fighting in the jungle or extracting a hostage from a freighter at sea.

Slater wasn't having any luck finding another vehicle for the team's extraction, and then Murphy's Law snuck up and kicked him in the nuts as a police vehicle came to a stop beside him, lights flashing.

CHAPTER 8

Phoenix couldn't believe their turn of luck as the Chinese-made JAC police truck screeched to a halt in front of his teammate Slater.

Despite his outward calm, Phoenix felt a jolt of adrenaline as his heart rate spiked. The four-door truck sported a roll bar with flashing red and blue lights now strobing across the wet pavement and reflecting off the windows of nearby shops and apartments.

The residential neighborhood provided little in the way of cover. Two-story or taller buildings lined each side of the street with gated or shuttered doorways and barred windows. There were no sidewalks, just narrow strips of concrete between the road and the buildings with cars parked close in, leaving barely enough room to pass between them and the apartment complexes. Phoenix knew any number of prying eyes were peering out from behind curtains or blinds, checking the police action on the street or keeping a close watch on the two strange men prowling through the neighborhood.

The downpour had stopped as suddenly as shutting off a spigot, and now the sun was shining brightly, raising steam from the pavement. The clean tang of ozone and the stench of wet garbage filled the air. Phoenix felt the weight of the Glock in the holster at the small of his back, with the suppressor weighing heavily in his pants pocket.

Squatting behind a parked car, he slipped the round metal tube out and held it loosely in his hand. He waited to see what the police would do before taking out his pistol.

From the police truck, two men in uniforms dismounted. The passenger had his Beretta Px4 Storm pistol out, and the driver had his hand on the butt of his, still in its holster.

Phoenix screwed the suppressor onto his Glock and then inched around the car toward the standoff. He kept a close eye on Slater through the car windows and tried not to make sudden movements that would alert the cops to his presence.

Slater listened to the cops tell him to put his hands up and then complied with their order. He said a few words in Spanish to let them know he understood them.

"We have a situation developing," Phoenix muttered into his comms unit, then gave Kendra and TJ precise directions to their location. "I need you guys to move up now."

"Moving," TJ confirmed.

"Be ready for action. If Slater can't work himself out of this jam, we'll have to go loud." Phoenix didn't like the idea of killing law enforcement officers even if half of them in Venezuela were on the take.

Slater pulled out his Canadian passport and handed it to the first cop.

"What are you doing here?" the cop asked, glancing down at the open passport.

"Scouting the talent," Slater replied, hooking his thumb over his shoulder. "There's some pretty good pussy up there."

The cop shook his head in disbelief, a thin smile playing across his lips at the man's arrogance. He tapped the closed passport against the palm of his other hand as if considering what to do with Slater.

Before the cop could make another move, three fighting-age males arrived on motorcycles. Phoenix recognized the bikes as Kawasaki KLRs by their distinctive front fairing, even though the owners had spray-painted them completely black. These new arrivals wore dirty blue jeans, black para-military boots, black shirts with the likeness of Che Guevara printed on the front, and ski masks to cover their faces. Two had colorful bandanas tied around their necks, and one sported a fanny pack, but the problem, Phoenix recognized, was that they all carried pistols and AK-style automatic rifles.

These men were *colectivos*—members of a government-funded group comprised of civilians or retired police and military. They acted as a state security force sanctioned by Chávez and Zarate to control various neighborhoods, suppressing political and criminal activities. Phoenix knew the *colectivos* were nothing more than ruthless criminals who preyed on the citizens of the neighborhoods they claimed to protect.

The masked man with the fanny pack snatched Slater's passport from the police officer's hand and ordered the police to leave. Without hesitation, the two uniforms hopped into their truck and drove away.

Phoenix felt his heart sink. At least Slater stood a fighting chance with the police. The *colectivos* like to rob or kidnap their victims, and on occasion, they would outright execute the "dissidents" in the street.

"You guys in position?" Phoenix whispered urgently into the comms.

"Say the word," TJ replied. "Kendra has the guy on the left. I've got the middle, and you've got Fanny Pack."

"Roger that," Phoenix replied as he watched the *colectivos* order Slater to his knees.

He rose from his crouch behind the car and strode toward the cluster of men. "Engage now."

Bringing up his pistol, Phoenix shot Fanny Pack in the

face, the bullet striking the man's eye through the opening in the ski mask. His head snapped back, and he fell to the ground, dropping his weapon and Slater's passport.

No sooner had Phoenix fired than Kendra and TJ took out their men, and all three *colectivos* lay dead in the street.

As Slater scrambled forward and snatched up his passport, a nearby woman, who had obviously witnessed the altercation, began to scream frantically.

Phoenix knew they had to get the hell out of there before more police or *colectivos* arrived. "We're taking the bikes. Let's ride."

He climbed aboard an idling Kawasaki. Slater, after snatching a ski mask off a dead man and pulling it over his head, jumped on another. TJ and Kendra climbed aboard the third bike.

Phoenix led the way out of the slum. Just ten minutes down the road, they crossed under Troncal 9, the major east-west four-lane highway that crisscrossed the country. They continued up the twisting pavement of an access road as it rose to a clearing dug into the side of the mountain.

The first obstacle they faced was a gated entrance to the heliport. Phoenix pressed the intercom button and spoke rapidly into it, telling whoever was on the other end that he was there to meet with Javier for a flight to Guyana City. The gate slowly rolled back, and the three motorcycles squeezed through.

At least Nightingale got something right on this op, Phoenix lamented as they made their way up through the final switchbacks to the heliport.

At the east end of the heliport sat a massive, modern-looking hangar constructed from red tin. Several helicopters sat on the apron in front of the hangar, while others, with fabric covers over their windscreens, occupied pads set off a taxiway.

The four team members parked their motorcycles in the

brush between the final switchbacks of the road and walked to the hangar.

As they approached, TJ spotted an MD500 chopper with the same paint scheme as the one from the television show *Magnum, P.I.* Pointing to it, he said, "Let's take that one."

"Cool your jets," Phoenix shot back. "Let's just find Javier and get out of here on whatever chopper he wants to fly."

Phoenix entered the hangar, his wet shoes squeaking on the concrete floor. The sun and wind had done little to dry his clothes during the ride.

The CIA officer knocked on the hangar's office door and asked to speak to Javier.

A short Venezuelan came to the door, his hair slicked back and aviator shades dangling from the neckline of his T-shirt.

"I am Javier. Are you Bowie?" the pilot asked when they were outside.

"I am. Nightingale said you could give us a ride."

Javier frowned. "Then, yes. Now, no. Someone has killed multiple SEBIN officers, and now they are on the warpath. The SEBIN has grounded all flights while they search for the murderers."

"How soon will you be able to resume flight ops?" Phoenix asked.

Javier shrugged. "Only time will tell."

"You're being well-compensated for this flight," Phoenix reminded the pilot. "We need to leave as soon as possible."

Javier shrugged again. "Money is not the problem. This is where I make my living, and I am telling you it is not possible right now."

"Fuck me," Phoenix grumbled. So far, this entire operation has been a bust. Cobalt Panther was dead, and now Javier refused to fly them out of the country while a roving band of *colectivos* and SEBIN troopers actively hunted for them. Phoenix wondered if things could get any worse. He reminded himself not to manifest more problems and to focus only on the solution.

"Javier, which helicopter is yours?" Phoenix asked.

"That one." The pilot pointed toward a Vietnam-era Huey with oil stains down its green flanks.

"Jiminy Christmas," Phoenix muttered. "That thing looks like it won't even get off the ground."

"It will fly," Javier assured him with a knowing grin.

Phoenix made some quick mental calculations. None of the helicopters would fly farther than three hundred nautical miles on a single tank of fuel, meaning they could fly to Colombia or Trinidad and Tobago but not to Guyana. He walked out of the hangar and back to his people. "Get the bikes. We're riding south. The SEBIN put up a no-fly order, and everything is grounded."

"That sucks," Slater lamented.

They returned to where they'd left their motorbikes and pulled them from the brush.

"What's the plan?" Kendra asked.

"We go south—Guyana City and then to San Martin de Turumban on the Cuyuní River. From there, we catch a ferry to Georgetown."

"Sounds better than getting smoked by a surface-to-air missile if we try to fly out of here," TJ said.

Phoenix climbed on his bike and started the engine. At least the *colectivos* had kept their equipment in excellent working order.

It was going to be a long ride to freedom, one he hoped they all survived.

CHAPTER 9

SEBIN Headquarters
Caracas, Venezuela

Major General Alejandro Salazar sat in the opulent office of the Director General of the SEBIN, Hector Calderón.

He listened to Calderón explain why he wanted Salazar to mobilize his regular Army troops to search for a group of American infiltrators who had supposedly come to rescue a spy. From time to time, the general would steal a glance at a third man in the room. Salazar had him pegged as an American.

The stranger sat in a chair with a view of both Venezuelans and silently sipped from his rocks glass. Salazar guessed the man was in his mid-forties. He appeared to be in excellent physical condition, his muscles ropy on his long limbs. He wore gray slacks and a white dress shirt, unbuttoned at the collar and sleeves. The man's hooded eyes under thick brown hair seemed to take in everything at once.

"Why wasn't I informed that you'd captured two spies?"

Salazar asked. "Both of whom you claim were CIA officers or assets."

"It wasn't your business, General," Calderón said, rebuffing him.

Salazar studied his contemporary. Calderón was in his late fifties with coppery skin and deep-set brown eyes beneath jet-black hair. Despite the long day at the office, Calderón's expensively tailored civilian suit remained neatly pressed. However, dark bags were visible under the director's eyes, a trait that Salazar had observed in Calderón's predecessors. He considered the eye bags to be just one of the hazards of running the country's secret service.

But Salazar had his own stressors, and in the brief time he'd been the general-in-chief of the Venezuelan Army, his once lustrous brown hair had turned white and begun to recede. Salazar was at the end of a career punctuated with the difficulties of a country riddled with corruption. When he'd first joined the Army after graduating from the Military Academy of Venezuela, the country had been the mightiest of all of South and Central America, with a roaring economy and a military second to none, but now, with the implementation of socialism and the current president using the fractured Army to run drugs, Salazar had been fighting tooth and nail to remove the criminal element and establish discipline throughout the ranks.

It was a tradition for the Army general and the SEBIN director to have a drink when they sat down behind closed doors. Salazar crossed his legs and picked a piece of lint off his dark green uniform slacks. He lifted his own rocks glass to his lips and sipped the Ron Añejo Carúpano 'Legendario' twenty-five-year-old single barrel rum. The five-hundred-dollar bottle of Venezuelan rum had been a gift to Calderón, or so he claimed. Salazar didn't mind. He liked the taste of the rum on his tongue and the burn as it slid down his throat.

It made hearing Calderón's news of American spies in their country more palatable.

"Tell me, Hector, when would it be my business to know of the spies?" Salazar finally asked.

Calderón's eyes flicked away and back, a momentary sign that he had lost control of the narrative. "Now, General. That's why we're having this meeting."

"Does this have something to do with the national lockdown of all air flights?"

Calderón nodded.

"Ah," was all Salazar said over the rim of his glass. He felt the stranger in the room had some control over these matters even if Calderón said nothing about the man's presence.

Eventually, Calderón elaborated. "We captured an American spy several weeks ago while he was collecting dead drops. We plucked him off the street and interrogated him. After much suffering, he gave us the name of his asset." The director used the tip of his index finger to move a sheet of paper on his desk and then read the name. "Miguel Tapia worked in the Ministry of Economy and Finance. We took him to a safe house in the mountains to interrogate him. While my men were just warming up on Tapia, a group of what we believe to be Americans mounted a rescue operation early this morning." Caldron paused his narrative to clear his throat. "Unfortunately, Tapia died in the ensuing firefight, and the would-be rescuers escaped."

"And what do you need from me?" Salazar asked, knowing Calderon was leading up to something. Salazar relished the thought of Calderón owing him a *huge* favor when he finally made his request.

Calderón leaned forward and placed his forearms on the desk, interlacing his fingers. There was no hemming and hawing now. "I need you to mobilize your forces and hunt down these criminals before they can escape our beloved country."

"What makes you think they're still in Venezuela?"

"Less than an hour ago, they attacked and killed several *colectivos* outside Boleita. They stole the *colectivos'* motorcycles and then rode to the heliport outside Mampate. The pilot turned them away. We have him in custody, and we will interrogate him for everything he knows."

Salazar nodded. The rescuers would have to flee the country on foot. The fastest way out would be by vehicle to the Caribbean coast and then by boat to one of the neighboring islands, but the Americans could just as easily commandeer a plane despite the no-fly order.

"Any idea which direction they went?" Salazar asked.

"The last report says they headed east from the heliport on three motorcycles," Calderón confirmed.

Salazar leaned forward in his seat. "May I use your phone?"

"Certainly." Calderón gestured to the instrument on his desk.

Salazar lifted the receiver and dialed a number from memory. When his adjunct came on the line, the general-in-chief briefly explained the situation and then ordered roadblocks, aerial patrols, and increased sea patrols along the coast. Before hanging up, Salazar glanced at Calderón. "Anything else, Director?"

Calderón shook his head, and Salazar ended his call before returning to his seat. He eyed the stranger in the corner, then addressed him. "Does this meet your approval?"

The man took a deep breath and then nodded. "You have done well, General."

Salazar couldn't place his accent. He figured the man had learned Spanish at some intense immersion school provided by the CIA or some other government agency, and his inflection resulted from whoever his teacher had been. Maybe Mexican, possibly Colombian, but then again, the flat accent could just be from too many years bouncing from one foreign duty station to the next, trying to learn the slang and speak like a local. It wasn't impressive to Salazar, a man who could speak Spanish, English, Portuguese, and a smattering of Russian and Chinese. His country had many foreign agents, and Salazar had to converse with them all.

"May I ask who you are and what your interest is in our operation?" Salazar asked the mystery man.

Calderón spoke before the other man could. "He's a *friendly* representative."

"I thought the CIA had ceased operations in Venezuela," Salazar conjectured. "It was my belief that we were an unfriendly nation, hostile toward the American government."

The mystery man said nothing.

Salazar pressed again. "Why is the CIA directing this operation when it is CIA agents that we're hunting?"

"I think you answered your own question, General," Calderón replied.

Salazar stared blankly at Calderón for a moment. As comprehension dawned on him, his eyes shifted toward the stranger in the corner. The man's eyes locked with Salazar's over the rim of his rum glass. The general knew there were two possible explanations. One, the man was CIA and directing operations against rogue agents, or two, and more likely in Salazar's mind, the man was a turncoat, outing his countrymen to the Venezuelans and then hunting down his fellow officers.

The CIA had been an active participant in funneling drugs to the U.S. and money to the cartels since the Nicaraguan Revolution in the 1970s. It made perfect sense for them to be in bed with the Venezuelans despite the denunciation of both the Chávez and Zarate regimes by the American government. While the CIA outright denied actually handling drugs, Salazar couldn't help but wonder if Zarate was the beneficiary of those well-established pipelines of transport for drugs and weapons in exchange for political protection. This was the corruption he sought to eliminate from his armed forces, and now he was climbing into bed with someone he didn't even know or trust.

Seeing the troubled look on Salazar's face, Calderón spoke up. "Don't worry, General, everything will be just fine, but we must stop these rogue agents before they can escape our country. With the help of our *friend*, we will be victorious."

Trying not to let the wonderment show on his face, Salazar pondered the unclear meaning of Calderón's words. The general realized that whatever favor Calderón now owed him also made him a CIA patsy. Salazar silently chastised himself for becoming a pawn in a larger game he did not understand.

The major general drained the last of his rum. Salazar didn't know if it was the burn of the liquid in his throat or the burn of betrayal in his gut that hurt the worst, but he knew everything would not be as copacetic as Calderón had tried to assure him it would be.

There was too much at stake. Zarate had commanded Salazar to fortify the Isla de Ankoko Territorial Security Base on the Guyana border. Money seemed to flow into the military's coffers despite the need to spend it on more pressing issues. Salazar figured it came from the Russians or the Chinese, and with the mysterious man sipping rum in the corner, the money might just be American tax dollars.

War was coming, and he felt this mobilization was just the first skirmish in a much larger battle.

CHAPTER 10

97th Special Forces Camp
La Paragua, Venezuela

Lieutenant Coralina Blanco finished cleaning her CAVIM Caribe machine gun and slipped a fresh magazine of 9x19mm rounds into the mag well of the bullpup-style weapon.

The Caribe was a Venezuelan original, built by state-owned *Compañía Anónima Venezolana de Industrias Militares*, or Venezuelan Company of Military Industries, and they'd issued it to Special Forces troopers to evaluate. And much like Blanco herself, who stood five-feet-nine-inches, or 175cm, the submachine gun was lean and sexy.

Blanco, however, preferred something with some knock-down punch rather than the spray of rounds needed to kill an enemy with the little SMG—even though it was deadly enough. She missed the old AK-103 with its much larger 7.62mm rounds. The kick of the bigger gun had always left her shoulder sore, but there was no doubt in her mind that a sore shoulder was better than a wounded enemy who continued to shoot back.

The flap of her tent burst open, and Major Silva barked, "Muster the troops, Lieutenant. Now!"

Without waiting for a reply, Silva was gone, leaving only the motion of the tent flap and the echo of his words in the nearly naked lieutenant's ears.

Rising from the cot, Blanco pulled on her camouflage uniform pants and shirt over her white cotton bra and panties. Even at dawn in the Paragua River basin, it was too hot to wear her fatigues in the tent. So, she had been cleaning her weapon in her underwear, skin already glistening with perspiration. The humidity made everything damp and sticky, plastering her clothing to her before she could even lace up her boots.

With her uniform in place, Blanco glanced into the metal mirror she kept on a tent post. Quickly, she ran a hand through her short brown hair and noted the fatigue in her gray eyes. She'd been beautiful enough to win pageants as a youth, but the army had hardened her into a warrior, and life had turned her into the stone-cold bitch that she needed to be to rise to the rank of lieutenant in a male-dominated institution.

Life had been good for her before Hugo Chávez had ruined the economy and stolen away her father's job with the state-owned Petróleos de Venezuela, S.A. for taking part in an industry strike in 2002-2003. Chávez gutted the company of crucial technical expertise, causing oil production to plummet and, with it, the intake of the vital tax dollars that drove the economy forward. Blanco's father became a shell of his former self, barely able to provide for his family as a janitor despite his degree in petroleum engineering. He had killed himself by jumping from the twelfth floor of the office building where he'd worked.

With nowhere else to turn, Blanco had traded in her

pageant dresses for camouflage, becoming just another face-less soldier in a sea of green. Yet, she demonstrated enough courage and tenacity in her newfound profession to be sent first to the Military Academy of the Army and then to Cuba to train with their elite Special Forces unit, the "Black Wasps." The training had been grueling and the instructors brutal, but Blanco had passed and earned her spot with the 97th Brigade of Special Forces.

Stepping outside her tent, Blanco slung her Caribe over her shoulder and began barking orders at the nearby sentries to roust the sleeping warriors of the 97th Brigade. While the sentries started running through the encampment, shouting for the troops to muster in front of the command tent, Blanco watched with pride and satisfaction. She could taste the adrenaline in the back of her throat. She hoped they were finally going to see some action.

The 97th was a fairly new regiment, brought into existence after a disastrous outing by regular Army troops on the Colombian border in April 2021. Two helicopters full of soldiers had landed near the town of La Victoria in the border state of Apure to fight former Colombian FARC rebels whom the Venezuelan government believed were acting as dissident forces against the Zarate regime. Two days after the helicopters had landed, the FARC called in local priests to administer the last rites to the dead. The FARC rebels had taken eight prisoners and slain the rest. Angered at his troops for being outfought by the rebels, who were masters at asymmetrical warfare, President Zarate had ordered Major General Salazar to establish the 97th to combat unconventional forces.

Blanco had volunteered immediately for the outfit, tired of the chaos of the conventional army and the willingness of the generals to use the troops under their command to fulfill Chávez's "Plan Bolivar 2000." Under the edict, the troops had become garbage collectors, filled potholes, refurbished schools, and carried out other public works. Forced out of their regular duties, the military continued to fragment, and commanders demanded the troops pledge their allegiance to Chávez and his Bolivarian project instead of to Venezuela. The ruling party slogan, "Fatherland, Socialism or Death," began echoing across parade grounds at every army post. It sickened Blanco to hear the troops chanting for more governmental control. She wondered how everyone around her could be so blind to the destruction the ruling class had brought to Venezuela.

Whatever Blanco's opinion, Zarate did not share it. He had removed Congressional oversight to name military officers, and soon anyone Zarate or his cronies desired to bless with an army rank got one. These new officers had little military training or leadership skills. Blanco had hoped the 97th would be different, and in some respects, it was, but there were always political games to play. The training was challenging, yet she had mastered it with ease, and Blanco routinely outshone the men of her unit, which did little to endear her to some of them. Her response had always been, "Fuck 'em. They don't need to be in my unit if they can't keep up."

When the men and women of the 97th Brigade, not quite seventy in total—more than a platoon but far less than the three to five thousand troops the brigade name assumed—had assembled in the tiny parade ground before the command tent, Blanco felt another swell of pride. Their numbers may have been small, but that just meant they had to be experts at guerilla warfare. Training under the command of former Russian Spetsnaz and civilian instructors from the Black Wasps, the members of the 97th were quickly mastering their new element.

"All accounted for, Lieutenant," Staff Sargeant Ariel Gomez barked when the troops had assembled into their respective squads.

Blanco turned to find Major Silva behind her, and she

reported to him that all troops were present. Military protocol remained despite their Special Forces designation and the oft-relaxed standards they enjoyed.

Silva, a sinewy man of thirty with thinning hair and a quiet demeanor, paced in front of the formation with his hands behind his back. He examined the first line of troops, inspecting their uniforms and kit.

"*¡Qué güevo!*" Blanco muttered under her breath. "*What a nuisance!*" She had hoped for action, but despite Silva's training at the Black Wasp base in Cuba, his actions showed he was just an incompetent blowhard like the rest of the officer appointees.

Silva must have overheard her as he wheeled to face her. "Do you have something to say, Lieutenant?"

"No, sir!" she barked.

Silva turned back to the assembly. "We have been tasked with hunting for four American spies who are traveling through our quarter. I want Squads One through Six to fan out across the region. Seven will stay as rear guard."

Blanco wanted to swear at him again, but she held her tongue. As the leader of Squad Seven, better known as *La Zorras* or "Blanco's Bitches," Blanco wanted them to see action. All ten members of Squad Seven were females. The other men often referred to them as the brigade's house-keepers—not there to fight alongside as equals, but to be their cooks, maids, and paper pushers, and on an early patrol, several of the men had tried to use the women as their playthings.

Blanco had caught a trooper trying to force himself upon Sergeant Aguilar. Wanting to set an example, the lieutenant had beaten the young soldier into unconsciousness and then tied him to a nearby tree. After jerking his pants down, she'd coated his penis with honey. The incessant bite of the fire ants had snapped the man awake into a screaming world of agony. Silva had turned a blind eye to the action until a giant anteater had shown up and began feasting on the offending ants, plucking them from the blubbering man's skin with his long snout. The major had cut the trooper free, and no one in the brigade had bothered the women since.

Lieutenant Blanco had fought Latino male chauvinism and sexism her entire career, but despite their intended glass ceiling, she had become a respected leader and feared by those who dared to cross her.

Silva wrapped up his orders to the brigade and shouted, "Loyal always!"

The troops responded in unison, "Traitors never!"

Blanco frowned. She hated those stupid sayings. They sounded like something straight from the Nazi regime.

As the other squads dispersed to carry out their assignments, *La Zorras* gathered at their leader's tent. Blanco, however, did not join them, heading instead into the command tent to confront Major Silva. She had no problem demanding better or equal treatment for her teams, no matter if they were male or female.

"Is there a problem, Lieutenant?" Silva asked, looking up from the map spread across the table in the center of the command tent.

"No, sir. I want to know what your orders are for my team."

"I know you want to join the fight, Blanco, but we must maintain a rotation to stay fresh. Tomorrow, you and your squad will go into the field. You're the best we have. For now, stand by to be a quick reaction force if needed, and when it's time, prepare the evening meal. The other squads will be hungry and tired when they come in."

"Yes, sir. Is there anything I can help you with—operational planning or tactics?"

"Right now, we don't know anything other than the enemy is traveling south on motorcycles. According to the report, they stole the bikes from some *colectivos*."

Blanco grunted in satisfaction. She had no love for the *colectivos*. She had seen firsthand the destruction they could wreak on the unsuspecting populace. They had raped many of her former female friends. The local gang had forced her older brother into service, and they had brutally murdered her youngest brother. "I hope the Americans killed the bastards."

"They did."

"Maybe we should give them safe passage for that action alone," Blanco suggested.

"Traitors never, Lieutenant," Silva reminded her.

"Yes, sir," Blanco replied, burning with the desire to get into the action. While she was grateful the Americans had killed the few *colectivos* that they had, she kept in mind they were also enemies treading on foreign soil, and it would be a career boon to anyone who put their heads on a stake. "I'll have the squad start the morning chores, sir. If you need anything, I'll be close by."

Blanco left the tent after Silva dismissed her, and she organized her squad to do the morning chores. Once those were complete, they would have free time before preparing the evening meal. Blanco had a job to do, and she preached all jobs were equal, be it gunning down American imperialists or scrubbing pots. When it was their time to go into the field, she and her *Zorras* would prove who the best hunters were.

And they would take no prisoners.

CHAPTER 11

The motorcycle engine sputtered between John Phoenix's legs, and his heart sank.

His Kawasaki KLR650 had run out of fuel. Reaching down to the bottom of the gas tank, he flipped the lever on the petcock to reserve, and the engine hummed back to life.

Half turning in his seat, Phoenix glanced back at the two bikes behind him. The third in line had two riders, TJ and Kendra. If his bike was out of fuel, theirs had to be already running on fumes with the added load.

The fuel in the Kawasaki's tank had lasted just over four hundred kilometers. Phoenix began watching the road for a gas station or even a house where they could purchase a few gallons of gasoline. Running out of fuel would leave them stranded again, and they didn't have time to waste searching for a new vehicle.

They were on Troncal 12, weaving their way south through the foothills away from Caracas, putting as much ground between themselves and anyone searching for them. Phoenix figured the SEBIN had mobilized their cells all across the country. If the SEBIN was desperate to find his team, they might just call out the Army to throw up roadblocks and provide roving patrols. Even the *colectivos* had loose associations with other criminal organizations who would hunt for them. Just thinking about the entirety of Venezuela's military and criminal elements crashing down on them made Phoenix's butthole pucker to the seat.

The motorcycle's engine sputtered and died. Phoenix punched the starter button to no avail. He even tried to bump start the single-cylinder thumper by dumping the clutch, but the engine would never run with no fuel in the tank. TJ came up behind Phoenix and put his right foot on the left foot peg of Phoenix's KLR. He effectively pushed the bike up the next hill as Phoenix pulled in the clutch and shifted the transmission into neutral.

At the top of the hill, Phoenix felt the weight of TJ's foot come off his peg, and he leaned forward, urging the big dual sport motorcycle to coast down the hill. To his right, about halfway up the next hill, he saw what appeared to be a village. He pointed to his tank and then at the houses to let TJ know he wanted to stop to see if they had any petrol for sale. TJ made a thumbs-up gesture and then turned to let Slater know.

When the speed bled off Phoenix's bike, TJ came alongside again and pushed Phoenix toward the small cluster of homes. As he entered the driveway, Phoenix grabbed too much front brake, and dust swirled around him as the wheel locked up in the dirt.

Reigning in his steed before he dropped it, Phoenix saw the others had stopped beside him. He glanced around at the small, tree-shaded shacks covered in tan stucco with rusty tin roofs. Behind them were little garden plots with pops of vibrant color from flowers planted amongst the vegetable greenery. Chickens, goats, and a lone pig wandered freely about. Two small children peeked out of a curtained window. Their faces were dirty but smiling. Phoenix hoped it meant good things were to come.

Climbing off the bikes, the group removed their helmets, and Phoenix approached the nearest house. He didn't need to knock on the door. A man in his late twenties came around the corner at the rear and asked what they needed.

In Spanish, Phoenix replied that he wanted to purchase some gasoline for the bikes. As the two men spoke, older children gathered around the motorcycles, chatting excitedly as if they'd never seen such marvelous creations before.

"I have some gasoline, but maybe not to fill all the bikes," the man named Jose said.

"We'll take whatever you can give us," Phoenix replied. He eyed the children, hoping they wouldn't rat them out to the police when the cops came calling about strangers in the area, especially those on motorcycles.

"Come with me," the younger man said, then yelled at the kids to play elsewhere. He led Phoenix to the back of the house, where a shed roof covered a fifty-five-gallon drum that Jose had been laid over on its side and rested on iron legs about five feet off the ground. A black hose ran from a hole in the drum to a makeshift nozzle. Jose dumped fuel into a metal pail, and Phoenix carried it to the bike, where he poured it into his gas tank, careful not to spill any.

As he carried the fuel bucket back and forth, Phoenix noticed Kendra squatting among the children, giving them small candies from her bag, causing them to smile and laugh.

Phoenix made three trips, putting fuel into all the bikes. Once Jose had given him all the fuel he could spare, the CIA man removed a wad of Bolivars from his pocket. He handed over the money, which Jose protested was entirely too much. But Phoenix insisted, saying the man was a lifesaver. He also hoped the money would buy the man's silence, although if someone threatened to harm the children, Phoenix knew Jose would give them up without a second thought.

Jose offered to feed them, but Phoenix refused, saying they needed to get back on the road even though his stomach growled at the smell of shredded beef and black beans wafting through the open kitchen window. It had been quite a while since he or any of the others had eaten anything other than protein bars. While Phoenix knew they desperately needed nourishment, they had to stay mobile. Getting bogged down only two hours outside of Caracas was a sure way to get pinned in by a roadblock.

For the entire ride, Phoenix had been apprehensive that around every curve would be a squad of SEBIN or *colectivos* waiting to gun them down. He felt the urgency to escape oozing from his pores. They *needed* to move.

Climbing back on the bikes, the team headed out again. They followed the roads south and east, angling for the safety of Guyana.

———

THE RIDERS WERE on Route 15 near Santa Mara de Ipire when the fuel in Kendra and TJ's bike gave out.

Phoenix used his boot on their foot peg to push them through the hills toward the next place they could find to refuel. By now, Phoenix's stomach felt like it was trying to turn itself inside out from hunger despite eating several protein bars while on the trip. It had been difficult to peel off the wrappers and eat while riding and wearing a full-face helmet, but he'd managed.

Slater led the way, finding three full-fledged service stations grouped together in the heart of town. He pulled into one, and they fed their steeds high-octane fuel straight from the pump.

While Phoenix and Slater stood guard over the bikes with their balaclavas firmly in place, Phoenix dispatched Kendra and TJ into the store to purchase supplies. This wasn't the United States, where every gas station was also a convenience store packed full of roller-warmed hot dogs, pork rinds, sodas, and beer. No, Venezuela was a third-world country with food shortages and empty shelves. The lovers returned with cold Coca-Colas and hot *paledonias*—a half cookie, half cake concoction that always reminded Phoenix of sponge cake.

"Let's find a spot out of town to eat," Phoenix suggested, disappointed they hadn't purchased anything with protein in it. His body craved some red meat, and as they rode, he thought about the venison stew his father used to make after shooting a white-tailed deer. He could almost taste the delicious mixture of meat and vegetables, and his mouth watered just thinking about it.

It had been a long time since John Phoenix had stalked anything other than his fellow man. He had become as good at that over the years as he'd been at stalking deer and coyotes back in Texas.

Maybe, he thought, *when I get out of this jam, I'll take a vacation and go sit in the woods somewhere.*

Then he smiled to himself. That was precisely what he'd been doing before Nightingale had summoned him out on this treacherous little operation. He'd been sitting in the woods, watching Russian surveyors on Ankoko Island, and that was probably where she'd send him back to if he made it out of Venezuela alive.

The team found a secluded pull-off not far out of town and parked the bikes in the brush to ensure they couldn't be seen from the road. While they ate their *paledonias* and drank their Cokes, Phoenix fired up his phone.

In Washington, D.C., Leslie Connelly picked up on the other end. "Talk to me, Bowie. Where are you?"

"In the middle of a giant shit storm," Phoenix replied. "The SEBIN shut down all flight ops, so we couldn't catch a ride on the whirlybird."

"Oh shit," Connelly muttered.

"You can say that again. We're on motorcycles just outside the town of Santa Mara de Ipire."

"What's your plan?" Connelly asked.

"Ride to Guyana. The problem is that our bikes have a limited fuel range, and we keep having to stop for gas. One of these times, we're gonna get popped."

"We're hearing a lot of radio traffic coming out of Caracas," Connelly said. "They've mobilized the Army to help search for you guys."

"Ain't that some luck," Phoenix muttered. "Look, there's something I gotta tell you, in case we don't make it out of here. Just before Cobalt Panther died, he said *'caballito del diablo,'* which translates to 'devil's little horse.'"

"What do you think it means?" she asked.

"It's Venezuelan slang for dragonfly. When I asked him what he'd said, he clarified by saying, *'libélula,'* which is the normal Spanish word. Any idea what he was talking about?"

"No," Connelly replied, but Phoenix could read the hard inflection in her voice. She was lying to him or at least not telling him the whole truth. "Head for the town of La Paragua. It's about six hours from where you are now," Connelly continued. "If you're intent on going on foot, you can take a boat down the Paragua River to Angel Falls, then go overland to Guyana."

Phoenix considered her suggestion for a moment before saying, "Sounds like a plan, but we gotta go through Ciudad Bolivar to get there. I'm sure they've got roadblocks on every bridge by now. And once we get to La Paragua, there's nothing but jungle between it and Guyana."

"You're a bright boy, Bowie. You'll figure it out. Call me when you get to La Paragua."

"Copy that," Phoenix replied glumly. He ended the call and shut off the phone before Nightingale could say anything else. He had to admit she had come up with a decent suggestion.

From La Paragua, they could get lost in the jungle where even the Venezuelans didn't like venturing if they didn't have to. Phoenix and his team could join the local natives, the illegal gold miners, and the smugglers as they all hid from the government.

"Get down!" Kendra hissed as the sound of an engine filled the air.

Everyone dove for cover. Phoenix jerked his pistol out of the holster and steeled himself for action. Through the trees, he could see a green Tiuna UR-53AR50 stop at the mouth of the clearing. Two uniformed soldiers disembarked from the rear and headed for the small trail that Phoenix and his fellow riders had taken into the clearing.

Suddenly, the soldiers began shouting about a trio of motorcycle tracks they'd spotted in the mud, and two more men jumped out of the Tiuna. They all carried AK rifles with folding wire stocks. Phoenix knew they'd been found and that these men were eager to make a name for themselves by bringing in a team of invading *Norte Americanos*.

He hoped everyone in his group was ready to rock and roll. From his vantage point, he had a clear view of the trail and the soldiers. Phoenix didn't know where any of the other members of his team were, so he was going to solo this op. Sliding his gun forward, he sighted on the opening the men would come through. If he were the only one shooting, he would wait until all four were in the clearing, then take the last man first, working his way up the line to the leader. With the suppressed shots fired from Phoenix's Glock, the leader of the soldiers wouldn't know the fate of his friends until it was too late, and then it would be his turn to die.

Phoenix let out his breath. He hated the fact he'd have to kill Army soldiers, but he also didn't want to spend the rest of his short life being tortured in the bowels of *El Helicoide* or *La Tumba*. He was CIA, which meant he had secrets—secrets the SEBIN would be desperate to pry out of him, but he also knew Kendra would have it the worst. They would rape and torture her just for the sheer pleasure of it. He couldn't imagine the humiliation she would have to endure. Between Phoenix's Special Forces training and his years working paramilitary operations, he'd been exposed to torture and its effects on his psyche. He had no desire to repeat those experiences or to suffer whatever the SEBIN would dish out.

The lead Venezuelan soldier entered the clearing and made a beeline toward the motorcycles, dropping all sense of operational awareness. Once the fourth man entered the clearing, Phoenix shot him in the head. The suppressed weapon bucked in his hand, and he used the movement to help swing his sights toward the next man in line. By now, the soldiers had spread out, but Phoenix found his target, and his gun bucked again in his hand when he pressed the trigger.

Two men down.

As he moved his sight picture to the third man, he heard more suppressed shots, and the other two soldiers toppled over dead.

"Cease fire," Phoenix called quietly to the other members of his team.

He got up and issued orders as he moved toward the dead men. "Slater, check the Tiuna for more troops, then get it off the road. The rest of you, help me get these dead guys into the brush."

The team worked quickly and soon had the chores done. Phoenix eyed the gas cans strapped to the rear of the Army vehicle and wished there was a way to take them with them. TJ came up with a plan. He found some bungee cords and ratchet straps in the back of the Tiuna and used them to secure a five-gallon steel can to his motorcycle before attaching the second can to Phoenix's Kawasaki. Slater found a length of hose, and they siphoned fuel from the Tiuna into the motorcycles' fuel tanks, topping them off again.

"What now?" Kendra asked as they mounted up.

"We get the hell outta here before they send more troops

to find these guys when they don't report in," Phoenix replied.

He kicked his bike into gear, and they headed out. Phoenix didn't know how soon these dead troops were due to check in via radio transmission, but he didn't want to be there when they missed the call, and the search teams came looking.

CHAPTER 12

CIA Headquarters
Washington D.C.

Leslie Connelly set the phone back in the cradle on her desk and put her hands on her hips as she stood in her windowless office.

The snippet of conversation she'd just shared with Phoenix played repeatedly in her mind. He had used the keyword "dragonfly," and now she knew she had to go to the Seventh Floor.

Director Cole Stratten needed to know about Phoenix's last transmission.

Connelly slipped on her low heels, raising her height an inch to five-eight, or 172cm, and tugged at her white dress shirt. She had naturally large breasts whose size she tried to minimize. Sports bras seemed to work the best, but they weren't always comfortable. Connelly wanted to be recognized for her hard work and intelligence, not for her figure. Still, she knew the guys at Headquarters had a ratings scale for every woman who worked there. According to the last poll she'd seen via an intercepted email that had landed its originator at HR, she'd rated an eight. And that had irritated her to no end. She figured she was at least a nine.

Still, Connelly recognized she worked in a male-dominated profession, and sometimes, she just needed to show off a little cleavage to get what she wanted. Going to see the director was not one of those times. She turned to the full-length mirror hanging from the back of her office door and smoothed the shirt again before she adjusted the belt at the top of her black slacks. After one more glance to ensure her hair was in place, Connelly opened the door and headed for the elevator.

Stepping out onto the Seventh Floor always gave her a sense of wonderment. This was where the big dogs played, and from her first day at the CIA, she had known she wanted to be a part of it.

Connelly strode briskly to the director's suite and told the executive assistant that she needed to see Director Stratten immediately.

"What's this concerning, Leslie?" the assistant asked, reading her badge.

"I need to update him on the situation in Venezuela."

"Ah. One moment." He picked up the phone and spoke to Stratten. "Can you wait five?" he asked Connelly. She nodded, and he confirmed it with Stratten before ending the call.

Connelly perched herself on the edge of a chair in the waiting area and crossed her legs under her at the ankles. She glanced at her Cartier watch, a present from her father after graduating college. It had languished in a safe deposit box for years while she traveled first as a junior executive for private equity firm Kohlberg Kravis Roberts & Co, better known as KKR, and then as she'd traipsed across South America as a young case officer. Now that she was in Washington full-time, it was suitable to wear the expensive watch. It made her feel like she "fit in" with some of the more elite citizens of the capital city.

Before college, her globetrotting parents had hauled Connelly all over the world. Her father had been a U.S. State Department official, or so he claimed. It wasn't until someone mentioned to Connelly that she was a legacy recruit for the CIA that she learned the truth about her father's real job. When she'd told him she'd gotten a job with the CIA, his only words of wisdom had been, "You'll do all right."

Connelly had learned to speak Spanish as a child while living in Buenos Aires, and later, she'd become fluent in Portuguese while attending school in Sao Paulo, Brazil. The CIA had also stationed her father in Europe during her teen years, but French and German seemed to elude her mastery.

"The director will see you now," the assistant said.

Connelly stirred from her memories and strode to the door. She opened it and stepped inside. Director Stratten had his jacket off and was sitting on the couch, files stacked on the coffee table beside a can of Red Bull. Coffee was out of vogue, and sugary caffeine was in.

"What is it, Leslie?" Stratten asked, motioning to the chair across from him.

She sat and again crossed her ankles under the seat. She gripped the chair's wooden armrests and clicked her manicured fingernails against the underside. "We have a situation in Venezuela."

"I'm aware the team was ambushed. How are they fairing?" he asked without looking up from jotting a notation in a file.

Connelly gave him a summary of Phoenix's movements and the complexities thrown at him by the SEBIN. "But there's something else, sir."

He raised his eyebrows. Stratten was a Washington insider. He'd been a case officer decades ago before quitting the CIA to join the private sector, where he'd become a colleague of the current president, Randy Mercia, which was how he'd received the appointment to be the nation's spy chief.

Connelly had also known Stratten for years. She'd watched him change from a handsome young man to a distinguished gentleman in his late fifties. His once black hair was now tinged with gray, but his blue eyes could still pierce her like a laser. Stratten had been friends with her father, but he never seemed to hold it against her or compare the two of them as case officers. In fact, she'd had a childhood crush on the man. It never bothered her that he was white. Living overseas had taught her to be color blind. Now, she considered the man across from her to be more of a father figure, helping guide her career.

She cleared her throat to get his full attention. "Phoenix said Cobalt Panther's last words were *'caballito del diablo.'* A rough translation would mean dragonfly."

"Dammit," Stratten muttered and leaned back in his seat. "I thought we'd taken him out in a drone strike last year."

"I did, too, but I don't know if Cobalt Panther meant him or something else."

Dragonfly had become the codename for a man they believed was a shadow operator with close ties to the CIA. Over the past several years, Dragonfly had exposed case officers and long-standing operations in China, Africa, and Latin America. It surprised Connelly that Phoenix's name had not been on the list of compromised assets.

Earlier intelligence had put Dragonfly in a terrorist training camp in Yemen, and President Mercia had authorized a Predator drone strike, dropping two Hellfire missiles onto the compound. Despite Ground Branch troops combing the training camp and confirming the death of the man they believed was Dragonfly, it now appeared as if he had faked his own death and was still operating against them.

"It has to be him," Stratten said. "He's giving up our officers to the Venezuelans now. That has to be how Anaconda and Cobalt Panther got swept up."

"It seems likely," Connelly acknowledged.

"What did Phoenix make of it?" Stratten asked.

"He doesn't know who Dragonfly is or was," Connelly replied. "He's not been read in."

"Keep it that way for now," Stratten said.

"Yes, sir," Connelly replied, hoping Phoenix hadn't become Dragonfly's next target.

"Stay on top of Phoenix and make sure he gets out of Venezuela. We need him down there. He's done excellent work, and I want him to go back to Ankoko Island. If what he reported about the Russian surveyors is true, we need to stay on top of that, too. Zarate and his new General-in-Chief Salazar are preparing for something."

"Yes, sir," Connelly said again.

Stratten fixed her with one of his infamous stares. "How's the relationship between you and John?"

"Tense, sir, but he knows the score."

Stratten nodded thoughtfully. He didn't have to tell her how inappropriate their relationship had been, but at least she'd declared it to the agency, even if it was after the fact, and in an effort to avoid becoming his handler.

Connelly knew Stratten wanted her to remain professional, yet she worried about Phoenix even if she'd grown accustomed to Phoenix's rudeness, which had only gotten worse since she'd broken off their brief but torrid relationship. He'd been an exceptional lover, skilled even before they'd slipped between the sheets, and he'd always been eager to learn new ways to please her, but he was emotionally distant and uncommunicative with Connelly when she'd needed him to express himself the most. He would often joke that he communicated best with her in the bedroom.

Phoenix had been through a succession of handlers until

they had passed him to her. Connelly had been reluctant to take him on, but it had been out of her hands despite her protests and the Seventh Floor knowing about their past relationship. Part of the reason they had assigned Phoenix to her was that, despite his problems, Connelly could read him like an open book. Stratten believed in Phoenix and wanted to keep him busily employed in South America.

While the Latin American Division had a multitude of COs and NOCs—CIA case officers with nonofficial cover placed in private businesses—Phoenix continued to give them the best information no matter where they sent him. He blended in easily with the population. He had a command of the language. And he was gregarious. Phoenix could make friends with anyone, yet he could be incredibly tight-lipped and standoffish when in a relationship with a woman.

One of Connelly's friends had put it best after listening to her complain about Phoenix over drinks for an hour. "Honey," she'd said with a laugh, "he's just being a man."

Stratten eased forward to the edge of his seat. "Let's keep this Dragonfly business to ourselves for now. There's no need to ruffle feathers when he might still be dead. Understand?"

"I agree," Connelly replied, thinking the unmasking of Anaconda and Cobalt Panther might just be the last tentacles of the dead man unwinding from the grave.

"Good. Keep me apprised of what's going on with John." Stratten reached for a file on his stack, and Connelly knew it was the signal for her to leave.

She stood and walked briskly from his office, taking the stairs to avoid the line at the elevator. Inside her own office, she closed the door and tried to read other reports from around the Western Hemisphere, but it wasn't easy to concentrate on them with Phoenix on the run for his life. Usually, when a gun came into play during a CIA operation, things had gone horribly wrong. She'd tried to convince Stratten to send a team of Ground Branch shooters, whose job was nothing but gunplay, but none were available on such short notice to rescue Cobalt Panther.

Connelly wanted to call her case officer to see how things were going, but she knew she would get no answers to her questions. Phoenix would call when he could—or not at all if he was dead. She felt her gut tighten at that last thought.

Despite how the physical relationship between her and Phoenix had ended, Connelly still cared deeply for him, and she couldn't lose him now—not as a case officer under her command nor as a friend. Even though they didn't always see eye to eye, she still counted John Phoenix among her friends. She hoped he would remain so, and that hope was the tickle in the back of her mind that kept her on the edge of her seat, praying for his safety.

CHAPTER 13

GDFS *Essequibo*
Atlantic Ocean
Off the coast of Guyana

Commander David Clarke was ready for action.

He stood on the bridge of the GDFS *Essequibo*—a brand new Defiant 115 patrol vessel built by Metal Shark in the United States. His whole body thrummed with anticipation. The *Essequibo* was his first command, and he felt a keen responsibility for the twenty-four souls aboard his vessel as they prepared for the coming conflict with the Venezuelan Navy.

The *Essequibo* was the second in a fleet of new Defiant-class boats that Guyana was slowly acquiring to protect its burgeoning offshore oil and gas industry, and to combat the intrusion of the Venezuelan Navy into Guyana's territorial waters. To staff the new ship, the navy commanders had selected experienced crew members from other vessels. Moreover, they trained new recruits at the small boot camp in

Kingston and provided them with technical training at schools in Trinidad and Tobago. Clarke himself was a product of officer training at the Britannia Royal Naval College in Dartmouth, and he'd been a Coast Guardsman his entire career. He'd devoted his life to the service of his country and wanted nothing but the best for it.

"I have the *Guaiqueri* on radar, now, sir," the radarman reported to Clarke.

"Roger that. Stand by," Clarke said. "If she makes a move, we'll go after her."

The captain glanced down at the large display screen mounted in the ship's dash. Just about everyone on the bridge could see what was happening on the radar or by glancing out the large windows that wrapped around the entire upper deck that constituted the bridge. Forward, on the bow, Clarke could make out the helmeted head of a crewman beside the Mark 38 MOD 2 25mm chain gun.

They'd been shadowing the PC-21 *Guaiqueri* for the past couple of days. So far, the Spanish-built offshore patrol vessel had stayed in Venezuelan waters, but the *Guaiqueri* had a habit of harassing fishing boats running along the disputed territorial demarcations between Venezuela and Guyana. Twice, the Venezuela crews had confiscated catches made by Guyanese fishermen and once they'd even sank a fishing boat they claimed had strayed into their territory. This time, Clarke wanted to be there to catch them in the act.

He had orders to prevent another incident from occurring. The telex communication Clarke had received just days ago had come straight from President Terrence Fredricks via Admiral Muhammad Issacs. President Fredricks had given Clarke carte blanche to take whatever measures he deemed necessary if a Venezuelan naval vessel strayed into Guyana's waters. Clarke felt reasonably assured that the *Essequibo* could handle anything the *Guaiqueri* might throw at them. Besides the Mark 38 gun on the bow, the *Essequibo* carried multiple crew-served M2 fifty-caliber machine guns and two sets of Mark 32 Surface Vessel Torpedo Tubes configured to carry three each of Raytheon's latest Mark 54 torpedoes.

"The *Guaiqueri* is now eighteen kilometers inside our territorial waters, sir," the radarman reported.

Clarke picked up the radio mic and keyed it to transmit. "This is Captain David Clarke of the Guyana Defence Force Ship *Essequibo* calling Venezuelan patrol vessel PC-21 *Guaiqueri*. Come in, please."

In perfect English, the PC-21's commander returned the call. "This is Captain Juan Domingez of the *Guaiqueri*. You are in Venezuelan territorial waters. If you do not return to your own seas, we will be forced to take action."

"It is you who are trespassing, Captain!" Clarke barked in reply. "Return to your dock at once." He knew Domingez was getting the better of him, but Clarke didn't care if he provoked the man into action. Something needed to be done about these incursions into Guyana's territory. He was already fed up with the Venezuelans making trouble for them when they clearly had so many problems in their own country.

"Stand clear, *Essequibo*, or you will be fired upon," the *Guaiqueri*'s captain answered calmly.

Clarke gritted his teeth. "Officer of the watch, prepare to take evasive action."

The claxon rang immediately, signaling to all aboard that trouble was brewing. Clarke had already called the crew to general quarters when they'd first spotted the *Guaiqueri* on the radar screen. Now, he wanted everyone to be on their toes and prepared for action.

"Sir, the *Guaiqueri* is approaching one of our fishing vessels," the radarman reported.

Clarke keyed the mic again. "*Guaiqueri*, you cannot prevent Guyanese vessels from conducting fishing operations. Stand clear and return to your own waters."

There was no reply from the Venezuelan captain.

"Flank speed, helmsman," Clarke ordered, wanting to position his ship to best assist the fishing vessel if Captain Domingez decided to become aggressive. His fervent hope was that the presence of the *Essequibo* would deter the *Guaiqueri* from doing anything openly hostile to the fishing vessel.

At the helm, Boatswain's Mate Glasgow ramped up the power to the twin 1,600 horsepower Caterpillar diesel engines, thrusting the ship's speed to twenty knots and racing them across the waves toward a date with destiny.

———

TEN MINUTES LATER, the radarman reported they had closed to within a kilometer of the *Guaiqueri*. Clarke ordered the *Essequibo* to slow. Through the binoculars, he could see that the *Guaiqueri* and the longliner fishing vessel lay side by side in the dead calm water.

The *Guaiqueri* had deployed one of her tenders along with a contingent of sailors, who were swarming over the long liner. Focusing on the boarding team, Clarke saw they carried marine-grade shotguns and holstered pistols. The wide bridge windows on the longliner allowed Clarke to see that two of the boarding crew held the vessel's captain at gunpoint. Inside him, Clarke's blood boiled. He couldn't believe the audacity of the Venezuelan crew.

"Bring us to within five hundred meters," Clarke ordered, then keyed the mic to speak to the *Guaiqueri*. "Now hear this, Captain Domingez, remove your boarding crew from the fishing vessel at once. You are trespassing in Guyanese waters and have no right to hold a Guyanese crew hostage while you search their vessel."

"Sir! They're swiveling their Oerlikon gun toward us," the boatswain's mate cried.

"Stand fast," Clarke ordered.

Domingez's voice came over the radio. "*Essequibo*, you are in violation of presidential decree number 1787, ratifying Venezuelan sovereignty over the coast of Guyana. Stand down and return to your own territorial waters."

Clarke sighed in disgust. The Venezuelans had been trying to claim half of Guyana and its territorial seas since Guyana had gained independence from Britain. Keying the radio mic, Clarke said, "Captain, may I remind you that made-up decrees have no legal standing. Only the Maritime Zones Act of 2010 is the rule of law. It clearly defines the territorial sea and exclusive economic zone of Guyana. If you'd like to consult international law and the United Nation's Law of the Sea Convention, I'll gladly give you two minutes in which to do so. And while you learn you are completely overstepping your boundaries, you may recall your boarding team."

The *Essequibo*'s captain could feel his blood pumping hard and fast through his veins. Naval college had taught him to not be a shrinking violet, but despite his training, Clarke could feel his hands shaking from the confrontation.

Clarke waited for a response but noticed that Domingez made no move to recall his boarding team, and now the 35mm gun was aimed squarely at them.

The silence on the bridge of the *Essequibo* was stifling. Every crewman awaited their captain's orders, and Clarke knew the eyes of the world would question his every move if he fired unprovoked on the *Guaiqueri* even though they were clearly operating in Guyanese waters and harassing Guyanese fishermen. Clarke picked up the satellite phone and dialed the number for Admiral Issacs, head of the GDF Coast Guard.

After Clarke had filled the admiral in on the situation, Issacs bemused the political points Clarke had made over the airwaves to the *Guaiqueri*, then said simply, "Return fire if fired upon."

"Yes, sir," Clarke said. He ended the call and reached for the mic.

"Gun mount is moving, sir!" the boatswain cried again.

A moment later, a puff of smoke followed a boom as a round left the barrel of the *Guaiqueri*'s Rheinmetall Oerlikon Millennium 35mm gun. The projectile crossed the bow of the *Essequibo* and fell harmlessly into the sea twenty meters off their starboard side, sending up a geyser of water.

Clarke gulped as sweat beaded on his forehead. While he'd wanted action, he certainly hadn't expected the *Guaiqueri* to fire upon them. The captain knew what he had to do to protect his ship and the sovereignty of his country. Admiral Issacs had ordered him to return fire, but Clarke felt momentarily paralyzed by indecision.

"You are in violation of Venezuela law, and we consider your vessel a hostile threat to our operations," the *Guaiqueri*'s captain called over the radio. "Return to your country's territorial waters at once."

The radio traffic shook Clarke from his daze. To no one in particular, he muttered, "Are we not in Guyana's territorial water?"

Boatswain's Mate Glasgow spoke up. "We are now twenty kilometers inside our territory, sir."

Someone shouted that the *Guaiqueri*'s 35mm gun mount was moving again.

The radio crackled to life as Captain Domingez spoke. "You've been warned, Captain Clarke."

Clarke felt his face redden. The Venezuelans had gone too far, and it was high time to make them pay. He lifted the sound-powered phone from its hook beside him. "Torpedo crews, target the *Guaiqueri*. I want a firing solution in sixty seconds."

It took a mere thirty for the Chief Weapons Officer Allicock to respond. "Firing solution is ready, Captain. We are standing by."

"The *Guaiqueri* is opening its missile hatches, sir," the boatswain's mate stated.

Still gripping the sound-powered phone, Clarke stared across the water at the openly hostile *Guaiqueri* and took a deep breath to calm his racing heart. Clarke then gave the order that would forever change the course of Guyana's history.

"Fire the torpedoes!"

CHAPTER 14

Santa Isabela, Venezuela

JOHN PHOENIX SHOOK HIS HANDS AND FEET TO GET THE BLOOD flowing back to them, then rolled up his poncho and stuck it back in his pack. He found a knot on a nearby tree and placed his back against it, digging the rough bark into the muscles between his spine and his right shoulder blade, acting as a makeshift acupuncture treatment and temporarily relieving the pain.

"What's wrong with you?" Kendra asked.

"Nothing," Phoenix replied. "Just trying to scratch an itch."

"Must be one helluva itch," Slater commented. "You've been digging at that spot since before we left Guyana. Maybe you should see a doctor."

"I've heard of tree huggers, but by the way you're working that thing, maybe you should buy it dinner first," TJ chimed in.

Phoenix gritted his teeth and growled in disapproval

about the team poking fun at his physical condition. They had been on the road for almost two full days, evading Army checkpoints and roving patrols of SEBIN troops and local police who had been alerted to the activity in their sectors.

The hardest part of the journey outside of the shootouts had been finding a way around the heavily populated Ciudad Bolívar that spread nineteen kilometers in length on the southern shore of the Orinoco River. All the bridges had barricades across them, with troops checking identification and stopping anyone on motorcycles for a closer inspection. Phoenix had led his people down dirt roads until they were well east of the city, and then he'd bribed a young local to ferry them across the river, one bike at a time, to the southern shore. From there, they had beat their way through the brush.

Despite the quality design of the Kawasaki motorcycle, Phoenix's bike had picked up a vibration that buzzed through the foot pegs and handlebars, causing him to have to shake out his hands and feet to keep them from going numb as he rode. Even then, his limbs tingled from the juddering of the vibration and the constant dodging of rocks and clumps of tussock. To top it all off, Phoenix's shoulder ached from the stress knot just under the bone. No amount of massaging or Tylenol he swallowed from the med kit in his pack seemed to ease the pain. He just had to keep pushing through, and once this mission was done, things would go back to normal. Or so he hoped.

The land had flattened out after they'd left the Orinoco River, turning into a savannah dotted with small trees, but it was primarily open grasslands with volcanic rocks that thrust through the soil to nibble on the rubber tires and poke holes in the inner tubes. Small river tributaries cut through the hills, and thick trees lined the streams in what Phoenix knew were called "gallery forests," much the same as in the arid areas of Texas where he'd grown up.

While the landscape appeared flat and smooth from a

distance, it was rough as a half-eaten sweet corn cob up close. There were no high-speed runs through the savannah. They had to pick and choose their lines, stop to fix the flats—fortunately, the *colectivos* had kept repair kits aboard—and wipe the sweat from their brows under the brutal sun as they pressed on.

Their lives depended on it.

Phoenix questioned Connelly's decision to send them toward La Paragua, which had one main road leading in and out of it. And eventually, Phoenix and his team would have no choice but to ride down it. He wanted to avoid that for as long as possible, which meant beating through the bush on the motorcycles and creating their own path.

The team squatted over their makeshift camp, cleaning up to head out again after a restless night. Phoenix had been studying the map as TJ and Slater gassed up the bikes with the remaining fuel from the five-gallon cans they'd confiscated after killing the soldiers what seemed like a lifetime ago. They'd refilled the cans several times at various roadside fuel stops that consisted of some guy with a drum of fuel in the back of his truck, but now the cans were empty again.

"Toss them in the bush," Phoenix said. "We can make one last push to this mining operation just south of the junction of Troncals 10 and 16. Once we get to the mine, we can ditch the bikes and find other transportation."

"What do you think our ETA will be on getting to the mine?" Kendra asked.

"Depends on if this weather holds," Phoenix replied.

Dark clouds had covered the skies, and thunder had rumbled around them for the last twelve hours. So far, they'd only received a smattering of rain, but Phoenix could tell by the way the birds were seeking shelter that a storm would soon be upon them.

"Let's get going," TJ suggested. "It's going to be a long

slog to this mine, and I don't want to be caught out in the rain."

They mounted the bikes and headed out, following an animal trail through the tufts of grass. The team had to scout the banks for the best place to cross at several creeks.

It was during one of those water crossings when it began to rain. The warm air chilled quickly as the breeze picked up. Phoenix shivered, barely able to see through the heavy mist and pounding rain.

"This is so much fun!" Kendra shouted sarcastically as they sought shelter under a large tree along the bank. Phoenix knew they couldn't stay there long. The risk of a flash flood swamping the creek was very real, and if caught in the swift-moving water, their chances of survival were slim.

Even though the trees had large leaves on their over-hanging branches, they did little to slow the rivulets of water that coursed down their bodies. All around them, the land had turned into a sucking quagmire of sticky red mud.

Phoenix wished he'd commandeered a helicopter and had taken their chances of getting shot down as they fled the country. A Javelin missile up their tailpipe would be preferable to the misery they'd subjected themselves to since leaving Caracas, but Phoenix didn't have time to feel sorry for himself. He just kept telling himself that he'd been in worse spots. Training to be a Green Beret had been more challenging than anything he'd been through in the last few days of riding motorcycles through the stunningly beautiful country-side of Venezuela, and he knew that where they were going the land would become even more spectacular.

The savannah would turn to high tepuis, or giant table-top mountains as high as three kilometers. La Paragua was one of the jumping-off points for tourist excursions to Angel Falls, the world's tallest waterfall, which fell from Auyán-tepui. Phoenix had been there once, having detoured from a mission to see the natural wonder with Connelly. Still smiling at the memory of them enjoying a much-needed break together, he tried to put it out of his mind. Maybe that was why he got grumpier as they got closer to La Paragua. The sweet memory and the reality of her dumping him weighed on his soul.

He knew why Connelly had sent him toward La Paragua. Phoenix was familiar with the lay of the land, and the jungle was impenetrable in places. The only people who ventured into the area were indigenous hunters and farmers or miners searching for illegal gold.

And, Phoenix thought ruefully, *outlaws on the run.*

The place seemed like the literal ends of the Earth and much like the town of Eteringbang, near Ankoko Island, the countryside had a Wild West feel about the place.

The downpour let up after an hour as they moved past the creek and onto higher ground, but the rain turned into a miserable drizzle, which was just as demoralizing for the team.

To add insult to injury, mud now caked the bikes' knobby tires, forcing the riders to peddle the bikes forward to gain traction as they sat on the seat. When the going got too bad, they had to get off and push, using the strength of all four of them to muscle the bikes forward. The reddish dirt covered everything from their bikes to their combat boots.

After two hours of minimal progress, TJ called a halt to the procession and said, "All we're doing is leaving a trail for someone to follow. I say we hoof it to the mine."

"How far is it?" Slater asked.

"Another mile," Phoenix replied. "You can see the peak over there." He pointed to the six-hundred-meter-high Cerro Bolívar.

"That's where we're going?" Slater asked. "I thought we were trying to avoid people."

"We are, but we need transportation. That's our best shot at getting something decent with four wheels unless you want to keep horsing the bikes around."

"I agree with TJ," Kendra chimed in. "We have to leave the bikes somewhere. It might as well be here."

Phoenix wasn't ready to give up yet, but his team was eager to push on without the excess weight of the mud and the motorbikes. Disgruntled but with no authority to push them harder, Phoenix reluctantly agreed. The plan had always been to ditch the bikes at some point, and it did seem like the perfect time. They were holding the team back, especially with the mud covering nearly every square inch of the engines, the frames, inside the cosmetic plastic bits, and packed between the rear wheel and the swingarm. All of it added nearly thirty pounds to each machine, and with their fading strength from the lack of sleep and proper nutrition, the team didn't have the fortitude to continue pushing the bikes up and down the hills between them and their destination.

"We'll park them under those trees." Phoenix pointed downhill toward a gallery forest along a creek bank at the bottom of the hill. "No sense leaving them out in the open for everyone to see."

While there was grumbling amongst the team, they knew Phoenix was right. Every countermeasure they took to protect themselves was one step toward getting out of Venezuela alive. Fortunately, it was easier going downhill. Kendra walked while the others rode their laboring machines. Phoenix dropped his KLR once, and Slater lost control of his twice. TJ managed to stay upright the entire way to the tree line and coasted to a stop beside the creek. When the others made it to where TJ had parked, they leaned their bikes against TJ's and shouldered their packs for the strenuous march ahead.

"Stay in single file and keep low as we crest the hills," Phoenix admonished, even though they were well-versed in operational doctrine. "We don't want to make ourselves easy targets for some sniper, who might be out there lying in wait."

The others nodded at his words of wisdom.

"Ready?" Phoenix asked.

"Let's go," Slater said, voicing everyone's opinion.

Phoenix led the way, moving slowly up the rocky and slippery slope. He had to admit that they were making much better progress without the bikes. They crossed several creeks, and the land was devoid of human life save for the four weary travelers.

Drawing closer to the mine, they had to advance uphill, and the trees grew much thicker, turning into a genuine forest instead of just trees sprouting from the creek banks. Phoenix paused and listened as they entered the woods.

"What do you know about this place?" TJ asked Phoenix.

Phoenix whispered a hurried explanation to the contractor, but the CIA case officer knew a lot more about the mining operation than he let on. At one time, the CIA had sought to coerce the mine workers into striking to prevent China from receiving the 42.96 million tons of iron ore they'd paid for by wiring a billion dollars into the Venezuelan Economic and Social Development Bank. The funds followed the traditional Chinese model of commodity-backed lending, proposing the development loan to improve production capacity at CVG Ferrominera Orinoco, the state owners of Cerro Bolívar, in exchange for iron ore. Based on actual commodity prices, the Venezuelans had ended up shipping a little over four billion dollars worth of iron ore to China. And if they hadn't delivered in time, the Venezuelans would have had to repay the loan plus a seventy-million-dollar penalty and still deliver the ore.

The CIA, having watched the ineptness of the deal and the original billion dollars disappear through corruption and misuse, realized Venezuela had shot itself in its own foot by getting into bed with the Chinese. Moving on to greener pastures, the CIA had given up on the strike idea, which suited Phoenix just fine. The workers at the mine needed their jobs regardless of who was in power, and he, for one, hadn't relished the idea of going undercover as a mine worker to help institute the strike.

Overall, Phoenix's history lesson meant nothing to his team on the ground. What it did mean was that they had the opportunity to get in and get out without being noticed since the mining extraction itself was 6.4 kilometers long and 1.2 kilometers wide, making the place easy to infiltrate as heavy machinery scraped the iron ore off the ground and dumped it into railroad cars.

Over the years, the miners had terraced the top of the hill and constructed wide roads that snaked up and down both sides of Cerro Bolívar. And the mining operation had some of the highest-grade iron ore in the world, with a half billion tons yet to be extracted.

What Phoenix had also discovered during his research was that Venezuela had been on the slow road to socialism since the early 1970s. He had erroneously thought Hugo Chávez had ushered in the age of nationalism, but it had been his predecessor, Carlos Andrés Pérez, in 1975, who had kicked out the capitalist pigs for exploiting Venezuela for its natural resources. Pérez had merged the mining operation into CVG Ferrominera Orinoco and the oil extraction into PDVSA, or Petróleos de Venezuela S.A. Chávez had politicized the two industries, merging them under a single leadership and appointing loyalists to the board. Following the end of an oil worker strike in 2003, Chávez had fired twenty thousand workers, prompting a mass exodus of talent to neighboring countries. While Pérez had sought to nationalize things to make money for Venezuela, Chávez had just fucked them up.

"Here's the plan," Phoenix said, having neither the time

nor the inclination to explain Venezuela's geopolitics to the team. "Kendra is going to walk up there and get us a truck."

"Why her?" TJ blurted out.

"Come on, man," Phoenix replied sarcastically. "Have you even looked at the woman you're dating? She's gorgeous, and no one will suspect a thing. Everyone will be on high alert if we all go traipsing in there."

Kendra shed her pack and looked down at her filthy, mud-caked clothes.

"Tell them you were hiking and got lost," Slater suggested.

Kendra rolled her eyes and then peeled off her shirt, exposing the sports bra she wore beneath it. She flicked the shirt onto her shoulder like a towel and headed for the mining operations office.

Glancing over her shoulder, she said, "Don't worry, boys. I've got this."

CHAPTER 15

Junction of Ciudad Piar Road and Troncal 16
Ciudad Piar, Venezuela

Since the early morning downpour, the sun had come out, and it was now baking the thick mud back into cracked clay. Lieutenant Carolina Blanco and her troop of *La Zorras* had set up one of their two roadblocks in a gallery forest along a tiny creek bed. For approximately forty meters, tall trees lined the south side of the road, encompassing a small pond where the landowner had dammed the creek.

Blanco had divided her troop into three teams, leaving her to float between them. She had assigned one team to stand guard on the road to Ciudad Piar while the other worked from an open-air booth in the middle of a roundabout at the junction of the two roads. When not checking vehicles for the fugitive Americans, Blanco's third team bivouacked beside the pond.

From her vantage point, Blanco could look east and see the abandoned and broken-down buildings of the old farm that had once occupied the area. Further on, at the intersection with Troncal 16, Squad Two checked the vehicles going north and south. To the west was the town of Piar, the administrative seat of Angostura Municipality, one of the eleven municipalities making up the State of Bolívar.

She was all too familiar with the area, having trained in and around Ciudad Piar for the last year. The search for the Americans was the largest operation the 97th Special Forces Brigade had conducted since taking part in the raids around Tumeremo to round up illegal gold miners and destroy their equipment. The sweep had been an effort to break the backs of the small mining operators to establish the government-run Orinoco Mining Arc to exploit the vast quantities of gold, bauxite, diamonds, and other minerals in both the states of Bolívar and Amazonia.

The miners had called the operation a "military incursion," claiming they had contracts with the Venezuelan Mining Corporation. It had been a crushing blow to the workers and another kick in the gut for Blanco. Despite wanting to serve her country, she saw the cruelty of its leaders and their desire to line their pockets over the needs of the people.

Pale red dust hung in the air as a truck approached the blockade they had set up in the middle of the road. The white Ford F-150, a vehicle ubiquitous to the mining operation as they'd purchased dozens of them, stopped, and the driver rolled his window down. Blanco could see the man staring at the soldiers in confusion.

Maria Ortega, Blanco's second in command, headed toward the truck. Decked out in their green utility uniforms, chest rigs, and black combat boots, the women looked every bit the professionals Blanco knew them to be. Each wore a boonie hat to cover their hair, which the women had pulled into ponytails or buns. In uniform, all ten of her *Zorras* looked alike, varying only in height.

The driver grinned when he saw Ortega was a woman and asked, "What's going on?"

"We're searching for four Americans," Ortega said. "Have you seen anyone suspicious at the mine?"

"Only all the of you." He chuckled mirthlessly. "Why would I tell the Army anything? You're a bunch of bullies who are probably going to destroy our equipment if we don't cooperate."

Ignoring the man's ire, Blanco flipped back a tarp in the truck bed to check for anyone hidden underneath it, then peered into the cab.

"Let him go," Blanco said, motioning for the other two women to move the barricade.

"We know what you're doing!" the man shouted as he drove away. "Stay away from our mine!"

"We're wasting our time," Ortega said.

"We have our orders," Blanco replied with a sharp glance at the Staff Sergeant. "This is our checkpoint."

Ortega was shorter than Blanco but just as physically fit. With their packs on, they could run for hours. Ortega had long brown hair pulled into a French braid and hard brown eyes behind wraparound sunglasses. Both women had been battle-tested against the FARC rebels, and it was Blanco who had recruited her into the 97th. She trusted the younger woman and knew how she thought in battle, but Ortega was a party hardliner who believed in Zarate's mission. Blanco wasn't such a believer.

"When were you ever one to follow orders?" Ortega scoffed.

"We have a job to do. Keep it together, Staff Sergeant," Blanco ordered.

But Blanco knew she was right. The Americans had successfully avoided all the roadblocks thus far, and she'd been pondering the thought of sending out a patrol to skirt the base of Cerro Bolívar. Deciding action was better than standing around checking vehicles, Blanco walked to the bivouac and gathered the women around her.

"We're going to recon along the northern edge of the mine. Mount up in the Tiuana."

The team quickly assembled at the vehicle and climbed aboard.

Keeping an eye on the map, Blanco gave directions to Sergeant Elaine Gomez. Once they passed through the town, she ordered Gomez to turn north, taking them to the railroad tracks. Gomez drove along the tracks toward the mine and stopped in a copse of trees where the four women disembarked.

"Keep your heads on a swivel and look sharp," Blanco instructed.

The women nodded, and Blanco told them to move out. The four women spread out in the trees, walking abreast of one other just six meters apart as they moved west.

Blanco couldn't help but think this was a waste of time, but it made her feel better to be doing something other than checking vehicles. If the Americans were smart, they would be well to the east, skirting the massive Lake Guri and making their way to Guyana, or they could be swimming to Aruba for all she knew. There were vague reports that four people on three motorbikes had passed through various towns and purchased food or fuel, but no actual sightings of them by Army troops. Even the four dead outside Santa Mara de Ipire didn't inspire Blanco to believe the Americans were stupid enough to leave such a path of destruction. She wondered if this whole exercise was another conspiracy cooked up by Zarate and his secret police.

"Heads up," Sergeant Karin Aguilar hissed.

Blanco snapped out of her reverie and concentrated on the situation at hand. Aguilar held two fingers up to her eyes, then thrust them forward toward something Blanco couldn't see. She began edging her way through the brush toward her subordinate.

Kneeling beside Aguilar, Blanco saw signs that someone had recently passed through the area. She didn't know if it had been mine workers or the Americans, so she decided she and Aguilar would check it out.

She ordered Sergeants Gomez and Vicki Torres to stay put.

In its infinite wisdom, the military had decided that any enlisted personnel who they hadn't already promoted to the rank of sergeant would automatically receive the promotion upon graduating from Special Forces training. Having so many sergeants in the chain of command could lead to confusion, but Blanco made things easier by just issuing orders and treating all the soldiers as equals.

Turning to Aguilar, she motioned the woman forward. She'd been the one to spot the trail so she would have the privilege of running point.

The two women moved like ghosts through the woods, following the faint track in the greenery.

Suddenly, Aguilar stopped. She threw up a closed fist to signal Blanco to pause, then pointed toward a man leaning against a tree. He was taller than the average Venezuelan, had long blond hair in a man bun, and carried an H&K MP5 on a sling across his chest. From his relaxed posture, he clearly wasn't expecting visitors.

Movement in the underbrush alerted Blanco to two more men, also facing outward from a central position. Blanco felt her gut tighten. She moved only her eyes as she looked for the team's fourth member, reportedly a woman, but she saw only the three men. Blanco wondered if the woman had gone to procure a vehicle as she didn't see the motorcycles anywhere nearby. This situation felt completely wrong, and she wondered how they'd gotten the drop on the Americans so easily.

Reaching for the fire selector on her Caribe, Blanco slowly

pushed it from "Safe" to "Blast-Your-Entire-Magazine-In-Two-Seconds-Full-Automatic." Blanco hated it. At least they had the long-awaited suppressors. She noticed Aguilar had her gun shouldered and aimed at the man to her left. Blanco aimed at the man leaning against the tree. She steadied the gun against her shoulder, and just as she was about to take her first shot, Aguilar opened up.

The problem with the Caribe was that it had such a short barrel, almost no longer than the average pistol, and coupled with the full-auto rate of fire, the muzzle tended to rise faster than most other automatics. When Aguilar took her first shot, the muzzle jumped, and then it rose with the recoil of each successive shot. Despite all their training and time on the range, Aguilar didn't control her muzzle rise or her rate of fire.

Blanco watched in disbelief as their targets dove for the forest floor and began returning fire. Leaves shredded off the trees and drifted through the air. Chips of bark sparked off the tree closest to Blanco, stinging her skin and causing her to yelp in pain and roll away. In the chaos, she lost her target.

Swearing in Spanish, Blanco moved toward Aguilar. The Americans had excellent fire discipline and had stopped shooting after their initial bursts. In the silence, she changed magazines, popping a fresh thirty-round mag into the Caribe.

Blanco unclipped her radio from her belt and softly called for Torres and Gomez to move up. They needed reinforcements. After her two teammates replied, Blanco radioed Ortega at the roadblock. "Send up Vargas and her team with the Tiuna. I want support from that twelve-point seven." The big machine gun would slow the American devils down.

"Say your position, Lieutenant," Ortega replied.

Lifting the radio again to her lips, Blanco said, "North side of the mountain. Come up the access road toward the rail cars."

After Ortega responded that Vargas' team was rolling,

Blanco moved forward, jammed herself against the trunk of a nearby tree, and then waved Aguilar up. They couldn't afford to lose the Americans now. In order to take them prisoner, they needed to keep pressing them until backup arrived.

She spotted movement and opened fire. Immediately, return fire poured into her position. Blanco dove to the ground and rolled through the leaves, dirt, and twigs. Coming back to her knees, she fired again where the Americans had been.

As Aguilar and Blanco tried to advance, more suppressed shots poured in around them.

When Aguilar screamed, Blanco twisted to see that the sergeant had been hit. Two rounds had struck Aguilar in the vest, and then more rounds had marched up her body to slice open the arteries in her neck. Hot, red blood pumped out in spurting streams between Aguilar's fingers as she feebly tried to cling to life. Blanco gagged and felt the burn of bile in the back of her throat. By the time Blanco made it to Aguilar's side, the woman was dead, glassy eyes staring into eternal nothingness.

Fiery rage flashed through Blanco. The fucking Americans had killed one of her troopers. She'd lost troops under her command before, but this was different. Blanco had grown close to her *La Zorras* and knew Aguilar's family. The anguish she now felt was the penalty for not remaining detached from the women under her command.

Blanco rose and fired blindly into the woods, sweeping the Caribe right and left, screaming like a banshee. She barely noticed her magazine had run dry and that she was just holding the trigger down on a non-firing weapon.

"Smoke out!" a man shouted, and a grenade bounced off a tree and rolled down the hill toward Blanco.

Torres tackled the lieutenant from behind. The two women rolled across the forest floor as thick white smoke billowed from the grenade.

Regaining her composure, Blanco realized the Americans had used the smoke to cover their retreat. Blanco jumped to her feet, shouting, "Torres and Gomez, flank them! I'm going up the middle!"

Blanco swapped magazines in the Caribe again and began creeping through the smoke. It was their only shot at catching the Americans before they could escape.

Aguilar was dead, and Blanco wanted revenge.

CHAPTER 16

"Smoke out!" TJ shouted and lobbed the grenade into the woods.

It bounced off a tree, and Phoenix thought it would ricochet right back into their redoubt, a fallen log they'd taken cover behind after retreating and regrouping during the first lull of the firefight.

The grenade fell to the ground and detonated, throwing thick, white smoke into the air. It drifted through the trees, obscuring the vision of whoever had been firing on them.

Once the smoke hung thick in the air like a dense fog, Phoenix shouted to the others, "Let's move!"

The CIA case officer jumped up and ran toward the road that ringed Cerro Bolívar. He wasn't sure where Kendra had disappeared to, but he hoped she would appear miraculously in a vehicle they could use for their escape. Hazarding a glance over his shoulder, he saw TJ and Slater were right on his heels.

The trio broke out of the trees onto a wide dirt road. A massive yellow dump truck lumbered straight for them, dust billowing up behind it. Phoenix ignored the truck, knowing it could never outrun whatever his pursuers were driving. The haul truck's tires were twice the average male's height, and with a top speed of only sixty kilometers per hour, the truck wasn't going anywhere fast. Although Phoenix figured he could use it to smash and destroy like the Bigfoot monster truck if the need arose.

Bullets smacked into the dirt at their feet, and Phoenix veered to his right, angling toward the line of train cars waiting to be loaded with ore. There would be safety behind their giant steel carriages and high metal walls.

As he ran, Phoenix keyed his radio mic and shouted, "We're taking fire, Kendra! Where the hell are you?"

"Getting a truck, Bowie. Keep your pants on. Aren't you a trained spooky spook?"

"We're by the train on the north side. Put some speed on things," Phoenix replied, ignoring her sarcasm.

Seconds later, Phoenix, TJ, and Slater peered out from behind the train cars to spot whoever was chasing them. Phoenix mentally shook his head. He'd let his guard down. He'd gotten complacent around the mine and hadn't expected anyone to come sneaking through the woods. Even though he'd posted the team in a circle, facing out, someone had gotten the drop on them. They had all let their guard down.

"I think we got one," TJ panted. "I heard someone screaming, but it sounded like a woman."

"Yeah, it did," Slater agreed.

Phoenix had heard the wail of the dying woman and the wicked screams of whoever had come up firing at them afterward. He'd heard stories about Venezuela's all-women combat teams, so it wasn't surprising to go up against them now.

The haul truck was just moving past them, and, in its wake, three figures came darting through the dust.

Phoenix brought his MP5 up, targeting the chest of the

first runner in his holographic sight. He pressed the trigger and let the muzzle rise a hair, streaking bullets out to catch the runner in the chest and then the head, knocking her off her feet.

He shifted his sight picture toward the second woman, but no sooner than he'd lined her up in his sights than TJ shouted, "We've got more company."

A hail of lead shattered against the empty railcar, marching across the steel. It sounded like someone was ringing a bell inside Phoenix's head as the gun atop the Tiuna continued to rain hellfire down on them.

The trio of Americans started running along the train cars, trying desperately to get away from the Tiuna, but the big utility vehicle easily kept pace with them.

Phoenix knew he had to do something drastic to escape the punishing rip of the 12.7mm bullets as the gunner concentrated her fire into the gaps between the train cars. Phoenix could see the red tracer round shoot through the openings and the sparks of ricochets as the bullets bounced off the carriages, car bodies, and the tracks.

Slowing, he let TJ and Slater gain a lead as he stopped beside a set of carriage wheels to mask himself from the shooter on the Tiuna. As the truck slowly rolled past his position, Phoenix stepped up on the car coupler and then dropped down on the other side. He braced himself against the rail car so only the barrel of his sub gun protruded from the corner and shot the Tiuna's gunner in the back of the head. Not knowing if the vehicle had been up-armored, he aimed at the tires and rippled off several bursts to see if they would go flat.

When Phoenix realized his shots did not affect the tires, he moved his sights higher and targeted the side window. His nine-millimeter rounds bounced off harmlessly as a new gunner with a long braid down her back took the place of the one that he'd just killed. Before he could transition his gun to take her out, someone else shot the woman.

Phoenix heard a horn honk from the far side of the train tracks. He wasn't sure if the driver had directed it at him or if the driver was trying to break up the shooting war happening on the miners' turf. Instead of checking to see who was blowing the horn, he kept his concentration on the Tiuna and the team of shooters trying to kill him and his people.

Quickly changing the mag in his MP5, Phoenix dropped the empty on the ground and hopped back over the railcar coupler. He started running west along the train cars, expecting to link up with Slater and TJ, but he didn't see either of them. Somehow, he wasn't surprised. He'd just have to take out the Venezuelans himself and deal with his deserting contractors later.

Phoenix grabbed the ladder on the corner of another railroad car and started to climb. He expected the ore car to be empty, but the miners had already filled it to the brim with loose dirt scraped from the earth. He pulled himself over the top lip of the car and rolled onto his belly. The dirt seemed to invade every opening of his clothing, and dust filled his mouth, nostrils, and eyes.

Blinking rapidly to clear his vision, Phoenix continued to wiggle toward the far edge of the car. He wanted a better vantage point to engage the Tiuna, and gaining the high ground would surprise them.

Once he had a view of the top of the Tiuna, Phoenix brought his gun up and started shooting again. Another woman had dumped Long Braid overboard and replaced her behind the machine gun. Phoenix was in the process of acquiring her in his sights when three women ran out from the safety of the Tiuna toward the railroad cars. There were too many targets for Phoenix to engage all at once.

Behind him, the vehicle horn blared incessantly like the wail of a petulant child.

"Frag out!" Slater shouted.

From his elevated position, Phoenix saw two grenades bounce across the hard-packed dirt road and roll under the Tiuna. Seconds later, they detonated, lifting the vehicle off its wheels and exploding the fuel tank. A giant ball of yellow flame and black smoke billowed into the air above the disabled vehicle, giving Phoenix the satisfaction of a victory in the running gun battle.

"Let's go, Bowie!" TJ shouted.

Phoenix rolled over, cognizant that there were still three shooters out there somewhere.

He had to tread slowly across the dirt to avoid sinking deeper than ankle-deep into the soft loam. His earlier sprawl on his belly had distributed his weight evenly enough to keep him from sinking in, but as he tried to move in an upright position, he found it much more difficult.

The horn blasted again, and Phoenix looked up to see one of the mining company's white Ford F-150s idling on the hill not far away. Kendra sat behind the wheel, with Slater and TJ sprinting toward it. Phoenix reached the edge of the railcar and was about to jump down when a woman's voice stopped him in his tracks.

"Don't try it," she warned. Her voice was a low, desperate growl of anger. "I will shoot you where you stand."

Phoenix raised his hands, letting the MP5 fall onto his chest and bounce on the end of its sling.

"Take the gun off, slowly," she ordered.

The Ford truck drove off, and Phoenix wondered if they were leaving him in his time of crisis. He would have shot this bitch right off her perch and mounted a rescue if he'd been in the Ford. Phoenix realized just how little he trusted his companions through his constant second-guessing of their actions.

Unfortunately, the truck disappeared along with his team. This was the last time he ever took contractors into the field with him. Even though they had proved their worth on several occasions, Phoenix was in no mood to change his mind, and he had no choice but to comply with the order of the woman holding him at gunpoint.

"I'm taking it off," Phoenix said. With deliberate slowness, he reached for the buckle, securing the sling around his body. He turned slightly to face the woman to let her see he was complying with her order. The submachine gun fell into the dirt at his feet when he tripped the buckle.

"Now the pistol," the short-haired woman ordered.

Phoenix sighed inwardly and tried to keep his composure. Giving up his sidearm left him defenseless, but then again, he had to comply as another woman took up station below him and aimed her Caribe in his direction. Gingerly, he pushed the button on the Kydex holster and slowly removed his Glock.

His gaze diverted from the woman when he saw the white truck reappear farther down the train track. Kendra had the gas pedal mashed to the floor, barreling straight for them. Dust billowed behind her in a long cloud that hung lifeless in the still air.

The woman on the ground turned to face the new threat and began shooting at the truck. Phoenix saw Slater standing in the bed of the bucking and swaying truck, trying to return fire at the woman on the ground. Without thinking, Phoenix dove to the side thrust out his Glock in a two-handed grip and drilled the woman next to him in the chest. The round smacked into her bulletproof vest and knocked her flat on her back.

Continuing to roll, Phoenix found the edge of the ore car and twisted so that he would land on his feet when he fell over the side. Bending his knees to help absorb the impact, he felt his heels dig hard into the ground, and pain flared up his spine, triggering starbursts of agony behind his eyes.

He'd wanted to hit the ground running, but instead, he

fell heavily on his side, realizing he was on the opposite side of the tracks from his rescuers. Shaking his head to clear the discomfort from his body and readying himself to move, he saw the legs of the other shooter through the gap between the train car and the tracks. He aimed his Glock at her thigh and snapped off a shot, hoping to scare, if not wound her. So far, she had held her ground against the speeding truck. His shot must have gone wide, as she didn't move.

Groaning in effort, Phoenix rolled to his knees and stood, bracing a hand against the coolness of the metal train car caught in its own shadow from the harsh sun. Phoenix knew he had to move, but all those parachute jumps during Special Forces training had left his knees on fire and his back aching. He took a test step forward and then another, reaching the coupler between the cars. The pain receded with movement, but it was still sharp enough to keep him aware of it.

Climbing over the coupler, he checked to his left and right for more shooters. There was a third woman out there somewhere, or if she was smart, she'd have gone to ground to wait out the gunfire.

The truck came to a stop beside him. Slater extended his hand and jerked Phoenix over the bedside. The case officer landed flat on his back. Staring up at the sky, he saw a woman leap off the top of the train car and land in the back of the truck. Kendra stomped on the gas, and the truck spun its tires in the dirt as it gathered speed.

Phoenix kept his eyes on the woman, crouched in the corner of the bed, her Caribe up and ready to gun them all down. He, Slater, and TJ all had their weapons aimed squarely at her. She was tall and lean with dark skin and shoulder-length brown hair. The stripes on the shoulder of her uniform said she was a lieutenant, and her name tape read: *Blanco.*

"Put it down, Lieutenant," Phoenix ordered in Spanish.

Blanco glanced around at the weaponry arrayed against her and jettisoned her Caribe over the side. She slid her feet out from under her and dropped into a seated position.

Staring at Phoenix, Blanco sized him up as the leader before saying, "Take me to America with you."

CHAPTER 17

Oval Office
Washington, D.C.

PRESIDENT OF THE UNITED STATES RANDY MERCIA PACED THE floor as Director of the Central Intelligence Agency (D/CIA) Cole Stratten and his protégé, Leslie Connelly, sat on the edge of the blue sofa, informing him of how the GDFS *Essequibo* had sunk the PC-21 *Guaiqueri*.

"You're telling me they sank a Venezuelan ship?" Mercia asked.

"Torpedoed it right out from under them, sir," Stratten replied.

"Who the fuck gave the Africans torpedoes?" Mercia demanded.

Connelly had to stifle a laugh. The leader of the free world thought Guyana was a country in Africa.

"What's so funny?" Mercia demanded as Connelly held the back of her hand to her mouth and coughed.

"Nothing is funny, Randy," Stratten replied. As good

friends, Mercia didn't mind if Stratten called him by his first name.

I'm glad he appointed Stratten to the CIA, Connelly thought in relief. *At least someone around here is competent.*

"Then why the hell is she laughing at me?" Mercia demanded.

"I'm not laughing, sir," Connelly replied, trying to repair the damage. "Guinea is a country in West Africa. Guyana is a country in South America. They're easy to confuse."

"I was wondering why some country in Africa was starting a war with Venezuela," Mercia said. "It didn't make any sense to me."

"The two countries have been in a border dispute for almost five hundred years," Connelly said. "Recent discoveries of oil off the coast of Guyana have heightened the tension between them."

"Why is she here?" Mercia suddenly asked Stratten. "I asked *you* for a briefing."

Stratten put a hand on Connelly's knee to calm her. "Leslie is our foremost expert on the situation between the two countries. She's been on the Latin American desk since she started her career, and she's now the division's assistant chief. And she still runs case officers and assets in the region. If I need to know what's going on down there, I call Leslie."

"You call Leslie," Mercia mocked.

"Look, Randy, I know you have your hands full with other things. If you want, I can work with the State Department and get this situation ironed out for you. You won't need to worry about it."

When women described their ideal man as tall, dark, and handsome, they probably had Mercia in mind. While Mercia might have looked presidential, like some guy who had just stepped out of central casting with chestnut brown hair and sea-blue eyes, Connelly thought he acted as dumb as a box of rocks at times.

There had been an actor, a reality television star, a community organizer, and plenty of gentlemen farmers who had been past presidents, but all of them seemed to have more common sense than Randall J. Mercia combined. Connelly, however, had learned never to underestimate people as some of them could rise to great heights when called upon, while others shrank into the bushes à la Homer Simpson.

Randall James Mercia had proved in the past to neither be a bloomer nor a shirker, and Connelly knew the man wasn't stupid. Like a lot of politicians, he'd ridden in on a wave of special interest money and patriotism. Mercia was not a flag-waving, gun-toting, red-meat-loving Republican. He was a moderate, and from day one in office, he strove to keep the status quo.

Mercia had grown up as the son of a wealthy oilman in Oklahoma, and he'd decided early on that being a wildcatter like the old man just wasn't his thing. He'd used his daddy's money to get himself elected to the city council in Norman, then worked his way up to become governor. After barely getting himself elected to a U.S. Senate seat, he was now, miraculously, the leader of the free world.

During an early primary debate between Republican candidates, one of them had made a slip of the tongue and called his opponent Randy 'Merica. Mercia's publicity hounds had run with it. His team quickly plastered the campaign slogan "Randy 'Merica" on hats, T-shirts, truck bumpers, and billboards. "Randy 'Merica—Good for the country." "Randy 'Merica—Patriot!" The man could play the redneck rube to perfection and now ended his speeches and press conferences by shouting, "'Merica!"

The president pressed a button on the desk phone. "Carl, get Asbury in here right away."

One thing Mercia had going for him, in Connelly's opinion, was that he'd surrounded himself with excellent people. His cabinet was chock-full of some of the smartest and brightest minds that Connelly had ever known personally or seen on television as a talking head. Mike Asbury, the current Secretary of State, had dedicated his life to being a statesman and knew international politics like the back of his hand. A student of history and a lifelong fan of the American football team, the Green Bay Packers, Asbury frequently counseled his boss never to do anything rash and to try to see the playing field from both sides of the ball.

Sitting in the Oval Office, waiting for Asbury to arrive from the Harry S. Truman Building several blocks away, Connelly realized she had a golden opportunity. If Guyana and Venezuela were on the brink of war, then she, as the leading intelligence officer in the region, would have the opportunity to shine in front of all these heads of state. If she played her cards right, she could win them over and take Cole Stratten's job. Connelly allowed herself an inward smile, savoring her first moments in the Oval Office and her new plan of action—even if she and the president had gotten off on the wrong foot.

It didn't take long for Asbury to arrive. In fact, he'd been on his way over to the White House after speaking to President Fredricks in Guyana and Felix Schweizer of the Swiss Federal Department of Foreign Affairs, since the Venezuelan Minister of Foreign Affairs, Ramón Ochoa, wouldn't take Asbury's calls.

"Well? What's happening?" Mercia demanded after Asbury had explained his phone calls. At sixty-five, he had a full head of salt-and-pepper hair on a rectangular face. He had aged gracefully and spent an hour a day working with a personal trainer to keep himself in shape.

"The Venezuelans are pissed," Asbury said bluntly.

"No shit, Mike. What's going to happen?" Mercia demanded.

"I asked the heads of state to sit down in a neutral location to see if we can work this out. As of right now, both militaries are on full alert. But there's something else going on in Venezuela. Schweizer claimed that there appeared to be some sort of nationwide manhunt." He turned to Stratten and Connelly. "I take it from your presence here that you know more about what's going on down there than he does."

"We do," Stratten replied. "We sent in a team to rescue one of our assets, but the SEBIN knew they were coming and ambushed them. The team escaped, but the Venezuelan Army and the SEBIN are searching for them."

"Sweet Mary and Joseph," Asbury muttered.

"Sorry, Mike," Stratten said. "It seems someone leaked the names of all our case officers and assets to the Venezuelans, and they've been hunting them down just like the Chinese did."

"I thought we pulled all Americans out of there when we closed the embassy in 2019," Mercia said.

"We pulled agency personnel," Connelly replied. "Our NOCs continued to run their assets to keep tabs on Venezuela's ongoing operations."

"So, we have more CIA personnel in Venezuela?" Asbury asked.

"Well, no," Connelly replied. "The only case officer in VZ is the one the Army is searching for. I spoke to him yesterday, and he's confident he can make his way out of the country. He's also reported seeing Russian military advisors on Ankoko Island, surveying the runway."

"Fucking Russians," Mercia muttered.

"And if he doesn't make it out?" Asbury asked.

"Then we'll probably have another incident like Operation Gideon back in 2020," Connelly replied, meaning the failed attempt to overthrow Zarate by members of the private military company Silvercorp USA. "That won't look good for us if they capture our case officer."

"And it will look like the CIA tried to stage a coup," Asbury concluded.

Everyone in the Oval Office fell silent as they inwardly digested the consequences of the Venezuelans capturing a CIA case officer and his merry band of mercenaries. Mercia continued to pace while rubbing the back of his neck.

Asbury was the first to speak, asking Stratten, "Do you have a mole in the agency leaking the names of your assets?"

"It would appear so," the D/CIA replied.

Mercia stopped pacing. "Why do we give a fuck about what happens between these Third World shitholes?"

"Oil, sir," Asbury replied. "There are a lot of U.S. companies heavily invested in the newly discovered fields off Guyana."

"Why is all the oil in the most dangerous quarters of the world?" Mercia asked rhetorically. "I say fuck 'em. We can drill for oil here. We were energy-independent until that last joker got into office. You know I'm pro-oil and that I'm ramping production up again here. We're going to drill, baby, drill, while those shitheads bomb the crap out of each other."

Connelly wished she could have recorded Mercia's comments. Selling them to the press would be like printing money, but she knew better than to repeat the private conversations that took place behind closed doors in the White House, even though audio and video recorders taped everything they said.

"What do you suggest we do, then, Mr. President?" Asbury asked.

Mercia sighed. He'd vented his frustrations, and now it was time to give the answer everyone wanted to hear, even if he thought it was complete bullshit. "Let's get them in a room together and see what we can work out. We have to protect American interests at home and abroad, and since oil is the lifeblood of our economy, we need these fuckheads more than they need us."

"We can restart the negotiations we started in 2021 in Mexico City," Asbury offered.

"And see if China will come to the table," Connelly suggested. "They're heavily invested in both countries, and their clout might swing Zarate away from taking further action."

"So, what do we bring to the table?" Mercia asked. "We've imposed so many sanctions on Zarate's government that he's not likely to listen to anything we have to say. Hell, we indicted the man and half his cabinet on narco-terrorism charges."

"Oil," Connelly repeated. "It's the only thing that matters right now. If Venezuela can start selling oil on the open market again, they can take steps to alleviate their humanitarian crisis, and it will be a show of good faith that we trust Zarate to move forward."

Asbury laughed. "Zarate isn't going to change his spots. He's a dictator and a bully."

"We deal with the Saudis on a daily basis," Mercia said. "They've got more human rights violations than half the world combined. I say we give him what he wants and refill our strategic reserves with sweet Venezuelan crude."

Connelly reappraised the president. While he might seem clueless on many other subjects, he had a handle on the oil business and a broader grasp on geopolitics than he let on.

"What Zarate wants," Stratten said, "is to reclaim the Essequibo region and control all the oil in Venezuela and Guyana. It would give him a virtual monopoly on the market. More so than the Saudis or even OPEC."

Asbury turned to Connelly, using Mercia's comments to segue into a new topic. "What's your assessment of the *Essequibo* Incident."

"It's been a long time coming," Connelly replied. "Venezuela has made claims of the Essequibo Region since 1835, and more recently, Zarate claimed all the Essequibo's territorial waters by presidential decree, going so far as to use the Venezuelan Navy to stop fishing and oil exploration vessels in Guyana's water. If the Venezuelans did fire first, then it was Guyana's right to return fire. We can let the two countries escalate things to an all-out war, in which case, I think the Venezuelans will win based on sheer numbers and military hardware. However, if we were to intervene and pick sides, I think we would become embroiled in another Ukrainian situation, bogged down in a long-term war the world doesn't need."

"And further deplete our military reserves to give the Chinese an opening to take Taiwan," Stratten added.

"Maybe that's what China wants," Mercia mused. "If we get involved down there like we are in Ukraine and Israel, the Chinese will take Taiwan uncontested and show the world who's really in charge. I, for one, don't like the sound of that, but I'm also not too fond of the commitment we've made to Taiwan. If China makes a move, we'll have no choice but to react. Our military is in a dangerous situation right now. We have low recruitment numbers and low reserves of munitions."

"I think we need to take a multipronged approach," Stratten advised. "Our first priority is to strengthen the military and reserves. The second should be to get Guyana and Venezuela to the negotiating table and hammer out a new pact between them. And finally, we pressure our NATO allies to offer greater support to Ukraine."

"You want to go back to America first," Asbury said.

"It's always been America first," Mercia snapped. "We need to do whatever is necessary to prevent war on two more fronts. China and Russia both have military and economic ties to Venezuela. If we get involved, it could be the start of World War Three."

"What happened to the Monroe Doctrine?" Asbury asked. "We used to believe that intervention in the political affairs of the Americas by any foreign power was a potentially hostile act against the United States."

"Are you suggesting we go back to the Monroe Doctrine being our guiding force in dealing with this situation?" Stratten asked.

"I don't think the Monroe Doctrine is the answer, but we need to do something," Connelly said. "China is eating our lunch in Central and South America and across the Caribbean with their Belt and Road Initiative. Not only are they providing funding for critical infrastructure projects and economic improvements, but they're also buying up mineral rights and leveraging loans for control of governments."

"Don't forget they control the key shipping choke point of the Panama Canal," Stratten injected.

"What do we do first?" Mercia asked.

"Get Venezuela and Guyana to the negotiating table," Connelly said. "Everything else pivots off that."

CHAPTER 18

Cerro Bolívar Mine
Ciudad Piar, Venezuela

JOHN PHOENIX STARED IN DISBELIEF AT THE WOMAN IN THE TRUCK bed with them. She had given up her gun and said, "Take me to America with you."

The Ford F-150 bounced and swayed as Kendra kept the hammer down, fleeing the ambush site where Blanco and her all-woman team had gotten the drop on them.

"What do you mean?" Phoenix asked, still trying to process that the woman had asked them to aid her in fleeing the country.

"I want to defect to the United States," Blanco declared. "I can guide you out of Venezuela." In a show of good faith, she added, "My team has a roadblock set up near Route 16, but I can order them to abandon the post."

"Do it," Phoenix ordered.

"I am going to use my radio now," Blanco stated.

Phoenix pounded on the rear window of the truck cab and

shouted for Kendra to pull over. He wanted to hear both sides of the radio conversation and didn't want the lieutenant to have to shout over the wind. Kendra reluctantly brought the truck to a stop at the top of a switchback that led down the southern side of the mountain.

"Go ahead," Phoenix told Blanco.

Blanco raised the radio to her lips. "Ortega! Ortega, come in!" she called breathlessly.

"Go for Ortega," the other woman replied stoically.

"I need you to bring your team to the north side of the mountain. We are taking heavy fire, and the Americans have killed all of my team. I need reinforcements!"

"My orders are to stay at the roadblock," Ortega responded.

"I'm ordering you to move up!" Blanco shouted back. "Didn't you hear me? The Americans are here."

"Major Silva has called personally and ordered me to take command of the roadblock."

Blanco tossed down the radio and swore in rapid-fire Spanish.

"What just happened?" TJ whispered to Slater. He was the only one on the team unable to speak Spanish, and he had no clue what was happening as the others continued to talk in the foreign language.

"We're fucked," Slater replied and explained the situation.

"Is there a way around the roadblock?" Phoenix asked Blanco, continuing in Spanish.

She nodded. "You'll have to follow the railroad tracks to the north. Once we cross Route 16, we'll head toward Lake Guri and cross by boat. From there, we can get to Guyana with ease."

"Why Guyana?" Phoenix asked.

"It's the closest border," Blanco replied. "Brazil is too far away."

Blanco's radio crackled to life, and a man's voice called for her.

"It's Major Silva," Blanco said to Phoenix. "I have to report in."

Silva repeated his call to the lieutenant. Phoenix nodded to her, hoping she was on the level. If Blanco wanted to defect, she would mislead the major, but if this was all a ruse, then she could be leading them straight into a trap. Unfortunately, he had to let her use the radio and then try to decipher her words and how she said them to her superior.

Blanco held the radio to her mouth and returned Silva's call.

"Say your situation and location," Silva said.

"We are on the north side of the mine, taking heavy fire. Five of my team are dead or injured. We need reinforcements."

"I'm sending the National Guard unit from Ciudad Piar to your location. They will contact you shortly via this channel."

"Copy, sir. Tell them to hurry," Blanco said.

She clipped the radio back to her belt. Looking up at Phoenix, she said, "We have to go. Follow the railroad tracks."

Kendra leaned out the window. "The tracks on the north side of the mine or the south?"

"They come together east of here. Either will work," Blanco replied.

Phoenix remembered this as well from studying the map in his pack.

Kendra put the truck in gear and headed down the mountain, following the steep road through the switchbacks. She started to turn at the first set of tracks, but Blanco shouted for her to continue. "These are just a siding. Go to the next track."

Straightening the wheel, Kendra continued to drive as fast as she dared, yet not fast enough to attract the attention of the other mine workers.

Phoenix felt the clock in his head winding down. Once Silva had said he'd dispatched a National Guard unit, Phoenix knew they had to get out of town before the unit could sweep through and find that Blanco had lied to her boss.

"What unit are you with?" Phoenix asked as Kendra turned onto the road beside the tracks and headed east toward Ciudad Piar.

"The 97th Special Forces Brigade," Blanco replied.

"Is that a new unit?" Phoenix asked. "I've never heard of it."

"We've been together a year. We're only seventy strong, operating in seven squads of ten."

"Are you an all-female squad?" Phoenix asked.

Blanco nodded. "We are called *La Zorras,*" she said proudly. "We are the fiercest fighters in the command."

Phoenix could attest to their competency. The women had gotten the drop on his team and then almost taken them all out. It was only by sheer luck that they'd been able to escape.

Blanco dug at the front of her chest rig, pulling out the bullet Phoenix had shot her with on top of the train car. The hollow-point round had mushroomed on impact with the ceramic plate. She flicked it over the side of the swaying truck into the brush.

They had entered a large stand of trees, and Kendra had taken to driving with one set of tires inside the railroad tracks and the other on the stone ballast. The truck shuddered as the tires ran over the wooden sleepers and rough gravel that filled the space between the ties. Phoenix pulled out his map and studied it. It gave topographical data, showing only the main roads through the countryside. It didn't show the railroad tracks, but he had a general idea of where they were. Knowing they needed to do something more drastic to escape, he fired up his satellite phone and opened a map application available to him through a clandestine CIA server.

Scooting over to where Blanco sat, wedged in the corner of the bed, Phoenix showed her the map on his phone. "What about this dirt road going south?"

"I haven't been down it," she said.

"Where will the guard unit come from?"

"There's a National Guard base on the south side of Piar," Blanco stated. "It will take some time to recall the troops. After that, the nearest regular Army unit will have to come from Guyana City."

"And your team is here?" Phoenix pointed to the junction of Troncal 16 and the road leading to Ciudad Piar.

"Yes. What's left of them."

Phoenix crawled back to the front of the truck bed and spoke to Kendra through the open slider in the rear window. "Once we break out of the trees, you need to switch sides of the track, then stay to the right at the junction. About a kilometer past the track junction, there will be a dirt road going south. Take that."

They rode in silence as Kendra kept the hammer down and then switched sides of the track to avoid crossing the junction where the northern and southern railroad tracks met. She tried several times to muscle the truck tires over the tracks with the steel rims grinding against the rails. Phoenix thought the rubber would shred off the rims as the truck bounced up and over the tracks.

Safely on the other side of the junction, they pulled onto a dirt maintenance road, allowing Kendra to increase her speed. Phoenix kept eyeing the attractive Venezuelan Special Forces officer, wondering when the other shoe would drop. She had quickly ingratiated herself with him by providing directions, advice, and false radio reports. Part of the reason he had deviated from her suggested egress route was that he still didn't trust her.

Phoenix and his team had beat across the savannah on the Kawasaki KLRs, and now they would do it in the truck if necessary. The dirt road he'd spotted on the map appeared to go all the way to Troncal 16, but there could be cattle gates or fences blocking their path, which might force them to back-track straight into the arms of the awaiting Army unit. Phoenix patted his chest rig, where he usually carried a pair of side-cut pliers for snipping zip cuffs. He wasn't backtrack-ing. He'd cut the damned fence if he had to or blow it up with some C-4.

Kendra turned away from the tracks onto the service road, and they had to climb several hundred meters to go over the top of the ridge. Phoenix glanced around from their high perch and scouted the land. The seventeen-kilometer-long ridge that tapered away from Cerro Bolívar to their east stood out in stark contrast to the surrounding savannah. He saw no approaching Army or National Guard units, and without binoculars, he couldn't see the roadblock set up by Blanco's *La Zorras*.

They plunged down the side of the mountain, Kendra accelerating quickly toward town. Suddenly, a Tiuna appeared out of the woods in front of them, a gunner strapped to the 12.7mm weapon in the gun turret. The big weapon opened up, and rounds slammed into the dirt all around the F-150.

At a Y in the road, Kendra spun the white truck around and headed back up the ridge toward the railroad tracks. Blanco flung herself face down in the truck bed so the attacking troops couldn't see her. The fleeing Ford raised so much dust that it was impossible for Phoenix to see the Tiuna, but it kept firing at them, missing wildly as the two vehicles bounced and bobbed over the rough road.

Phoenix glanced over his shoulder at the road ahead, then down at Blanco. He wondered how the troops in the Tiuna had found them since he had deviated from the plan Blanco had set to follow the tracks. Now, they had no choice but to go along with her egress plan.

The CIA case officer fished beneath the lieutenant and came up with the radio. She had fixed the transmit button so that a hair band and a small chunk of wood held it down, giving real-time updates to the enemy. Phoenix reared back and threw the radio as hard as he could at the Tiuna, hoping it would shatter against the windshield.

"I ought to throw you out of this truck right now!" Phoenix shouted.

"I had to do it!" Blanco yelled back. "If you left me on the side of the road, I had to tell them I did everything I could to prevent you from escaping."

Phoenix understood her logic, and he hated himself for it. He might have done the same thing if he was in her shoes.

"Hold on!" Kendra called through the open rear window. She spun the truck to the right onto the railroad access road and mashed the accelerator to the floor. Dust continued to obscure their view of the Tiuna, but Phoenix knew it was back there. He could hear the machine gun chattering, and occasionally, a bullet would punch through the metal truck bed or shatter a window.

"Is that Tiuna armored?" Slater asked Blanco in Spanish.

She looked up at him with defeat on her face and shrugged.

"Frag out!" TJ shouted and lobbed a grenade into the road behind the Ford. Seconds later, the grenade detonated, and the Tiuna swerved up on the ballast at the edge of the railroad track.

With a clear view of their opponent, Slater lobbed his grenade. It landed a few feet in front of the light utility vehicle and detonated under the engine as the Tiuna rolled forward. The hood blew off, and a ball of fire rose from the engine bay.

"Hell yeah!" Slater shouted.

"Stay on the tracks," Phoenix urged Kendra.

He settled back to watch Blanco as Kendra kept them at a

steady speed along the train tracks. Closing his eyes, Phoenix tried to breathe deeply through his nose and swell his belly before exhaling. The action helped to quell the rapid upper chest breathing associated with the body's flight or fight response. He also considered what to do with the woman in the truck bed with him. While getting her out of the country would provide the agency with a one-time intel dump, it would be better if Phoenix could turn her and run Blanco as an asset. Since the Special Forces were usually the first to fight, she would be on the front lines, able to provide him with immediate battle information.

Phoenix's eyes snapped open as he felt the truck pitch up at an angle as Kendra drove onto the ballast embankment and then bounced the truck tires over the first track. She steadied the vehicle as it ran across the sleepers. Then she jerked the wheel hard again, forcing the truck to straddle the train tracks between its wheels, having learned how to do it more proficiently from her last try.

The truck ping-ponged off the rails for a moment before she could gather it in. Once she did, Kendra held the truck in a straight line and sped up, which Phoenix absolutely couldn't believe. They were barreling straight for a truss bridge constructed over a small creek. Unable to look at the impending crash, Phoenix put his back against the cab so that he wouldn't fly out of the truck if they hit the trusses.

Kendra's aim was true, keeping the truck centered between the trusses, but the metal uprights clipped the mirrors off both sides of the vehicle. Once past the bridge, she followed the track around a bend and then gunned it down the straight. Back on the open savannah with only gallery forests to block their view, they could better see if the enemy approached.

At what seemed like an abandoned siding yard, Phoenix directed Kendra to exit the track and proceed toward Troncal 16.

Just as she turned onto the pavement to head north, they saw a twin-engine Dornier 228 airplane come in for a landing at an airstrip up ahead. The plane didn't have any military markings, leaving Phoenix to wonder if the SEBIN had lifted the flight restrictions. The answer to their problems lay ahead, and Phoenix could feel the momentum turning in their favor.

The case officer shouted a command through the window. "Head for that plane!"

Turning back to his companions, Phoenix explained his plan. TJ and Slater grinned wildly at the prospect of flying out of danger.

Kendra cut off the main road, following a sign that directed them toward the landing strip. The Dornier was taxiing onto the parking ramp as they pulled up in the truck.

Phoenix told Kendra to wait until the airplane stopped and then tapped the roof to tell her to drive up behind the plane once it found a parking spot. She came alongside the tailfin, and all three men bailed out, running for the door of the Dornier. Phoenix jumped up and tripped the latch, letting the door swing open, and the airstairs fall into place before charging into the plane. There were four passengers inside, along with the pilot and co-pilot.

"Everybody out and leave the engines running," the CIA officer ordered, motioning with his pistol. While TJ and Slater stood at the airstairs, Phoenix prodded everyone out. He glanced at the fuel gauge to see the tanks were nearly full. He was familiar with the Dornier, having flown one in and out of Afghanistan when his Special Forces team needed a ride and there was no one else to take them. The plane required just eight hundred meters of runway to take off and had an operating range of 715 nautical miles, more than enough to get them out of Venezuela.

Yeah, he thought with a grin, *this will do nicely*.

After escorting the passengers and pilots off the plane,

Phoenix walked back to talk to Blanco while Slater and TJ stood guard.

"Take me with you," she pleaded.

"How about you work for me?" he countered. "I'm a CIA case officer. I want you to report troop movements and activities to me. I'll give you a phone number to call."

"Why?" Blanco demanded.

"The government in Caracas needs to be toppled," Phoenix said. "I think you can help us with that."

"And if I don't?" she asked, crossing her arms.

Phoenix shrugged. "Nice knowing you," then called to his team, "We're out of here. Everyone get in."

Blanco's cheeks flexed as she worked her jaw muscles. She shifted from one foot to the other. She could see he wasn't taking her with him. "Fine. Give me a number to call."

Phoenix took a slip of paper from his chest rig and held it out to her. "That's my sat number. Call anytime."

"If I do this for you? What then?"

"Let's see what kind of information you provide, then we'll talk about the end game."

"Let's go!" Slater shouted.

"I'll be a traitor to my country," Blanco said. "You know what the SEBIN will do if they find out?"

"I've got a pretty good idea," Phoenix replied.

"That's it?" Blanco shouted.

"It's all I can give you right now." And it was. He had no prior authorization to take her out of the country, and while he wanted to whisk her away from the depravity of her homeland, it would be a better deal all around if she remained embedded with her unit. "If you get me information, I can wire you some money. That's what all my assets want."

"But I want to leave," Blanco said emphatically.

Phoenix placed his hands on her shoulders and looked her in the eyes. "You can do this, Blanco. Be my asset, and we'll get you and your family safely out of Venezuela. If you leave now, you'll lose whatever negotiating power you might have."

Blanco stared in disbelief at the CIA officer trying to coerce her into turning on her own country. But if working for him provided an opportunity to get her family safely out of Venezuela, then she would do as he asked.

She nodded. "Okay. I'll do it, but you have to promise to get my family out."

"I swear," Phoenix replied.

"Go. I will think of something to tell Major Silva."

Phoenix patted her shoulders. "Thank you, Lieutenant." He turned and bounded up the airstairs with TJ pulling them shut behind him.

Phoenix hopped into the pilot's seat and pulled on the headset. Glancing over his shoulder, he saw that TJ had shut the door and that all his passengers had their seatbelts fastened.

The plane only needed half the runway to take off, and once they were in the air, Phoenix turned southeast and headed toward Guyana.

CHAPTER 19

Miraflores Palace
Caracas, Venezuela

MAJOR GENERAL ALEJANDRO SALAZAR HAD BEEN INSIDE THE presidential palace many times over the course of his career, and he had always marveled at the beauty and majesty of the old building. If there was a visible symbol of what a wealthy and powerful nation Venezuela had once been, it was the opulent palace.

The original occupant had been Joaquin Crespo, a military officer and politician who had served as president for two terms between 1884 and 1898. The most interesting thing about Crespo's term, in Salazar's opinion, was that he'd presided over the Venezuelan Crisis of 1895. By then, the dispute over the Essequibo Region had already lasted three hundred years, but it came to a head when Venezuela hired William Lindsey Scruggs, a former American ambassador, to lobby Washington on their behalf, claiming British aggression in Latin America violated the Monroe Doctrine.

The 1895 crisis boiled down to arbitration between Venezuela, Great Britain, and the United States. The joint panel unanimously decided to give British Guiana control of the modern-day border lines, including the Essequibo Region. However, in 1949, U.S. jurist Otto Schoenrich slipped a memorandum written by Severo Mallet-Prevost to the Venezuelan government. And in it, Mallet-Prevost claimed that Russian diplomat Friedrich Martens, who had served as the head of the arbitration panel, had colluded with the British in return for their support of Russian aggression elsewhere in the world. While no one knew how Mallet-Prevost learned of this deal, the Venezuelans seized upon it to renew their efforts to reclaim the Essequibo Region.

Salazar knew that Martens, often referred to as "Lord Chief Justice of Christendom" for his track record of impartially adjudicating international disputes, had kept a diary of the arbitration of the Essequibo Region. In it, he never once referred to any such deal as Mallet-Prevost claimed. The Venezuelan government, never one to let facts stand in their way, used the memo to continue their push for the reclamation of their territorial lands.

But Salazar hadn't been summoned to the meeting with President Zarate to admire oil paintings and original bronze lamps hand forged in the late 1880s or to relive ancient history. As Salazar walked through the halls of power, a presidential aide came alongside him and guided him toward the Ayacucho Room.

When Salazar stepped into the room, he saw his fellow officers—the heads of the Navy, Air Force, and the National Guard—already seated at a polished mahogany table. Salazar, wearing his dress uniform the same as the others, set his briefing folder on the table in front of his chair, just to the right of the head of the table where the president would sit.

Moments later, President Michel Zarate strode into the room, wearing a black suit with a striped blue and white tie.

He was tall with a barrel chest and a thick mustache, but his hair had left him long ago, resulting in a gleaming dome that some claimed his mistress waxed and polished on a daily basis. Salazar figured that whoever had started that rumor needed clarification about which head a mistress normally polished.

The military leaders stood in respect for their commander-in-chief. After Zarate had taken his seat at the head of the table, the military council sat back down, and the meeting came to order. Besides the president and the council, there were stenographers, aides-de-camp, and various palace servants in attendance. Salazar felt there were too many ears in the room, but who was he to give the president an order to clear the room?

"Give me a report of the *Essequibo* Incident," Zarate said to Admiral Lester Valenzuela.

The Chief of Naval Operations, a compact officer with blond hair and a misshaped nose, launched a detailed summary of the high-seas encounter between the former PC-21 *Guaiqueri* and the GDFS *Essequibo*.

Salazar ignored the verbal report since he had already been briefed on the incident. He gazed around the room, admiring the life-size portraits of Simón Bolívar, José Antonio Páez, the first president of Venezuela, and Hugo Chávez dressed to look like Bolívar in colonial-era clothing and a feathered hat. Underfoot, bright red carpet offset the white walls gilded with gold trim. With a seating capacity of 250, the president typically reserved the Ayacucho Room for official events or for when he addressed the nation. Thankfully, the galley was empty today.

The commanding general tuned back into the conversation just in time to hear Valenzuela say, "Once the *Guaiqueri* opened their missile hatches, the *Essequibo* fired two torpedoes. Both hit the *Guaiqueri* broadside amidships, quickly sinking her. There were few survivors, and either the *Essequibo* or the nearby fishing vessel picked them up. They are now being held in a jail in Georgetown.

"I've spoken to Vice President Franklin Singh," Valenzuela continued. "He says they will release the prisoners *if* we agree to withdraw all claims to the Essequibo Region and its territorial waters."

Zarate shook his head. General Salazar knew his commander-in-chief was unwilling to give up any claim to the Essequibo Region. It was their territory, no matter what any court had to say on the matter. And with Guyana sinking the *Guaiqueri*, Salazar knew it was just a matter of time before Zarate ordered them to run rampant over their weaker neighbor and reclaim what was rightfully theirs.

"What should be our response, *El Jefe*?" Valenzuela asked.

"We must retaliate," Zarate replied. "We cannot let this action go unanswered. I want Guyana to know who its master is."

"We propose to step up sea patrols in the area and block all Guyanese fishing vessels from operating in our waters, as well as stop the offshore exploration and drilling efforts," Valenzuela stated.

Salazar knew Valenzuela meant the territorial waters of the Essequibo Region that Zarate had designated as their own under presidential decree number 1787.

Changing the subject, Zarate asked, "When will they pave our new runway on Ankoko Island?"

"We have surveyed it, and we're moving our heavy equipment into place as we speak," Salazar said. "According to our Russian advisors, it should take no more than six months from breaking ground to having a completed runway with navigation lights and aids installed."

"Unacceptable," Zarate stated.

"We did not anticipate how far Guyana would escalate the situation," Salazar replied. "I will speak with the contractors and let them know we need to accelerate the timetable."

"I want to fly our Flanker jets into Ankoko within thirty days," Zarate commanded.

"We still have very few jets capable of flying, sir," Air Force General-in-Chief Martin Rolando reported. "We've grounded all the F-16s for lack of parts, and only a handful of the Su-30 Flankers are operational."

"Call Putin," Zarate ordered. "Have him send parts and more planes."

"They are embroiled in the Ukrainian Conflict, sir," Rolando replied. "They are limited in what they can provide."

Zarate sighed. "Must I do everything?"

Rolando cleared his throat. "No, *El Jefe*. I have spoken to one of Minister Xi's representatives. Xi is willing to send ten of his Chengdu J-10s fighter jets and complete armament packages for each. The Chinese will open a supply line with us if we desire."

Having been fleeced by the Chinese several times, Zarate asked warily, "What will that cost us?"

"Oil, sir," Rolando replied.

"That's what everyone wants," Zarate muttered.

Salazar knew there was no way they could ramp up production to pay for the fighters, and taking the Essequibo fields would do little good as most had yet to come online.

While Salazar had made it his mission to clean up and reorganize the army, he'd also been begging Zarate to modernize their air fleet by purchasing new planes and helicopters. Heavy forests covered much of Venezuela, and Salazar wanted to use the airmobile tactic the U.S. had employed during their war in Vietnam. Not only did Salazar desire to use Chinese-made Harbin Z-20s, dubbed by many as the "Copy Hawk" because it looked exactly like the Sikorsky UH-60 Black Hawk helicopter used extensively by the U.S. military, but he also wanted Changhe Z-10s, an AH-64 Apache equivalent that could provide air support for his cavalry troops.

His request languished on Zarate's desk for several reasons that he knew. The first was obvious—Venezuela could barely afford to feed its people, let alone purchase new military hardware—and the other was the fact that Zarate had ties to many of the criminal elements Salazar wanted to pursue, including former FARC rebels in Colombia, various cartels running drugs through Venezuela, and Hezbollah raising funds for terror operations by illegally mining Venezuelan gold.

Even if Salazar were to get his request for the helicopters approved, it would boil down to support, like the twenty aging Mi-17 Panare and Mi-35 Hind helicopters in his fleet and every vehicle, aircraft, and ship in Venezuela's military.

If he didn't have a steady stream of spare parts or the ability to replace the helicopters because of mechanical issues or combat losses, then there was no point in having them. And if Salazar did have them, he would have to train pilots, aircrewmen, crew chiefs, and weapons officers to fly the new aircraft and retrain troops in air assault tactics. There just wasn't time to do any of that if *El Jefe* wanted to go to war tomorrow.

"We need to strike fast," Salazar offered, trying to bolster support for his position and for the new aircraft order. "If you want to declare war on Guyana, we should deploy Air Cav units to take Georgetown and set up a naval blockade with Admiral Valenzuela's ships. The new fleet of helicopters can provide close air support along with our Flankers and the Chengdu J-10s."

"It sounds like you've been working on a plan of attack," Zarate stated.

"Yes, sir. I thought it was prudent," Salazar replied.

"Is that why you've been lobbying for more helicopters?" the president asked.

"Yes, it is, sir," Salazar said. "Air superiority is an established doctrine for controlling the war on the ground."

"That's not working so well in Ukraine," Valenzuela chimed in. "Nor for the Americans in Afghanistan or Iraq. Air superiority can't stop a fervent counter-insurgency."

"You're correct, Lester, but the Ukrainians are receiving outside aid," Salazar replied.

"So will the people of Guyana," Rolando added. "I feel I have to be the voice of reason here, *El Jefe*. The people of Guyana will not roll over and allow us to take the Essequibo Region, nor will the world. We know Russia and China, our own allies, are doing business in Guyana, and so is the United States, Guyana's most strategic trading partner. If we go to war with Guyana, we'll be going to war with the U.S."

Zarate chuckled. "They're sending so much money and war materiel to Ukraine that they can't support a war on a second front. Besides, they care more about climate change than Guyana's oil and gas industry. They want to power their country with solar and wind—useless in a modern war."

"No matter what the Americans do, we'll still be fighting a war with weapons from the Cold War Era, *El Jefe*," Rolando pointed out. "We need to modernize or at least get spare parts for the equipment we have before we commit to a full-scale war."

Salazar knew his contemporary was scoring valid points, but he was also questioning the wisdom of their president. He wondered how far out of the office Rolando would get before Zarate had him arrested for treason. One simply didn't question the orders of President Zarate, even if they were questions that any sane person would ask on the brink of war.

Zarate drew in a deep breath and glanced around at the men at the table. "We are going to war with the army we have. Do your best to prepare your equipment and your troops. I will set a timetable that is amiable to our plans and one that will take into account the negotiations I know are coming. But first, we must strike a retaliatory blow against

Guyana to let them know we will not take their actions lying down."

Salazar waited to be excused from the meeting. He had plans to work on, and his first wave of troops would be the most important. If Ankoko Island was to be a staging base for jets, then *El Jefe* needed a place to land his birds. Salazar needed to go on a scouting trip to the border.

The president ran a finger over his mustache and then stood, marking the end of the meeting. He thumped the table hard with his fist. "Gentlemen, we are at war!"

CHAPTER 20

University Hospital of Caracas
Caracas, Venezuela

Evelyn Acevedo knew she had to remain true to the Chavistas and to Michel Zarate to keep her job, but this humanitarian crisis was really pissing her off.

Dressed in green scrubs and a white surgical cap, she was hot from the lack of air conditioning in the hospital. *It's just another injustice in the world.*

Washing her hands in the sink, Acevedo pondered the felonious actions of the president of her country. She'd just finished performing surgery on a college-age male who had contracted gangrene in his leg from a bullet wound. While the youth hadn't sought medical attention until it was too late, it still galled Acevedo that she didn't have the proper antibiotics and medical care required to treat him, even if he had come to the hospital when first wounded. During surgery, the damage done by the swiftly moving gangrene had forced her to cut off the kid's leg just above the knee. Now an amputee, the young man would be just another in a rather lengthy line of Venezuelans unable to get a good prosthesis or to earn a decent living. It infuriated her to no end that she had to perform these needless surgeries.

While Acevedo didn't consider herself a capitalist, she believed there was a better system than what that asshole Zarate currently administered. Even the Communist Party of Venezuela (PCV) had broken with Zarate, claiming he supported crony capitalism and not the rights of the people. The PCV demanded better wages and had recently called for an investigation into Zarate and his support of corruption at top government levels. Zarate had turned to the highly politicized Supreme Court and forced them to denounce and disqualify the PCV from participating in national elections as he had with other political parties, consolidating his power to ensure he remained on the throne.

Being on the healthcare front lines, Acevedo saw firsthand the effects of Zarate's political machinations. She had also seen the opposite side of Zarate's policies while attending Duke University en route to becoming a medical doctor. In the U.S., medical supplies were cheap and plentiful, and hospitals never lacked running water and electricity.

Between the brutal violence of the *colectivos*, the ever-present fear of the SEBIN, and the uncaring government in Caracas, coming home to Venezuela was like waking up in a shocking nightmare turned into real life.

Zarate seemed to have orchestrated a crisis on almost every front, and she saw every day the desperate plight of the people, especially those who needed serious medical care. Widespread shortages of essential health products, critical medicines, running water and electricity, and fuel for the hospital's generators plagued the Venezuelan medical system.

While medical care was free to all in Venezuela, there was still a pay-as-you-go hierarchy where wealthier patrons often received better care and services than those less fortunate.

And there were few medical professionals to go around, just two doctors per one thousand patients. Nurses and technicians were even harder to come by as they continued to flee the country in droves.

While working for the hospital and teaching part-time at the Central University of Venezuela, Acevedo also held an active role in politics as she had been elected to the National Assembly during the last general election. The assembly was more of a figurehead post since Zarate did whatever he pleased without consulting anyone else.

It irritated Acevedo that her own people couldn't see just how corrupt Zarate was, or, if they did, they turned a blind eye toward Caracas, especially the poor who relied on Zarate's social programs for their daily sustenance. So many people were out of work or hungry that it seemed like a tipping point had to be close at hand.

And if one spoke out about the living conditions or complained too loudly about the Zarate regime, the SEBIN seemed to be right there to sweep them up for interrogation and reeducation. For Acevedo to state that she was, a free-dom-loving woman who favored a mixed economy over strict government intervention was akin to inviting herself to her own hanging.

But she didn't discount socialism as a governing mecha-nism. There was more than enough oil money to go around, and Acevedo believed every man, woman, and child in Venezuela should receive a check from the residual profits. The problem was corruption at the highest level, which prevented socialism from working properly.

Acevedo had hoped that things would change when Juan Guaidó had set up an interim government after declaring himself the victor of the last presidential election, but the world had recognized Zarate as the winner, legitimizing his presidency again. To put the icing on the cake in support of Zarate and his dictatorship, former President Joseph Brandon had struck a deal to send workers from Chevron to restart the oil fields so the United States could purchase oil from Venezuela.

It also befuddled Acevedo to no end how the United States, a country she considered her adopted home, could strike repeated deals with terrorists, dictators, and oligarchs in the name of cheap oil. It made no sense. Not when a free country like Guyana was next door with vast quantities of newly discovered oil reserves. By President Brandon giving his blessing to Venezuela, he had all but assured Zarate that he didn't care what Zarate did to his people or to other countries.

But then again, Acevedo thought, *Brandon hadn't given a fuck about the people in his own country.*

"Doctor," a female nurse said, opening the scrub room door. "A man is here to see you."

Acevedo straightened and reached for a hand towel. She dried her hands and arms, then dabbed at the sweat on her forehead. Pulling off her surgical cap, she asked, "Who is he? What does he want?"

The dark eyes of the nurse darted away, her face turning down. "He's from SEBIN."

Acevedo rolled her eyes. The SEBIN kept coming to her to patch up their wounded officers after they'd been in some type of skirmish, so she figured she would need to grab her surgical bag and head into the field again. She glanced down at her scrubs to see if she'd gotten any blood on them during surgery and if she needed to change. They appeared clean, so she shook out her loose, deep brown hair and ran her fingers through it several times before she pulled it back into a ponytail. After glancing in the mirror one last time to check her appearance, she licked her lips, wishing she had a little gloss or perhaps a hint of cover-up to conceal the lines under her soulful brown eyes.

Prepared to head out, Acevedo pushed through the door

and came face to face with a tall man in blue jeans and a dress shirt. Acevedo then noticed the two other men in black stormtrooper outfits armed with automatic rifles and handguns. The stranger with curly brown hair flipped open a wallet and showed her his identification. His name was Marcus de los Rios.

Acevedo instantly went on high alert. Typically, the SEBIN sent a car and driver to take her to the injured men, not an armed escort. One rarely saw the troopers in their black uniforms unless they were performing some sort of operation. She gulped as she prayed that they weren't there to haul her off to solitary confinement.

Mustering her courage, she snapped, "What do you want? Can't you see I'm busy here?"

"You need to come with us, Doctor," de los Rios replied flatly.

"What for?" Acevedo demanded. "I have another surgery to prep for."

De los Rios tilted his head, and the stormtrooper on his left stepped forward, holding a set of handcuffs. The agent in civilian clothes said, "There is the easy way, and there is the hard way, Doctor. Which do you prefer?"

Acevedo knew there was no use in resisting the SEBIN.

The three men escorted Acevedo out of the hospital to a waiting car. They drove through the city center toward the high rise near Plaza Venezuela known as *La Tumba*, or "The Tomb," for a detention facility in its basement. Acevedo felt her gut tighten. She'd heard the horror stories of the strip searches, the white noise interrogations, and the prisoners who slowly went out of their minds inside the tiny concrete cells with no fresh air or sunlight. If someone was looking for hell on earth, the SEBIN prisons were an excellent place to start.

Coming to a stop at the front entrance of The Tomb, de los

Rios assured his passenger that she was not under arrest or about to be imprisoned.

A wave of relief washed over the doctor, but the prospect of entering the building still frightened her. Disappearing was a fact of life in Venezuela.

De los Rios opened the car door and bid the good doctor to exit. He accompanied her through the front doors and onto an elevator. Acevedo closed her eyes, not wanting to see which button he pushed. Down meant hell. Up meant a meeting that could be just as bad.

The elevator car started to rise. Acevedo let out the breath she'd been holding. The car rose higher until it reached the top floor.

She'd faced down *colectivos* in Venezuelan streets and been mugged in Raleigh-Durham when she was a sophomore in college. Now, she would face the greatest threat of them all—the Director General of the SEBIN.

"This way, Doctor," de los Rios said, ushering Acevedo out of the elevator and into an opulent lobby. Behind a wood and granite counter sat a woman in uniform, her blonde hair pulled back in a severe bun. She looked both menacing and professional at the same time. Acevedo felt out of place in her scrubs and wished de los Rios had allowed her to change into something more appropriate for the meeting.

Without a word to the woman behind the counter, de los Rios opened the door to Hector Calderón's office and stood aside so Acevedo could enter. She glanced around at the polished marble floor tiles, the large portraits of former SEBIN directors on the wall, and, of course, Simón. He was always present—the great liberator. *How we need you now*, Acevedo mused.

Calderón sat behind a massive wooden desk. It was devoid of anything on its surface. To one side was an office station with a neatly arranged computer, printer, and other accoutrements he might need.

The director of the nation's intelligence apparatus stood as de los Rios shut the door. Calderón extended his hand and smiled. "Welcome, Evelyn."

After a polite shake, Acevedo said, "You may call me Doctor Acevedo, thank you."

"My apologies, Doctor. I thought you and I could be on a first-name basis."

"Why did you bring me here, Director?" she asked with exasperation.

"You're in the running to be the head of the National Assembly, are you not?"

Acevedo crossed her arms, showing her frustration through physical action. "I am."

"Come now, Doctor, there's no need to be upset. My intention was for this visit to be enjoyable.

"I have work to do. I'm on the surgical rotation, and thanks to the ineptness of our government, the job is much harder than it needs to be."

"Please, sit," the director said with a gesture toward a chair across from his desk. "This won't take long. Can I get you a drink, perhaps a dash of that Aviation Gin you liked so much during your time at Duke University?"

Acevedo felt surprised by his knowledge of her past, but she longed for a taste of the gin. She hadn't had a good drink in years. Acevedo continued to stand with her arms crossed. "What do you want from me?" she asked, trying to remain resolute.

Calderón stepped to a small cabinet near the wide window with a stunning view of Caracas beyond. He opened the door, produced two glasses, and poured gin into both. He set one glass on the desk near Acevedo and then stood by the window with his free hand in the pocket of his neatly pressed dress slacks, sipping from his own glass of gin.

After a few moments of silence, Calderón finally got down

to business. "What I wanted to talk about is potentially moving you into the position of vice president."

Acevedo tried to figure out the angle Calderón was playing. The vice president was the first successor in line to Zarate and acted more like a prime minister, serving as the head of the government. In Venezuela, it was just another ceremonial position with no real power. There was no other power than Zarate.

Flabbergasted, Acevedo asked, "But why?"

"You're an intelligent, attractive woman, much more so than our current VP, Delcy Rodriguez. She's outlived her usefulness. She's been sanctioned by numerous countries, and many more refuse to cooperate with her."

Acevedo ignored the jab at her good looks. Men had been trying to sleep with her since she was a thirteen-year-old girl, and even in her late thirties, she was still highly attractive. Standing on her bare feet, she was five-four, or 163cm, and was lean from the lack of food and working long hours. Her firm breasts still needed no bra, but she wore one anyway, preferring something lacey and delicate to make her feel more feminine under the unisexual surgical scrubs.

She tried again to sound out Calderón. "I still don't understand your desire to replace Rodriguez."

"We want to establish better relations with the U.S. now that Chevron is back at work in our oil fields. Not only have you spent time in the United States, earning your degree and traveling, but you seem to have a grasp of their political system and how the average American thinks."

Acevedo nodded, still trying to comprehend the depth of Calderón's knowledge of her past.

The director of the SEBIN continued, "You have no skeletons in your closet and no international bank accounts stuffed with ill-gotten gains that we know about." He paused and smiled. "Do you?" The doctor shook her head, and Calderón added, "And I believe you're a moderate, which is needed to temper Zarate's often crazy whims."

The conversation still puzzled Acevedo. "Zarate isn't going to want a moderate as his second-in-command. He's not going to listen to me."

Calderón sighed as he took a seat on the corner of his desk. "Evelyn, hear me out. We want to place a moderate in the office to show the world we're capable of change. You seem to be immune to too many foreign influences on our country. As a physician, you've seen firsthand the shortages and the perils of our economy. As the VP, you'll be able to do some real good, maybe even whisper into Zarate's ear and keep us from going to war over this *Essequibo* Incident."

"Is he calling for war?" she asked.

Calderón nodded. "How do you feel about the *Zona en Reclamación?*"

Acevedo knew the history and the politics of the disputed Essequibo Region—the Zone of Reclamation. She also understood why Zarate had been goading Guyana. She believed Calderón would back whatever decision Zarate would make, so she gave him an answer that she felt would satisfy him. "I think it belongs to Venezuela in accordance with the creation of the Kingdom of Venezuela in 1777, which established the border on the Essequibo River between the Spanish and Dutch colonies."

"Excellent, Doctor. That is an answer we can approve of."

"Who is pushing for me to be vice president? You keep using the term 'we.'"

"That is not for you to worry about. I'm just the one floating the idea out to you. Think about it and let me know by Tuesday."

"But I am worried," Acevedo countered. "I feel I'm being offered up on a silver platter to be a sacrificial lamb."

Calderón chuckled, then sipped his gin. "If we wanted a

sacrificial lamb, we would give them Rodriguez. What you're being offered is a golden ticket."

Acevedo had to admit it would only be a true golden ticket if Zarate was dead and she could ascend to the highest position in the land. The very thought of wishing ill on someone felt like a punch to her gut. *I'm a doctor! How could I wish death on anyone?*

But she had to admit, the offer was tantalizing. It was almost too good to be true for such a young politico like herself who didn't run in Zarate's circle and had no military experience. She couldn't say no to an opportunity to help all the people of Venezuela. This was a once-in-a-lifetime shot at actual power to enact much-needed change. Being a doctor, Acevedo held the lives of her patients in her hands. Being a politician, she held the lives of her fellow citizens in her hands.

And she could see where Calderón was leading her by asking about the Zone of Reclamation. If Venezuela controlled it, they would own the vast majority of the oil in the world, and everyone would be at their mercy. She could do so much for her people with the power and the wealth that came with that control. But the border was the border, sovereign and set, upheld by court decree. Venezuela had more than enough oil to power itself into the next millennium without invading another country.

Reaching forward, she took hold of the gin glass and shot the liquor back. It felt delicious on her taste buds as it washed down her throat. It had been a long time since she'd tasted good gin, and she chastised herself for not savoring it. Yet, she felt she needed the fortification of liquid courage for what she was about to agree to.

"I don't need to wait until Tuesday, Hector. I'll take the job, and since I'll be your direct boss, we should be on a first-name basis."

CHAPTER 21

CIA Safe House
Triumph, Guyana

Connelly was back in Guyana, and Phoenix was tired of being grilled.

They were in a two-bedroom house near Eugene F. Correia International Airport, where the CIA kept a hanger for Orville Wright and his Cessna. The shuttered house had no air conditioning, which worsened the oppressive heat outside. Tired and sweaty, Phoenix wanted Connelly's incessant questions to end so he could get on with the next mission.

While he knew that briefings and after-action reports were an essential part of his Army and his CIA career, that didn't mean he enjoyed doing them, especially when he had to sit in front of a computer and craft a detailed summary. Too much time staring at a screen made him restless, and being cooped up in the house with Connelly was driving him crazy.

He peeled off his T-shirt and used it to mop the sweat

from his forehead. "You guys couldn't have sprung for a place with air conditioning?"

"It wasn't my call," Connelly said. She, too, had stripped down to just her sports bra and shorts.

Phoenix rolled his shoulder, trying to relieve the ache in his muscles. "So anyway, just before we get on the plane, I throw the recruitment pitch at Lieutenant Blanco, but she hasn't called, so I don't know where we stand with her."

"What's the matter, John?" Connelly asked, watching him contort his body to ease the pain in his back.

"It's my shoulder. Same old bullshit."

Connelly got up from the table and stepped behind the muscular case officer. She placed her hands on his shoulders and then dug her thumbs into the exact spot between his shoulder blade and spine where his muscles had twisted themselves into a knot.

"You need to take better care of yourself," his handler said. "Take some time off."

"Will you let me?" Phoenix asked. "With the possibility of war between Venezuela and Guyana on the horizon, I don't think … Oh, yeah," he moaned. "That's the spot."

Connelly continued to massage his shoulders, loosening the tension he kept there. Whenever he was in D.C., Phoenix made time to get frequent massages and acupuncture treatments. The acupuncturist was also a homeopathic doctor who had told Phoenix that he carried a lot of resentment in his gall bladder, which resulted in swelling that irritated the phrenic nerve and caused his shoulder pain. Being the wiseass that he was, Phoenix looked at her and said, "Let's stick a pin in it, yeah, doc." And she had, literally.

But he'd often pondered her statement, wondering what he was so resentful about. He figured it was the premature death of both his parents, or maybe it was the way the judge had forced him to join the Army in handcuffs, although he'd excelled at being an enlisted man and then as a CIA case officer.

"You're right," Connelly agreed. "I don't think anyone will be taking time off." She moved both hands to his right deltoid and continued to massage him. "Tell me about the lieutenant."

"Not much to tell. She works for the 97th Special Forces Brigade and runs her own all-woman A-team that she claimed was called 'La Zorras.' Although, I'm not sure how many are left after the gunfight we had at the mine."

"I've never heard of the 97th," Connelly said. "They have the 99th, which has been around for quite a few years."

"She said it's a fairly new unit, stood up in the last year."

"Did she train in Venezuela for the SF brigade or somewhere else? What's her direct chain of command? Who are the other members of her team? Can we turn any of those?"

Phoenix shrugged off Connelly's hands and stood. "We were in a running fucking gun battle, Leslie. When was I supposed to ask her all those questions?"

"Why didn't you bring her out?"

"Because I hoped she would contact me and become an asset," he barked back. "I had to make a snap decision. She's still in the country, and I'm here."

"Take it easy, John," Connelly replied soothingly. "I'm just trying to get all the information I can for my report."

"Yeah. I know." Phoenix sat back down, placed his elbows on the table, and rubbed both temples with his fingertips. He was hot, and he was tired, and he was ready to sleep in a soft bed with an air conditioner blasting frigid air across his naked body. The safehouse felt stifling and confining. Not even the iced Coca-Cola in a sweating glass helped to cool his body. Fortunately for them, the ice maker in the fridge still worked while the A/C had yet to be repaired. Phoenix popped an ice cube into his mouth after swallowing some Coke and sucked greedily on the frozen cube.

Connelly sat before her laptop and started to type. Even the computer seemed to protest the heat as the fan blew constantly to cool the electronics inside.

"What's next?" he asked. "Am I going back to Ankoko Island?"

"That's the plan," Connelly said, still typing.

"I gotta get out of here," Phoenix stood and grabbed his shirt. "I'm going to get a hotel room with A/C. You want to join me?"

"What?" Connelly asked, glancing up at him.

"I asked if you wanted to find a quiet spot to go skinny dipping. Remember that place near Angel Falls?"

"It's over, John. Please don't ask me again."

"Roger that," the ex-Green Beret replied. So much for wooing her back into the sack. Once she'd set her sights on the Seventh Floor, Connelly had cast him off like some old hat, worn out and forgotten. He still didn't understand why she was his handler. He placed a hand on her shoulder, feeling her muscles tense. "When you're back in D.C., find me another handler, will you?"

She glanced up at him. "Why? What do you mean?"

"I don't want to hold you back, Les. It's obvious you don't like having to deal with me, so let's cut the crap and move on."

"I wish I could, but you've alienated too many people in the LA division." Connelly sighed. "Dammit, John, you're great at your job, but your people skills, especially with those in your chain of command, absolutely suck."

Phoenix grinned, thinking of a witty comeback that was most sexual in nature about sucking, but he didn't voice it.

As if reading his dirty mind, Connelly said, "There's something wrong with you."

"You used to like my jokes, but I guess they don't fly when you're bucking for promotion under the director's desk."

"That's the kind of shit that I'm talking about, John. You know I'm not doing anything more than my job."

Phoenix grinned. "Blow *job*."

"Fuck. Off."

Phoenix headed for the door, pulling on his shirt as he went, and slung the overstuffed backpack he'd retrieved from the airport hangar after returning from Venezuela over his shoulder. He stepped outside and took a deep breath before walking down the steps to the ground from the elevated stilt house. With no car, Phoenix had no choice but to walk, so he headed east, knowing most of the hotels were near the Demerara River.

While seaside lodging would be spectacular, Phoenix was more accustomed to hostels or places with three stars or less in their reviews. It wasn't that they were any better than the more expensive Marriotts or Holiday Inns, but he could pay cash, and the smaller establishments didn't require a credit card for "incidentals" like if the room were to get smashed up while someone was trying to black bag him—it wouldn't be the first time. Had Connelly been along, Phoenix would have sprung for the Guyana Marriott Hotel Georgetown. The four-hundred-dollar-a-night room fee came with crisp white sheets, room service, and a full bar.

He had to put their past relationship out of his mind. Connelly had moved on, or so she claimed. Phoenix knew he wasn't destined for upper management or a job at Headquarters. His place was in the field, running assets, spying on foreign operatives, and breaking shit. As he walked, Phoenix ran a surveillance detection route (SDR). The CIA officer had spent enough time in Georgetown and the surrounding suburbs to move quickly toward his destination, a quiet little place near the Guyana National Museum, but the SDR allowed him to notice if there was anyone following him either by foot or in a vehicle.

After walking a little more than a kilometer, Phoenix was

sure no one was watching him, but the walk had left him hotter and more tired than he'd been at the safe house. Deciding he needed a break, he stepped into a nearby bar and sat under the lazily turning ceiling fan. He placed the back-pack between his feet and slipped one strap around his leg. As pro wrestler "Stone Cold" Steve Austin used to say, "DTA —don't trust anybody." Phoenix wasn't about to have his bag stolen.

The case officer ordered an ice-cold Banks DIH Caribbean Lager, the same beer he'd drank in Eteringbang before Connelly sent him on the ill-fated trip to rescue Cobalt Panther. As he sipped his beer, he thought about his relation-ship with his handler.

He had loved her, or at least the hot sex had made him believe that he'd loved her. She'd always joked that most men made too many decisions with their small head, and maybe that was the muscle that ached for her now, not his heart. With a snort of derision, he wondered if perhaps he just needed to exercise his muscle a little, and that would help him get over her. Yet, when a skinny young woman approached and asked if he was new in town, Phoenix gave her the brush off. He wasn't so desperate that he needed to pay for the exercise.

After his second beer, Phoenix felt more relaxed, and while he'd been sipping, he'd checked out his surroundings and the people coming and going from the bar. No one but the hookers seemed to be interested in him. He left cash under his empty bottle and stood, making his way outside.

Once on the sidewalk, he hailed a passing taxi and asked the driver to take him to the Le Grande Penthouse Hotel. The place really wasn't grand, and Pheonix had never seen the penthouse, but it was cheap and had all the essentials. Once in his room, Phoenix stripped down and took a long shower. He got out, wrapped a towel around his waist, and then lay on the bed, enjoying the mechanically chilled seventy-degree room temperature. He made the calculation in his mind and decided that saying it was twenty-two degrees Celsius just made him feel like he was in a walk-in freezer.

Closing his eyes, Phoenix breathed deeply, swelling his stomach and concentrating on the air flowing past the tip of his nose. Within a few breaths, he was sound asleep.

———

THE RINGING of a telephone woke John Phoenix from a dream. He and his father had been hunting whitetail deer, and the younger Phoenix was about to press the trigger on his rifle. Once the deer was down, his dad would clap him on the back, and they would spend the rest of the day smiling and joking about what an excellent hunter John had become. It was one of his fondest memories. He wished he could remember his mother that well, but he only had wisps of images of her, and they seemed to grow more fleeting every day.

Before Phoenix could get off the bed and dig the phone out of his backpack, the phone stopped ringing.

Curious about who had called, he rolled to his feet and checked the Caller ID. Fucking Connelly. He glanced at the clock on the nightstand and realized he'd only been asleep for two hours.

He was about to punch the number to redial Nightingale when he saw he had a voice message and a missed call. Figuring it was her, Phoenix scrolled down, and his eyebrows shot up when he saw the Venezuelan +58 country code. Quickly, he punched in his PIN to access his voicemail.

"Something big is happening. We're mobilizing back to Maracay to train with the airborne battalions. Rumor has it we're going to war with Guyana," Lieutenant Coralina Blanco said into the recorder.

The voicemail ended with a click. Phoenix listened to the

message again, then called Connelly back. "What?" he barked when she answered the phone.

"Where are you?" she barked back.

"Le Grande. Rob Street and Avenue of the Republic."

"What room number?"

"Why?" he asked, voice lowering into a coyer tone. "Did you decide to join me after all?"

"Grow up, John. I need to talk to you. Get back to the safe house as soon as possible."

"You don't want to come here?"

"I don't know if the room is compromised. I know this place is clean. We *need* to talk," Connelly emphasized through her teeth.

"Can't it wait, Les? I need a break."

"I'll be sure to tell Cole you needed a break the next time I talk to him."

Phoenix knew she meant Director Cole Stratten, her personal friend and the man she claimed was her rabbi, helping guide her career. "Fine," he said. "I'll be there as soon as I can."

One of the reasons that Phoenix had picked the Le Grande Hotel was its location near the port and the infamous indoor Stabroek Market. After dressing in shorts and a T-shirt, Phoenix left the hotel carrying his pack. He slipped out the back door and meandered through the haphazardly parked cars belonging to port workers or destined to be shipped via cargo container to another terminal. Once past America Street, Phoenix entered a world of vendor stalls under canopies or umbrellas. Moving through the crowd wasn't always easy, and the swirling mob frequently bumped and jostled him.

Occasionally, he would veer off into an alcove or stop between vendor booths to watch the surging mass of people. No one seemed to pay him any attention. It helped that Phoenix looked so much like these people with their brown skin and dark hair. When he mimicked their actions and speech patterns, the Guyanese frequently mistook him for one of their own.

Entering the market proper was an assault on the senses. Not only was it loud with constant chattering, bargaining, and shouting, but the smells of spices, raw fish, fresh vegetables, chemically tainted hair products, and cooking food filled his nostrils. Everywhere he looked, Phoenix saw a vibrant rainbow of color, from the vegetable stands to the patrons' clothing. The CIA officer grinned to himself as he moved through the crowd. This was his kind of place. While he loved the solitude of the forest, his body seemed to vibrate with the market's energy, filling him with a keen sense of invigoration.

Moving back outside, Phoenix stopped at a food stall and ordered fried iguana tail and cook-up rice, Guyana's version of fried rice made with peas, beans, and coconut milk. He slathered everything with a judicial coating of pepper sauce—blended Wiri Wiri peppers in lime juice—and added some scotch bonnet peppers on the side. He ate, holding the food carton in one hand and the fork in the other, scooping the spicy concoction into his mouth as he watched his surroundings.

Once he finished his meal, Phoenix chased the spicy heat with a cold Banks I-Cee orange soda, sipping it as he walked toward the Parliament Building, where he hailed a passing taxi. The driver came to a stop with such a loud squeal of brakes that it made Phoenix wonder if the car had any pads left to grab the rotors.

He had the driver drop him at a bar in Triumph. Phoenix drank a beer and then headed for the safe house, walking the last few blocks while checking for tails as he ran an SDR. He wished the place wasn't up on stilts, meaning there was one entrance and one exit so he couldn't slip in the back door. Anyone watching the house could clearly see who was coming and going. Connelly had said the agency owned it, and whoever had been in charge of the purchase didn't know their ass from a hole in the ground when it came to tradecraft.

"Fucking bureaucrats," Phoenix muttered.

Inside the house, he peeked out the curtains to see if there were any visible signs of counter-surveillance. If someone was watching them, they would have been smart to rent a house across the street. From there, they could use a long lens camera to snap photos and train a parabolic mic on the agency safe house to eavesdrop on the officers' conversations. It was all basic tradecraft, and once the case officer had left, it would be easy for foreign agents to place bugs, wiring them into the electrical system so they could listen forever, or at least while the power worked.

"No one is out there. No one is listening," Connelly assured him. "I've swept the place three times since I've been here."

"What do we *need* to talk about?" Phoenix finally asked, done making his rounds.

"Sit down, John."

"This can't be good," Phoenix mumbled, reaching into the fridge for a Coke. He'd rather have a beer, but Connelly wasn't much of a drinker, especially when on the job.

As Phoenix settled into his chair at the table again, he cracked open the soda bottle and then used the tail of his shirt to wipe sweat from his face. "How can you stand being here?"

Without missing a beat, she said, "It's my punishment for having to work with you."

Phoenix snorted. He wondered how long Connelly had worked on that line. "So, talk."

"I'm sending you back to Caracas."

Phoenix almost spat out his Coke. "What the hell did you just say?"

"I'm sending you back to Caracas. We have the opportunity to turn the next vice-president of Venezuela. She worked for us after leaving Duke University, but when she went back to Venezuela, she dropped off the radar."

"I would, too. Just look what the SEBIN did to all our assets and officers there. We have a leak."

"I also want you to stop by Anaconda's office and check it out."

"Fuck that," Phoenix replied.

"You see, John, this is why no one wants to work with you."

"No one in their right mind would go anywhere near that office. Especially me, the guy you're sending back to Caracas —after I just escaped a nationwide manhunt."

"John," Connelly said sternly as if admonishing a child. *"Leslie …"*

"You're *going* to that office."

"No. I'm not. The SEBIN is likely aware that it's a cover for a CIA operation. Anaconda's records were either taken or destroyed. And I bet those fuckers are watching the place like a hawk, just waiting for a guy like me to come waltzing in there to check the place out. So, no. I'm not going anywhere near that office."

Connelly shook her head in disappointment.

"What's the VP's name, and where am I meeting her?" Phoenix asked, moving the conversation forward.

"Her name is Evelyn Acevedo. She was born in Caracas to a board member of PDVSA. He apparently embezzled enough funds to send his daughter to college in the U.S., where she earned a medical degree from Duke. Like I said, she worked for us for a few years when she was with Doctors Without Borders. She ended all contact with the agency when she returned to Venezuela."

"So, whoever outed all our agents in Venezuela doesn't know about her?" Phoenix confirmed.

"Most likely not."

"Any idea who the mole is?" Phoenix asked.

"No." Connelly shook her head.

Both case officers had undergone training in multiple methods for detecting facial microexpressions made by a mark, and based on Phoenix's training, he could discern that she was lying her ass off.

"Fine. Don't tell me, but if my name is on that list and you send me in there to get whacked, I'm coming back to haunt you."

Connelly eyed him coldly over the top of her laptop screen.

"Where am I meeting Acevedo, and do we have a code-name for her?"

"Unicorn."

"Nice," Phoenix muttered. Landing her would be like landing a unicorn. Acevedo would become the highest-placed asset the agency ever had in Venezuela.

"You'll have to bump her," Connelly stated. "We *think* she'll be amiable to being our asset, but we don't know for sure. If she wants money, we'll set up an offshore account for her for when we relocate her later. I'll give you some cash to take with you to show her that we're serious."

A "bump" in CIA terms was when an officer found a target of interest in a public place and manufactured a reason to get them talking. The bump would hopefully lead to a "second meeting," which was an opportunity to continue the conversation at a later date. Through these meetings, the case officer hoped to build a relationship with the target and gain access to whatever information they might have access to or wish to share. In Unicorn's case, it could be a treasure trove if she became vice president.

"I'd certainly like to bump her," Phoenix said, studying a photo of the attractive doctor.

Connelly rolled her eyes. "There really is something wrong with you."

Phoenix chuckled. "When do I leave, and how am I getting into Caracas?"

"An asset will take you across from Chaguaramas on the island of Trinidad. His contact will meet you in Puerto de Hierro and drive you to Caracas." She went on to fill Phoenix in on the infiltration details, including descriptions of the men he would meet and the code phrases they would use to identify one another. To help keep the infiltration off the mole's radar, Connelly had used a cut-out to set up the meeting in Chaguaramas.

"What about communications?" Phoenix asked. "Is the DS&T going to set Acevedo up with something secure like our NOCs use?"

The Department of Science and Technology (DS&T) operated as the CIA's premier branch for collecting and analyzing data and technology used in intelligence gathering. A special department within the DS&T designed communication devices for Non-Official Cover operatives. In one case, the NOC had a special market bag with the comms device inside, and for others, it might be hidden in a shoe or some other Inspector Gadget-type device. Phoenix preferred his sat phone with a secure messaging app such as Signal. It was better not to stick out like a sore thumb to some foreign intel specialist monitoring signals for a comms device operating on a frequency beyond what he would typically see. It was like throwing up a beacon and saying, "Come get me."

Connelly sat back in her chair. "I spoke to McNeal at DS&T. He's working up a unit in a leather satchel. You can hand it over if you get a second meeting."

"How soon will the comms be here?"

"Two days tops. They're flying it down, especially for your trip."

"Then I have two days of R&R before I have to be in Chaguaramas."

Connelly reconfirmed the time Phoenix needed to meet

his contact at the port on Trinidad. Romeo would have the satchel and any other tech Phoenix would need.

Phoenix stood and reached for his pack. "By the way, Lieutenant Blanco says hi. She's moving to Maracay to train with the airborne battalions. She says the rumor is that they're going to war with Guyana."

"Wait! What?" Connelly shot back. "When did you hear from her?"

"She called while I was asleep."

"And you waited until now to throw out that tidbit?"

"You were worried about frying bigger fish," Phoenix replied.

"What else did she say?"

Phoenix played the phone message for Connelly.

"Okay. I need to assign her a code name—"

Phoenix cut her off. "Cobra. She'd like that, and she's about as venomous as one. You two would get along like houses on fire."

"Fuck you, John," Connelly replied.

"I'd love to, Leslie. We used to be good together." He bumped the table with his hip. "Move that laptop, and we can do it right here or maybe up against the counter."

"Go!" She pointed toward the door. "Be in Chaguaramas on time."

Phoenix smirked. He loved getting under her skin.

With new orders in hand, he knew his assignment would be dangerous, and he wanted some time to relax before heading back into the fray. If a mole was compromising CIA operations and assets in Venezuela, which Connelly had all but confirmed with her microexpressions and silence on the matter, then he needed to approach this mission with extreme caution.

CHAPTER 22

Parliament Building
Georgetown, Guyana

Commander David Clarke tried not to let his hands shake as he stepped back from the lectern after addressing the president, prime minister, vice president, twenty-two cabinet members, and the fifty-six members of Guyana's parliament. He took a seat on the stage beside Admiral Muhammed Issacs and the head of the Guyana Defence Force, Brigadier General Wesley Patrick.

Clarke felt more at ease ordering the sinking of the *Guaiqueri* than he did standing before the elected representatives of his own government. He reminded himself he had trained for war, not politics, but the higher up the ranks Clarke rose, the more the two seemed to intertwine, especially as he spoke about the *Essequibo* Incident in length to the parliament and had answered their questions for more than an hour.

In addition to his testimony, Clarke had played the voice recording from the *Essequibo*'s bridge and a video recording from a high-definition camera that Metal Shark had mounted on the communications mast before delivering the vessel to Guyana. The video demonstrated the warning shot fired from the *Guaiqueri* and then the opening of its missile hatches. As President Terrance Fredricks had introduced the video, he'd pointed to the screen and, like a lawyer giving an opening statement, had said, "You will see clear evidence of the aggressiveness of the Venezuelans."

Clarke wanted to fade into the background as President Fredricks, a short bald man with a fringe of hair above his ears, returned to the lectern. The man favored suits in various shades of brown and added color to his wardrobe via neckties. By all appearances, Fredricks was a modest man from a humble background, yet his looks could be deceiving. Fredricks was cunning and shrewd, and he'd cut deals with the biggest oil companies, trying to bring prosperity to Guyana.

Fredricks gripped both sides of the lectern and stared out at the members of his government. "Ladies and gentlemen, what we just saw and heard from Commander Clarke is Venezuela acting as aggressively as we have ever seen her. The actions of the *Guaiqueri*, not only in boarding and detaining fishing vessels in Guyanese waters, but also firing upon and then continuing to show hostile intent to our own vessel, are all actions tantamount to war."

Silence greeted his words. Every person in the room understood the predicament Guyana was in now. Venezuela was the bully on the street, backed by Russia, China, and Cuba, and they would soon be out for blood.

"The Venezuelan military has gone on high alert. Not only are they mobilizing troops, but they are now training new crews to put old ships and submarines to sea. We cannot stand by and let them take our country from us." Fredricks paused and glanced around again. "What I am asking from you today is a vote to go to war."

The place erupted in shouts as all parliamentary procedures fell by the wayside.

Clarke felt like someone had punched him in the gut. He knew the words were coming, but hearing Fredricks utter them was still a shock. There was no way they could go to war with Venezuela. The Guyana Defence Force only mustered forty-six-hundred active-duty troops with another three thousand in reserve. Ground combat forces consisted of three infantry battalions, a Special Forces unit, and an artillery company.

Meanwhile, the Coast Guard had a growing group of offshore patrol vessels and a few smaller patrol boats, but more were desperately needed. To top it off, they had no air support. While the GDF had plenty of planes, they were all designed to support ground operations by providing tactical observation, casualty evacuation, and transport. They had no jet fighters or attack helicopters. And the planes the GDF did have weren't designed to carry weapons.

Fredricks let them go on shouting for several minutes before he called the room to order.

"We can't win against Venezuela!" one parliamentarian shouted.

"Not a blade of grass!" another cried out.

"We'll mount a resistance like Ukraine," Gail Warren, Minister of Labor, called out. "The U.S. will support us."

"They don't want to buy our oil. Why would they want to give us guns?" someone else decried.

Fredricks smacked his hands together to gain everyone's attention, then called the room to order again. "Please, ladies and gentlemen. Let me amend my words. I will ask you to *prepare* for war. We know Venezuela will continue its hostilities. In fact, they have Russian advisors on Ankoko Island as we speak, measuring the runway so they can pave it."

"We disproved that rumor," Vice President Singh stated.

"I have seen photographic proof of the surveyors at

work," Fredricks replied. "Our committee failed to do a proper job, and soon, we will have Venezuelan fighter jets on our doorstep. What we must understand is that Michel Zarate refuses to accept the court ruling that gave the Essequibo Region to Guyana, and he's even convinced mapmakers to mark our territory as belonging to Venezuela. Zarate is a bully, and the only way to stop a bully is to punch back. To this effect, I ask that you appropriate funds to build our military, train new troops, acquire new equipment, and modernize for the future. Not only do we have Venezuela to the north but Suriname to the south, which also claims a piece of our country. If we do not stand against these long-time adversaries, they will eventually come for us!"

The president gripped the lectern again and lowered his voice to a normal level. "With our ever-increasing oil revenue, we can now prepare for the future. As we build new infrastructure and repair the old, we must also purchase bullets, guns, airplanes, helicopters, troop transports, new patrol craft, and naval vessels. As long as Venezuela lays claim to our territory, we will never be safe. We must prepare to fight at a moment's notice." He banged his fist against the lectern and shouted, "Not a blade of grass!"

The fervor displayed by Fredricks shocked Clarke. Usually, the man was soft-spoken and reserved. Yet, Clarke also felt heartened that, finally, someone was taking the threat seriously. It had been Clarke's actions, forced by the hand of the enemy, which had ultimately propelled them to act.

Once again, as he had on the bridge of his ship after sinking the *Guaiqueri*, David Clarke felt as if he had irrevocably changed the course of Guyana's history.

CHAPTER 23

Five Islands Yacht Club
Chaguaramas, Trinidad & Tobago

Patrons packed the little bar at the marina.

As one of the largest hurricane-protected ports in the Caribbean, Chaguaramas bustled with sailors settling their boats to ride out the summer storms while others used it as a jumping-off point to head west to Panama.

John Phoenix sat in the shade at the bar, sipping a beer and watching a couple argue about which route to take through the myriad islands along the northern coast of Venezuela on their way to the ABCs—Aruba, Bonaire, and Curaçao.

"I'm telling you, we should sail straight through," the pretty blonde said.

"I want to stop and see some of the islands," the man countered. "They're supposed to be ecologically protected and offer some of the best scuba diving in the Caribbean."

Phoenix tried not to bother himself with their trivial argument. The guy was a complete idiot if he thought sailing his little dinghy through Venezuelan waters was a novel idea, but Phoenix kept listening for the entertainment value as he waited for his contact, Ramesh, the owner of Five Islands Yacht Club, who was overdue to make an appearance.

The blonde at the table wore a blue bikini top that showed ample cleavage, and Phoenix tried not to picture her being gang-raped by pirates, or *colectivos*, or sailors from the Venezuelan Navy. He signaled the bartender, a beautiful Asian woman with lustrous black hair and warm almond eyes. Phoenix had heard others call her Bridgid. It always amazed him just how much information one could pick up in a bar by listening and observing. Normally, he'd butter her up and ask probing questions about Ramesh, obliquely trying to learn why the man was late, but she had an enormous rock on her finger, and Phoenix figured whoever had given it to her had staked his claim and would be willing to back it up.

So Phoenix settled for ordering another beer from her. He signaled by waving his empty bottle. As Bridgid approached, wiping her hands on a towel, she asked, "What can I get for you?"

Phoenix tried the direct approach. "Another Presidente and two Corona Lights. And can you tell me where I can find Ramesh? I'm supposed to meet him here."

"I can call him. Who be askin' about him?"

"Tell him that Bowie says he's late."

She arched her dark brows and then nodded ever so slightly. Phoenix had the feeling that she'd been appraising him all along, and the glint in her eye meant she knew more about him than she'd let on.

Getting the beer was the easy part. After she brought the beer and took his money, Bridgid walked out of the bar. Phoenix figured she was going to find Ramesh. He picked up the two Corona Lights and his own Presidente and headed for the table where the two sailors were still arguing. He set the beers down between them and then took one of the empty seats at their table.

The younger man stared at him with horrific fascination as if he couldn't believe a stranger would blatantly interrupt their private conversation.

Before the man could speak, his wife asked with a hint of hostility, "What do *you* want?"

"I want to give you a little friendly advice—free of charge," Phoenix replied.

The woman sat back and crossed her arms. "About what?"

"Have you listened to the local news lately?" Phoenix asked.

"I listen to the cruisers' safety report every day," the man said.

Phoenix took a sip of beer and pondered the man's statement. The cruisers' net was an informal safety and security brief given daily over the single-side-band radio. It generally provided regional updates on theft, piracy, and safety precautions, along with the best routes to take to avoid troubled areas.

"Have they said anything about the Guyana Defence Force sinking a Venezuelan patrol boat?" Phoenix asked.

"No," the man said.

"What about pirate reports here in the Gulf of Paria?" Phoenix questioned. "Refugee boats are crossing nightly, and among them are pirates ready to prey on pretty young things like yourselves."

"We won't be long in the Gulf," the man replied. "I plan to sail straight out of the Dragon's Mouth into the Caribbean and go west. We're just here to refuel and resupply."

With a nod, Phoenix said, "Okay. Here's my free and unsolicited advice. Venezuela is beating the war drum over the sinking of its ship. Their military is on high alert, and it doesn't matter that you're two Americans on a little sailboat; you *are* Americans. They won't bother to ask questions before they arrest you for trespassing in their territorial waters and accuse you of being spies. The prisons in Venezuela are no joke. If I were you, I would stay as far away from Venezuela as possible. Arc up over their entire archipelago and aim for the ABCs like your wife suggested, but whichever way you decide to go, stay the hell away from Venezuela because you're in a war zone."

Stunned, the young couple just stared at Phoenix as he took a drink from his Presidente. When the couple had nothing else to say, Phoenix stood, feeling he'd done his duty for the day. For added measure, he threw in a topper, saying to the man, "You better hope your wife is a good waitress because she'll be getting a lot of tips from the guards in prison —if you know what I mean."

Smiling at his joke, Phoenix ambled back toward the bar, where a large black man stood with his arms crossed and a bemused smile on his face. He wore white sneakers, gray shorts, and a tank top that showcased his beefy upper body. Phoenix knew immediately that he'd finally met Ramesh.

"You give dem kids some pretty good advice," the yacht club owner said in a strong island accent.

Phoenix shrugged. "If they take it, that's up to them."

Ramesh nodded toward the anchorage beyond the crowded docks. "What ya think about tonight? Weather gonna hold?"

Phoenix's brow furrowed momentarily, wondering if Ramesh was actually Romeo. He figured he'd give it a shot and uttered his code phrase. "The barometer is dropping. Is it safe to cross the bay?"

"Only if you watch for de pirates."

With the code exchanged, Phoenix shook the man's hand, having to crane his neck to look up at his face. Ramesh seemed to take satisfaction in towering over the shorter man and, after letting go of his crushing grip, led the CIA officer back to his office. Phoenix glanced around the place, checking out the photos on the wall, when he spied a picture that made him laugh. Pointing to it, he asked, "You know, Ryan Weller?"

"That boy be crazy. Let me tell you, this one time, I took that boy all the way to Margarita Island. He got himself locked up there. Killed a man, they say."

"I heard that," Phoenix replied. "I also heard he escaped."

"Yeah, that's what de say. You seen the boy lately?" Ramesh asked.

"Not for a long time," Phoenix lied. "What about tonight? Are we a go?"

"Meet me at de dock at one a.m. It be about fifty-five kilometers to your destination. A two-hour ride, give or take."

"We're leaving from here?" Phoenix asked. "Won't that look suspicious?"

"Naw, man," the big Trini replied. "The fishing boats come and go all hours."

Phoenix glanced at the photo of Weller and Ramesh again. The two men stood in front of a sailboat with Ramesh's thick arm wrapped around the back of Weller's neck. Weller had earned Phoenix's trust on the Dark Angel operation, so Phoenix had confidence in what the owner of Five Islands Yacht Club had to tell him. "I'll be there," he confirmed.

"Dock Two," Ramesh said. "Challenge code 'squire.' Acknowledge, 'page'."

Phoenix recounted the challenge and response words and then asked about the package DS&T had sent for him.

Ramesh motioned toward a cardboard box in the corner of the room. "I'll give ya some privacy. I need to check de bar, anyway. Don't want my wife Bridgid to get into no trouble with you tourists."

"I should have known she was your wife," Phoenix said, disappointed with himself that he hadn't made the connection. Usually, he had those things pegged within minutes.

"Don't worry. I take good care of Brigid. She's so tiny I feel like I have to protect her all the time."

"I think she can take care of herself just fine," Phoenix replied. "She seems kinda bossy."

"Oh, she is," Ramesh agreed. "I get to wear the pants in the relationship, but she tells me which ones to put on." The big Trini laughed as he slapped Phoenix on the back before heading out the door.

Phoenix picked up the cardboard box and set it on the corner of Ramesh's cluttered desk. He flicked open his tactical folding knife and sliced through the tape. Inside was a beautiful leather satchel handbag with two carry handles and a shoulder strap. A note in the box gave directions on how to operate the communications device. Phoenix memorized them and then opened the satchel.

His eyes widened at the stacks of Venezuelan Bolivars and American dollars tucked inside. Connelly had been serious about showing the money. A smaller package wrapped in brown paper carried a note that instructed Phoenix to leave it for Romeo. Phoenix set it on Ramesh's desk, figuring it was payment for Romeo's service.

He then stuffed the satchel into his backpack and backed out of the office. He headed for a little motel just down the road to get some rest before the night passage. Before settling in on the bed, he checked the weather. The weather guessers called for intermittent bands of rain to pass over the gulf, but that just meant it would make it harder for someone to spot them in their high-speed boat as they made the crossing. At least, he hoped.

After texting Connelly an update through the Signal app, Phoenix took a hot shower to help him relax, climbed into bed, and set the alarm on the bedside table. He had a full eight hours before he had to meet Ramesh at the dock.

Despite the deep breathing exercises he'd learned in the Special Forces to help calm his body, Phoenix couldn't relax. He was going back to Venezuela, one of the most dangerous countries he'd ever been to outside of Afghanistan and Iraq.

Not only had he just escaped a nationwide manhunt for his person there, but the CIA also wanted him to walk straight into the waiting arms of the SEBIN by going to check out Anaconda's office.

While Phoenix had abjectly protested to Connelly, he knew he'd go to the office. Still, he doubted the SEBIN would have left anything of value there, especially code books or comms devices. And just thinking about it made his shoulder ache. Maybe he was resentful. He hated that Connelly had ended their relationship and was now his handler, and he hated that she kept telling him what to do, especially ordering him deliberately into danger. It was just plain stupid.

Phoenix wished he could call Lieutenant Blanco and ask her to feel out the situation. He wondered how much fast-talking Blanco had done to get herself off the hook after he'd left her at the airport.

Instead of getting any rest, Phoenix tossed and turned. Finally, he got up and went to the front desk. He asked if there was a masseuse nearby. The clerk gave him an address to one just down the street. Phoenix carried his pack with him as he walked to the massage parlor, stripped down, and got on the table. An Asian woman came in and began oiling his skin, digging her elbow into the exact spot on his back that radiated pain. Phoenix closed his eyes and tried to relax as the masseuse worked to loosen his muscles.

He wasn't looking forward to going back to Venezuela. Bumping the future VP would not be a simple task, but it was one they had ordered him to do, so he vowed to himself that he'd do his best.

CHAPTER 24

Oval Office
Washington D.C.

RANDY MERCIA THREW THE PAPERS BACK ONTO THE COFFEE TABLE as he stalked past it. "What is this shit? I thought we were Guyana's number one trading partner."

"Not since Brandon chose Zarate over Fredricks," Cole Stratten said. "Your predecessor royally fucked us."

Mercia's growing knowledge of Guyanese politics impressed Leslie Connelly. Since her last visit to the Oval Office several days ago, Randy 'Merica had learned a great deal about the growing conflict. She wondered if Mercia's chief of staff, Carlton Choi, had been keeping the president appraised of the events circling the two South American countries on the brink of war. Beyond whatever Choi had briefed the president on, it seemed like the *Essequibo* Incident was all the television talking heads could speculate about. Just like anytime there was a looming conflict, they kept asking if it would lead to World War III.

While China and Russia had not commented on the *Esse-quibo* Incident and which side they would back if war broke out, it was more than clear who the United States had to support. Over the years of sanctions and rhetoric between Venezuela and the U.S., the U.S. had backed itself into a corner. They couldn't support anything Venezuela did other than demilitarize and hold free and open elections, and Zarate had, in essence, told everyone who'd suggested such things to go fuck themselves.

When Brandon's administration had sat down in Mexico City and negotiated Chevron's right to expand oil field production, they had not uttered a word about diplomatic relations. Zarate was the clear winner. The U.S. got more oil, and Zarate had to give no concessions.

Effectively, the United States had blinked.

"How exactly are we being fucked?" Mike Asbury asked.

Stratten motioned to his protégé. "I'll let Leslie explain."

Connelly shifted in her seat, a momentary show of nervousness amongst the men of power. "Here's the way I explained it to Director Stratten. When President Brandon purchased oil from Zarate instead of the Guyanese, there were some in Guyana who saw it as a betrayal and a lost opportunity to continue the stranglehold of sanctions on Venezuela."

"Not to relieve the humanitarian crisis, as Brandon claimed?" Mercia asked.

"No, sir," Connelly replied. "There are a lot of factors involved in Venezuela being in as bad a shape as it's in, and what we pay them for oil doesn't make a bit of difference. It boils down to corruption in the Zarate regime. Zarate and his cronies get the first crack at embezzling our funds instead of them going into a U.N. administered account to relieve the humanitarian crisis as Brandon's people had negotiated."

"What about the Guyanese?" Mercia demanded. "I could give a rat's ass about Venezuela."

"Like I said, some people in the government there see Brandon's deal as a betrayal," Connelly continued. "We're supposed to be Guyana's strongest economic and military ally, yet we chose differently. And, as you can see by the papers you just read, they've chosen to purchase their military hardware elsewhere."

"A big fuck you," Mercia said in understanding.

"Kinda," Connelly replied, "but we really don't have the aircraft to support their orders. Most of our helicopters and planes are going to Ukraine or coming online to replace aging units in our own military. Supply chains are taxed as it is, making it a struggle to get parts and supplies to build new aircraft or even repair old ones."

"Let me guess, China and the COVID virus?" Mercia asked sarcastically.

"Both, yes," Connelly said. "However, there's also a severe drought in Panama, causing record low water levels. They're having to limit gross ship weight and the number of ships that pass through the canal, which is impacting our supply chain significantly."

"Why aren't we building all this military shit in our own backyard?" Mercia asked. "Why are we having to ship it in from overseas?"

"That's how your predecessors have ordained it through deals like NAFTA and treaties with the Pacific Rim countries. We also struggle to procure the rare earth elements and other resources needed to build high-tech military systems," Connelly said matter-of-factly.

"Are Leonardo and Embraer capable of fulfilling the orders for Guyana?" Asbury asked.

"We're still trying to find that out," Connelly replied. "We do know that Embraer will deliver the first batch of Super Tucanos within the next week—five total. Eventually, Guyana will field twenty-four of them, making two squadrons. One will be based in Georgetown and the other in Linden, at one of their primary military training facilities."

The Embraer A-29 Super Tucano light attack aircraft, powered by a turboprop engine, had been designed by the Brazilians to provide close air support for ground troops. It carried a variety of rockets, bombs, gun pods, and air-to-air and air-to-surface missiles. In Connelly's opinion, Guyana had made an excellent choice since over fourteen countries around the world flew Super Tucanos in their militaries. The plane had a dependable track record of service in Afghanistan and many of the bush wars in Africa.

Mercia was angry about the next two contracts, and rightfully so. He wanted Guyana to purchase American military hardware. While Embraer assembled many of their Super Tucanos at their plant in Jacksonville, Florida, Guyana had given the helicopter contracts to Leonardo, an Italian aerospace defense firm who owned the Agusta and AgustaWestland brands. What Guyana wanted specifically was a fleet of twelve Agusta A129D Mangusta attack helicopters that reminded everyone of a Boeing AH-64 Apache when seen from a distance. The Super Tucanos and the Mangustas would support squadrons of AgustaWestland AW149s, a fifteen-passenger, multi-purpose version of the Sikorsky UH-60 Black Hawk.

"What are they going to do with all these aircraft?" Mercia asked.

"What we did in Vietnam, sir, and every war after," Connelly explained.

"And what is that?" Mercia asked, *"Lose?"*

Connelly had to suppress a surprised laugh with a cough before saying, "Well, we have done plenty of that, sir, but Guyana is interested in airmobile operations. Guyana and Venezuela have mountainous and jungle topography, making access via road virtually impossible. Having helicopters to move troops is essential to any plan that either country might cook up. We already have intelligence out of Venezuela that suggests they're training for these types of operations as we speak."

"That's news to me," Stratten said.

"My apologies, sir. Bowie turned an asset in the Special Forces brigade during his escape from the disastrous Cobalt Panther rescue op. His asset reports that her SF unit is moving to Maracay to train with airborne regiments."

"Venezuela will be able to set the negotiation terms if they set a naval blockade around Georgetown and strike a quick blow with air operations," Asbury stated.

"Yes, sir," Connelly agreed. "We also know there are Russian advisors on Ankoko Island. We suspect they're surveying the runway to pave it. Zarate has wanted to park fighter jets there for years."

"Fucking Russians," Mercia muttered.

"Do we have eyes on the situation?" Asbury asked.

"We planned to send Bowie back in, but we had to retask him," Stratten said.

"Don't we have other agents down there?" the president asked.

"We're *case officers*, sir," Connelly replied coldly, then added. "We moved some officers to Guyana when we shuttered ops in Venezuela, but it's a small country, and we can only hide so many officers in plain sight. Most ended up in Panama or Colombia."

"You approved of this?" Mercia asked his friend.

Stratten tilted his head and pursed his lips as if to say yes and no at the same time. "At the time, we had other stations with more pressing matters like China, Russia, and East Asia."

"South America always gets the short shaft," Asbury said.

"Not necessarily, sir," Connelly countered. "The agency spends a great deal of time and money on operations in Central and South America. We geared most of them toward countering communist influence or aiding in our War on Drugs. Cuba is a *huge* target as they're always training counter-revolutionary and paramilitary operatives to send to South American countries. The old joke around the water cooler is that Cuba has so much influence on Zarate that we should conjoin the two states and call them 'Venecuba.'"

No one laughed about the proposed name, and Connelly wanted to shift in her seat again but wiggled her toes in her shoes instead to release some of her nervous tension. She wondered if Phoenix had made it to Caracas yet and if he'd talked to Cobra again. *Why don't you check in, John?* She felt heat rise on her neck as she thought about his proposition to make love on the table. She had wanted nothing more at the time, and his silly, boyish grin seemed to haunt her even now. *Get it together, Leslie.*

"What are you focused on now, Cole?" Mercia asked.

"We're trying to get officers back into Venezuela and have them bump high-value political and military targets."

"What about the mole?" Asbury asked.

"Only Connelly and I know who these officers are, and we're keeping everything off the books, so to speak."

"But there *are* records of these officers and their work?" the Secretary of State asked.

"Yes, sir," Connelly replied. "By off-book, Director Stratten meant compartmentalized."

"Exactly. Until we figure out who the mole is, we have to be careful who we tell about our current officer and asset relationships in Venezuela," Stratten clarified. "Which is why we've chosen to meet with only the two of you for the time being since both of you were at our first meeting."

"Any progress on the mole hunt?" Asbury asked.

"Not at this time," Stratten replied, "but I have people on it."

Mercia paced the length of the room as he listened to the conversation. He suddenly stopped. "Who's going to fly all those new planes and helicopters Guyana is buying? Certainly, they don't have enough pilots to go around."

"Guyana has had people lined up at the recruiters' offices since the *Essequibo* Incident. They're tired of being at the mercy of the Venezuelans," Connelly said. "And from what I understand, Guyana is offering high pay to any trained pilots who want to come fly for them. They're effectively assembling a foreign legion of pilots, boat crews, and ground forces."

"They've also reached out to our Air Force to ask them to train some of their current pilots and aircrew on the Super Tucanos and Augusta helicopters like we did for the Afghanis," Stratten added.

"What else can we do to help?" Mercia asked. "I remember one of you telling me the head of Southern Command signed a pact with Guyana for military acquisition and cross-training."

"The proposal on the table from the Joint Chiefs is to step up patrols in the area with littoral combat ships and destroyers out of Mayport, Florida, to send an Army Special Forces unit down to help train ground troops, and to provide some ground-to-air missile defense batteries to combat Venezuela's jet fighters."

"Do it," Mercia said. "And I want some Marines on the ground. What about those ships Guyana is purchasing? Can we speed that up?"

Connelly had entered a zone. She felt as if she had all the information in the world at her fingertips as her brain rapidly shifted through the material provided to her through intelligence reports and other agency assets. "Metal Shark is working around the clock to complete two more Defiant 115 patrol vessels, which they should finish in the next thirty days. Guyana is also actively seeking to purchase some fast-attack craft from Israel or Sweden. Both have ships for sale and crews ready to train the GDF."

"Okay, so Guyana wants to go to war, and we're feeding the machine," Mercia said. "What are we doing to prevent a war?"

Asbury took over the conversation. "I've had extensive talks with President Fredricks and Felix Schweizer in Switzerland. Both agree we should reopen negotiations. According to Schweizer, Zarate is open to meeting with Fredricks to iron this situation out. He's ready to pick up the Mexico City talks again. Everyone has agreed to stand down until they can happen next month."

"In the meantime?" Mercia asked.

"Status quo. They're all training for war," Asbury replied.

CHAPTER 25

Caracas, Venezuela

From his initial assessment, Phoenix thought bumping Evelyn Acevedo would be damned near impossible.

While Washington talked and Guyana ordered weapons of war, Zarate had ousted his former vice president, Delcy Rodriguez, and installed Acevedo as his new top lieutenant. The doctor's first order of business had been to make a phone call to the Swiss Federal Department of Foreign Affairs and, through Felix Schweizer, restart the Mexico City negotiations, this time with bigger stakes than reviving a couple of oil fields. The annexation of an entire nation was at stake, and if the world had yawned as Russia reclaimed Crimea, it realized its mistake when Russia had invaded Ukraine. No one on the international scene wanted to see Venezuela and Guyana go to war.

Acevedo had agreed to sit down with the United States, Switzerland, and Turkey. After America had withdrawn personnel in 2019, the Swiss became caretakers of the U.S. embassy in Caracas. They provided consular support for Americans still in the country. Venezuela, however, hadn't agreed to the deal. Zarate wanted Turkey to provide the same service in the U.S., which the U.S. State Department had balked at, claiming Turkey actively engaged in aiding terrorism. Not only did it strain tensions further, but it also left half a million Venezuelans in the U.S. high and dry. Unable to renew their passports at a Venezuelan embassy in the States, they had to travel to a country that had relations with the Zarate government and renew them there.

And while Acevedo supported the Mexico City talks, she had also surrounded herself with SEBIN agents to protect her from rogue factions in Venezuela who would rather see the country go to war than negotiate peace. These plain-clothed men rotated around her like the planets around the sun. When she walked, the agents formed a curtain. When she rode in a car, they supplied armored limousines and civilian vehicles to cover her.

The only way for Phoenix to get to Acevedo was at her home, and even then, he'd have to get past the SEBIN. Caracas seemed like a tinder box, ready to ignite. People milled about on the streets, constantly searching for food or jobs or protesting the Zarate regime. Cops in full battle rattle stood on street corners, brandishing automatic weapons. It wasn't uncommon to see the police beating down a citizen or dragging them off the streets to some hellish prison.

Even Phoenix's stomach grumbled in protest at the lack of protein he supplied to his body. Street vendors sold everything they could get their hands on, from ice cream dished out of one-gallon pails to second-hand clothes and tube-type televisions, but there never seemed to be enough to go around.

As he walked the streets around Acevedo's apartment

near the Central University of Venezuela, Phoenix wondered why she hadn't moved to a more secure location, but he was also thankful she hadn't, as the apartment complex had things Phoenix could exploit. Since it was common to see men just sitting on the street, Phoenix had taken to doing the same, chatting amiably with the passersby and learning the neighborhood as he surveilled her building.

The second problem that troubled him involved hiding the cash he'd smuggled into the country. Any number of people would slit his throat for a pittance of the money he carried in his pack. He needed a safe place to hide it and decided maybe the easiest place was in plain sight.

Leaving Acevedo for a while, Phoenix traveled to the neighborhood around Anaconda's old base of operations. The LGT Imports office was on the second floor of a two-story building. After twelve hours of surveillance, Phoenix saw no sign of the SEBIN, which surprised him. He had to wonder if they felt that since they had taken Anaconda and the rest of the CIA's assets and officers off the playing board that, no one would come prowling around. Or they had better things to do than to babysit an office building.

Phoenix took a last look around the neighborhood, then headed for the rear door to the office complex. Once inside, he took the stairs to the second floor. He avoided taking elevators when there was no apparent reason to trap himself in a metal cage. Even if he'd wanted to use the one in Anaconda's building, the elevator had a sign on it saying it was out of order. *Typical.* Either the elevator was mechanically broken, or management had placed a sign on the door to prevent people from using it since the electricity in the city operated sporadically, and they didn't want anyone to become trapped inside.

Venezuela had chosen not to generate electricity with fossil fuels but via hydroelectricity. One of the primary generating plants for Caracas was on Lake Guri, and over the years, they'd neglected to perform proper maintenance. Combining that with a drought that caused Lake Guri to reach record low levels, the generator plant had overheated and shut down, effectively leaving millions in the dark. The failure at the Guri plant had forced the country to switch to coal power, but even then, the government rationed electricity.

In typical fashion, Zarate had blamed the problems at the Simón Bolívar hydroelectric plant on sabotage.

On the second floor of Anaconda's office building, Phoenix stopped to observe the situation. Most of the doors opened into small lobbies where secretaries would normally have sat, but many of the desks had signs that asked clients to knock on the interior office doors for help.

Moving quickly to the door of LGT Imports, Phoenix removed a lockpick set from his pocket and prepared to do battle with the old door. Instinctively, he tried the knob first and found it unlocked. He pushed his way inside and closed the door, glancing through the inset glass window to see if anyone noticed his movements.

The hallway remained empty and quiet.

Avoiding the secretarial desk, where previous searchers had ripped out the drawers and dumped their contents onto the floor, Phoenix directed his attention to the first office door. Not much remained, but rusty paper clips and some random papers. Someone had stripped this office, too. Apparently, once word had spread that Anaconda wasn't coming back to the office, the Venezuelans had cleaned house. They had carried off the furniture, and the only way Phoenix knew there had been paintings or pictures hanging on the wall was by the hooks embedded in the plaster.

He hurried into the second office only to find that someone had ripped the old safe from the wall.

"So much for that idea," he muttered to himself, feeling the knot beneath his shoulder tighten.

After snapping a couple of photos with his phone to send to Connelly, Phoenix exited the office and took the stairs back outside into the sweltering heat. The money weighed on his consciousness, and the pain in his shoulder had turned into a throbbing ache.

"What the hell am I doing here?" he asked himself.

Walking through the streets, he knew he had two options: find a place to store the money or give it to Acevedo so she could worry about it. As he walked, he schemed out a plan to get close to the vice president. He knew she had worked with the CIA previously, so maybe a bump wouldn't necessarily need to take place. Then his eyebrows shot up as he came upon a plan.

On his way back across town, Phoenix's phone buzzed in his pocket. He'd picked up a cell phone and a prepaid card from Movistar, the largest cellular provider in Venezuela. His sat phone needed a clear view of the sky to work properly, and he didn't want to use such an expensive piece of equipment in public, advertising his wealth or status, so he'd forwarded his calls. The display on the compact smartphone showed a +58 number he didn't recognize, but he answered anyway with a cautious, "*Hola?*"

"This is Lieutenant Blanco."

"Nice to hear from you, Lieutenant," Phoenix said, glancing around. "How are you?"

"Hungry and tired," Blanco replied.

"Are you still in Maracay?" he asked.

"Yes. Where are you?" Blanco asked. "I hope you're someplace safe with a full belly."

"Nope. Caracas. And I'm starving."

"Caracas? What for?" she asked, surprise in her voice.

"Work," Phoenix replied cryptically.

"Can you come to Maracay?" she asked.

"Sounds like fun," Phoenix said, eager to see the beautiful Army officer again. "When and where?"

"Plaza España at noon," Blanco instructed.

"I'll be there."

Blanco ended the call without another word, and Phoenix pocketed his phone. His plan for breaking into the vice president's home would have to wait.

CHAPTER 26

Hutchinson, Kansas

William Pounder pulled the control stick back into his gut and felt his stomach sink as the plane began to rise. He let the nose climb almost vertical before tipping the plane over on its right wing and diving for the ground again. Leveling off, he flicked on the sprayers and zoomed over the top of the cornfield, his wheels almost touching the green stalks. Just before the end of the field, he shut off the sprayers and climbed again.

Crop dusting had turned out to be fun and lucrative for the young man. Pounder always felt invigorated as he roared in at tree-top height and dusted the fields. Sometimes, he'd play a game of dodge the semi-truck as traffic passed on nearby roads, or he'd stay low and have to hop up over obstacles before kicking on the sprayers and dousing the crops with fungicides and insecticides.

He'd only gotten in trouble a handful of times. Once, he'd accidentally sprayed the wrong field, and another, he'd showered chemicals on farm workers, but buzzing a cop car on the highway had gotten him in the hottest water.

Pounder loved flying, and he was damned good at it. When he wasn't dusting crops, he taught flight lessons at the local airport. The Cessna 172 wasn't nearly as fun to fly as the bright yellow Air Tractor 802A. The Cessna had an anemic one-hundred-eighty horsepower compared to the AT's 1,295 ponies. A crop duster needed to muster all the power it could to repeatedly carry the weight of a fully loaded B-17 bomber into the air.

Once the chemical tank had run dry, Pounder gained altitude and leveled off his Air Tractor, heading for Hutchinson Regional, where his boss kept his fleet of six crop dusters. After completing the required post-flight checks and maintenance, Pounder decided it was high time to have a drink. He could afford to unwind a bit before heading home with no flight lessons scheduled for the day.

Pounder walked down the road to the main terminal building and then into Airport Steakhouse. It was a decent place to eat, and the bartender had a heavy hand when she poured.

"What's up, Max?" Pounder asked as he sat down on a stool near the end of the bar.

"Same as always, Will," she replied with a grin. "You want the usual?"

"Yeah." The usual was a Captain and Coke with a couple of lime slices.

"How was your flight?" she asked.

"It was good. I sprayed some weeds over near Pawnee Rock. So, what about it, Max? Are we going on a date, or what?"

"I told you, Will, I don't date the customers."

"And I told you I'd stop coming in."

"Yet, here you are," she said, spreading her hands like a magician pulling a rabbit from her hat.

Pounder snorted. He'd lost count of how many times he'd asked Maxine Gilespie out. He found her quite attractive with her long dark hair and big brown eyes. She had all the right curves in all the right places. Some would have called her chubby, but Pounder didn't care. He thought she looked just right. Pounder wasn't a bad-looking kid, either. At six feet, he had thick brown hair and an affable grin that lit up his blue eyes. He had a natural charm that his intensity could easily offset.

"You still hitting on Max?" Steve Gruber said, patting Pounder on the shoulder as he walked past. "I told you she'll never go out with a dirty crop duster. She likes jet pilots."

"She doesn't have daddy issues, old man," Pounder shot back.

Gruber laughed and smacked the bar playfully. "Pour me a tall one, Max, and put it on I Will Pound Her's tab." The stocky fifty-year-old with graying hair and sharp green eyes grinned down the bar at Pounder and gave him a wink.

Pounder had heard all the jokes about his name and had even made a few himself. When he'd been in the Army, serving as a paratrooper with the 82nd Airborne at Fort Benning, Georgia, his buddies had called him "Fatty" Pounder because he had a thing for the heftier ladies. When someone tried to pick on him for his choice of women, Pounder always shot back, "Fat chicks need loving, too." And when the other guys were standing around at the bar, waiting for some skinny young thing to give them the time of day, he was usually headed out the door to a one-night stand with a bigger girl. He wasn't overly choosy, but he *liked* Max. She was the kind of girl he could settle down with.

But as much as he liked Max, he detested Gruber. The old man always rubbed Pounder the wrong way. He flew a Bombardier Challenger 3500 in and out of Hutchinson for some company that sold fractional ownership shares in personal business jets. Whenever he passed through, Gruber liked to stop at the bar and swap stories with other pilots.

"Seriously, Gruber, when was the last time you flew an actual jet?" Pounder demanded. "Not one of those pussy machines you're flying now."

"2005," Gruber replied with a faraway look in his eye before taking a sip of beer. "My last flight in a *real* jet was in 2005. I flew out to the *Harry S. Truman*, did two carrier landings, and then returned to Oceana. I parked my F-14 Tomcat and walked away."

"You flew Tomcats!" Max exclaimed. "Like in *Top Gun?*"

"Honey, I *was* Top Gun," Gruber boasted. "Got the certificate and everything." He turned to look at Pounder. "But you know what makes me sick?"

Pounder shook his head. He had a newfound respect for the man, knowing he was a former Navy pilot, but he still didn't like the cocky son of a bitch.

"I could have crossed over to F/A-18s and kept flying in the Navy, but I took my ball and went home. I didn't want to be in the Navy if I couldn't fly Tomcats. They retired them in 2006, and now I'm stuck flying rich, pampered douchebags around instead of doing Mach Three with my hair on fire. That, my friend, was a royal screw-up on my part."

Gruber settled back into his chair, and Pounder let him stew in silence. After a few moments, he turned to Pounder again. "I know why you fly that Air Tractor. It's like grabbing life by the balls. Cling to that feeling, son. Take it from an old man: life goes fast. You get an opportunity to do something great; you take it. You hear me? You fucking take it."

Pounder nodded, thinking Gruber had finally given him some good advice, but he'd been living like that for years. He was a bit of an adrenaline junkie. Wanting to leave Kansas and obtain the G.I. Bill, Pounder had enlisted in the Army at eighteen. He'd learned to jump out of planes and still jumped for fun when he had the chance. After a couple of tours in

Iraq, pounding the sand, he'd gotten out and taken flying lessons, although those assholes at the VA had made him pony up his own money for a private pilot's license before they'd pay for additional training, which was why he had a professional pilot degree from K-State Salina.

While he attended college, Pounder had moved back into his old bedroom at his mom and dad's house just because he didn't care about getting his own place, and they enjoyed having him around to mow the yard and rake the leaves and clean the gutters—stuff the old man no longer wanted to do.

Pounder's problem now was that he was bored. While he loved the adrenaline of crop dusting, the shine had quickly come off the penny.

"I gotta go," Pounder said, standing. "Put Hans Gruber's beer on my tab. By the way, best Christmas movie ever."

Gruber held up his middle finger as Pounder walked out the door.

Pounder wandered back to the hangar where his boss kept the crop dusters and climbed into his truck, an older model GMC pickup with thirty-five-inch tires and a roll bar with extremely bright LED lights attached to it. As he started the beefed-up V8, he wished Max was riding shotgun.

Driving slowly back to his parent's house, Pounder thought about what Gruber had said about grabbing life by the balls and holding on for the ride. He didn't feel like he was doing that anymore. Things felt stale and bland. Parking the truck in the driveway, Pounder slid out of the driver's seat and found his parents sitting on the front porch. He sighed, feeling like he was just marking time.

There had to be something better out there.

Adventure was calling his name, but Will Pounder didn't know it yet.

CHAPTER 27

Plaza España
Maracay, Venezuela

JOHN PHOENIX CHECKED HIS ROLEX SUBMARINER. CAROLINA Blanco was fifteen minutes late for their noon rendezvous.

He sat on a park bench under the shade of some tall trees, watching kids happily climbing around on the playground equipment, utterly oblivious to the socioeconomic and spy dynamics swirling around them.

While Phoenix had hoped for a quiet spot to make this meeting, he understood why Blanco had chosen this place. It was centrally located and not too far from the military bases and airfields that surrounded the city. While Phoenix waited, he monitored his surroundings and munched on an empanada he'd purchased from a nearby street vendor.

The backpack containing his gear and the cash for Vice President Acevedo sat on his lap with his arms looped through the straps. Having so much money with him made him uncomfortable, and that made his shoulder continue to ache.

When he spotted Blanco, it took him a moment to recognize her. Instead of the olive-green tunic and pants he'd last seen her in, she wore a bright yellow sundress that fell just short of her knees. She'd pulled her brown hair into a clip, but two loose strands fell on either side of her face, framing it in their curl. Phoenix had to admit that she looked a lot prettier out of uniform. He could now see her for the lovely woman she was instead of the ballsy badass she'd portrayed herself to be during his wild escape.

Instead of making a beeline for the man she knew as Bowie, Blanco bought herself an empanada and then joined him on the bench. He nodded to her and kept eating his own food as Blanco slid closer.

"We can't talk here," Blanco whispered. "I have a place nearby—an apartment." She pressed her thigh against his. Looping her arm around his back, Blanco leaned in and brushed her lips across his ear, sending a shiver down his spine. "Kiss me. Make it look like we're lovers. It won't be as conspicuous when we walk off together."

Phoenix had done a lot of things to further his career, and he'd slept with a woman or two to get information from them, so kissing this beautiful asset was one of the easiest tasks he'd had to do since entering Venezuela. He cocked his head as he turned to gaze into her eyes. Blanco slid her hand up the back of his neck, fingers entwining in his hair. Their lips hovered just millimeters apart in what seemed like rabid anticipation. He could smell a hint of perfume on her skin and the spiciness of the empanada on her breath.

Gently, they pressed their lips together, and Blanco's fingers tightened in his hair, prolonging the kiss. Phoenix didn't mind one bit. He slipped his arm around her and pulled the lieutenant into his embrace. It had been a long time since he'd felt something for a woman not named Leslie Connelly.

Finally, breaking apart to take a deep breath, Blanco kept Phoenix's hair clenched in her fist and her mouth close to his ear. "I'm supposed to hate you. You're an imperialist Yankee." She nibbled on his earlobe. "I should hate you for leaving me at the airport."

Phoenix didn't know what to say.

"Let's walk to my apartment. Major Silva gave my team and me the afternoon off. We have plenty of time ..." Blanco nibbled his ear again. "To get to know one another." She stood and smoothed her sundress, and Phoenix rose to his feet. She linked her arm in his after he'd donned his backpack and then led him out of the park toward her apartment on San Miguel Street.

Like most of the buildings in the area, it had seen better days. The stairwell smelled of rotten garbage and stale urine. Inside Blanco's third-floor apartment, everything appeared clean and neat. Besides the built-in kitchen and small bathroom, there was a table, two chairs, a bed, a small television set, and a tattered cloth recliner.

White curtains with embroidered blue and yellow flowers hung over the open windows, swaying in the intermittent breeze. He set his pack on the table and removed a small electronic device. He began sweeping it over the walls, light fixtures, outlets, and windowsills. Blanco started to ask what he was doing, but Phoenix raised a finger to his lips.

His hand trembled as he worked the bug finder around the room. He wanted to rush over to Coralina Blanco and kiss her again, but he chastised himself into remaining professional, and not doing exactly as Connelly always claimed he did—think with his little head.

But he couldn't help it. He was a man first, a case officer second, and he was alone in this apparently bug-free apartment with a beautiful woman from the enemy force. It was too cliché. The lack of listening devices puzzled him some-what. He figured the SEBIN would have tapped her phone, suspecting she might have become a CIA asset.

Phoenix finished checking the bedroom and found no bugs in the apartment. He knew he needed to get serious and put his amorous thoughts out of his head, but his mind kept returning to the kiss on the park bench. *Be a professional, John.*

After tucking away the bug detector, he turned to Blanco. "The place is clean."

"I could have told you that," she replied. "I sweep it routinely."

"How? Where did you get the equipment?"

"I was an intelligence officer with a leg unit before I joined the 97th. I had access to whatever equipment I needed. Since our system is rife with corruption, it was easy to make a simple radiofrequency scanner disappear from the record."

Phoenix nodded, wishing he could write all this down, but he'd trained himself to remember reams of information for situations just like this. If the SEBIN caught him, he didn't want to have any notes on him about Army units or troop movements, especially personal information about Blanco.

"What unit were you with before joining SF?"

"The 93rd Caribbean Brigade," she replied. "I'm surprised you haven't asked me about what happened at the airport."

"I'm getting to that," Phoenix replied.

Blanco seemed to notice the switch from being a chatty lovebird to a serious handler. She picked up a handmade paper fan from the table as she sat in one of the straight-back wooden chairs.

Now that she'd brought the subject up, Phoenix began to pry. "How did you convince the Army you weren't a traitor?"

"I did what I had to do to survive."

"And what was that?" Phoenix asked, frustrated she wasn't more forthcoming.

"Actually, the guys you kicked off the plane vouched for

me. They told both the military investigators and the SEBIN that I was your hostage and that you left me stranded just like them."

"Did either of those organizations interrogate you?" he asked.

"The SEBIN hooked me to a polygraph and spent hours asking me questions. Fortunately for you, I learned how to beat the machine while training with the Black Wasps in Cuba."

Phoenix's eyebrows rose in surprise. "You trained with the Black Wasps?"

"It was required to become a part of the 97th. Everyone trained with them, including Major Silva."

"What's your role with the 97th now?" Phoenix asked.

"I'm second-in-command and the intelligence officer. I had my own team, but you killed most of them. Now, we have men integrated into *La Zorras* since there aren't enough women who've been through the training in Cuba. We're setting up a special training camp here in Maracay to reinforce our numbers, and the rumor is that they may integrate us into the 99th Special Forces Brigade to combine resources and expand their operations."

"What's the purpose of your current training?" Phoenix asked.

"Is it hot in here?" Blanco asked, getting up and going to the window.

"You said you're training for something big; do you know what that is?" Phoenix pressed, joining her at the window to keep his voice low. He suspected the apartment walls were paper thin, and anyone nearby could overhear their conversation.

She turned to face him and grimly said, "An airborne assault on Georgetown, Guyana."

Seeing the perfect opportunity to get a leg up on the

Venezuelans, Phoenix asked, "Can you get me a copy of the plans?"

"Impossible," she said. "I feel like I'm burning up." Blanco crossed her arms at the waist, bunched the dress in her hands, and then pulled it over her head. She tossed it across the chair back where she'd previously been sitting.

If Phoenix had been distracted by her beauty and the softness of her kisses before, then seeing her only in her underwear made him even more so.

Phoenix swallowed hard, trying to keep his hormones in check. While the U.S. had no official records of what Black Wasp training included, Phoenix recalled a rumor that they frequently trained their female recruits in the art of seduction. Taking off her dress wasn't a subtle move, but it made Phoenix think about something other than the mission at hand. Luring him into bed could result in hidden cameras snapping blackmail photos, but as Phoenix's gaze slipped to the pale yellow lace at the top of her bra, he wondered if it might be worth it.

"I … uh … what … what are the invasion plans?" he finally stammered out.

"You're so cute when you're nervous," Blanco said, touching his cheek.

Phoenix savored their skin-on-skin contact for a moment, then ducked away and went to his pack. "My boss has set up an account for when we relocate you. For now, I'm going to give you some money to show you how much we appreciate your help." He took a bundle of Venezuelan Bolívars from his pack and set them on the table.

"Are you kidding me?" Blanco asked, stepping over and picking up the bundle of cash. She ran her thumb over the end, seeing every bill in the stack was real. She tossed it on the table. "I don't want your fucking money. I'm not a whore. I want you to take me and my family out of here. Give us asylum in the U.S."

"Those aren't my orders."

"Fuck your orders and fuck you, Bowie!"

"I'm sorry, Coralina. I'm only doing what I'm told."

She picked up her phone and opened the screen to a preset number. "I have the SEBIN on speed dial. They can be here within minutes."

"Coralina … I'm begging you. I have my orders, too."

"I'll do what I have to do to survive," she said flatly.

"Get me the invasion plans, and I'll take you out," Phoenix replied, trying to de-escalate the situation. "I'll come back for your family."

"Bullshit." Her finger hovered over the contact button.

"Let's not do anything rash," Phoenix replied, holding his hands out to show her he was being compliant. His mind whirled. If she called the SEBIN, then all his plans to bump the vice president would be for naught. He'd have to flee the country again, and he doubted Connelly or her pals on the Seventh Floor would let him try again.

As it was, he didn't think the SEBIN had a photo of him or if they knew his true identity, but if they came to arrest him, they would definitely know who he was and what he looked like. There were other people around, in the park and on the street, if not in the apartment complex, who could identify him. And if the SEBIN were any good at their job, they'd have a composite sketch of his face within hours.

Blanco set the phone on the table and sank into a chair. "I want to leave," she whispered, tears forming at the corners of her eyes. "I don't believe in this war and don't want to die for a leader who cares nothing about his people."

Phoenix squatted in front of her and put a hand on her knee. Her skin was warm and smooth to his touch, and he felt himself slipping under her spell again. "I understand, Coralina. Maybe there's a way."

She looked at him, brown eyes shining with excitement.

"How long do you have off work? You said they gave you

an afternoon reprieve."

"I have the weekend, and then I am to report to the new Special Forces training camp as a member of the training cadre."

"Can you get your hands on the invasion plans?"

"Not after I report to the training camp."

"What about today?" he asked, excitement building in his chest. "Can you go back and get them?"

She shrugged. "Maybe."

Phoenix took Blanco's face in both his hands, kneeling on the floor to stabilize himself. "If you can get those plans, we'll go to Caracas. I have a job to do there. You can help me. Once that's done, we can leave."

She nodded, then leaned in and kissed Phoenix again, slow and tender, her fingertips grazing his cheeks.

Phoenix felt like a shitbird, using their feelings of sexual desire to coerce her into doing something dangerous with the promise of escape at the end. But then what? Would he ever see her again once the agency had moved her and her family?

Blanco stood and pulled on her dress, settling it around her breasts and hips with quick tugs at the hem. She headed for the door. "You better not wait here. Go out the back exit when I'm gone. I'll meet you in the park."

Phoenix nodded. "Here, you need to take this." He handed her an oversized pen. "It can take video and still photos."

After a quick tutorial, Blanco put the pen in her clutch and started for the door. She turned back to kiss Phoenix one more time before heading out.

Now, Phoenix felt a new flutter in his belly—fear. He had sent her on an ultra-dangerous mission inside a military base where, if they caught her, he couldn't help her. Ever.

Once she was gone, and he could no longer smell her scent lingering in the air, he went out the rear exit of the building, careful to check for any watchers.

Phoenix had run plenty of assets as a case officer, working either in the field or from an embassy office, and he'd never had a qualm about asking any of them to turn against their country. They wanted to do it for the benefits that would come in the end, like a fat bank account or relocating to another country, where they and their family members would be safe from reprisal. But as Phoenix walked the streets of Maracay, running an SDR, he couldn't help but fear for Blanco's life. He had put her in the worst of situations. If she got caught while stealing the invasion plans, then she would end up in a hell hole or be shot dead for being a traitor.

He kept checking his watch. Unsure which base in Maracay she had gone to, he didn't have a reference for how long it would take her to travel there and back.

After an hour, the pain in his shoulder was almost unbearable. He wanted to jam his back against something hard and sharp to help relieve the pain, but he also didn't want to be too conspicuous. This work as a spy was going to be the death of him, either slow and painful like the ache in his shoulder or quick and loud in a dark alley with a bullet to the back of his head.

It's time to get out.

He could turn in his resignation as soon as he got out of Venezuela. *But then what?*

Phoenix took a breath. He couldn't afford to think like this during an op, especially when he had to go back to Caracas and finish his plan to coerce Acevedo into working for the CIA.

Slowly, he took a deep breath, swelling his belly and exhaling, trying to kill the fight-or-flight mechanism ripping through his body. Everything screamed for him to run, but he couldn't until he knew Blanco was safe or that she wasn't coming back at all.

How long am I willing to wait for her? he asked himself.

CHAPTER 28

Lieutenant Coralina Blanco left the apartment and boarded a bus for the San Jacinto Barracks, home of the 99th Special Forces Brigade, where she had been training since the SEBIN had released her from questioning.

Once she was clear of Plaza España, she sent a text message via her phone.

The response came back within seconds. The sender told her to meet him at Mercado Market and also gave the challenge and response codes.

Blanco passed through the gate at the army base after showing her ID to the guard and then headed for the training barracks, where she kept her uniforms. Slipping off her sundress, she pulled on her green utilities, followed by her chest rig, before zipping it closed. She had to wiggle the rig around a bit to get her breasts to settle into place. Then she stood straight and gave a crisp salute to the woman in the mirror to ensure her uniform fit her properly.

As the intelligence officer for the 97th, it wasn't unusual for her to visit the command headquarters building to review sensitive documents, orders, and strategic combat plans. Leaving the barracks, Blanco returned the salutes of several of the enlisted staff on her way to headquarters, a single-story white stucco building surrounded by palm trees. As she walked, she formulated a ruse for returning to headquarters after being given the weekend off.

In the back of her mind, she had a ticking clock. The thought that weighed on her was that she had cut a deal with the CIA officer—the plans for her freedom. *If I can't deliver, will he dump me like he did before?*

Blanco knew that successfully completing the mission was the only way forward. Putting on an air of confidence she didn't feel in her gut, she pulled open the door to headquarters and stepped inside. For every soldier, there was a sense of pride and awe about entering the inner sanctum. Blanco had busted her ass to make it to where she was now, but she intended to throw all her hard work right into the dumpster to get the hell out of Venezuela before the shooting started.

Her combat boots squeaked on the polished marble floor. She kept her gaze straight ahead, not glancing at the framed photos of her chain of command from Brigadier General Riley Tomas to Command Sergeant Major Edward Brizola. She wondered if others could hear her heartbeat echoing in the hallway.

Blanco had to punch her security code into a numbered keypad to enter the secure room where the brass kept the war plans. She knew a camera in the ceiling recorded her every move, but she felt she could explain away her presence, and had concocted a lie on the bus ride over.

She went directly to the cabinet containing the battle plan map and pulled it out, discreetly using the pen Bowie had given to her to photograph the map after spreading it out on the central table. Once photographed, she rolled the map up and replaced it in the cabinet, then retrieved the file that outlined the Special Forces operation in the upcoming war with Guyana.

Behind her, the door opened. Blanco's heart rate, already

elevated, felt like it tripled, and her breath caught in her throat.

Major Silva stepped inside. "I thought I gave you the weekend off," he commented.

"Yes, sir. You did, sir," she replied, coming to attention.

She was about to snap off a salute when he waved a hand. "As you were, Lieutenant. What brings you back to the base?"

"I felt I needed to get a handle on the planning for Operation Takeback. If I know the tactics we'll use, then I can better incorporate them into our new training regimen."

"Excellent thinking," Silva said, clasping his hands behind his back as he circled the table. He paused to look down at the folder she had just opened. After a moment, he asked, "How are you doing, Lieutenant? We haven't had a chance to talk since your return."

"I'm fine, sir. Ready to take charge on Monday when the new class begins."

"I hope so, Lieutenant. I would hate to think that you haven't been completely truthful during the investigation into the disappearance of the American CIA team."

Frowning, she said, "I don't know what you mean, sir."

"You and I had the same training, Lieutenant. We can beat a polygraph machine."

"We did receive training on how to defeat the machine, sir, but I was truthful. The Americans held me hostage. I used my radio to bring the National Guard troops to the Americans' location, but you've probably read their testimony already. The Americans used grenades to disable their vehicle."

What she had just told Major Silva was a complete lie. Blanco had failed the polygraph from the first question, but Director General Hector Calderón had believed she showed promise as a double agent. Blanco had undergone intense psychological brainwashing through hypnosis and routine, bending her mind from wanting to leave Venezuela to believing she was one of their last great hopes to foil the Western imperialism aligned against Venezuela. And her training had included the planned seduction of the case officer named Bowie.

"Did you do anything to try to overpower them?" Major Silva asked, hands still behind his back.

"It was a three-on-one situation in the truck bed, sir. They would have killed me immediately."

"And why didn't you jump from the vehicle at the first opportunity?"

"I stayed, hoping to find a way to bring them to justice, sir. The board of inquisition covered all of this." Blanco tried to keep her breathing steady and focus on the task at hand, but Silva's questions were testing her patience. She didn't have time for this tête-à-tête.

Discretely, Blanco glanced at her watch. It had been two hours since she'd last tasted the empanada on Bowie's lips.

"Am I keeping you from something, Lieutenant?" Silva asked.

"Only from finishing my training rubric and leaving to enjoy my weekend."

"Monday. Zero five hundred. I want you in my office with a copy of your training doctrine."

"Yes, sir."

Major Silva cocked his head as he slowly made his way around the table. Blanco couldn't tell if he was eyeing her or the pen she'd laid beside the folder. He'd never made any overt sexual advances toward her, but she'd heard through the grapevine that he'd made multiple comments to his fellow officers about how he thought she should spend more time on her knees under his desk than in the field.

Indignation welled inside her as Silva stopped at the door with his hand on the knob and gave her a lecherous look.

"Zero-five hundred, sir," she said crisply.

Silva pushed through the door, leaving Blanco alone with

her folder. She pretended to chew on the end of the pen and thoughtfully read the pages, forcing herself to go slowly through the material to document everything with the camera, figuring Silva was watching her. Using a piece of scrap paper, she scribbled some illegible notes. With each turn of the page, she clicked the pen.

After reading through the Special Forces folder, she replaced it in the cabinet and removed the file for the 42nd Parachute Brigade, a unit the Special Forces worked closely with to establish air assault plans. Blanco photographed the pages within and made more notes before replacing the folder in the drawer and shoving the spy pen into her breast pocket.

Back outside, Blanco marched to the barracks and changed back into her civilian attire. Putting the pen in her clutch, she made sure she had switched it off so it wouldn't give off an electronic signal as she passed through security on her way off the base.

Her heart still beating fast, Blanco headed for the front gate. Passing through, she wished the soldiers a happy weekend and then hailed a taxi, not wanting to wait for the bus.

Time had passed surprisingly quickly inside the compound. Four hours had elapsed since she'd left the apartment. Blanco wondered if Bowie had grown anxious in her absence or if he'd given up, thinking they had caught her in an act of espionage.

Blanco kept glancing out the rear window of the taxi to see if they were being followed. She didn't know Bowie's plan for leaving Maracay, but she hoped it would be in a private car where she could hide on the floorboard until they were in Caracas.

"Turn here," she instructed the driver, who made an immediate right.

Blanco told the driver to stop in front of a small grocery store. She paid the driver in cash and then stepped out of the cab. Glancing around, she tried to determine again if anyone had followed her. As the taxi pulled away, she entered Mercado Market and strolled through the isles of nearly empty shelves. At the rear of the building, she met a man wearing blue jeans and a T-shirt with a picture of a sun setting behind mountains.

"Sunset," Blanco stated.

"Summit," the man replied.

Satisfied Blanco had passed the codeword test, the stranger led her out of the market and down an alley, where he used a key to open a heavy steel security door. After walking up a short flight of stairs, the man pointed toward another door and then took up a guard position outside it as she entered alone.

Inside, Blanco found the American she'd met during her polygraph interrogation and psychological reprogramming. He'd identified himself as Terry Martin, although she was sure it was a false name.

"Is he here?" Martin asked.

"Bowie is waiting for me near Plaza España," she replied.

"What did he ask you to do?"

"Steal the plans for the invasion of Guyana." Blanco pulled the pen from her clutch and held it up for Martin to see. "I have video and photographs on this."

Martin took the pen and examined it, pulling it apart to see the SD card and the USB connector hidden inside. He seemed to have been prepared for this turn of events as he removed the original SD card from the pen and replaced it with one he pulled from his pocket. Giving Blanco a wink, Martin put the pen back together and returned it to her. "Did Bowie tell you what you need to do next?"

Blanco nodded. "He has a job to do in Caracas. He wants my help, then he'll take me to the States."

Martin nodded. "Do the job but manufacture a reason to stay behind. I want you to keep feeding him disinformation."

Blanco agreed.

"I'm going to scare him a bit," Martin said. "I'll have two men follow you around the plaza. You and Bowie will work together to escape. It will build his trust in you."

"I understand," Blanco replied.

"Do what you have to do to keep him on the hook. He's the only officer the CIA has working in Venezuela right now. I helped Director Calderón eliminate the rest of them. Don't be a hero, Lieutenant, and don't dare to think of double-crossing me."

Blanco had heard the threat before. Martin had laid out how her life would change after Bowie had escaped Venezuela the first time. She was to return to her unit and contact Bowie, feeding him tidbits of real and manufactured information. If she refused to comply or if she tried to defect, Martin had assured her that he could find her wherever the CIA had stashed her. Once he found her, he would personally oversee her excruciatingly slow death. Martin had gone into great detail about what he would do to her, and just thinking about it now made Blanco shudder.

"Are we on the same page, Lieutenant?" Martin asked.

"Yes, sir. I'll contact you to let you know what happens in Caracas."

"Good." Martin stood. "Go meet Bowie."

Blanco left the building and went back out through the market, finding a car containing two men waiting at the curb to take her to Plaza España.

Two blocks from the plaza, Blanco ordered the driver to stop. He pulled into a parking space, and the three of them climbed out.

"I'll run an SDR. Pick me up near the far side of the plaza and make sure Bowie sees you," Blanco coached, then headed out without a reply.

She started her SDR, picking up Bowie as a tail about half a block from Plaza España. Blanco hoped he hadn't seen her talking to the SEBIN agents. Her heart fluttered momentarily, thinking about the scheme she was running on him. Bowie was handsome and a fabulous kisser, but Martin had convinced her that Bowie was actively working against Venezuela and against her by proxy. While the brainwashing had worked to an extent, she still had an overwhelming desire to get herself and her family safely out of Venezuela. Martin had tempered those desires with his promise of excruciating pain.

The two SEBIN agents stepped out of the shadows and moved toward her. Blanco thought about running or crying out to Bowie. Instead, she kept walking, checking the window reflections for the two men, drawing the trap even tighter.

They followed her just as she'd planned. She could tell Bowie had immediately alerted to them by reading his body language. Blanco smiled. She had gotten to him with her kisses. He had fallen into the honey trap. Deep in her heart, she wished things could have been different. She could easily love Bowie in another life, but in this one, she had to keep herself in check. It felt like being squeezed in a vise.

Blanco steeled herself. She would do what she had to do to survive.

CHAPTER 29

Plaza España
Maracay, Venezuela

John Phoenix knew he would have to murder the two men in suits who were following his asset.

He just had to figure out how and where. Once they'd done the deed, they would need to hide the bodies, so he and Coralina Blanco had time in Caracas to break into Vice President Evelyn Acevedo's apartment before the SEBIN caught up to them.

At first, Phoenix had felt a genuine sense of relief when he'd spotted Blanco walking along the sidewalk, but his relief had turned to dread at the sight of the men following her.

Operational doctrine told him to hold back and not rush toward the asset, putting them both in danger in case someone was following the asset. Phoenix was glad he'd forced himself to follow protocol, enjoying the view of Blanco moving in the pretty dress, but his gaze constantly roved over the people on the streets and his surroundings, searching for anything out of place.

Phoenix tracked the trio of two suits and Blanco, moving closer to them with each step. He tried to reason out how the suits would take Blanco or to where. She, too, had spotted them and kept glancing over her shoulder. The fear was clearly etched on her face, and the crowd seemed to part as they made their way down the street.

He would have to wait until they were alone, either in an alley or in her apartment, but killing them there was a problem. The apartment would be one of the first places the SEBIN would check if their operatives never returned. Phoenix needed a better game plan.

Pulling out his phone, Phoenix called Blanco. As he watched, she stopped and removed her ringing cell phone from her clutch. She put it to her ear and said, "Hello, sweetheart."

"Keep walking," Phoenix instructed her. "We need a quiet place where we can dump these guys."

Blanco resumed walking, her phone to her ear. "What do you mean by 'dump'?"

"You're a pro, Coralina. You know what I mean. Do you have a Bluetooth headset?"

"No," she replied.

"Okay." Phoenix knew she'd just have to walk with the phone to her ear. "Where are we taking these guys?"

"Don't you have a car we can escape in?" she asked, desperation in her voice.

"I do, but I'd rather not lead these guys to it. Stay calm, Coralina. Deep breaths."

He could hear her trying to control her breathing as she walked.

"I'm scared, Bowie."

"I know. Me, too, but we've got this. We're Special Forces. We know how to handle ourselves."

"Where's your car?" Blanco asked. "We can put them in the trunk and drive them into the hills. It would be best there."

Phoenix debated what to tell her. He really didn't want to take out her pursuers on the street in plain view of anyone watching or lead the agents on a high-speed chase out of the city. However, he didn't know what other alternatives he had. Phoenix didn't know the city of Maracay well enough to take them to a more convenient location for a force-on-force encounter. With little other choice, he finally said, "My car is parked on the street in front of an auto parts store at the corner of Carabobo and Suroeste Street."

"That's a rough neighborhood. Are you sure your car is still there?" Blanco asked.

"Let's hope so. It's a white Toyota Hilux truck."

Phoenix's contact in Puerto de Hierro had gotten his hands on a single-cab version of the truck with the venerable 22R motor in it. Despite being used and abused over the years, the 1989 pickup still tracked straight, and the engine started with every turn of the key. Truly, Phoenix reasoned, the vehicle's life span was a testament to the ingenuity and resourcefulness of the Venezuelan people. The contact, having been previously informed by Chief of Station Trinidad and Tobago that it was too dangerous for him to leave the village in the company of the American, had handed Phoenix the keys and wished him good luck. The chief had been a wise man since someone had burned all the VZ assets. So, after Ramesh had smuggled him into Venezuela, Phoenix had driven across the country to Caracas by himself.

Knowing where Phoenix had parked his truck, Blanco turned toward the auto parts store.

Instead of following his asset, Phoenix went the other way, planning to meet up with her at the truck. He was still at a loss about what to do with the two men following Blanco, but as he approached the truck, Phoenix struck upon an idea. It would be best to cause a public scene and get the local populace involved and then stuff the lieutenant in the truck and drive away.

Once he arrived at the Hilux, Phoenix took in the situation. There were few people around, and the case officer wondered if his plan would work. As he unlocked the driver's doors with his key, he mentally scrambled for a way to get rid of the two SEBIN agents following Blanco.

Phoenix still had his earbuds in place, and he could hear Blanco breathing on the other end of the line. "You still with me, Coralina?"

"I'm here," she said, her voice tight with anxiety.

"Where are you?"

"Coming down Suroeste."

"How far back are the agents?" Phoenix asked.

"Half a block."

"I'm in the truck." He turned the key, and the little four-cylinder engine started up. "Can you start running?"

"Yes."

"Good. End your call, and I'll have the door open."

"I'll cross the street when I see you turn the corner."

Phoenix pulled away from the curb and shifted the transmission into second gear, riding the clutch to keep up his momentum. Closing on Suroeste, he checked the cross traffic and then turned left.

"I'm here!" he shouted.

The phone line went dead, and he saw Blanco sprinting across the street, sundress swishing around her legs. Behind her, the two agents appeared momentarily startled into inaction but then began giving chase.

Blanco bounded onto the sidewalk as Phoenix came alongside her and threw the passenger door open. Without waiting for him to come to a complete stop, Blanco launched herself into the truck and landed on her left hip, legs still dangling out the open door.

Phoenix mashed the accelerator as he reached down and grabbed the back of Blanco's thigh to help haul her in. The engine whined with the need to shift gears. He let go of his charge and grabbed the stick shifter.

Ahead of him, the two agents had stopped in the middle of the street and drawn their pistols. Blanco struggled to get into the truck, kicking her feet against the open door. The truck's windshield and rear window exploded with violent cracks, showering both driver and passenger with tiny squares of broken safety glass.

Phoenix ducked as another shot slammed into the hood of the truck.

Angling the Toyota Hilux toward the two agents now blasting away with their handguns, Phoenix shifted again and jammed the gas pedal to the floor. The two agents must not have thought he would intentionally run them over as they stood their ground and kept firing.

The truck's chrome front bumper hit the first guy in the legs, knocking him to the ground as the second SEBIN agent dove out of the way.

Blanco sat up in the seat and slammed the door closed before glancing over her shoulder. Phoenix had just enough time to look in the side mirror to see he had severely mangled the first agent before he cut the wheel hard right onto the nearest side street.

"What the hell was that?" Blanco demanded.

"I call it getting out of a jam," Phoenix answered with a grim smile.

"Now we have to ditch this truck and find another mode of transportation!" Blanco exclaimed.

"Yeah. No shit!" Phoenix replied, feeling the wind blasting him in the face as it whipped through the cab. He was pissed at the SEBIN agents for trying to gun them down in the street and at himself for not coming up with a better plan. He liked this truck, and now he'd have to find a replacement. "Got any bright ideas, L.T.?"

"Turn right on the next street."

They burst out on Constitution Avenue across from the Museum of Contemporary Art, reminding Phoenix that people craved to create and see beautiful things even amid destitution. The truck's tires squealed as he accelerated east.

The traffic lights on Constitution Avenue turned out to be Phoenix's next problem, and the first one he came to was red. He hooked another right, but that brought them back onto Carabobo Street, just where he'd started. Glancing out the passenger window, he saw a crowd of people gathered around the prostrate man on the street, backing up traffic. He kept the accelerator down and rocketed along Carabobo toward Troncal 1, the east-west freeway that would take them rapidly out of the city.

Phoenix wanted to put some distance between himself and the scene of the crime, so he kept going south, barely slowing for the intersections.

"Stay on Carabobo," Blanco instructed. "There's a parking lot just before the freeway. We'll get a new vehicle there."

"Are you sure?" Phoenix asked.

"I'm a professional soldier. I know my way around this city."

Phoenix just kept driving, the wind howling through the cab and people staring as they rolled past. While it wasn't unusual to hear gunfire on Venezuelan streets or to see vehicles with bullet holes parked off to the side of the road, it was rare to see them fleeing the scene of a crime when normally the police would have overwhelmed the offenders and left them for dead. Anyone who saw them knew they had been in an altercation with either the police, the SEBIN, or a group of *colectivos.*

Carabobo Street ended at Aragua Avenue, and once Phoenix had crossed the intersection, he was on Mérida

Avenue, which split to go around a long plaza decorated with an ornate reflecting pool, a massive flagpole shaped like an anchor, and a bronze statue of the Maracay chief, created by Italian artist Gaetano Chiaromonte in 1957.

"Great," Phoenix mumbled when he saw there was no parking lot near the freeway as Blanco had claimed. It should have been the last time he trusted her, but he knew it wouldn't be.

"Keep going," Blanco said. "There are plenty of factories on the other side of the overpass."

Phoenix had no other choice. It wasn't like they could just get out and walk to Caracas, but the sooner they could ditch the truck, the better.

Once past Troncal 1, they entered La Hamaca Industrial Zone, a large area full of warehouses and factories sand-wiched between the freeway and Lake Valencia, where firms such as Coca-Cola, Biotech Labs, and Pfizer had manufac-turing plants.

Phoenix kept his head on a swivel as he drove, looking for the most likely place to stash the truck and steal a new ride. He finally pulled into a parking lot and climbed out of the truck, leaving the keys in the ignition. Shouldering his pack, Phoenix headed for the nearest exit and started up the street.

"Where are you going?" Blanco asked, hurrying to catch up.

"We're going to find another vehicle and get out of here."

Phoenix glanced at her as she took his hand and interlaced their fingers. While he was as forgettable as the average male on the street, she was a stunner in that dress, and he wondered if someone would remember her if the SEBIN canvased the neighborhood after finding the abandoned pickup truck.

As they passed another parking lot, Blanco veered into it and began checking door handles, finding one open. Sliding behind the wheel of a Toyota Cressida, she quickly hot-wired it.

As Phoenix climbed into the passenger seat, Blanco put the car in gear, and they headed for Caracas and a date with Vice President Evelyn Acevedo.

CHAPTER 30

Airport Steakhouse
Hutchinson, Kansas

Will Pounder took his usual stool at the bar and ordered his usual drink.

Life had become full of "the usual" lately.

Max sashayed toward him, wearing a plaid schoolgirl skirt with a white top tucked tightly into it. Pounder thought she looked amazing. She set his Captain and Coke on the bar and leaned on the bar rail. Whether or not she meant to give him a show, Pounder enjoyed the view down her shirt.

"Put your tits away, Max, unless you're gonna finally go out with him," Steve Gruber said as he walked in. As usual, he clapped Pounder on the shoulder as he passed. Gruber sat a couple of stools down from Pounder and ordered a frosty beer from the tap.

Max rolled her eyes as she pushed off the bar and grabbed a clean beer mug from the stack.

Gruber studied Pounder as Max poured his beer. "I heard you flew corporate jets for a while."

Pounder nodded.

"What happened?" Gruber asked.

Pounder shrugged. "Let's just say I'm more of a crop duster kinda guy than a corporate jet kinda guy."

Gruber nodded, but Pounder didn't think the man understood. Flying jets for rich folks just didn't make Pounder happy. Sure, he'd flown all over the U.S., but he'd mostly visited airports and had seen the rest of the country from thirty-thousand feet. It didn't make his hair stand on end like buzzing semis or grazing corn tassels.

They sat silently, sipping their drinks as the dinner crowd arrived. Max drifted away and served other customers, leaving Pounder to watch from afar.

As the bar filled up, Pounder finished his drink and stood to leave, but Gruber moved two stools down to sit beside him.

"You remember the other day when I told you that you needed to keep grabbing life by the balls?"

"Yeah. What about it?" Pounder asked, annoyed that the jet jockey was still talking to him.

"What if I told you there was a way to do that?" Gruber asked.

"There are lots of ways, old man," Pounder shot back.

"Sure, there are, kid," Gruber said, "but you and me—we want our thrills in an airplane. The great wild blue yonder."

Please don't break out into the Air Force theme song! Pounder silently pleaded.

When Gruber didn't sing or elaborate, Pounder said, "So? What's your point?"

He wished he had another drink if he had to keep listing to Hans Fucking Gruber drone on. Pounder wondered how good it must have felt when John McClane finally threw the terrorist off the top of Nakatomi Plaza.

Gruber pulled out his phone. "Let me show you something." He opened the Internet browser to a saved tab and set it on the bar top by Pounder's empty glass. "Guyana and Venezuela are about to go to war. You hear about the *Essequibo* Incident?"

Pounder nodded, vaguely remembering his parents watching something about it on the nightly news.

"Anyway, Guyana is buying twenty-four Super Tucanos—know what those are?"

Pounder shook his head.

"It's basically an Air Tractor that carries a shit load of bombs, guns, and missiles. They use them for close air support."

"So what?" Pounder said.

"They're looking for pilots, Will. They've got like five thousand people in their whole military, tops. Guyana's putting together a flying foreign legion, like the old Eagle Squadrons back in World War II when Americans flew for the RAF before the U.S. joined the war."

"What's your point, Steve?"

"You and I should join," Gruber said earnestly. "They're doing all the training down at Moody Air Force Base in Georgia. If we sign up and complete the training, Guyana will give us two-hundred-fifty grand apiece. On top of that, we'll get flight pay and a regular wage just like we were in their military."

"Are you serious?" Pounder asked, his interest now peeked.

"Check it out." Gruber pointed to his phone. He signaled Max over to order another round as Pounder took his seat on the stool again and read through the article Gruber had pulled up on his phone.

When Max set their drinks down, she asked, "When did you two become best buds?"

"Since we decided to fly Super Tucanos for the Guyana Defense Force," Gruber cheerily replied.

"What?" Max asked, reaching over the bar for the cell phone Pounder had in his hand. She snatched it away and scrolled quickly through the article. "You can't be serious?"

"Deadly," Gruber replied with a devilish grin.

"Will …?" Max asked hesitantly.

Pounder shrugged. "Looks like I'm not going to be a regular at the bar anymore, babe."

Gruber slapped Pounder on the back and about made him spit out the drink he was taking. "This kid is gonna be a war hero, Max. You better give him some of that sweet poontang before he ships out."

"Poontang, Steve? Really?" Max asked. "Just how old are you?"

Gruber shrugged. "I don't know what you kids call it these days."

Max rolled her eyes again as she turned to face Pounder. "Are you really going to do this—go fight for some stupid country over oil?"

"I've already done that once, Max. This one seems like a better deal," Pounder replied.

"I can't believe the two of you. What the hell has gotten into you?" she demanded.

Gruber grinned like a little kid at Christmas. "Adventure, Max. We're gonna go grab life by the balls."

"The only balls you're gonna grab are your own, Steve," Max shot back, then gave Pounder another concerned look. He shrugged his shoulders as he polished off his drink.

Excitement bubbled through him. Pounder hadn't felt this giddy about anything in years. He was going back into combat again. Well, training for it anyway. The two sides would probably come to a mutual agreement of sorts before more bullets flew. But how could he pass up the chance to fly a Super Tucano? If he got the training, there were probably other countries looking for qualified pilots to drop bombs. He could become a flying mercenary.

"You got the drinks tonight, Gruber," Pounder said. "I gotta go home and pack."

"The training starts in a couple of days, Will. I'll meet you in Georgia," Gruber called over his shoulder.

Pounder wandered out to the parking lot in a daze. Thoughts swirled through his brain so fast he could barely keep up with them. He was climbing into his truck when Max came running out of the bar. She threw her arms around him and hugged Pounder with a ferocity he didn't know she felt for him.

"Damn you, Will Pounder. Don't do this," she begged.

"What's keeping me here, Max?" he asked as she released him.

"Me. I should have said yes to you a long time ago, but it was like a game, you know. I liked you coming in to bug me and asking me out."

"I can't stay, Max. I like you, but it seems like the only reason you're out here right now is because I'm leaving. You better go back inside before you get fired."

She stared up at him, her eyes full of tears and a deeply wounded look on her face. Shaking her head in consternation, Max turned and ran back toward the bar.

Pounder didn't want the complications of a long-distance relationship. Maybe if she'd said yes last year, he wouldn't be going, but Max just kept toying with him, and now he'd cut her out of his life. It was a hard but necessary thing to do.

———

THE RED NUMBERS on the alarm clock on Pounder's nightstand told him it was three-fifteen in the morning. Someone outside was shouting his name and cussing a blue streak while doing it. What sounded like a glass bottle shattering against the wall just below his window brought him quickly out of bed.

Outside, a light snapped on, and Pounder's father shouted, "Go away! I've got a shotgun."

"Send that fucking pussy Will out here!" Maxine Gilespie cried.

"He's asleep. We all were. Now go away before I call the police," Keith Pounder yelled back.

"Fuck you and fuck him!" Max cried.

Will Pounder looked out his bedroom window just in time to see Max flip off his father with both middle fingers. He ran down the stairs in his boxer shorts and onto the porch. "What the hell, Max?"

"There you are, you lousy son of a bitch!" she muttered, staggering across the lawn toward him.

Pounder's dad pointed at Max. "Watch your mouth, missy!"

"Max, get up here and quiet down," Will Pounder ordered.

She made it to the porch before she doubled over and puked into the bushes. Finished heaving, Max collapsed on the front steps, sobbing.

"Get her in the house, Will," the elder Pounder said.

"Yes, sir." He hooked Max under the arms and pulled her to her feet. "Let's get you inside, babe."

"I love you, Will."

"No, you don't," he replied. "You're just drunk."

Inside the house, Pounder helped Max into a chair at the kitchen table. Mama Marlene already had a pot of coffee brewing. Once the water had run through the grounds, she poured two steaming mugs and sat one in front of Max as she eased into a chair across from her. She glanced over at the Pounder men before turning back to Max. "Tell me what this is all about, honey. Did Will knock you up?"

Max snorted. "I wish he had. Then maybe he wouldn't be

doing something *really* stupid."

Keith and Marlene turned toward their son.

"What's going on, Will?" Marlene asked.

"It's nothing, Mom. I'm going to Georgia for flight training. That's all."

"Tell them why," Max growled.

"It's just training, Max," Pounder insisted.

"Training so you can join some fucking mercenary squadron in Guyana, so when they go to war, you'll be there to fight it for them," Max stated.

Pounder swiveled his neck in consternation. He closed his eyes and breathed deeply into the silence that filled the kitchen. It was the same silence his parents had greeted him with when he'd told them he was joining the Army years ago.

When he opened his eyes, he found his father staring at him. Pounder knew what he would say, and he hated the tone of disapproval and disappointment that would come with the words.

"You're a grown man, Will," Keith admitted. "You can decide to do whatever you want, but how am I supposed to stand at the pulpit come Sunday morning and preach the love of Christ when my son, my very own son, is out there killing people?"

Pounder had no answer for his father, just like he'd had no answer for him when he'd been a paratrooper. It was never about going out to shoot people. It was about patriotism and loyalty and maybe a little about proving himself.

"I've gotta pack," Pounder said, heading for his room.

It didn't take long for him to throw jeans, shorts, T-shirts, and underwear into his old Army duffel. He added his combat knife, a Glock 19 pistol, his shaving kit, and an extra pair of running shoes to the mix before he zipped the bag closed.

Downstairs, three people sat at the table in silence. He loved two of them more than anybody else in the world, but joining the Army had fractured their relationship, and leaving again probably meant the end of his time in Hutchinson, Kansas. Max was the one other person he would miss and probably the only reason he'd even contemplate returning. While he loved his parents, his father's disapproval of his lifestyle choices had always been a wedge between them.

"Come on, Max," Pounder said. "I'll drive you home."

Max glanced over at Marlene. "Thanks for the coffee, ma'am, and I'm real sorry I woke you all up."

Marlene jumped up and hugged her son. "I know I can't stop you. You're a grown man and can make your own choices. All I'll say is that I love you, and be safe down there."

"I will, Momma." Pounder nodded at the old man who sat with his arms crossed. He snorted his disapproval, but Pounder still said, "Love you, Pops."

Max walked on shaky legs beside Pounder out to the big GMC. Pounder helped her up inside and then went around to the driver's side. Pausing at the door, he looked up at the porch to where his parents stood, having followed them out.

A Bible verse sprang into Pounder's mind. He'd memorized a lot of them when he was younger. He used to love to throw them back at the old man when they'd argued. This morning, Pounder felt tired, sad, and alone. Gazing back at his father, the pilot said, "Remember John 15:13, Pops. *Greater love hath no man than this, that a man lay down his life for his friends.*"

Keith Pounder pursed his lips and said nothing, merely crossing his arms again like he always had when they'd come to an impasse in their disagreements. It usually meant Pounder was about to get the belt across his bare ass. Discipline was how his old man showed his love, tempered with the occasional grunt of approval.

Pounder felt a lump in his throat as he climbed into his truck. He started the engine and backed out of the driveway.

He didn't know if he'd ever come back again.

CHAPTER 31

Oval Office
Washington D.C.

PRESIDENT RANDY MERCIA PACED THE FLOOR AS HE USUALLY DID to burn off energy during meetings.

Seated on the couch was Carlton Choi, a Korean American whose ancestors had immigrated to California in the waning days of the Korean Conflict. They had settled in San Francisco, and Choi was a fourth-generation American, born and bred in the liberal incubator under influences like Phillip Burton, Willie Brown, and Diane Feinstein, the woman who had pressed Choi into service as a Senate staffer. From there, he'd had a swift and steady rise to his current position as the president's chief of staff. While Choi's politics seemed diametrically opposed to Randy 'Merica's good old boy image, the two men had developed a loose friendship over the past year.

Mercia figured they'd never be drinking buddies, but he did like the guy.

"I still don't understand why you keep meeting with the Director of the CIA and the Secretary of State without me being present," Choi complained.

"Some things don't need your approval, Carlton."

"But I'm your Chief of Staff, sir. I'm not saying that I need to know everything, but I am supposed to oversee policy development and protect your interests. As the man who's *also* supposed to be your *closest* advisor, I feel you should allow me to attend those meetings."

"Here's the gist," Mercia said. "Guyana and Venezuela are at each other's throats and threatening to go to war. As Guyana's ally, we are supposed to step up and help them, but we've given them a raw deal in the past, and it's time to make it right."

"How so?" Choi asked.

"I want oil," Mercia replied. "While the liberal queens around here demand solar and wind power with their New Green Deal, those *renewable* energies don't work worth a damn. Just go ask the people down in Texas or over in Germany."

Choi started to object.

Mercia held his hand up to stop him. In Mercia's mind, the Green New Deal was a death knell for America. "My daddy is an oilman, and by default, I'm an oilman. If we can't drill here, we're gonna drill somewhere, and I'll be damned if we keep supporting that son of a bitch Michel Zarate. I want Guyanese oil, and I want to make them a deal. They owe us a lot of money for past loans. We take oil in payment, and we trade military hardware for black gold."

"We're committed to Ukraine, sir."

"Carlton, do you know who isn't committed to Ukraine?" Mercia asked sarcastically before answering his own question. "The American people. That's who. The latest polling numbers show they're tired of giving money and war materiel to them, and frankly, I get it."

"But supporting Guyana isn't any different," Choi argued.

"You're absolutely right," Mercia replied. "It's a no-win situation, but the upside to Guyana is this: if Guyana wins this war, we get two *big* wins. Not only do they owe us oil for life, but we also get to settle this Venezuelan crisis."

"What about the peace negotiations in Mexico City?" Choi asked.

"Look, Carlton," Mercia put on his best country rube accent, "y'all wanna talk and make nice, discuss thoughts and feelings, and try to understand everyone better." Mercia's voice shifted into a harsher tone. "That's horseshit. It just doesn't work. Your buddy Brandon proved that, but he screwed the pooch and us right along with it. Zarate isn't going to talk. Zarate isn't going to budge. We—and by that, I mean everyone who can read an Internet article—know where Zarate stands on everything from reclaiming the Essequibo Region to silencing political opponents. He will never change his mind. People like that don't just throw up their hands and turn *laissez-faire*. Zarate doesn't give a fuck about free and fair elections." Mercia slowed his cadence to enunciate every word of his next sentence. "Zarate will do everything possible to remain in power."

"Zarate is looking for world support, and we've been sanctioning Venezuela into collapse," Choi replied.

"Bullshit. Chávez and his asshole buddy Zarate have killed that country's economy from day one. We had nothing to do with it. In fact, the way your leftist buddies turn their back on the oppression of the Venezuelan people is setting a dangerous precedent. It empowers others like Zarate to try the same thing."

Choi vehemently shook his head. "Zarate was democratically elected and, in some instances, is being oppressed by American policies and sanctions."

"We sanctioned him because he's a fucking criminal, Carlton. "If I were to arrest my political opponents, try to nationalize every company in this country, and help known gangs and drug cartels move their products, I'd be impeached and thrown in jail."

"You're associating with a known gang by conspiring with the CIA."

Mercia rolled his eyes. He'd been saddled with Choi by the big wig donors who had helped to sweep Randy 'Merica into office. While he and Choi may have become "friends," their ideologies were about as far apart as they could get, especially regarding communism and the support of regimes like Castro's in Cuba or Zarate's in Venezuela.

"The way I see it, Carlton, is that the left has lumped Castro and Zarate into the same mold and are holding them up as demigods. The more one of you leftists sympathizes with either of those criminals, the more points they score with their Marxist friends. Cuba is a rallying point for you all, pointing to the fact that the country has defied the West and survived by the skin of its teeth. Notwithstanding everything Castro has done to his people, the longer he and his family are in power, the more it becomes legend—the 'idyllic paradise' of Carl Marx. And now Cuba has imported its brand of oppression, poverty, and suffering to Venezuela. People are not happy to be unencumbered by materialism despite everything the liberals want us to believe.

"No matter where they live, people want the same thing— to provide for their families, put food on the table, gas in their cars, and for their children's lives to be better than the ones they lived.

"America has fought against tyranny since its founding, and we've stood as the world's policeman against it, no matter what name it bears. So, if Guyana chooses to fight Venezuela, then we need to back them to the hilt."

"And Ukraine," Choi stated.

Mercia saw he'd backed himself into a corner. "All right, Ukraine, too. Reagan did paint Russia as the 'Evil Empire' and therefore, by my little speech, we must continue to support them." Mercia sank on the couch opposite his chief of staff. "I'd rather just leave them alone and let them fight it out, but we still face the same problem. We're running dangerously low on munitions, armament, and war materiel. That makes us vulnerable to attacks on many fronts."

"Are you thinking China and Taiwan?" Choi asked.

"Yes," Mercia said with a nod.

"I don't believe President Xi wants to suffer the same economic sanctions that we've put on Russia, and besides, his economy is in a recession."

"If Xi was focused on his economy, he would have implemented more of his sixty-point reform plan to fix an obsolete growth model. It's true that China is suffering under a critical debt load, but most of it is internal, and despite all their economic woes, there are signals that he plans to reacquire Taiwan."

"I agree, but just look at the economy."

"I don't give a rat's ass about the economy in China," Mercia barked. "We have to listen to what the man is saying. Xi is intent on bringing Taiwan back into the fold. Zarate is intent on remaining in power and reclaiming the Essequibo Region. China, Russia, Iran, and Cuba are all supportive of Zarate. If there was an axis of evil as my predecessor liked to claim, then they're it."

"This is why I'm here, Randy," Choi admitted. "You're too much of a hawk. We're supposed to be maintaining the status quo, not getting involved in every bush war on the planet."

"I'm not a hawk. I'm a realist," Mercia shot back. "I put the best people in place to help guide U.S. policy, and they recommend we back Guyana to the hilt. So that's what we're doing. Kennedy made the Russians blink. I'm gonna make Zarate blink, and when he does, we're gonna kick his ass, and if I have my way, we'll roll right straight north and put that Miguel Díaz-Canel fuck out on his ear, too."

"No! Absolutely not," Choi declared. "Never say that again."

"Why? Because you want Cuba to live on as a 'dream' of what's possible."

"Cuba hasn't given us cause to invade. We can't simply remove the president of Cuba from power because you don't like his politics. If we go in there with guns blazing, it will be like the debacle in the Dominican Republic all over again."

On April 28, 1965, President Lyndon B. Johnson had ordered troops into the Dominican Republic through "Operation Power Pack," fearing President Juan Bosch would lead the DR into a Cuba-style communist dictatorship. People around the world had openly condemned the U.S. intervention, claiming it was only to protect U.S. business interests in the country.

Mercia ignored the DR reference. "Let's talk to the people Castro shot to death with his kill squads or starved to death with his economic policies. Oh, wait. We can't. They're fucking dead!"

"Calm down, Randy," Choi pleaded.

Mercia rose from the couch and started pacing again. He would love to fire Choi, but there were strong donor hands thrust deep into his pockets, and should he wiggle, they might grab him by the balls. He pursed his lips as he paced across the presidential seal woven into the carpet. Guyana had their struggles, and he had his.

"We've forgotten our history, Choi."

The chief of staff knew he was in trouble when Mercia started using his last name.

"We used to adhere to the Monroe Doctrine, which asked Europe to limit its participation in Latin America to their existing colonies and to dissuade them from pursuing further colonial ambitions. The original principle stands even though China and Russia have run roughshod over it. But what we should be concerned with is the Johnson Doctrine. It specifies that we intervene if there is a threat of a communist takeover of a government—like the Dominican Republic, as you mentioned. With China actively pursuing their Belt and Road Initiative in Latin America and the Caribbean, we have communist-affiliated countries all across the Western Hemisphere. I think it might be time to act and put these regimes out of business, not for the good of the United States, but for the good of the people suffering under their oppression."

"No, Randy!" Choi cried, leaping to his feet. "We can't go to war with half of South America. You need to rethink everything you just said. If anything, we need another 'Good Neighbor' policy."

"Non-intervention has gotten us nowhere. The drug cartels and the guerillas and the political thugs think they can run a government, but they've proven ineffective time and again."

"Listen to what you're saying!" Choi argued. "War is not the answer."

"You want isolation?"

"That's not a good policy either," Choi admitted.

"I can do either one. Whichever one we choose, we're going to do it with every ounce of our being. I'm tired of these half-hearted efforts and of the U.S. always losing wars. Do you know the U.S. hasn't won a war since the donkey was a major form of transportation? A big fat zero in the win column from Korea forward. No wonder no one takes us seriously."

"Status quo, Randy. Those are our orders. *Status quo.*"

"I'm getting really tired of orders," Mercia muttered.

CHAPTER 32

Caracas, Venezuela

JOHN PHOENIX KNELT ON THE THREAD-BARE CARPET OF THE apartment complex hallway as he raked the lock pick set across the tumblers of Vice President Evelyn Acevedo's door lock. He already had the deadbolt unlatched, and in another thirty seconds, he'd be inside.

It surprised him that the SEBIN agents hadn't installed a better lock or a burglar alarm. If he were in charge of her detail, Phoenix would have insisted she move from the tiny apartment she'd occupied since her return to Venezuela. Getting her into one of the official political residences would have protected her from harm and from guys like Phoenix.

Once Phoenix and Blanco had escaped from Maracay in their stolen Toyota Cressida, they had found a place to hole up across from Acevedo's apartment so they could monitor her schedule. Blanco had dumped the Cressida and returned with a newer model Nissan Patrol. Phoenix didn't bother to ask where she'd gotten it, and Blanco had volunteered nothing beyond that she'd "found it."

Phoenix's tension wrench seated at the bottom of the lock, simulating the key's flat portion, and Phoenix dragged the rake across the tumbler pins. He could feel them give beneath the tension, lifting the pins into their precise locations inside the lock. Keeping the wrench and rake in place, he carefully twisted the doorknob with his gloved hand.

Part of his and Blanco's reconnaissance of the place had been to use the cover of maintenance workers to climb past Acevedo's window on a ladder and photograph the interior of her place with a small digital camera. Those photos, combined with some taken from a longer range, had allowed Phoenix to examine a portion of Acevedo's living room and bedroom. He'd also determined there was no alarm by checking the window casing as he'd climbed past on the ladder.

As he eased through the door, Phoenix prayed he was correct. If he'd missed a silent alarm, the case officer knew he would be screwed. The SEBIN would roll in to arrest him, and he'd disappear into The Tomb.

Once he was inside the apartment, Phoenix closed and locked the door behind him. He stood perfectly still, listening to the sounds of traffic passing on the street below and the hum of a window air conditioner, which also surprised Phoenix, given the rolling blackouts and energy rationing happening across the country. Quite possibly, it was a perk for the building to have electricity since the new VP lived there. When Phoenix saw the candles strategically placed around the various rooms, they reminded him of an old joke: what did Venezuelans use to light their homes before candles? Electricity.

As he chuckled to himself, Phoenix inhaled a faint odor of perfume. He recognized the lavender and sandalwood for something Connelly liked to wear. Phoenix felt a rush of heat through his body as he suddenly felt he was cheating on Connelly by having slept with Blanco shortly after their arrival in Caracas. He hadn't planned for it to happen. It had just occurred naturally as an extension of the passionate kisses they'd shared in Maracay.

Switching his mind back to the work at hand, Phoenix glanced about the place again. Rich woven carpets adorned the hardwood floor under a small dining table, and a red couch faced a low entertainment cabinet under a wall-mounted flat-screen television. Phoenix moved through the apartment on his toes, examining the bedroom, the bathroom, and then an office furnished with a wooden desk, a small filing cabinet, and a bookshelf loaded with medical texts.

Feeling this was the best place to lay his trap, Phoenix opened a desk drawer and placed the bag that DS&T had prepared for Acevedo inside. He carefully arranged the currency into neat stacks and then set a note he'd written earlier on the top. It read: "This is a gift from the friends you frequently talked to while traveling with Doctors Without Borders." The note also gave her a phone number to call should she decide to cooperate. Once she called in, her handler would instruct her on how to use the communication device secreted into the bag.

Stepping back, he took several photos of the bag, the currency, and the note before gently closing the drawer. The photos were to be blackmail. If Acevedo didn't call her CIA handler, Phoenix would send her a photo and remind her of just how easy it would be to send the others to the SEBIN or even to Zarate himself to show them where her loyalties lay. A payment from the CIA would be damning to her political appointment, and might send her to The Tomb for inter-rogation.

After much contemplation, Phoenix had decided this was the easiest route to take. Bumping her on the street meant he had to devise a plausible reason for being there and another reason for a second meeting. If, by magic, he did get the VP of Venezuela alone to hand her a bag full of American dollars, there was no reason to believe she might take it. While her old handler at Headquarters believed Acevedo might be willing to continue her relationship with the agency, that didn't guarantee she would. Spying on her own country was a lot different from the work she'd done for the agency while traveling for Doctors Without Borders. And between then and now, Acevedo's attitude might have changed, become more nationalistic, or she might outright refuse to inform on her own countrymen.

Planting the DS&T bag, cash, and note ensured they would end up in Acevedo's possession no matter what. What she did from there was on her, as the onus had always been. Even if Phoenix had met with the VP twice, she might balk at continuing to be a CIA asset. Phoenix had pitched a lot of potential recruits, and he had a seventy percent failure rate. Running such a high-level asset would be a boon for his career, but Phoenix was also risking his life by just being in Venezuela. He had no official cover, and the CIA would probably disavow him if he were caught. Leaving the money in the drawer had turned out to be his best option.

Once Phoenix had plenty of photographs, he stepped over to her bookcase and planted a bug under the lowest shelf. To his surprise, there was another bug already there. Straightening, he wondered who else was listening in on the vice president. His listening device had a forty-eight-hour battery life, and Phoenix figured he'd know which direction Acevedo would take by the time his bug died.

Before exiting the apartment, Phoenix called Blanco on the new cell phone he'd gotten for her after he'd tossed her old one out the window on the way to Caracas. The Army or the SEBIN could have been tracking her with it, and he wanted no more problems with law enforcement than he already had.

"Is it done?" Blanco asked.

"Yes," Phoenix confirmed. "How's it looking out there? Is the coast clear?"

"Looks beautiful," Blanco confirmed.

————

THE SPECIAL FORCES lieutenant stood on a street corner across from Acevedo's apartment complex, sipping coffee diluted with a lot of milk that she'd purchased from a nearby café. She'd been texting her Venezuelan handler, Terry Martin, since Phoenix entered the apartment. Martin had decided to let the situation play itself out rather than interfere with Phoenix's efforts.

Even though the morning was warm, Blanco had opted for blue jeans and a blouse. Bowie had complimented her on the way her jeans fit her ass, and she liked the fact that he looked at her in that way. It meant she was doing her job right. She'd seen that look in a guy's eyes before and enjoyed seeing it in Bowie's.

Blanco had set the hook with the kisses in the SEBIN-provided apartment in Maracay. And she'd sunk it even deeper by sleeping with the CIA officer. Since their first torrid and passionate affair, they had made love several more times.

The brainwashing she'd received hadn't erased any prior thoughts she might have had of caring for him. He was to be nothing more than an asset, and they had programmed her to do whatever she needed to keep him on the hook. Blanco tried not to allow herself to get attached, thinking she was only in bed with Bowie for the good of her country, but when that first orgasm had rocked her, she'd decided that she might as well enjoy it.

Blanco glanced over at the café. Terry Martin hadn't come himself but had sent one of his Venezuelan agents in his stead. The dark-haired man sat under an umbrella with his legs crossed as he sipped from a steaming mug and scrolled through his phone.

Bowie walked out of the apartment complex and turned right on the sidewalk without slowing down. He crossed the street, dodging cars and receiving a couple of rabid horn honks in return, but he ignored them and kept going, reaching the café. He disappeared inside and returned a few minutes later with a cup of coffee in a cardboard cup.

Like a criminal returning to the scene of the crime to watch the police at work, Bowie took a table on the sidewalk with his back to the wall. His gaze seemed to rove every-where and take in everything, and when his eyes locked with Blanco's, Bowie's mouth twitched into a smirk as if to say he was happy to be with her.

Ironically, he'd sat right down beside Martin's proxy, which made Blanco chuckle to herself as she returned Bowie's grin. She decided she would join Bowie at the table and possibly get him and Martin's agent to engage in conversa-tion, if for no other reason but her own entertainment. Before sitting across from Bowie, she bussed her lover on the cheek.

Blanco and Bowie made small talk about the weather and the local gossip about the impending war with Guyana. The news on the radio and television—when they worked—was replete with Guyana's purchase of war machines and materiel. She let her fingers trail along the back of Bowie's hand or trace little patterns across his skin. He didn't seem to mind, smiling at her in such a manner that she knew he wanted to make love to her.

"What do you think?" Blanco asked the agent.

The man glanced up from his phone. "*Es un arroz con mang,*" he replied, then returned to his coffee without another word.

While her handler's agent had literally said, "It's rice with mango," in the vernacular of the local slang, the meaning was, "It's complicated." Blanco had also heard the saying used in Cuba to describe a "clusterfuck," which certainly applied to the political tension between Guyana and Venezuela.

Once Bowie finished his coffee, he signaled to Blanco that it was time to leave, and they stood. Blanco interlaced her fingers into his as they walked down the street, appearing to be a happy couple out for a stroll, but as they walked, Blanco tried to manufacture a reason for her to remain in Venezuela. While she did not want to stay, Terry Martin's threats terrified her, and she feared for her safety and that of her family. And she didn't know if Bowie could fulfill his promise of extracting all of them from Venezuela.

Then, she struck upon an idea.

If Bowie thought she was dead, he would flee without her and take the fake documents with him.

She would have to text Martin the plan forming in her mind.

CHAPTER 33

Evelyn Acevedo felt bone-weary, caught between the demands of President Zarate and the needs of the people of her country. More often than not, those two things stood in direct opposition.

Zarate wanted to remain in power no matter what the cost to anyone around him or to his country. Acevedo wasn't a violent woman, but she sometimes thought a bullet in the right spot would make the world a better place. Sometimes, she still wondered why Director Calderón had chosen her to replace Delcy Rodriguez. There were angles within angles that she had yet to figure out. What she did know was that Calderón had thrust her feet first into the battle for the survival of her country.

While not particularly religious, Acevedo had grown up a Catholic, attending mass on holidays and for special events. When she prayed now, she asked God to help her free her people from the oppression they suffered as he had freed the Israelites. *Just don't let us wander in the wilderness for forty years.*

Acevedo often wished for a sign to show her which direction she should turn, whether to align herself with the hardline party attitude of her president or to move against him.

Climbing the steps to her apartment with SEBIN Agent Marcus de los Rios on her heels, she prayed again for a sign. She couldn't go on feeling like they'd trapped her in a blender. Eventually, the blender would grind her up and spit her out.

De los Rios went ahead of her in the hallway and opened her apartment door. He allowed her to stand just inside the doorway as he swept the place for potential hostiles. Returning to where she waited by the front door, he said, "All clear. We'll be right outside if you need us, ma'am."

Acevedo nodded to the agent as he stepped outside and closed the door behind him. She turned the lock on the knob and then shot the deadbolt home. She stared at it for a moment, puzzled as to why de los Rios hadn't unlocked it when he opened the door. In her memory, he had only opened the lock on the doorknob.

She tried to remember if she had locked the deadbolt when leaving earlier that morning. Sighing, Acevedo decided she had missed de los Rios using the key to open the dead-bolt. She was tired, after all.

Making her way into her home office, Acevedo set down her leather briefcase and reached into the drawer for the bottle of Aviator Gin that Calderón had presented to her as a gift when she'd accepted the vice presidency. After pouring the glass two fingers full, she sat back and sipped the liquor, trying to relax and forget about the troubles of the day. The problem she realized as she sat in her office, sipping the expensive and hard-to-source liquor, was that she was now part of the *enchufados*, or plugged-ins, for her government connections.

Not wanting to waste the excellent gin by throwing it out, Acevedo continued to sip it as her mind shifted gears to the upcoming peace summit in Mexico City. Zarate had agreed to it only in spirit since he had no desire to reconcile with President Fredricks or to speak to anyone from the U.S. delegation. They had all known that the dispute over the Essequibo Region would eventually come to blows, but no one had expected the *Essequibo* to attack and sink the *Guaiqueri* unprovoked.

Zarate had ordered Acevedo to take charge of the preparations and scheduling for the conference while he tended to other things. Chief among them, Acevedo knew, was the drug trafficking operation he ran with the help of Diosdado Cabello Rondón, a captain in the armed forces, and a man they called "The Octopus" because he had his tentacles in everything. Many claimed he was the head of an international drug trafficking organization called Cartel of the Suns, composed of various high-ranking members of the Venezuelan military.

The cartel was less of a ruthless operation like the Mexicans ran, but a way to regulate the drug trafficking system via collection of trafficking "taxes," providing corridors for safe passage of drug shipments, and sometimes military transportation of the drugs themselves from the Colombian border to air- and seaports in Venezuela. While cocaine was a lethal drug, it provided something the broken and bankrupt Venezuela desperately needed—hard currency. The protection of shipments became a way for soldiers to earn extra pay, and the Cartel of the Suns used the money accumulated from the trafficking operations to buy political loyalties or just outright bribe armed groups to turn a blind eye to drugs being moved through their territories.

Acevedo knew that eliminating Zarate would cause a power vacuum in which The Octopus might just rise from the depths where he'd been hiding and establish himself as the chief power broker of the entire country. She had to wonder if other people would fight against him or if the military would simply provide support for his presidency so they didn't lose their power base or ability to profit from the drug trade. Many of the political-appointed generals were involved in the drug trade in some fashion. And Acevedo had to believe that Major General Alejandro Salazar was an active part of the corruption despite his efforts to clean up the military.

Maybe Zarate isn't wrong to want a war. We could wipe out some of the corruption.

Even if she wanted war, Acevedo knew she had to talk peace in Mexico City. War was coming, no doubt about it. Zarate had made sure of that by his recent maneuvering. Sadly, Acevedo accepted that a war might be the reset button Venezuela so desperately needed. However, it would probably kill the hard-working enlisted men and women, not the generals and admirals in the Cartel of the Suns.

Reaching into the drawer where she kept a notebook to record her thoughts, Acevedo found herself staring at a bag full of U.S. one-hundred-dollar bills in ten-thousand-dollar bundles. A note sat atop the pile of cash, subtly telling her to call her old handler at the Central Intelligence Agency.

Stunned, Acevedo slammed the drawer closed and clamped her hands over her mouth. Hoping it was just a figment of her imagination, the vice president slid the drawer back open and stared at the money again. Acevedo hadn't expected the CIA to brazenly place a bag of money in her desk drawer, even though she had figured someone from the agency would try to contact her after she'd become the VP.

Slowly, Acevedo closed the drawer and unscrewed the cap from the gin bottle again. She poured more of the clear liquor into her glass and then stood and paced the floor as she sipped.

What do I do now?

Calderón had led Acevedo to believe that the CIA case officers and NOCs had fled the country when the embassy had closed, then the SEBIN had hunted down the last vestiges of their network and eliminated their assets. Obviously, that wasn't true, or the CIA had decided the possible death of a case officer was worth the attempt to contact her. While she had done work for the agency when she was a young doctor, it had been little more than reporting on conditions in her host country or counting rifles if she operated in a hostile environment.

If this was an answer to her prayer, then Acevedo wondered if she'd been asking for the wrong thing. The appearance of the money and the note could damage her image of purity. If the wrong person found either, she would be in real trouble, although she could claim the money as a political donation and burn the note. Without realizing it, her handler's phone number popped into her mind.

Acevedo pulled out a box of matches and struck one across the side, lighting the sulfurous head with a flare. She stared at the dancing flame, trying to discern in which direction she should turn.

Knowing she needed to trust someone, she blew out the flickering match before it could burn her fingertips and reached for her cell phone. Acevedo dialed the number for Director Calderón. The man had been nothing but friendly since she'd taken her new job, and she hoped he would provide her with advice now.

After taking the office of vice president, she had discreetly inquired about Calderón's loyalties to Zarate and to the military. Everyone she talked to claimed Calderón to be a man of integrity. He wasn't a Chavista, and he wasn't embroiled in the drug trade, but he still had close ties to both Zarate and The Octopus, which she supposed any man would need to rise to the directorship of the SEBIN.

Calderón answered on the third ring. "Madam Vice President, what can I do for you?"

"Are you free at the moment, Director?"

"As a bird for you, Evelyn."

She was still uncomfortable with him using her first name, but Acevedo let it slide.

"Would you be available to come by my apartment?" she asked.

"Of course. Is this a social visit?"

"More of a work thing," Acevedo replied evasively.

"I will be there in an hour," Calderón assured her.

Acevedo stood and paced again after ending the phone call. Her stomach roiled, and she felt like vomiting. Calderón's reaction to the money and the note would determine her fate. She went to the kitchen, drank a bottle of warm water, then opened the door and summoned Agent de los Rios into the apartment. "Director Calderón will be here in an hour. Ensure everything is ready for his arrival."

"We already have a security cordon set up," de los Rios notified her.

Acevedo nodded. She didn't know what precautions the SEBIN took when the director traveled. De los Rios stepped back outside and closed the door. Acevedo went back to her desk and sat down. She opened the drawer, moved the note to the desktop, and then counted the stacks of currency. Twenty-five bundles in total—two-hundred-fifty-thousand dollars. A quarter of a million U.S. and worth over eight million in Bolívars. She figured whoever had smuggled this cash into the country must have gotten an ulcer from carrying it around. Acevedo was getting heartburn from just looking at it. Once she knew how much it was worth, she replaced the bundles in the bag.

She stared at the bag of money and sipped more gin to calm her nerves until she heard a knock on the apartment's front door. Getting up, Acevedo brushed a hand over her hair to ensure she was presentable, then twisted the locks free and opened the door for Hector Calderón.

The director of the SEBIN stepped inside, leaving his

usual retinue in the hallway. He glanced around the cozy apartment. "You have a nice place, Ma'am."

"Thank you," Acevedo replied, closing the door.

She ushered Calderón into her office. "Can I pour you a drink, Hector?" It felt a little formal to address him by his title or last name as they stood in her apartment.

"I'm fine. I'm on my way to dinner with my wife."

Acevedo motioned for the man to step behind her desk, and after he did so, she opened the drawer with the money in it.

Calderón's eyes widened, but it was the only outward display of emotion he expressed.

"I wanted to ask your opinion on the possibility of spies infiltrating our agency."

With the tip of his shoe, Calderón pushed the drawer closed.

Acevedo opened her mouth to speak, but Calderón held a finger to his lips. He tapped the wall and then pointed to his ear as if to say, "The walls have ears."

The VP nodded.

"An interesting question about spies," Calderón finally said. "I want you to come to my office tomorrow, and we'll discuss this further."

He led Acevedo to the front door, then said, "Good evening, Doctor."

After opening the door, Calderón motioned for her to step outside. Once he'd closed the door, he ordered de los Rios to continue to stand guard over the apartment and not to let anyone inside. The agent nodded, and the two men who acted as Calderón's bodyguards started for the stairs. The director of the SEBIN placed his hand on Acevedo's elbow and guided her down the hall.

When they were alone, Calderón said, "Where can we speak in private?"

She motioned toward the stairs, and the two went up, stepping onto the roof of the building.

Acevedo used a brick to wedge the door open, something she and the other residents often did when they wanted some fresh air at night instead of walking the dangerous streets. With the brick in place, Acevedo straightened.

Calderón looked her square in the eye. "Where did the money come from?"

"I don't know," she replied. "It was there when I came home."

"And the note? Is this true? You worked for the CIA?"

"When I was with Doctors Without Borders, I reported to them from time to time about things I saw in my host countries."

Calderón nodded, rubbing his chin in thought.

"I thought you'd hunted down all the CIA officers in Venezuela," Acevedo said.

"The CIA is like a cancer. You can cut it all out, but it always returns."

"What should I do?" she asked.

"Put the money somewhere safe. We all have funds to fall back on. I will think about how we should proceed. There are many forces at play in our country right now. I'm not sure inviting the CIA back in is such a good idea."

Acevedo nodded.

"Come see me tomorrow. One p.m."

Acevedo hugged herself, feeling the need for comfort. Calderón had not given her any indication of which direction he would take, so walking into his office tomorrow could either be a prison sentence or turn her into a CIA asset. She wasn't sure which was the better option. Her stomach churned with dread.

Calderón placed both hands on Acevedo's shoulders. "Tomorrow, we will decide the future. Rest easy, Doctor. This is a game I love to play."

Acevedo felt a chill course through her body, even in the dying heat of the tropical day. She barely understood the politics of the National Assembly, but Acevedo knew how to triage a wound, and Venezuela was hemorrhaging from deep trauma. It was time to operate as if she were trying to save a life—and not just her own.

CHAPTER 34

Across the street from Evelyn Acevedo's apartment, John Phoenix listened intently to the dead air coming from the bug he'd planted in her bookcase. He strained to hear something beyond the brief conversation she'd had with Director Calderón before they'd gone out the front door.

"They're on the roof," Coralina Blanco said a moment later.

Phoenix stepped to the window where he, too, could see the VP and the SEBIN director standing near the open door of the roof access stairwell. He wished he could hear what they were saying. So far, his trap had been for naught.

Never in his career would Phoenix have bet on Acevedo calling the director of the SEBIN to her apartment to discuss the appearance of the cash. Their brief conversation about spies in their agencies didn't warrant Calderón's trip to her apartment. That was a conversation they could have had anywhere, so Phoenix's best guess was that Acevedo had called Calderón to show him the bag of cash and the note. The American case officer had to assume Acevedo had turned her back on the CIA and had become a wholly owned subsidiary of the Venezuelan government.

Disgusted, he took off his earphones and threw them on the desk.

"What do you think they're talking about?" Blanco asked.

"The money is my best guess, but I don't know," Phoenix said with a shake of his head. Whatever it was, it didn't bode well for him. Acevedo and Calderón now knew a CIA officer was operating in their country. The last time the SEBIN had learned he was in-country, they had engaged the Army to help try to track him down, and he prayed the weight of the nation didn't fall upon him again.

Standing, Phoenix began packing his equipment into his backpack. It was a lot lighter than when he'd come into the country since he'd passed the DS&T satchel and the money to Acevedo. He tossed in the headphones and the camera he'd used to photograph the staged scene at Acevedo's desk, now realizing that Acevedo had trumped him at every move. The blackmail photos were useless if he couldn't leverage her against the SEBIN.

"What are you doing?" Blanco asked.

Phoenix straightened and gave Blanco a steely gaze. "We're leaving Venezuela, and once we cross the border, it'll be time to uphold your end of the bargain. You'll have to give me the plans."

"I promise. I'll uphold my end of the deal," she replied curtly. "You don't trust me after all I've done. I'm giving up my country for you."

Phoenix glanced up at her. "We have a job to do. My mission here is over, and now we have to get the war plans back to my colleagues."

"Don't you trust me, Bowie?"

"I trust you, Coralina," he replied, zipping his pack closed and then moving over to take her into his arms. He kissed her gently on the lips, then stepped away before the kisses became something more. While he'd slept with her and felt the urge to do so now, he still adhered to Stone

Cold's adage: "DTA—don't trust anybody." Especially in Venezuela, where everyone seemed to be out for themselves.

In that spirit, Phoenix placed his essentials into a money belt around his waist in case he had to ditch the pack. With his preparations complete, he slung the backpack over his shoulder and reached for the lieutenant's hand. Together, they walked out of the apartment building and onto the street. The Nissan Patrol sat on the curb, waiting for them to get in and drive away.

But there was something about the vehicle that bothered Phoenix. He'd hot-wired many cars and trucks over his career, and he would have avoided the newer model Nissan like the plague. Touching the wrong wires together could cause myriad issues, including setting off the airbag or the alarm.

But Blanco had somehow secured the Patrol with the ignition intact and key in hand. She claimed she'd found the Nissan in a government lot and that the keys had been under the driver's side floor mat. It didn't sit right with Phoenix, so instead of getting into the Patrol and putting as much distance between himself and Caracas as possible, he led Blanco down the street and out into the night.

"We're not taking the Patrol?" she asked.

Phoenix kept walking. "We're running an SDR."

———

After a half hour of walking, the CIA case officer and the Venezuelan Special Forces lieutenant were back where they'd started. He'd dumped their disabled Movistar cell phones into various garbage bins along the route.

During their walk, Phoenix had seen nothing out of the ordinary, not realizing the enemy had switched tactics, using an overhead surveillance drone, a tracker planted in the

Nissan, and the switched-on location tracker in Blanco's former phone to watch their every move.

"Let's go," Phoenix said, heading for the Patrol.

Even though it was an eleven-hour drive to Puerto de Hierro, their exit point to Trinidad, Phoenix opted for a longer, more circuitous route to check for tails.

In the fading light of the day, it didn't matter which way he turned or how fast or slow he drove, John Phoenix couldn't pick out a tail. He couldn't help but feel there was something wrong, which made the knot in his shoulder tighten and his entire right arm ache.

He should have been grateful to be leaving Caracas without so much as a second glance from the Army or the SEBIN, but he'd been inside the VP's apartment, and he'd expected there to be some sort of fallout from the planted money.

———

Four hours after leaving Caracas, Phoenix stopped the Nissan at the junction of Troncols 9 and 11. He watched as a semi-truck lumbered past and then eased out into traffic.

The clock on the dash said it was almost eleven p.m., and Phoenix hoped the cover of darkness would help them pass easily through Clarines. There were both national police and National Guard command posts with traffic checkpoints in front of each station just six hundred meters apart. He'd successfully navigated around both checkpoints before by taking side streets, and he planned to do the same this time.

After crossing the bridge over the Unare River, which had swollen over its banks from the torrential rains that had drenched the state of Anzoátegui over the last couple of days, Phoenix slowed again and prepared to turn onto a dirt road that would take him into the city and around the checkpoints.

The headlights of the Nissan Patrol swung from the

scarred asphalt and swept across the entrance to the dirt road, illuminating an orange shipping container that someone had wedged between two large trees, effectively blocking traffic.

Phoenix cursed his luck and pulled back onto Troncal 9. He checked the road ahead for other side streets, but there was nothing between him and the first of the two check-points, this one manned by National Guard troops. They had erected a high metal roof over the paved road to provide shade for the guardsmen as they inspected the industrial vehicle traffic, allowing the residential vehicles to pass for inspection farther down the line at the police checkpoint. Blazing lights affixed to the support posts and under the roof illuminated the checkpoint and its surroundings.

As Phoenix approached the checkpoint, heart hammering in his chest, he hoped they would just let him pass through, but if an alert guard had been watching the road, they would certainly ask why he was trying to circumnavigate the check-point. And at this time of night, his actions would be highly suspicious.

In the line ahead of them were two cars and a motorcycle, and the guardsman, wearing a reflective safety vest and carrying an AK-103 rifle, waved the other vehicles through, then dropped the metal gate pole across the road and held up his hand for Phoenix to stop his Nissan Patrol.

Phoenix cursed under his breath for the second time since arriving in Clarines. The guards had witnessed his attempt to take the dirt road. As Phoenix inched towards the gate, the Patrol's brakes squeaked in protest. Beyond the gate arm, the guard stepped into the road and aimed his rifle at Phoenix through the windshield. Two other guardsmen came charging out from a booth on the other side of the street. They all carried automatic weapons and screamed for Phoenix and Blanco to exit the vehicle.

"Fuck that," Phoenix said and jammed the transmission lever into reverse while the car was still rolling forward. The entire vehicle shuddered as the transmission ground and squealed in protest. Phoenix mashed the gas, and the vehicle seemed to pause for a moment as the transmission tried to decide which direction the Patrol should go. Then the rear tires chirped on the asphalt, and suddenly, they were flying backward, away from the checkpoint. Phoenix threw his arm over the seatback and turned to stare out the rear window, effectively driving the SUV in reverse.

The National Guardsmen opened fire with a barrage of bullets that shattered the windshield and sliced through the seat upholstery. The rounds narrowly missed Phoenix, but one guard had a better aim than the others, and his shot struck Blanco in the center of her chest. Blood began pouring from the wound.

Phoenix jerked the wheel, sending the Patrol skidding into the dirt on the side of the road to avoid ramming an oncoming semi-tractor. Back on the pavement, he executed a Rockford turn, spinning the Patrol 180 degrees before jamming the transmission back into "Drive" and speeding away from the checkpoint.

The problem Phoenix now faced was that an armored personnel carrier had moved up and blocked the road on the far side of the bridge over the Unare River. The APC's bright lights shown across the pavement. They illuminated the bridge and the troops pouring out of the back of the vehicle.

Phoenix glanced over at Blanco. She had her hand pressed against the chest wound, and blood seeped through the gaps between her fingers.

"I'm sorry," he said.

Blanco reached over with her free hand and squeezed his forearm. He could see she was fading fast. She had lost so much blood that her shirt appeared black in the darkness. With the effort to speak, she began gasping and frothing at the mouth.

Phoenix decided it was over for her. As much as he hated

to leave her, he knew there was no way he could triage her wound and escape the National Guard troops with her in such critical condition. His focus now turned to finding a method of extraction for himself. Beyond the bridge, troops knelt in front of the APC, aiming their rifles at him. A man with a bullhorn commanded Phoenix to stop his vehicle, or the troops would open fire.

Phoenix brought the Patrol to a halt in the middle of the bridge. A single headlight threw a weak yellow beam onto the faded asphalt. Steam hissed from the radiator, and the temperature gauge redlined. He twisted in his seat to look out of the opening where the rear window had been. More National Guard troops were running up behind them. A police siren wailed somewhere in the distance.

"Give me the pen!" Phoenix shouted to Blanco, wanting to take the war plans with him. At least he could salvage something from this clusterfuck of an operation.

Weakly, Blanco pointed to her clutch. Phoenix grabbed it and ripped it open, using the glow of the dashboard lights to help find the pen in the bottom beneath her wallet. Opening the money belt on his waist, where he kept his agency cell phone, his wallet, and a thick bundle of U.S. dollars and Bolívars, Phoenix jammed the pen inside to keep it safe and resealed the pouch. He would have to abandon his backpack. The spy pen was the most essential item for him to take.

Phoenix glanced wildly about, taking in the situation. The man on the bullhorn gave them another order to exit the vehicle. As if knowing it had traveled its last mile, the Patrol's engine suddenly seized and died. He wasn't going anywhere in the Nissan.

He glanced at Blanco again. She was in a bad way. Her eyes were closed, and her breathing had slowed to shallow gasps. Unable to keep her hand on her wound, it had dropped into her lap, and in the glare of the lights shining from the APC, Phoenix could see the pucker of the bullet wound in her blouse. He found something strangely curious about the scene. The blouse appeared to have blown outward instead of being punched in by the bullet, but he didn't have time to investigate.

Blanco pawed the air with her hand, and it finally came to rest on Bowie's forearm. "I … I love … you."

He squeezed her hand and softly replied, "I love you, too."

Without waiting another moment, Phoenix kicked open the door, ran across the asphalt, and leaped over the bridge railing into the muddy water below.

CHAPTER 35

PHOENIX'S LEAP OF DESPERATION LANDED HIM IN THE RIPPING current of the Unare River. When his feet hit the bottom of the river, he didn't shove off. Instead, he allowed his body to go with the current and prayed the turbid water and the darkness of the night would cover his escape.

Recent torrential rains had caused the river to flood over its banks, and the current surged with debris. Phoenix hoped that if the soldiers above had no target, they would refrain from shooting, but over the roar of the water in his ears, he could hear the rattle of automatic weapons. He figured they were reconning by fire, hoping to strike him and cause him to float to the surface.

The fleeing American twisted his body around, so he floated feet first along the river bottom. While whitewater rafting guides taught their clients to float on the surface and keep their feet up to avoid "foot entrapment," where the foot becomes lodged in debris and traps the rafter underwater, Phoenix wanted to stay underwater for as long as possible, which meant he couldn't see what was coming and brace for impact. Having his feet in front of him gave him a bit of protection, but if he became entangled, he would likely die underwater.

Phoenix's lungs burned from the lack of oxygen. He'd once been able to hold his breath for up to five minutes, but that had been when he was a combat diver in top physical condition. Over the past couple of years, he hadn't had time to maintain peak physical readiness as he would have liked. But he also knew his body and the superhuman feats it was capable of by shutting out the pain and running on instinct alone. And the instinct lodged in his gut told him that for him to stay alive, he had to remain underwater for as long as possible.

Even if it hadn't been almost midnight, Phoenix couldn't see his hand in front of his face in the heavily stained river water, let alone the hands on his Rolex Submariner. He worried the troopers had riddled Blanco's body with bullets for not getting out of the Patrol and wondered if that had been the source of the gunfire he'd heard.

A sudden impact to his chest drove the remaining air from his lungs as Phoenix came to a dead stop. The rush of water pinned him against whatever he'd hit, and if he didn't get free in the next few seconds, he would drown.

Forcing himself to remain calm, Phoenix ran his hands around the obstruction. It was rough to the touch, and he guessed he had struck the trunk of a submerged tree. His feet and hands remained free, and there seemed to be some clearance below the tree trunk. Gambling with his last ounce of strength, Phoenix let his body go limp and slid off the trunk. The water carried him below the tree trunk, his knees and elbows scraping against the smooth rocks on the river bottom.

Gathering his feet beneath him, Phoenix raised his hand above his head to protect it from anything floating on the surface above, then launched himself straight up. His head came out of the water, and he drew in a deep breath before submerging again, still caught in the heavy current.

On his next trip to the surface, Phoenix saw he'd traveled some distance from his entry point. A slight bend in the river would take him out of sight of the troops on the bridge. Phoenix kept his body as submerged as possible, only lifting his head to breathe every thirty seconds or so. Now that his survival didn't depend on the distance he could swim underwater, he relished the luxury of breathing more freely.

Once Phoenix had traveled around a bend in the river and the trees blocked his view of the APC lighting up the bridge, he brought his feet up and floated on his back, letting the surge carry him along.

Out of immediate danger of being shot by the National Guard troops, Phoenix faced a fresh problem. Traveling down the river limited his options for escape. At any moment, the guard troops could pull up on the bank and begin shooting at him again.

With that thought in mind, Phoenix knew he had to get out of the water and start making his way overland. Once again, the SEBIN had exposed his cover, and Phoenix didn't want to risk the lives of Ramesh or his contact in Puerto de Hierro by going there. Remembering the conversation he'd had with the two sailboat cruisers in Chaguaramas while awaiting Ramesh's arrival at the marina, Phoenix decided his best option was to get to the coast and steal a boat.

But first, he had to get out of the river. With scant moonlight to see by, he could barely make out the trees along the bank. He kept his feet up and spread his arms, using his hands like rudders to angle his body toward shore. Visualizing the map he'd memorized, Phoenix knew that all roads on the west bank led to Troncal 9, so he steered for the east bank, hoping to steal a vehicle at one of the small farms nearby. He realized that stealing a vehicle from these poor farmers would probably set them back a few decades, but it was their livelihood or his life. Phoenix chose his own life.

It took several minutes for him to maneuver closer to the

bank, and then he had to swim the last couple of yards into the trees to where the water was still knee-deep. He waded through the water, shuffling his feet to prevent himself from tripping over hidden debris or stepping in a hole that might twist his ankle or, worse, break his leg.

After wading a good ten meters, Phoenix finally stepped onto dry ground and began moving parallel through the trees. His first objective was to find transportation.

Thankfully, a sliver of a moon lit the path on his hike. He passed several houses, but they were all a good distance from the river, and he was loath to strike out overland in the darkness for fear of running across National Guard troops or local police units he knew were probably out searching for him.

Approximately a kilometer down the riverbank, Phoenix came to a farmhouse with several large barns. The overflowing river lapped at the low fence that enclosed their backyard. A dog barked and darted off the back porch toward a gate at the rear of the fence. Phoenix stepped behind a tree and used it as a cover to observe the property. When no one appeared at the back door of the house, he figured the occupants were asleep or not at home. Since the fence kept the dog corralled, Phoenix made for the largest of the barns.

He was about to step into the pitch blackness of the barn's interior when Phoenix felt the muzzle of a double-barrel shotgun press into his belly. A voice growled out of the darkness. "You better run, mister. If you're the one the police are looking for, I don't have a problem shooting a trespasser."

Phoenix backed cautiously away. While Venezuela had confiscated guns from registered owners, there were still plenty of weapons to go around. This farmer had obviously chosen not to adhere to the letter of the law to better protect his property.

"I need a ride to the nearest town," Phoenix said, throwing up his hands involuntarily.

"You better start walking," the voice said aggressively. "My truck broke down last night."

Phoenix backed up a few steps, then turned and headed into the trees along the river again. He glanced over his shoulder once, but he could see nothing but the dark outline of the building with a darker opening where the farmer probably still tracked him with the scattergun. From what the man had said, Phoenix guessed the police had already been there, and the case officer had been lucky to make it out alive.

Moving quickly through the brush, Phoenix followed the horseshoe bend of the river and had to climb over several fences to continue his journey. He acutely felt the pressure of time. The longer he was on the run along the river, the easier it would be for the cops and soldiers to track him down.

When a dirt road came close to the river, Phoenix struck out along it, figuring he could make better time jogging on the road than traipsing through the trees. He had just come to an abandoned building and started searching the interior for weapons or a vehicle when a police car pulled up in front, lights shining straight inside. Cursing his luck, Phoenix climbed into the building's rafters, dislodging a pigeon into the air and getting bird shit on his hands.

The cops walked into the building with their guns drawn, having apparently seen his silhouette in their headlights. Phoenix crouched on the rafter and prayed the ancient wood wouldn't give way beneath him. Then, the shaky truss creaked and splintered with a loud crack, spilling the American spy onto the hard-packed earth below.

Turning to see what the commotion was about, the cops trained their guns on Phoenix and ordered him not to move. From the pain flaring through his body, Phoenix wondered if he even could. Lying on his back, Phoenix mustered his reserves as he waited for them to cuff him.

As the first cop moved in, Phoenix whipped his legs around and caught the man in the side of the knee, knocking him off his feet. The second cop charged in as Phoenix tried to get up off the ground, and he kicked the CIA officer square in the ribs. Grunting with pain, Phoenix rolled across the floor and came back to his knees, straining to his feet as the cop closed in on him again, gun up and ready.

Phoenix grabbed the man's pistol by the barrel and pushed it up and away, feeling the heat of the triggered round seer through the steel. With his hand locked around the slide, it prevented the gun from cycling a new round into the chamber. As the cop continued to pull the useless trigger, Phoenix punched the man in the throat. The blow crushed the cop's trachea, and he immediately let go of his gun to clutch his throat, falling to the ground as he struggled to breathe.

As Phoenix spun the gun in his hand to grip it properly, another shot rang out. He dove for the ground as a third gunshot thundered inside the building, reverberating off the concrete block walls. Phoenix rolled behind the cop he'd punched in the throat to use him as cover from the first cop, who was lying on his back with his arms extended and gun between his knees. Another shot streaked overhead and hit the wall, showering Phoenix with dust and tiny shards of cement that stung the back of his neck.

Wiggling forward, Phoenix brought up the Glock 19 he'd confiscated off the cop and cycled the action to let the slide ram a fresh round into the chamber. Thrusting the gun out, he snapped off two quick shots, knowing he needed to end the fight as soon as possible and get on the move before more cops showed up.

Phoenix's first shot struck his attacker in the leg, and the man howled with pain. The wounded cop hammered his trigger and emptied the rest of his magazine. Most of the shots went wide, but one struck his partner in the head, exploding blood and brain matter all over Phoenix's face. He wiped away the gore with his free hand and rose to his knees, shooting the cop dead as the man attempted to reload his gun.

After removing the uniform top from the cop he'd punched in the throat, Phoenix ripped off the man's undershirt and used it to wipe away the dead man's blood and brain matter from his face. As clean as he could make himself without a mirror, he tossed the shirt away and liberated two extra magazines from the man's duty belt. Phoenix dumped his partially used mag on the ground and replenished his Glock. He patted both cops down and found the keys to their cruiser and a usable cell phone.

Before entering the barn, Phoenix's clothes had been soaked from his swim in the river, and now dust and dirt covered them from rolling around on the ground. His hand still smelled like bird shit and his back ached from the hard landing after the rafter had given way, but he now had a gun and a vehicle. He shrugged into the least bloody police uniform shirt and buttoned it up, then climbed behind the wheel of the JAC J6 pickup truck and started the engine.

The patrol vehicle had an excellent GPS unit, and Phoenix used it to locate his position. To the north of him, road crews were constructing what appeared to be a new bypass for Troncal 9. He figured traveling up the unpaved road would be the best way to avoid traffic.

With one more glance at the barn to ensure the cops hadn't moved, Phoenix put the truck in gear and headed out into the night.

The GPS unit led him about a kilometer down the road, where he found a dirt access road to the new bypass nearly hidden by a grove of trees. He turned onto the little-used road and headed north, bouncing through the potholes and gunning the motor to help propel him through the heavy mud. After another kilometer, he broke out of the trees that lined the smaller road onto the wider avenue for the soon-to-be four-lane interstate.

Again, the thick mud dragged on the tires, and standing water lay in large puddles in every dip of the road. Fortunately, the JAC truck came equipped with four-wheel drive, a necessity for the many dirt roads traversing Anzoátegui State. Phoenix flipped on every light he could find on the truck, except the red and blues, and kept the pedal to the floor and the transmission in a lower gear so he could quickly build the revs should the truck bog down.

Once or twice, he had to downshift and blast through a large puddle to keep his momentum going. Still, he made excellent time traveling along the unimproved road, buoying his hopes of getting out of Venezuela alive.

CHAPTER 36

Around three a.m., Phoenix dumped the police truck in a lot near the Barcelona International Airport as a Sukhoi Su-30 Flanker fighter jet streaked overhead. The airport was also the home to a fighter wing, reminding Phoenix that a heavy military and police presence still surrounded him no matter where he went.

John Phoenix wished he knew how to fly a Sukhoi jet so he could boogie on out of Venezuela in style. He tossed the police uniform shirt into the cab of the truck but kept the Glock under his T-shirt at the small of his back and the extra mags and the police badge in his pocket. The contents of his money belt were still soaking wet, and his CIA-issued cell phone had long stopped functioning after its river bath. He clung to it anyhow, wanting to take the tech out of the country lest it fall into the wrong hands. The geeks at DS&T had encased the SD card compartment in the spy pen in a waterproof capsule to keep it dry, and Phoenix wasn't about to open it. He'd let the DS&T guys have that honor.

While his clothes had dried somewhat during his drive to Barcelona, they remained damp and chaffed at his thighs and armpits as he walked. Part of the reason he'd dumped the truck at the airport was so that he might catch a cab, but he wondered if there were any running at this early hour of the morning. To answer his unspoken question, a cabbie snapped his headlights on and then headed Phoenix's way. The cab pulled alongside Phoenix as he was just about to raise his arm to hail it.

Once seated inside, Phoenix asked the man to take him to a scuba diving resort he'd spotted on the truck's GPS unit along the El Morro River canal. He'd decided his best bet was to find a boat there since Lecheria, a resort suburb sandwiched between the cities of Barcelona and Puerto La Cruz, had large recreational yacht clubs and ferry services to and from the islands just offshore. If nothing else, he could catch a ride to Margarita Island and then figure out his next move from there.

"The shop won't be open at this time of the morning," the cabbie stated.

"But it will be in a few hours," Phoenix replied. "Just take me there."

Now, in the cab, the exhaustion from the long day kicked in, and Phoenix had trouble keeping his eyes open. He concentrated on the scene at the bridge to keep himself awake. Something nagged at him about the death of Coralina Blanco. He had charged himself with keeping her safe, and he'd failed. There was an ache in his heart and his shoulder. He wanted to punch something but kept his cool around the cabbie. Two dead cops didn't seem like an even trade for the life of a woman he'd fallen for.

After arriving at the dive shop, Phoenix paid the cabbie with wet Bolívars and then climbed out. Once he saw the cabbie had turned around, Phoenix headed for the dive shop. As the cabbie had said, a closed sign hung in the window, and no lights were on inside the shop.

But glancing around, Phoenix saw he'd picked the right spot to go boat shopping. The dive shop sat at the edge of

Marina Américo Vespucio, which Phoenix figured they'd named after the avenue that ended in a roundabout where the cab had dropped him off. The marina complex consisted of a rectangular basin where boats floated alongside finger piers, dry boat storage and repair facilities, and an office complex that housed a small convenience store, a restaurant, and a nightclub.

Walking along the El Morro River Canal, Phoenix observed more marinas, boat rental services, and tour agencies. As he searched for a boat, he wanted desperately to call Headquarters just to hear Connelly's soothing voice. Yet, he also dreaded making the call, believing she would see right through him and the feelings he'd developed for Coralina Blanco—God rest her soul. The last update he'd sent via the Signal app had been just before leaving Caracas last evening, informing Connelly of his decision to stage the money in Acevedo's apartment and the arrival of the SEBIN director.

Phoenix tried to look the part of a wealthy tourist out for a stroll, but he was tired, his clothes were wet and dirty, his ears still rang from the gunfight in the enclosed building, and his heart ached for Coralina Blanco and the misery he'd brought to her short life. All she'd wanted was to leave Venezuela with her family. Phoenix chastised himself for not taking her out on the plane when he and his team had taken off from Ciudad Piar. He could have saved her life then, but he'd left her to fend for herself, and now she was dead.

"Don't play this game, John," he whispered to himself as he walked. "You both knew the consequences."

Phoenix refocused his thoughts on the job at hand—finding the perfect boat. One of the massive sportfishers would be nice since it was a forty-six-hundred-kilometer run to Bonaire. He could travel in style and luxury, but a smaller craft with twin outboards and a T-top would do just as nicely.

As if to answer his prayers, Phoenix spotted a newer model Cobia 35 center console with twin Yamaha 425XTOs on the stern. It sat on the far side of a larger sportfisher, which perfectly blocked the view of anyone watching from the office or the mainland. Phoenix stepped down into the boat and used his pocketknife to jimmy the lock on a compartment under the steering wheel. The compartment door flopped open, exposing the wiring he needed to hotwire the boat. He popped the wiring off the ignition switches for the engines one at a time, stripped them with his knife, and then touched the ends of the bare wires together.

Nothing happened.

Disgruntled with himself for not checking the batteries first, Phoenix went to the rear of the boat and lifted the hatches to find them. The owner had installed knife switches to prevent the batteries from draining, feeding power only to the bilge pumps. Once Phoenix engaged the battery switches, the Yamaha outboards fired right up.

The American thief took a moment to power up the giant Garmin GPS units. Once everything had come online, he cast off the bow and stern lines, then engaged the throttles. The big center console rammed hard against the sportfisher before Phoenix could steady the wheel. It had been a long time since he'd driven a boat, and most of them had been small rubber raiding crafts not nearly as large as the Cobia.

Idling out of the marina, Phoenix followed the canal toward the protected harbor entrance to the Caribbean Sea. He passed a maze of small housing complexes, marinas, and individual boat slips. Many of the hotels showed signs of neglect, with long grass growing in their yards. Most buildings needed a fresh coat of paint. Phoenix even passed half-sunken boats still moored to the piers, their hulls delaminating and their tenders deteriorating with age.

He tapped the glass over the electronic fuel gauge. It read half full. To avoid drawing any more attention to himself by stopping for fuel, he decided to head for Gran Roque, an island that sat halfway between himself and Bonaire. Phoenix was confident he would find fuel for the boat, food for his belly, and a place to rest his weary bones in the tourist town.

Once he reached open water, Phoenix followed the information the owner had written in his logbook and set the throttles to four thousand RPM, ensuring maximum efficiency from the engines. The case officer yawned and settled back into his seat after setting the boat's autopilot for Gran Roque.

He was finally on his way home.

CHAPTER 37

SEBIN Headquarters
Caracas, Venezuela

Venezuelan Vice President Evelyn Acevedo found Director General Hector Caldron staring out the window of his top-floor office that overlooked downtown Caracas. He wore a dark blue Dolce & Gabbana suit with a crisp black shirt and a matching tie as he stood with a glass of gin in his hand.

A little over sixteen hours had elapsed since Acevedo had found a satchel full of American greenbacks in her desk drawer. After her brief rooftop meeting with Calderón, she had packed half the money into a bag and taken it to the personal residence of the director of the University Hospital of Caracas. She had handed him the money and told him to use it as he wished. When the man had asked how she had gotten her hands on so much cash, she'd politely told him it was a donation from an anonymous source and not to ask any more questions. Grateful, he accepted the gift and assured Acevedo he'd put it to good use at the hospital.

Even though many now considered Acevedo a member of the "bolibourgeoisie"—a term coined by journalist Juan Carlos Zapata to define the corrupt Venezuelans who funneled billions of dollars out of government coffers for their own private use under the guise of socialism—she hated being a part of it. Seeing Calderón in a three-thousand-dollar suit turned her stomach, and she seethed over the cost of the fabric when so many people were starving on the streets.

Sadly, she had seen the same thing on the streets of Washington, D.C. Power brokers in thousand-dollar suits strutted past beggars on the sidewalks who rattled their change cups for just a pittance of what those men carried in their pockets.

Long ago, Acevedo had determined that the world was the same no matter which end of the political spectrum one stood. Capitalists raised themselves up on the backs of others, and dictators suppressed their people to remain in power. Everything boiled down to those two things: money and power. When she'd worked with the CIA, Acevedo had quickly come to realize they'd only wanted to maintain the foreign investment interests of capitalist businessmen in the United States in whatever corner of the world they'd chosen to invest. And she was loath to go back to work for them, which was why she had called Calderón about the money.

He seemed disinterested in a quarter of a million dollars, which was a mere drop in the bucket for someone with his hands in the pocket of the PDVSA. One didn't rise to be the director of the SEBIN without being Zarate's crony and enjoying the perks that came with the job. Acevedo could also dip into the funds, but she held herself to a higher standard. In a true socialist society, the government would redistribute the money to every individual in the country. No one would be above the station or wealth of another. But she also knew that was just a pipe dream Marx had shared with the world.

The reality was often very different. The elite at the top always benefited at their people's expense.

If allowed to become president of Venezuela, Acevedo had a laundry list of improvements to transform the country into the mighty power it once had been in the 1970s and early 80s. Yet, as VP, Zarate had only tasked her with minor projects and saddled her with the upcoming summit in Mexico City.

"The problem we face is that spies are still infiltrating our country," Calderón said while still staring out the window. Acevedo had to drag herself back to the present to focus on what he was saying. "The man who planted the money in your apartment is a CIA officer. His name is John Phoenix, but he goes by the codename, Bowie."

"How do you know that?" Acevedo asked.

"I have my sources within the U.S. government and a local source who knows Phoenix intimately, you might say."

Acevedo cocked her head, not understanding the director's meaning.

"We have an opportunity, Evelyn," Calderón stated.

"How so?" she asked.

Instead of answering her question, Calderón asked one of his own. "Do you know why I fought for you to become vice president?"

Acevedo shook her head, trying to understand exactly what Caldron was talking about.

"Our country is in disarray. Our president is the best there ever will be. However, there is always room for improvement."

Acevedo wondered if Calderón suspected Zarate had planted listening devices in his office or if the man spouted platitudes out of habit. She reached forward to the desk for pen and paper and scribbled a note to that effect.

"No," Calderón stated. "I sweep it daily, but we did find bugs in your apartment. We recovered some of the American's gear from the vehicle he'd been driving. My techs correlated it to a listening device in your office, placed, I assume, to record your reaction to finding the money in your desk."

Acevedo felt angry and vulnerable that someone had creeped her apartment.

"The other listening device we found belongs to a man we know as Terry Martin. He is also a CIA asset, but one with a dubious track record of aiding terrorists and selling his services to the highest bidder. He provided us with the information to hunt down the CIA operatives in our country. Despite his assurances to the contrary, I have long suspected that he is playing us for nothing more than money."

"What are we going to do about it?" Acevedo asked the spy chief.

Calderón sipped his gin, drawing out the moment, before saying, "We are going to play a very dangerous game."

"What do you mean?" the vice president asked, her interest piqued.

"Martin has assets within our government and military that he relies upon. He has brainwashed some to act as double agents." Calderón held up a finger to stave off Acevedo's question. "Meaning Martin has resources feeding him information from all sides. Not only will we be threading the needle to ensure he does not find out what we're doing, but *El Jefe* must never know either. If you play the game with me, Evelyn, they will consider us traitors if we fail and heroes akin to Simón Bolívar if we succeed."

"What do you have in mind, Director?" Acevedo asked.

The corner of Calderón's mouth rose in a smile as he turned to face her and said simply, "Revolution."

CHAPTER 38

Two days later
Moody Air Force Base
Valdosta, Georgia

"All right, you big corn-fed ape, we're coming over the target again. Let's see if you can actually hit something this time," Colonel Ceasar "Salad" Romano said from the backseat of the U.S. Air Force training plane, an AT-802U Sky Warden, one of the first of seventy-five planes that U.S. Special Operations Command had ordered.

Will Pounder knew the controls of the Sky Warden intimately, as Air Tractor-L3Harris had built the warplane on the same platform as his old crop duster. The key differences between his crop duster and the plane he flew now were that he had old Ceasar Salad yacking in his ear, bomb pylons on the wings equipped with dummy bombs, and armored windows restricting his view. Pounder had already pickled two bombs and had come up short of the target. He concentrated on the sight as he flew, training it on the ground target.

As he zoomed overhead, Pounder hit the release button on his stick to drop the remaining bombs.

He felt the plane jerk as the load came off the wings, but he held it steady, and the bombs flew true. Once he was off the bomb run, Pounder pulled the stick back and drove the plane straight up into the sky until he felt the engine stall, then tipped the Sky Warden over on one wing and flew straight for the target again.

"What the hell are you doing, Pounder?" the colonel barked from the backseat.

"Just having some fun, sir. Keep your pee in your bladder." Pounder could see the dummy bombs lying almost dead center of the target zone. He flicked the switch to activate the machine guns mounted in each wing and sent a stream of lead into the target, hitting the dummy bombs and making them skitter along the ground. Letting off the trigger, Pounder kept diving until he was just fifty feet above the ground before he pulled back on the stick.

"Land this plane immediately!" Romano screamed into the radio.

Pounder popped the plane over the trees and aligned himself with the flight path, calling the tower to let them know he was inbound. Moments later, he was on the ground, taxiing toward the hangar where the 81st Fighter Squadron had based their operations.

The 81st had a long history as a training command, dating back to World War II when they had flown P-40 Warhawks. Converting to F-4 Phantoms in 1973, the 81st flew them until 1994 before swapping the obsolete fighters for A-10 Warthogs. When the Air Force pulled the last of the A-10s out of Europe, they deactivated the 81st.

As the War on Terror heated up, the U.S. needed to train Afghani pilots to fly the A-29 Super Tucanos they'd purchased for the Afghanistan Air Force. So they had reactivated the 81st Fighter Squadron at Moody AFB.

Between October 2014 and November 2020, the squadron had trained thirty pilots and seventy maintenance techs, but President Brandon had allowed the Taliban to regain control of Afghanistan, and the entire training effort had been for naught. The 81st had then trained personnel from the Nigerian Air Force on the Super Tucano before being deactivated again in December 2022.

With President Mercia's order to help train and equip the Guyanese military, the Air Force had once again stood up the 81st, quickly reestablishing the training command by pulling past pilots, maintainers, and administrative personnel from other billets. They had even hired civilian pilots and mechanics from Sierra Nevada Corporation, the builder of the Super Tucano in the United States, to help expedite the needs of the Guyanese mercenary force now known as the Flying Jaguars after the national animal of Guyana.

Newly minted "Lieutenant" William Pounder of the Guyana Defence Force brought the Sky Warden to a stop under the metal awning that shaded the flight line and shut down the engine. He still wore a big grin at having been able to unleash some creative control over the rigorous training, but he knew he'd overstepped the boundaries with his trainer.

Romano tilted the canopy out of the way and climbed down from the cockpit. Pounder could practically see the steam rolling out of the man's ears. He stepped out onto the port wing and then used the step on the landing gear to lower himself to the ground, helmet in hand.

Once both men had descended from the aircraft, the colonel wheeled on his student in front of a group of ground maintainers and other pilots, including Steve Gruber. "Your flying was completely unacceptable up there. This ain't the fucking movies, and you ain't Tom Fucking Cruise. Between your propensity for fat chicks and your inability to do anything right, you're just one big fucking dumpster fire. If I had my way, I'd bust your ass out of here so fast it would make your head spin."

Pounder tried to keep a straight face, but the guys behind Ceasar Salad had cracked up with laughter, and Pounder found it contagious. While Romano was commanding officer of the 81st and a fount of knowledge about the Super Tucano, Pounder had a tough time taking the man seriously. A guy named "Salad" reminded Pounder of the Presto SaladShooter his mom used to have at home. Then the old Veg-O-Matic TV commercial trope popped into his head, and he mentally modified it to, "He slices, he dices … but wait, there's more! He flies in from the sky!"

When Pounder didn't respond to Colonel Romano's tirade, the CO turned and stalked toward the hangar. Pounder began walking around the Sky Warden, doing his usual post-flight checks ingrained in him since he'd first gotten his private pilot's license.

"What was that about?" Gruber asked, stepping over to speak privately with Pounder.

"I deviated from the flight plan," Pounder replied simply.

"You might want to start taking this seriously, Will. This is the opportunity of a lifetime. I don't want you to blow it."

Pounder sighed and nodded. "I got out of the Army because I got tired of being told what to do all the time. I guess it's the rebellious streak in me."

"That streak makes you a great pilot," Gruber stated, "but you gotta temper it with the ability to take instruction."

"Yeah. I get it," Pounder said.

One of the maintenance crewmen walked over and said, "Hey, Dumpster. Do you want us to load her up again, or are you done for the day?"

"Dumpster?" Pounder asked.

The crewman laughed. "Yeah. Short for Dumpster Fire."

"Fuck!" Pounder muttered. He preferred being called

Fatty by his old Airborne buddies, but when someone hung a call sign on a pilot, it generally stuck.

On his way to the hangar for the flight debrief, Pounder made the mistake of handing off his survival gear and helmet to a rigger. Before the end of the day, the rigger would stencil "Dumpster" on Pounder's helmet.

Pounder pushed through the door to the flight-ready room and came face to face with his superior from Guyana, Colonel Jorge Mansoor, a short, wiry Black man raised on the banks of the Essequibo River where his parents still worked the Omai Gold Mine. Unsatisfied with the backbreaking labor, Mansoor had joined the military and had distinguished himself enough to attend officer school in Great Britain, where he'd learned to fly. His time overseas had left him with a bit of a British accent. While Mansoor held qualifications to fly all four types of prop planes in the GDF's arsenal, he was not an A-29 driver. He was undergoing the same training as the rest of the new recruits.

"Colonel Mansoor." Pounder came to attention and saluted.

"At ease, Lieutenant," Mansoor replied, placing his hands behind his back. "Are you having trouble settling in?"

"No, sir."

"Then why am I hearing disreputable reports from the training cadre?"

"Sir, I was overzealous and showing off."

Mansoor nodded, taking in Pounder's report of his actions.

"You served in the Army, is that correct?" Mansoor asked.

"Yes, sir," Pounder replied. "I was a sergeant in the 82nd Airborne."

Mansoor nodded appreciatively. "Then you understand the need for professionalism."

"I do, sir," Pounder replied.

"Excellent," Colonel Mansoor replied. "One more bad fit rep, and you'll be on your way home. Understood?"

"Yes, sir!" Pounder enthused.

He would straighten up and literally "fly right" because he loved flying, and the thought of doing it in combat exhilarated him. Pounder had been doing his homework in his downtime, reading up on the National Bolivarian Armed Forces of Venezuela, and he knew that while the Venezuelans mostly had a fleet of aging fighter jets for air dominance and ground combat support, they also had a large fleet of prop planes they used as transports.

While not designed for air-to-air combat, the Super Tucano could undoubtedly handle a fat C-130 Hercules or Dornier 228, and he planned to sneak up on one of them and blow it out of the sky.

They can call me Ace *Dumpster.*

Five kills made a pilot an ace, and Pounder planned to put a hash mark on the side of his Super Tucano to signify everyone he downed.

"Now that we've come to an understanding, Lieutenant, I want to ask you about your experience in the Sky Warden. I understand you flew the civilian version as a crop duster?"

"Yes, sir. That was my job back in Kansas."

"Is it as good a plane as the Air Force thinks?"

"I believe it will be beloved by our troops, sir. It has plenty of ISR capabilities, a six-hour loiter time, and can carry plenty of bombs and ammunitions."

Mansoor nodded. "I feel you might offer valuable insight into the flight characteristics of a prop plane. Many of your fellow squadron mates are commercial jet pilots and haven't flown a prop plane in years, let alone down and dirty like you have. I'm not asking you to take the place of the training cadre, as they have this training down to a science."

Pounder seemed a little confused. "I'm not following you, sir."

"I've been observing you, Pounder—the rest of the new pilots as well. You're a man of action. You're an excellent pilot. A natural if I've ever seen one, and you have a certain leadership quality that I believe you should harness." Mansoor sighed. "Let me put it bluntly for you, Lieutenant. We might not have a year to train these men. If the war starts, I believe we'll have to battle with the army we have, not the army we want. You're going to be one of the first men I send."

Pounder felt a flush of adrenaline course through his system, and the hairs on his arms and neck stood on end. He'd be first in the fight if he played his cards right. Not knowing what else to say, he replied, "Thank you, sir."

"I don't want you to thank me, Lieutenant. I want you to prove my thinking to be correct. Adhere to the training schedule and listen to your instructors. When the time for war comes, we'll all benefit from the discipline, but there's always room for rogue pilots. Do you know of Gregory "Pappy" Boyington?"

"He was a Marine Corps aviator, sir. He led the Black Sheep squadron during the liberation of the Pacific in World War II until the Japs shot him down and captured him."

Mansoor nodded. "He won your country's Medal of Honor, a Navy Cross, and many other awards. Boyington was a hero and a legend who frequently defied his commanding officers, but his excellent results speak for themselves. And he's credited with shooting down twenty-eight planes. What I'm saying to you is that we need the same fighting spirit Pappy Boyington had—tempered by excellent tactics and doctrine, of course."

"Understood, sir."

"Now. Colonel Romano would like to speak to you. And for your sake, might I suggest contrition."

"Yes, sir. Thank you for the pep talk, sir."

Colonel Mansoor patted his younger pilot on the shoulder on his way out of the room. Pounder waited a few moments, then exited the ready room and headed for the Colonel's office. He knocked on the ante-room door, and a second lieutenant let Pounder in. "He said for you to wait in his office."

Pounder stepped into the room and stood at attention. Normally, an office like this would have photos and awards covering the walls—the typical "I love me" wall—but Romano's office lacked any decorations, except for a computer on the desk and a model of an in-flight Super Tucano on a pedestal.

The clock on the wall loudly ticked off the seconds as Lieutenant Pounder waited for his ass chewing. After a few minutes, Pounder relaxed his posture. He strained to hear any sound indicating Colonel Salad Shooter was on his way into the office.

When Romano entered the anteroom, he commented to the second lieutenant, loud enough for Pounder to hear, that Pounder had picked up a new call sign based on the ass chewing he'd given him on the parking ramp. The two men laughed. Pounder seethed inside as he came back to attention, ready to tell Salad to get tossed, but then he remembered his conversation with Mansoor. He wanted to be the first to fight. Mansoor had recommended contrition, and Pounder would just be one contrite motherfucker.

Colonel Romano opened the door and then slammed it so hard that it felt like the entire building would fall down around them. Romano stalked around to his desk, started to sit, then rose back to his full height—a little less than Pounder's six feet—and came back around the desk to get into Pounder's face.

"I understand you already talked to Colonel Mansoor. He sees something in you that I don't get. You're a cowboy, and I don't like cowboys in my unit. If I had my way, I'd send you packing right now, Pounder. You can go back to Iowa and dust crops."

"Kansas, sir," Pounder responded automatically.

"What the fuck did you just say to me?" Romano said, bowing out his chest as he stood toe to toe with Pounder.

"If you're going to insult me, at least get your facts straight, *sir*." Pounder barked out the last word for effect. All thoughts of contrition had disappeared out the window.

"I haven't begun to insult you, Pounder. In fact, I think you're living up to my previous statement. You are a living, breathing dumpster fire, and you're going to crash and burn. If you somehow, by a miracle of our Creator, make it through my course and into battle, God help us all, Pounder, because you're going to get someone killed."

At the reminder that he would be first to fight, Pounder decided to shut up and take the verbal beating. He knew he deserved it for going rogue on the training course and correcting the colonel had not been the brightest of his ideas.

"You're walking a thin line, Lieutenant. You screw up again, and you *will* be going home. Back to Kansas, Dorothy."

Pounder breathed a sigh of relief. *Thank God he didn't utter that statement on the flight line. I'd be Will* Dorothy *Pounder. I'll take Dumpster any day.*

Romano stepped to the window to stare out at the flight line, hands clasped behind his back. "Tomorrow, we'll receive our first A-29, and I'll never know why the saints have blessed you, but Colonel Mansoor wants you to be the first to fly it."

Again, Pounder kept his scathing retort about being a superior pilot to himself and mentally noted that Mansoor knew the best when he saw the best.

"So, we're going to see what you can do in a Super Tucano," Romano said. "And God help me; I'm going to be riding in the backseat. I want to see if you really are the best, Pounder, or if you're just another smoking dumpster fire that we'll have to put out after you auger in." He turned to face Pounder and shouted, "Now, get *the fuck* out of my office!"

Without hesitation, Pounder snapped off a crisp salute, executed a perfect about-face, and exited the office.

As he walked across the hangar deck, someone yelled in a mocking joke to the movie *Top Gun*, "Hey Dumpster, your ego is writing checks your body can't cash!"

Pounder held his middle finger aloft for all to see and then headed for the ready room to check the flight schedule.

Let them laugh and joke. Tomorrow, I'll be flying a Super Tucano.

CHAPTER 39

Lieutenant Luis del Valle García Air Base
Barcelona, Venezuela

Colonel Carlos Xavier climbed into his Su-30 Flanker fighter jet and ran his hands over the flight control surfaces in reverence and delight.

It had been months since he'd been inside a Flanker cockpit and even longer since he'd flown one of them. After a Flanker crashed during an airshow in July, the overly cautious generals in Caracas had decided to ground the fleet and only fly the planes when necessary. Xavier relished the feel of the cockpit—the coolness of the metal, the soft click of the rubber-covered switches, and the smoothness of the worn plastic grip of the control stick. Then there was the ever-present smell of jet fuel, which to Xavier was as pleasant as the smell of frying bacon was to a cook. He pulled the safety harness around his G-suit and buckled himself in. Wiggling against the belts to get them as tight as possible, Xavier prayed this flight would end as safely as all his others.

As commanding officer of Air Hunting Group 13, Xavier had chosen himself to fly this mission and then let the other pilots draw straws for the other three planes in their covert-action flight. The four planes were among the only operational units of the eleven jets that made up their squadron.

Unfortunately, the Russians had been slacking in their maintenance agreement as they tended to the war in Ukraine. Out of twenty-two fighter jets in Venezuela's Flanker fleet, only twelve were flight-worthy, and this concerned Xavier to no end. He'd lobbied his generals to bring the Russians back to Venezuela to provide maintenance and technical support for the jets they'd sold them, but Russia had its own problems, and Venezuela hadn't purchased the technical support package offered by the Sukhoi factory.

"We ready, Bobby?" he asked his crew chief, who stood on the ladder outside the cockpit.

"Yes, sir. I made sure to service and fuel the aircraft fully, and I personally pulled all the pins on the ordnance."

"You're a good man, Sergeant."

Bobby saluted. "Have a safe flight, sir."

Xavier saluted back and then pressed the button to lower the canopy. Today, in addition to his normal load of 150 auto-cannon rounds, he carried two Kh-29 air-to-surface missiles and two KAB-1500L laser-guided bombs. Others in his flight carried cluster bombs and air-to-air missiles should they encounter hostiles during their flight. He didn't expect a midair dogfight since Guyana had no fighter jets. The only aircraft equipped with any weapon in their meager fleet was an old Huey with a machine gun mounted in the door. It didn't matter if the Guyanese had aircraft to scramble anyway, as his jets would be in and out of Guyana before the GDF could muster a response.

Once all the other pilots were in their Flankers, Xavier started his preflight checks and then switched on his batteries.

He lit the fires on both turbofan engines and scanned the gauges as the engines came up to temperature.

Moments later, Colonel Xavier checked in with his other pilots via radio. They, too, were online and ready to fly. After wiggling his control stick again to ensure his flight surfaces moved freely, Xavier released the brakes and began taxiing toward the runway. Their military base sat on the western side of Barcelona International Airport, so Xavier and his flight had to roll past a waiting passenger jetliner to get to the end of the runway. Once there, the four jets received priority clearance from the control tower and went to full power. The four Sukhoi Flankers raced down the runway and sprang into the air.

Turning his craft to the east over the sparkling blue of the Caribbean Sea, Xavier checked his navigation equipment and the GPS coordinates preset into the mission computer. Today's target was Base Camp Seweyo near Low Wood, Guyana, approximately forty miles south of Georgetown. According to the information on his screen, it was just 951 kilometers to the target—less than an hour of flight time with the cruise set on Mach One.

Xavier glanced out of the canopy to find his jets had assembled correctly into a figure-four formation. As element leader, Xavier was to the rear left of the flight leader, Major Suarez, and on Suarez's rear right was the second element, comprised of two jets flown by First Lieutenants Infante and Nicodemo.

Formed up, Suarez led them into a turn to the southeast, leaving the Caribbean behind and clearing the Venezuelan Coastal Mountain Range, then dropping low to the carpet of green treetops spread out over the Orinoco River Delta. Suarez had carefully chosen their flight path as the area below them was less populated than the Essequibo Region of Guyana. Dense rainforest and low swampy ground made building roads through the thick jungle difficult, leaving Guyana open and vulnerable to attack.

The flight's mission was to exact revenge for the sinking of the PC-21 *Guaiqueri*. The signature on Xavier's orders had been from *El Jefe* himself, Michel Zarate.

It didn't take the flight of Sukhoi Flankers long to cover the distance to the Guyanese base camp that had recently hosted Tradewinds 2023, a multinational military exercise led by U.S. forces to support security and training for Central American and Caribbean countries.

Xavier figured that President Fredricks was plotting an attack on his homeland, so Xavier had no qualms in dropping bombs on the putrid little turds who'd fired the first shots in a war he had prayed would happen during his lifetime. Despite Venezuela's lack of maintenance on their military equipment, they were still a superior fighting force with better equipment and more troops than Guyana could ever hope to muster. Xavier had always wanted to test his mettle in combat, and while it wasn't a dogfight as every jet pilot prayed for, leading this flight was the opportunity of his career.

The mission computer on the dash of Xavier's cockpit flashed, showing they were only fifty kilometers from their target. He flipped the switch to arm his weapons and advised his colleagues to do the same, even though he knew they had received the same warning on the computers in their aircraft.

"All right, boys, let's light them up," Xavier said.

The second element peeled off and circled around to come in behind the first element. Flying on Major Suarez's wingtip, Xavier lined up his aircraft with a visual sighting of Base Camp Seweyo and then locked his laser-guided bombs on the headquarters building nestled in a group of trees.

On the ground, Guyana Defence Force personnel stopped to stare up at the rapidly approaching planes. Some ran, hoping to escape the coming conflagration, while others appeared to be frozen in place, marveling at the approach of the high-speed jets.

"Sweet dreams, assholes," Xavier whispered as he pickled off his bombs. He saw Suarez do the same an instant before him, and once they were clear of the target, they pulled back on their controls and climbed into the sky.

Out over the frothing Atlantic, the lead element waited for the second element to join up with them. Once they returned to the figure-four pattern, the four planes commenced a second bombing run over the military base.

From a distance, Xavier could see that his four-ship flight had wrecked Base Camp Seweyo during their first pass over the place. The laser-guided bombs and cluster munitions had destroyed most of the buildings. Fires raged through the trees, devouring the dry wood of the camp's barracks, galley, and muster hall. Dead GDF troops lay strewn across the ground while others who had survived were running for safety. Xavier felt no mercy for the enemy.

With all the destruction, there was no reason for Xavier and his pilots to drop the rest of their ordnance load other than sheer spite. But Xavier gladly locked his Kh-29 missiles onto a burning building and let them fly. The missiles added to the flames and debris scattered about the camp. As the lead element closed in for a battle damage assessment, Xavier stroked the trigger on his GSh-30-1 autocannon and chased a running man through the trees with the massive rounds from his gun. He didn't know if he'd hit the man, but it felt good to fire the gun in anger instead of just clicking the trigger on an empty chamber during practice.

Once the four-ship element had expended all their ordnance on the second pass, the jet fighters headed for their base, assured they had struck a resounding blow in the coming Guyana-Venezuelan War.

CHAPTER 40

The Tomb
Caracas, Venezuela

Venezuelan Special Forces Lieutenant Coralina Blanco tried to open her eyes, but it required too much effort to come fully awake.

A coldness had crept into her bones, and her naked body shivered under the thin white sheet that covered her. Drawing in a breath made her chest ache, and when the putrid stench of body odor and human waste entered her nostrils, she tried to fight down a wave of nausea. She wished she could go back to sleep.

Beneath her was a thin mattress pad, and her arm brushed rough, cold concrete as she moved her hand up to cover her mouth. Vomit rose in her throat, and she turned her body, almost falling off the bunk cast into the prison cell where she now lay.

Rolling made her dizzy, and vomiting made her entire body ache. Blanco curled into a fetal position, trying to ward off the pain and the cold and the questions burning in the back of her mind. Blanco wondered where she was and how she had gotten there. The last thing she truly remembered was the soldiers at the checkpoint opening fire on their Nissan Patrol. She had a vague memory of gripping Bowie's arm and telling him she loved him. Then he'd disappeared, leaving her all alone again.

Bowie. A fresh wave of nausea hit her hard, and she vomited again, spitting out nothing but stomach bile and dry heaving for what seemed like an eternity. When her stomach finally stopped heaving, Blanco drifted into a dream-like state, reliving the past few days with the case officer. She had loved playing the spy game both for and against him. Terry Martin floated into her mind, and she recalled the psychological torture he had inflicted on her after Bowie had first escaped.

Suddenly wide awake, Blanco sat up and jammed her body into the corner of the cell, pulling her legs to her chest and wrapping her arms around them under the sheet. She shivered from the cold and from the memories. Martin had somehow blocked off her feelings for Bowie, but as she sat in the cell, she felt an overwhelming surge of emotion. Bowie thought she was dead, and he was never coming back for her.

Whatever had happened in the Nissan Patrol had flipped the switch in her mind back to before Martin had bent her to his will. Blanco glanced around her cell as if coming out of a daze. The austere concrete room was no larger than three meters by three meters, with a bunk molded into the concrete and a bucket to do her business in. The door was a solid sheet of steel save for a slot cut in just above the floor for passing a food tray and a window higher up with a sliding cover over it. She knew there was no use trying to escape. Blanco had been on the other side of the door as a soldier who had jailed her share of prisoners.

Wherever she was, Blanco knew she was there for the

duration. Unless someone came to rescue her, she felt certain she would die in the cell.

And that thought terrified her.

CHAPTER 41

CIA Headquarters
Langley, Virginia

STANDING IN THE DS&T OFFICE SPACE, JOHN PHOENIX FELT OUT of place in his Brooks Brothers suit and tie. Anytime he rotated back to Washington, he had to wear a monkey suit to work, and he much preferred the relaxed standards of dress he encountered while working in South America, where slacks and guayaberas were the order of the day.

After arriving in Gran Roque, Phoenix called Connelly, ate, slept, and refueled his stolen boat before continuing to Bonaire. Connelly had cleared his way into the Dutch protectorate, and members of the Dutch Caribbean Coast Guard had met him at sea. The coasties had taken control of the stolen Cobia 35 and then whisked Phoenix to the airport, where he'd boarded an awaiting CIA-owned jet bound for D.C.

Now, he and Connelly stood with two DS&T techs as they examined the spy pen Blanco had used to photograph Operation Takeback.

"It looks intact," said the first tech, a bespectacled geek of a man who Phoenix suspected hadn't gotten laid in over a decade.

"I agree. However, you said you got the pen wet?" asked the other tech, a pudgy man going bald on the top of his head.

"I told you I took it for a swim," Phoenix replied, having already gone into depth about what the pen had endured during his escape from Venezuela. "Just open the damned thing already."

"In due time," Tech One said.

Phoenix sighed. If these two useless tools didn't open the pen soon, Phoenix just might choke one of them to death.

Finally, the techs unscrewed the cap and found that water had seeped past the O-ring seal and flooded what should have been a waterproof compartment. Phoenix swore and slammed his fist into the workbench, rattling their equipment and tools.

"Calm down," Tech Two said. "We might recover something from the SD card."

They inserted the card into an air-gapped laptop computer and tried to access the intel. The files were badly corrupted.

"This isn't from water damage," Tech One stated. "We can usually pull some data from a waterlogged SD card."

"What caused it?" Phoenix asked. He had a sinking feeling in his gut that he'd been double-crossed. While he had wanted to trust Blanco, and they'd bonded as lovers, there was something just not quite right about her actions from their meeting in Maracay to her death.

Tech Two stepped over to a magnifying glass on a swiveling arm and snapped on an attached light. He placed the SD card he'd removed from the reader on a gray rubber mat and moved the magnifier closer to the card. "This isn't the SD card we gave you. Did you swap it out?"

"I never opened the pen. After I gave it to Cobra in Maracay, she had it in her possession until she surrendered it at the bridge."

Motioning for Connelly to peer through the magnifying glass, the tech said, "Our card was a black SanDisk that could hold three terabytes of data. This is a commercially available card that will hold only one terabyte."

Perplexed, Phoenix asked more of himself than anyone else, "Why would she swap the card?"

"Anything else?" Connelly asked the tech.

"No, ma'am."

Connelly sent a quick text on her phone and then turned to Phoenix. "Come on, Bowie. Let's go up to my office." Connelly led the way to the door.

Phoenix followed, stepping onto the elevator for the ride up from the basement cavern where the DS&T geeks had been sequestered.

During his time on the boat, fleeing Venezuela, Phoenix had replayed the ambush at the National Guard checkpoint over and over in his mind. There had been three Guardsmen with automatic weapons, yet they had only disabled the vehicle and put one round into Blanco. Phoenix wanted to attribute it to their poor shooting ability and his superior training, but he just couldn't. Then, on the bridge, the troops should have opened fire as soon as they were set, but they had refrained from doing anything until he had gone over the rail into the river. Now, with the wrong SD card in the spy pen, he had the feeling that someone had set him up. The question was, whom? But the why was obvious—the Venezuelans didn't want their battle plans to fall into American hands, and someone knew he worked for the CIA and that Blanco had been helping him.

Standing in the elevator car with Connelly, Phoenix caught a hint of her perfume and noticed the quality of her tailored skirt, blouse, and jacket. Her overall presence reminded Phoenix of why he'd been so attracted to her in the first place and why he still loved her despite the tryst with Coralina Blanco. He restrained himself from complimenting Connelly on her new suit and how nice her ass looked in it.

Nightingale's phone chimed as they were about to step off the elevator onto the floor housing the Latin American Division and Connelly's office. After reading the text, she stopped Phoenix from exiting the car through the open doors.

Pressing the button for the Seventh Floor, she said, "The director wants to see us."

The doors closed, and the elevator rose to the Seventh Floor. Connelly led the way to the director's office, and the executive assistant buzzed them right in as if he knew Cole Stratten expected them at any moment.

Stratten rose from behind his desk, greeted Connelly with a smile, and shook Phoenix's hand. "I've heard good things about your work in South America."

"Thank you, sir," Phoenix replied. He wanted to say it wasn't all sunshine and roses, and allowing his asset to get killed certainly wasn't anything to brag about. In reality, his entire mission had failed. He'd lost Blanco, hadn't recovered the plans, and Acevedo hadn't returned to the CIA fold.

"Tell me about the intelligence you brought back," Stratten said.

"There is none," Phoenix replied. Stratten's brow furrowed as the case officer continued. "Someone switched the SD cards, so I don't even know if my asset photographed the plans."

"How well did you know this asset?" Stratten asked.

"I've only been her handler for a few days," Phoenix responded.

"What was your take on her?" the director asked.

Phoenix looked the D/CIA in the eye. "I thought she would be the key to rebuilding our network in Venezuela, sir."

Stratten nodded thoughtfully. "What do you think happened?"

"I think someone got to her and forced her to swap the SD cards. She *really* wanted to leave Venezuela, and I think she withheld the pen from me so I wouldn't leave her behind again. And I think the encounter with the National Guard was a setup. Whoever swapped the cards had to have been tracking us, and they killed her for helping me just like they killed the rest of our network down there."

"How do you think they were tracking you?" Stratten asked.

"I'm not sure."

"What about Vice President Acevedo?" Stratten asked. "I read your report, but what's your take on her?"

"From her rooftop meeting, I'd say she's in bed with Calderón," Phoenix replied. "Whatever affiliation she had with our agency is over."

"But we don't know that for sure?" the director said.

"I'm not holding my breath for her to call," Phoenix said. "She looked pretty cozy with Calderón, and we know Calderón is good buddies with Zarate."

Stratten seemed to ponder what Phoenix had said as he walked back to his desk and sat down. He leaned back in his chair, put his elbows on the armrests, and steepled his fingers. "The trip was a waste of time."

"Not really," Connelly stated. "We have a clearer picture of where Acevedo stands, and we know we still have a leak."

Stratten shot Connelly a quick look as if to tell her to keep quiet.

"It's no secret, sir," Phoenix added, "it's obvious someone ratted out our operations and assets to the Venezuelans."

"I think it's time to read him in, sir," Connelly added. "Bowie could certainly help us ferret out the mole, especially if he's in Venezuela now."

Stratten remained silent and deep in thought, and Phoenix

took the time to gaze around the room at the many photos on the wall of Stratten with world leaders and some of the most influential people in Washington. There was even one of him with a teenage Connelly and her father. He glanced at his former lover. She'd only gotten more beautiful with age.

After a long moment of silence had passed, Stratten said, "Bowie, we haven't been truthful with you. We know there's a mole in the agency. He's been giving up our officers and NOCs to the highest bidder for several years now. We thought we'd nailed him with a drone strike last year, but, unfortunately, it appears he's resurfaced in Venezuela."

Connelly picked up the narrative from the director. "We didn't know he was there until you reported Cobalt Panther had said the word 'Dragonfly,' which is a code name the mole has used for himself in the past. We picked it up here at Headquarters and have used it ever since."

"So, how many officers has Dragonfly outed?" Phoenix asked.

"We think he's been active as far back as 2010 when China began killing or imprisoning CIA sources. China claimed they had broken the code to our communication system, but we believe it was Dragonfly's first foray as a double agent."

"And you think he still works for the agency?" Phoenix asked.

"It's our belief that he does since much of the intelligence he's sold was available only to someone inside Headquarters," Stratten replied.

"Or he has some highly placed sources feeding him information," Phoenix suggested.

"That is a possibility," Connelly conceded.

"What are *you* doing about it?" Phoenix asked.

"We're doing an internal audit, and we want to start a task force," Connelly said. "We want you to be a part of it, which might involve you returning to Venezuela."

Phoenix's jaw muscles tightened involuntarily. He wanted

to bark, "Not happening!" but held his tongue. Going back to Venezuela after escaping not once but twice by the skin of his teeth wasn't a wise idea. They should allow things to cool down a bit before he snuck back in, but then again, he was a case officer with a job to do, and if that meant going back into the fray, then that's exactly where he expected to be sent.

"And what am I supposed to do in Venezuela?" Phoenix asked.

"For now, it's something we're kicking around," Stratten said. "We want you on the task force, and when the peace talks begin, we'll send you to Mexico City."

"To track the mole?" Phoenix asked. "What makes you certain he'll be there?"

"We want you to bump Acevedo. Push her. See what her reaction is. If she won't budge, find someone else in the government willing to work with us," Stratten said.

"The SEBIN has to know who I am by now," Phoenix replied. "If they had Blanco under surveillance, then they'll have plenty of pictures of me. Trying to get close to Acevedo could be pretty risky."

"It's a risk worth taking," Stratten said. "They know you, and so does Dragonfly."

"Seems he's more like a remora, sucking the flesh off its host," Phoenix stated.

Stratten swiveled in his chair and folded his hands on his desk. "That's an excellent analogy and very fitting."

"If you can get close to Acevedo, we might find Dragonfly," Connelly added.

And there it is. I'm going to be bait. Director Stratten and Connely had just told him that his life was as expendable as all the rest of the case officers and assets Dragonfly had outed during his tenure.

"I'll go with Bowie to Mexico City," Connelly volunteered. "Together, we have a better chance of getting to Acevedo."

"Fine. Let's do it your way," Stratten said, "but however

you do it, bring her back into the fold. We need all the help we can get in infiltrating the Venezuelans' operations. She's the perfect mark."

"And hopefully, Dragonfly will be there, whispering in her ear," Connelly added.

Phoenix felt the ache in his shoulder intensify with the stress of having to put his life on the line again. He wanted to resign right then and there, but he knew this was a fight he would stay in until the end.

If that meant going to Mexico or even back to Venezuela to hunt the most dangerous of prey, then it was a game he was willing to play.

ABOUT THE AUTHOR

Evan Graver is the author of the Ryan Weller Thriller Series, the John Phoenix Thrillers, and the stand alone Liberty Brigade. Before becoming a writer, Graver worked as a motorcycle mechanic, property manager, and in the scuba industry. He also served in the U.S. Navy as an aviation electronics technician (AT) until they medically retired him following a motorcycle accident that left him paralyzed. Graver lives in Hollywood, Florida, with his wife and son. His passions are fishing, scuba diving, and writing.

To see his full biography, visit the About Section at www. evangraver.com.

While you're there, sign up for his newsletter and receive the free Ryan Weller Thriller short story, *Dark Days*.

www.ingramcontent.com/pod-product-compliance
Lightning Source LLC
Chambersburg PA
CBHW040855010826
48978CB00013BA/1035